KTIMENE

Founder of Civilizations

Luan Brunson Haynes

TREATY OAK PUBLISHERS

PUBLISHER'S NOTE

This is a work of fiction. Except for historical records of ancient tales of the Odyssey based on the author's research, none of the other characters or events is based on actual people, living or dead, or their lives or circumstances. Any similarities are a coincidence and purely unintentional.

Printed and published in the United States of America

TREATY OAK PUBLISHERS

ISBN-978-1-943658-47-3

Available in print and digital from Amazon

DEDICATION

To my blended family who have seen me through this project
in many different ways:

Bill (1924-1988), Kent, James (1958-1981), John,
Elizabeth and Cody, Ann, Stephen,
Deborah and John, Kevin (1958-1978), Julie.

TABLE OF CONTENTS

GREECE (HELLAS) AND THE IONIAN AND AEGEAN SEAS

PART ONE

KALLISTO

THE ISLAND OF KEPHALLENIA

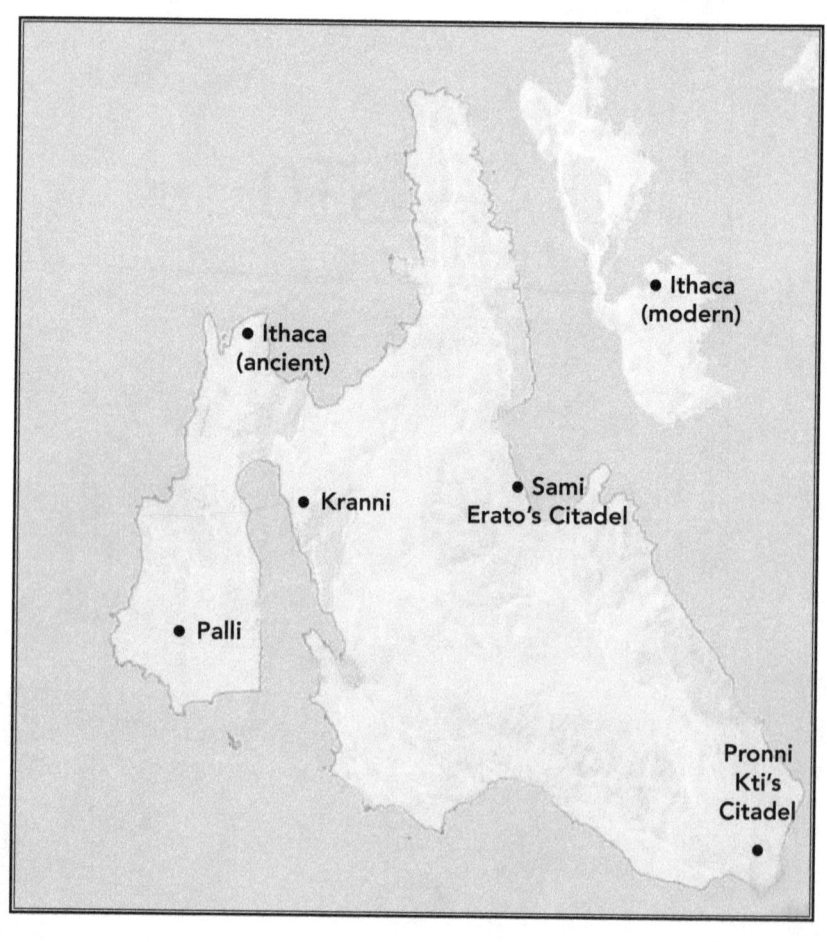

Starlight beams through the ages, young one,
sparking forth to enter you more deeply this day.

Chapter One

Through the western window of the robing house, Kallisto gazed at the late afternoon sun, thankful that the breezes of the Korinthian Sea tempered the heat. With a sigh, she reached high to guide the lavender chiton of the initiate over her head and wriggled it downward until it surrounded her slender body. "I will never get this straight," she said.

Her mother Antikleia stood behind her, tugging at the seams of the side stitches. Clad in white garb of a matron, her practiced hands sped through the dressing. "How the years have flown, Kalli. Now, with first blood, you are ready to partake of the shrine ritual and receive your public name. The proper time of the moon has arrived. Your new name will mark the path to your star."

"I hope I am ready."

"Kalli, you have a deep understanding of the rituals of the Great Mother. You administer to the needs of the hill people already. Now that you have learned to recite the rituals, you can go without me to give our hill people words of wisdom as well as sustenance."

Kalli bent her head, "Mother, I never shall I be as effective as you are."

"Nonsense, child, no more chatter. Your talents as a teller and a scribe enhance the rituals far beyond my pronouncements. Yes, Kalli, you are ready."

Antikleia stepped to the window that faced the outdoor circle where the women gathered. "The holy women awaiting you have prepared many generations of strong women for regal and ritual roles. Long before the warriors came, my ancestors gathered for rituals here on Mount Parnassus and at other shrines in the south near our ancestral home on Mount Kyllene. Then, all youths received their names from Great Gaia. Now the men, who brought the traditions of their ancestors, choose names for young men who compete in hunts to gain an animal prize. Because the men seldom bother us women, we keep our ancient rituals."

Kalli stepped closer to her mother. "Perhaps, Mother, I can speak publicly of our former traditions to convince the men to join us once again."

"Ah, difficult, but who can tell?" Smoothing the other side of Kalli's lavender chiton, Antikleia said, "Today belongs to you, Kalli. When you enter the circle by the sacred pool formed by the gushing springs, a gift of Mother Gaia herself, the holy women, after confirming what you have learned, will pronounce your new name, Great Gaia's choice. Your name presages your star path to our ancestors already in the skies, the great source from which we came. You may miss your childhood name that honors our revered ancestor, Kallisto. Never doubt, she will always guide you. When you need her, her words will come to you from the skies."

Antikleia closed Kalli's purple cloak with a clasp Kalli designed herself. "I wonder how you imagined this design."

"The design came in a dream voice. 'You are a lioness and seven cubs are yours.' I did not follow the meaning, but I knew the golden clasp must represent the words."

"Strange," Antikleia said. She embraced Kalli, then opened the door. "Now, dear one, gather your thoughts for a time of reflection. Let your mind travel into your memories. When I return, your Grandmother Neaira, my own dear mother, will come with me. We shall lead you to the stone circle, but you will advance to its center alone to greet the shrine women."

Absorbed into the quiet, Kalli stared at the steep mountainside of Parnassus and the sharp drops into the valleys of Delphi. She shifted her vision to the spring flowers, their dazzling yellow blossoms swaying in the evening breeze. "The contrast of the spring flowers with the stark peaks of Parnassus takes me to the rolling hillsides dotted with multi-colored spring flowers below tall Mount Aenos of my home citadel on Kephallenia Island." She wrapped her arms around her body. "I feel the comfort of my bed chamber where I sought refuge from the activities of the great hall. I see me, a child set free to wander for hours on the hillsides of Pronni."

Kalli raised her hands to shade her eyes. "Now I see me older, a student and assistant to my mother in the family shrine below the citadel. Mother speaks. 'Remember you are a part of Gaia's circle. You trod this earth to learn, grow, and rejoin your star home when your time comes.'"

Kalli pulled at her ear. She heard the booming words of Laertes, her father: 'Long ago, your birth filled a void in the household after a winter chill. Arkos, your oldest sibling, returned to his rest in the stars, leaving you to be friend as well as confidante to Lykos, your brother. No longer a child but comely woman, your time approaches for our ship to sail to Delphi's port. There, you and your mother can finish your studies at Parnassus. Then Sybil Pythia will pronounce your name at the women's shrine just as our priest at the prompting of your grandfather, Autolykos, gave Lykos his adult name, Odysseus, after his successful boar hunt on the slopes.'

Then she had answered before the family embarked for Parnassus, 'Yes Father, I shall go.'

Kalli shook her head. Her father's voice silenced and she shifted her vision. "I see a special day from my early times with Ody," she said, "when we practiced the art of the teller with our scope, Phemios. Eumaios, my dearest friend and our constant companion, tells first of his homeland, of his being kidnapped at four years of age by a serving maid for her passage home and of his being sold into our household when she died at sea. Then Ody tells of Kephalos and Prokris, progenitors of the line of our father, Laertes. Next, I tell of Mother's ancestral line. I hear my finishing words. 'Neaira came from Kyllene to Parnassus where she tended family lands until she found her mate, Autolykos. Together, they raised their daughter Antikleia, now beloved queen of Pronni and my mother."

Kti leaned against the windowsill to hear Phemios' words echo. 'Your voice blends perfectly with the instrument. When you speak of Kallisto's disappearance, her son Arkos appearing thereafter on the hillside near the bear caves of Kyllene, you make me wonder if you might solve the mystery of what happened to Kallisto whose name you bear. Later, when you remind your listeners that your parents will follow the family tradition of passing the ancestral home to their youngest daughter, you mark your birthright. In *this* household, child, *you* are that youngest daughter. You will manage this citadel, so you can keep its story alive and chart its destiny. What a responsibility.'

Kalli ran her hand through her dark hair that matched her mother's, then straightened her shoulders when footsteps interrupted her reverie. When the white robes of her mother and grandmother appeared, she smiled. "Ah, dear ones, accept my embrace, and to you, Grandmother, I add a special welcome."

Neaira held Kalli at arm's length. "Just look at you. You are a picture of your mother and, no doubt, a great comfort to her for all of your help. I am grateful to be able to witness your naming today."

After looking first at her mother, Kalli's eyes then met those of her grandmother. "I have travelled deeply into my childhood. I know that the star marker of my new name will bring light to my path forward. I ask Mother Gaia for the wisdom to choose the best turns of the path. I know I face changes. Above all, I know I must keep our citadel safe as it one day becomes my own, and I must keep the Great Gaia present in the world." She beamed. "Mother, may I now tell your view of the deeds of the Olympians."

Her mother shook her head. "We must tolerate Zeus, Poseidon, and Hades. For years, men have brought that trio to us for supplication. They keep adding deities that come from their trading ports and occupied territories. First, there were Hermes, Hephaestus, Ares, and now, Apollo, whom they name brother of Artemis. They scheme to supplant Mother Gaia with Apollo here at Parnassus where they would take over the oracle of Sibyl Pythia. For that matter, they would take over the oracles of the other Sibyls who preside at shrines all over the Great Sea."

Antikleia tugged at her daughter's shift, then picked up

the hair-smoothing stone to give her daughter's hair a vigorous brush. "People laugh at the strange ways of the Gods. 'Too whimsical, too flawed,' they say. The warriors endow the good qualities of the Mother upon their upstart gods any way they can. They diminish Hekate, Kirke, Kalypso, Medea, and Medusa by making them enchantresses and whores to be feared for their evil, seductive powers. If they allow Mother forms stature at all, they become wives, daughters, and sisters of the gods."

She banged down the stone as she guided them toward the doorway. "What lessons they attempt to instill in us."

After a few steps, Antikleia slowed her pace. "You will know what to tell and how to tell it when the time comes. Now we take you to the shrine women awaiting you in the circle."

Hours later, the procession came from the sacred stones.

"Ktimene, we call you henceforth," her mother said. "What does such a name suggest for your future? When 'ktios,' a strong word that suggests a creator, joins 'mene,' a female designation, anything might come your way."

"Mother, I hope I meet the challenge of the meaning the Sibyl gave it: "Founder of Civilizations.""

But Ktimene kept to herself the question she dared not speak: "How will such a name, which implies marriage, fit with my plans to work in the shrines of the Great Mother?"

Ktimene received blessings and embraces of many cousins, aunts and friends. Among the greeters came her closest companions: Cousin Penelope, daughter of Periboea and Ikarios, from the Argive mountain stronghold across the Arkadian valley from Mount Kyllene, and Cousin Helen, daughter of Leda and Tyndareus, from Sparta deeper into the southern Peloponnese. As they led Ktimene to the great feast, Helen asked, "What shall we call you, dear cousin: 'Kti' or 'Mene'?"

Ktimene's answer came right away. "Kti."

Late in the evening, an attendant rushed toward Autolykos, Kti's wolfish grandfather who with the other men had joined in the feasting. Autolykos stopped the feasting. "Women, you must go into the citadel. Men, we have work to do."

"But Grandfather," Kti said, hands on hips, "we women must hear the cause of such haste to shelter us."

Sighing, the brusque man said, "Very well, stay. Your direct challenge reminds me of me in my youth. All of you listen. At the eastern edge of our sea, a bandit assembles brigands who have no homeland. They plan invasion. Any threat to our lands and our shrines must be quelled. We must never lose this stronghold that protects all of our homes here and in the Western Isles. They want Sibyl Pythia's shrine plus our citadel that many in Thebes and that upstart village of Athens covet. Men, to the ships. We sail immediately. Surprise is our aim."

PART TWO

KTIMENE

GREECE (HELLAS) AND THE IONIAN AND AEGEAN SEAS

Look to the stars. Through your heart's eye, find wisdom.

Chapter Two

The household gathered in the mighty hall of Parnassus to greet the men after their successful skirmish. Neaira gave the men the grape of Sybil Pythia's altar to commemorate the victory.

Kti watched her grandfather's twinkling eyes scan the group. "How fortunate so many hearty men gathered here to help my warriors dispatch those scoundrels. Now, you may return to the safety of your homes. Those renegades will not come our way again." He saw my expectant gaze. "You two eager ones must board my ship for Thresprotia if you wish to visit the Shrine of Dione and Themis in Dodona."

Some weeks passed before Kti returned from Dodona to Pronni. Helen would visit until she studied at Demeter's shrine in Eleusis. Kti feasted her eyes on Eumaios when he met the ship to help them up the hill to the citadel. She ran ahead when Antikleia and Laertes rushed into the courtyard. Entwined in outstretched arms, Kti disappeared with the happy party into the great hall leaving Eumaios to see to their gear.

Some days later, Kti stood by as Helen spoke to Antikleia. "Dear Aunt, I go with you to take food to the hill people as Kti works at the shrine."

Eumaios, when Kti entered the valley shrine, dismissed the young boys he instructed. "How am I to remember the shift of Kallisto to Ktimene or, even more personal, Kalli to Kti?"

Kti almost said, "Eumaios, it is just a name," but the intensity of his gaze silenced her for a moment. "We must honor you with an adult name. The Mother of your land would have named you by now."

"Though young, I do remember my mother saying 'My son, you will go with me to the teachers of the Magna Mother for lessons as well as naming.' Yes, the wise women would have given me a name."

"Well, tomorrow, I shall pronounce your naming ritual. Then, you will open the Great Mother's ways even more strongly to the males here. They must know the Mother as well as Zeus."

Silent for a moment, Eumaios then said, "Kti, you honor me. Gladly shall I receive my name from you."

Kti turned her head with a shake. "Listen to this, Eumaios. Grandfather rushed Helen and me to his ship for sailing to Thresprotia, for us to start our walk into Dodona. When we sailed from Parnassus, he told us not to be swallowed at Thresprotia by the whirling waters leading to the Underworld, Hades' domain. We knew the Underworld belonged not to Hades but to Persephone, our lady of transforming rebirth who prepares us to ascend to our star, but we saw it as fruitless to debate Grandfather."

Eumaios laughed. "You survived your arrival; then what?"

"From Thresprotia, we followed the tall trees into the sun-filled valley of the shrine. None of the family had travelled to Dodona for years. The ancient wisdom, along with the handling of practical politics we found there, gave us valuable insights.

"You two will always treasure what you learned. Were you good traveling companions?"

"Our friendship deepened as we journeyed. All nature bent to Helen, who always attracts Gaia's creations. She sparkled like the sunlight that filtered through the embracing trees of the Kalamas River. Small animals and birds gathered around her wherever she walked. Never aware of her aura, her attraction or her beauty, she exuded mature, yet innocent wisdom."

"What an experience you enjoyed. Entering Helen's world invited you to a deep connection with her, I know." Eumaios grazed Kti's arm as he spoke.

Kti shifted her stance. "Helen departs for Eleusis tonight for her studies with the women of Demeter's shrine. I shall miss her. Old Tyndareus and his new wife want Helen away. She returns to Sparta after the study year to attend the wedding of her half-sister Klytemnestra to Prince Agamemnon of Mycenae."

"You must be present, of course, but will all your family attend the wedding?"

"We plan to make the trip. I hope Mother will be well enough to go." Kti replaced the vessels she had cleaned and stepped toward the entry. "Now I must return to meet Mother and Helen." She turned to face Eumaios, "Remember, we meet at dawn for your naming ceremony."

"I shall meet you at first light." Eumaios grinned.

As the sun rose, Kti confirmed Eumaios' name. "Come forth, Jamin. You receive the name you once told me your mother used to call you from play. The name marks your destiny, Eumaios. When you return to your citadel, you will find your family and claim your birthright." She paused. "Jamin, your name in private, must remain Eumaios in public. Know that we function as equals in the eyes of the Mother. Now you can approach me—"

"Kti, you must not see me as an equal. I am not free. If I were to go home, establish my birth right and come back with many gifts, then perhaps..." His face contorted in wistful silence.

"Well then, tomorrow I shall ask Father to give you freedom before he sets you on your way home. Then I shall expect your return."

Eumaios raised his eyebrows, then regained his composure. "No, Kti, you must not. We shall always look after one another. We shall work side by side. We have a higher purpose, that of serving the Mother. As for me, I have important work here."

Kti blinked. She knew the wisdom of his words. "Yes, my Eumaios, my Jamin, we have a bond so strong no one can separate us. We have larger duties than our personal whims. Our work binds us at a deeper level."

After a long silence, they went their separate ways: Ktimene to her mother, Eumaios to his work.

Kti intensified her work with her mother. One day shortly after Helen departed, she spoke of Dodona. "Tribes from all directions migrate into the region. Before the warriors brought Zeus, the people followed wise Mother, Dione, whom the warriors tried to match with Zeus as subordinate wife. One shrine woman told me Dione came south for refuge here. Have you heard of that?"

Antikleia wrinkled her brow. "No, Kti, I have never heard of such a connection. We must ask the women of Palli who keep the history at the main Mother shrine of our island."

"In Dione's absence, Themis, her Titan sister, with her great snake, appeared to guard Dione's temple. When Dione returned, Themis stayed and the two competed for the people's hearts. Zeus's followers, seeing the division as a way to supplant them both, took over giving advice from the oracular whispering of the leaves of the sacred oak. We watched the excitement of the women's regaining the oak before we left. One of the holy women admitted at our departure that the splits confuse the people who justify abandoning all rituals. Indeed, the region, fast becoming a harsh waste, serves as a refuge for scoundrels and robbers."

"Ktimene, you have brought us valuable information. We must see that our people flourish in these changing times."

Kti turned to Helen's status in Sparta after the death of her mother.

Antikleia knew the story. Still she listened. "My daughter, you show much wisdom as you sort out the problems caused by Tyndareus's quick marriage to Klytemnestra's mother. Helen lives in confusion about her place in the household and in her father's heart."

Kti wondered, "Whatever will become of Helen, now a stepchild?"

"We both know Helen can take care of herself." Antikleaia shrugged. "After all, the warrior's lore already calls her Zeus' child."

Antikleia established ways for Kti to increase her work. "During my illness last year, you discharged my duties. I am confident you can carry out all of them except my welcoming special guests and performing rituals when I am called to do them. Beyond tending to the needs of the hill people along with the household, you will counsel them when they come to you. You will keep all household records and see to needed supplies. Best of all, you will script the family history, a task you will enjoy beyond the telling you already do. I shall enhance Eumaios' role. In addition to instructing the male youth and counseling the men, Eumaios will join you to intone rituals."

"Yes, Mother, you must rest more. I shall do my best with my duties. I shall consult you when I need counsel, of course." She paused. "I am glad Eumaios will work with me. I admire him and his abilities."

Kti, cautious not to reveal her love for Eumaios, could not hide her feelings from her mother.

Because Eumaios showed the restraint of a true prince, despite being a slave-servant, Antikleia admired his character. Still, a love match with Eumaios would foil family plans for Kti to marry a nearby prince, a son of Palli, Krani, or Sami—all of the line of Kephalos. "Surely, she will find one to her liking and continue the line."

Antikleia found a diversion. "Your parents have a surprise for you, dear daughter. We found you a companion, a servant to take care of your needs. You will see that she becomes a loyal retainer."

Kti eyes widened, "I shall emulate your way of training her. Like my cousin Erato, who became mistress of a servant after she returned from Parnassus, I shall now have mine. Thank you, dear Mother."

"Your father secured a young girl with promising abilities. She already knows the local language, but her characteristics place her very far north beyond the bounds of Hyperborea. Until recently, our traders little dreamed they could travel so far beyond the home of the winds."

Kti said, "Why has she come so far south?"

"My inquisitive one, always you want answers. You will learn her background once you gain her confidence. No one, so far, can coax her history from her. Laertes tells me her name sounds like 'Freya,' a word we do not know, but the captain spoke with awe and claimed she had royal lineage. He said no man has touched her. Ancient Eurykleia, your nurse and before you, mine, will assist you."

Eurykleia brought the girl to Kti in her bedchamber. Kti smiled, then extended her hand to welcome her. "May I call you Freya?"

The young girl approached, lowered her head, and bowed. "You may, mistress."

Kti, her arms moving to her side, said, "You may call me Ktimene, or better still Kti."

She surveyed Freya's round face of childhood from which surfaced angles of high cheekbones and full, round lips—the marks of her forming mature beauty that matched her stately stature. She wore a rough-woven shift, the simple garb of the household. Entwined in her golden braid, a glistening metallic cord served as her only adornment. *If she had not been taken from her home, she would be training her own servant.*

Helpless to rescue Freya from her exile, Kti softened her expression. Taking Freya's hand, she said, "Freya, let us be good friends. Like others of our household who have lost their homeland, I want you to feel at home." She stepped back. "Now I shall acquaint with the chamber."

Shape your inner nature. See. Learn.

Chapter Three

K ti and Freya crossed the valley below Pronni's citadel. The women, of the same stature, presented a contrasting tableau of beauty. The sun highlighted Kti's olive skin while it added luster to Freya's pale porcelain face; the breeze tossed the tips of Kti's long black tresses, but barely moved Freya's close coif of golden hair.

"I am glad you enjoy our outings," Kti said. "Today, we take Eumaios his midday meal. He adds chambers to the royal tomb to make room for the bones of my parents. He stays busy tending the swine and instructing the herders of cattle and sheep. Added to that, he supervises workers who construct a new shrine center dedicated to Mother Trimetria, our Gaian protector of our people. His most important work is helping me at the shrine. Too much work, I say, but he enjoys all he does."

"The other servants admire him," Freya said. "They tell me he is wise."

"Eumaios was taken in youth from a land where the Great Mother conducted most of the rituals. He is deeply involved with our work here."

Freya shifted the reed basket full of food to her other hip. "Being able to do so much, especially doing his shrine work must give him great pleasure."

Kti nodded. "You tell me that you and your mother saw shrine work dwindle to favor the men as well as the Gods of the North. We also have lost the rituals for the men to the Skygods that Father favors."

Freya stopped and looked to the north. "How sad we felt when we moved to our southern lands; for then, Father turned mostly to a male shaman for conducting the rituals, healing, and advising of the people, and the burying of the dead. Those roles had been the work of everyone in our northern home."

"Here, too," Kti said, "the warriors bring their gods. Just as you and your mother did, we still keep our rituals alive. My mother, learning of your experiences with your mother, wants to teach you our ways so that you can help us. Then you can join Eumaios and me in our work."

"Gladly will I do the Magna Mother's work here and share what I know." Freya's eyes glowed. "I look forward working with you."

They approached Eumaios who worked deep inside the layered rock tomb, Eumaios climbed out of the cavernous tomb and leaned against a wall that he, together with his workers, had formed.

"To give you strength," Kti said, "we bring you fresh figs, last year's best olives, cheese just seasoned, and wheat cakes from the hot stones. We have first presses of wine from our north vineyard that I slipped from the storeroom without Pontrakles suspecting.

Eumaios laughed. "You spoil me, Kti."

"While we eat, Freya will speak to us of her life in the North. Soon, because she knows the Great Mother in her northern form, Mother wants time together to instruct her in our ways so that she can help us."

Eumaios titled his head at Freya. "How good that you know the Great Mother. I shall welcome your help. How you came here interests me."

Freya leaned against the wall and stared into space. "An older relative—my uncle, the brother of my father, who likely saw me as a threat to my younger brother's inheritance—arranged an excursion for my family to his seaside villa. He lived far to the south of my mother's people, but near to our new home. Although my mother had spent her life in the north, she had agreed to lead part of the tribe to the southern shores of our land. There she and my father were developing trade. Soon after we arrived at my uncle's villa, my uncle organized a buying expedition for me. Traders from farther south brought exotic goods. 'A rare treat,' he said. 'We must go soon; they leave immediately,' he told my parents. 'I want your daughter to select a special gift from their treasures to celebrate her coming of age, an outing just for her'."

"For some time, my chaperone and I admired fine cloths of gold, red, rare blues and purples; jewels, mounted in gold or silver, some jasper, lapis and turquoise; rare spices and oils and implements of ornamented metals, even those that shone back my own reflections. I ran my fingers over many vessels of clay, metal or ebony, all filled with oils, wines or perfumes. Before I could make my selection, I missed my uncle and my attendant. The captain of the vessel assured me he would find my uncle, but as he continued to prepare the ship for departure, I realized I had been abandoned. I could not leave, although I tried."

With a shake of his head, Eumaios looked down. "What

a plight. You were older than I, but I remember vividly being stowed in a small hold where I saw no light for many days."

Freya sighed and was silent for a moment. "I remained in a small enclosure. I tried the door, but it was barred. For some days at sea, the captain left me to myself, his crew seeing to my basic needs. On the third day, the captain came."

Kti pressed her hands together. "That must have frightened you."

"He remained aloof. He revealed what I already suspected. My uncle controlled the servant my mother trusted as a chaperone. He acted out of fear that I, not my brother, would soon gain the family leadership according to my mother's customs."

Freya stared into the distance at a lone bird flying. "I remembered then the helpless look of my mother when my uncle took me from the room. Yes, my mother's eyes showed me that I, even at twelve, just receiving the rite of adulthood, could take care of myself in all circumstances. My mother's eyes, I hold ever in my heart to comfort and guide me."

Kti and Eumaios exchanged glances. "What became of you on the voyage?" Kti said. "But only if you want to tell us more."

"The captain told me he hoped for high payment for me. He believed I had more value than the furs. He stopped often to barter the hides of elk, bear, mink, seal, deer, or precious white ermine. He did not trade me, but allowed no one to touch me. He became my mentor in the languages of the Great Sea."

"That must have been a comfort, said Kti."

Freya shrugged. "The men grew restless about my presence, blaming me for any rough seas. The day before we came to Pronni's port, since I understood their language better than they realized, I told the captain the men planned mutiny. His eyes saddened. He told me he had hoped to make me a member of his own household, a gift to his wife. Still some days from his homeland, he saw the danger. Indeed, he realized that his wife, possibly believing untruths about us, might mistreat me should they make it safely home."

Freya gave half a grimace and shook her head. "The next day, he hastened from Pronni port, all smiles. I would have a good place among the servants of King Laertes, whose young daughter needed a genteel servant. He assured me Laertes, along with all his relatives from neighboring Sami, traders themselves, stood in good repute throughout the Great Sea. He said their trade extended from the ports of this island ruled by ancestors of Kephalos and Prokris's four sons to far eastern ports, one being Samos Island to the east not far from his home port. Laertes no longer took to the seas, he said, instead tending his orchards, herds, and a large retinue of followers."

"He spoke well of us," Kti said. "I am grateful. I hope that gave you comfort when he left."

After an eastward glance, Freya continued. "He wished me happiness in my new position, shook his head, then said, 'I am told, Laertes once helped Jason of Korinth and his Argives bring home a golden fleece from the sacred sheep of a chieftain who abided deep into the Dark Sea past Truva. Some say not he but his ancestor of the same name led them.'" Freya softened her gaze with a flickered a smile. "How well my friend placed me. I hope he made it safely home."

Kti shifted closer to Freya and took her hand. "I know you miss your home and your family. That your misfortune benefits us saddens me. I am pleased that you love the Great Mother as we do and are versed in her ways. As soon as my mother instructs you, we shall welcome you as a shrine worker."

Young one, still, but wiser, learn from others' ways.

Chapter Four

Kti , with her mother and Eumaios, sat by the warm fire, watching the smoke of the blazing logs whirl upward through the hole above the hearth of the great hall. "Freya, come warm yourself and join with us as we discuss the Great Mother. Now that Mother has trained you in serving the inner needs of our people, we want you to sit with our spirit circle."

Freya warmed her hands then joined the group. "What your mother has taught me builds upon my work at home. I know how you heal, bring harmony in conflict, bury loved ones and mark passages to youth, womanhood and marriage. The warriors of the north do more to hamper the women than your men do. Even so, we followed the Mother Way of our ancestors in secret every time we could. I thought Mother would revolt when I could not use the name, Freya, given to me in womanhood. The name honored a powerful form of our Great Mother, but in our new home, Od, a warrior god, took her as suppliant wife. To my surprise, Mother stayed calm, placed a hand on my arm and said, 'We have larger battles to fight'."

Antikleia, swathed in a loomed woolen shawl and lap robe sat closest to the fire. She stirred the fire with automatic strokes. "Freya, may we agree that the Great Mother of your people follows the same family of Gaia that we do? Even though you may call Her and her family by different names and pronounce different rituals, their characteristics have similarities."

Freya turned her head northward, then back. She arose from her seat and knelt before Antikleia. "My queen, long we have discussed Gaia and her children. I agree that those who guide us, no matter the name, are the same. But our gods in both places would change us."

As Freya seated herself next to Kti, Eumaios said, "Yes, our Great Gaia remains constant while the gods both there and here control and entangle lives with conflict, duplicity, and trickery."

Kti stepped to her loom. Freya arose to help her carry it back to the hearth. Once settled, Kti took her shuttle in hand and began to weave. "Even our way of dying would change if the Gods had their way. Fates, once helpmates of the Mother, under the warriors hold life of each human by a single thread to cut at a whim. Such uncertainty causes their believers to depend on outer forces instead of their inner strengths. The gods would eclipse the peaceful life to which the Great Mother guides us who makes people responsible for forming their stars."

"Our Mother as yours," Freya agreed, "clearly knows no bounds to her work that both Zeus, here, and Od, in the North, limit."

Antikleia stared into the fire. "Our Mother disallows ridiculous pettiness. Instead, she shows us how to live harmoniously. Her powers eclipse subduing outer forces."

Eumaios stirred the fire. "By analyzing patterns of entrails of sacrificed animals and birds spread upon an altar, the leaders of warriors claim they read signs of how people should live. Such acts the Mother never condones. Instead, she protects all nature as part of a larger pattern of life. We have better ways of guiding our people. We use their dreams, good diet, proper breathing, inner stillness, and healthy movement to keep them vital."

"Because the Mother emphasizes good health, her healers rarely prescribe herbs to renew the breath of life. The Mother never resorts to superstitions that cause fear, guilt or pain. With gladness, we receive followers of the Skygods who come to us for healing and direction." Antikleia said.

Kti stopped her work. "Burials, the Mother makes a part of the life cycle to be treated with simplicity and reverence. Leaders of the gods both north and south change the ritual to superficial displays of spectacle and power."

"Yes, the women of my land followed our ancestors' way of burial," Freya said. "We await the journey to the afterworld on a simple hollowed log, male and female equally honored. The body faces the mellow light of the setting sun that draws it out of a simple mound to its star place. Men display more outward show in their burial rites. They richly clothe the body and transport it in a fine carriage followed by an entourage, each dressed in finery. They place the body on a barge amidst its riches and send it into to sea as a sign of a journey. After that, they pull the barge back again and carry it to its place in the burial mound. You can see remnants of the old way, but I wonder if Father's shaman will have difficulty with the women at the time of my mother's death." At these words, Freya sighed. "Now, secret or public, I shall not be there to perform her rites as she did at her mother's burial."

"When the time comes, you will be with your mother," said Eumaios as he patted her hand. "You will sing to her on the winds. You will see her take her place among the stars. You will know the time. Some, in the present world, cannot understand what connects us to the Mother's world. The Way, past their imagining, we will keep open to those who listen, those who see deeply with an inner vision that awakens their hearts."

Kti added, "My studies taught me the deeper meaning of the words of our Way. They connect us to the Mother at all times. We must guard the words but hold them in memory. I worry that more of us do not learn them. At times, I believe the Way to which the words point will disappear."

Freya said, "We imprint sacred signals on the rocks of the mounds, the old places and the ceremonial circles. When we bury, we encode them in the beading, the decoration of the burial garments. Surely, with care, others will understand the signs and keep the meaning of the sacred alive."

Eumaios, with knitted brow, said, "I hope so. Our mission must be to assure that some know the signs."

Kti said, "Traders tell me in the islands farther east, people skilled in stone chiseling created a language with figures they placed in the stone-lined graves of their dead. The uninstructed would not know what they saw, but surely someone will always know. We must instruct some to read the signs. Better than that, now that we script, we should consider scripting our secrets for future generations. That would cause a fire storm across our world."

Both Freya and Eumaios nodded although Antikleia said nothing.

Kti glanced at her mother. "Look, Mother sleeps. She has not heard us discuss scripting the secret codes and rituals. When we discuss it again, she will have insights we must hear."

Then Kti shifted in her seat. "Klytemnestra detached

herself from our concerns at Parnassus. She and her mother went through the forms of the rituals openly rejected the Way of the Mother held by Helen and her ancestors. When Helen's mother died, Helen dedicated her life to perpetuating the Way. Klytemnestra said that she and her household, one generation hence, would not remember the Mother's teachings. She created quite a stir. I wonder if those who bury her will place the signs of the Mother in her fancy tomb that she and Agamemnon plan in the valley below Mycenae to match his great beehive monument already constructed there to hold his body with treasures of his conquests."

"Now, Kti," Eumaios said, shaking his head at her, "you know you wish Klytemnestra well. You seldom jest bitterly about such serious matters. I think you feel concern that Klytemnestra's thinking may dominate now."

"True, Eumaios," Kti agreed, "I hope that women will always have a part in public ceremonies.

Kti looked toward her mother. "Mother still sleeps. Let us leave her in the care of Eurykleia while we walk in the chill to the shrine to meet the youth who gather there for instruction."

Your sister calls.

CHAPTER FIVE

Springtime came to the hills of Pronni. Before daybreak one morning, Kti awakened with a start. The cries of a young woman intermixed with sounds of winds from the east. "Strange dream," she uttered as she slept on.

At morning's light Kti found her mother with a stranger. "Kti, your cousin, Helen, needs us. You must go immediately with Orkemedes, our Arkadian kinsman. Some months ago, early in her time at Eleusis, Helen caught the attention of a local chieftain. The sacred women of Eleusis discovered that Helen expects a child, but she will not speak of it. She refused herbs to cease the birth while insisting the child belongs to Demeter. Helen calls for our healing hands to deliver the child."

"Will you go with me?"

"Freya will accompany you. The rough journey would be my death. You know how to deliver a child. You must leave with the shift of the winds. With good timing, you will arrive in five days."

Orkemedes still in his traveling cloak, his dark beard covering his ruddy face, spoke in the slow words of a Peloponnesian mountaineer. "The chieftain will send guards to the port beyond Korinth and Parnassus' ports. He assures us safe, swift passage overland to the shrine which lies farther east. Eleusis lies west of the village of Athens, where the descendants of an earlier chieftain, Theseus, still rule."

Antikleia raised her frail hand. "That small settlement sits on the eastern rim of a vast wasteland full of bandits who prey on travelers. Our kinsman will help you, but depend mostly on yourself and your dagger. Trust no one there except the sisters at the shrine."

Following their hasty preparation, Kti departed with Freya and Orkemedes. Early on the fifth day, as the entourage entered the shrine grounds, shrieks of pain pierced the air. "I believe," Kti said, "Helen has begun labor,"

Kti determined that Helen made steady progress to a normal delivery. She took Helen's hand. "You will be just fine, dear Helen," she said in a soothing tone.

As she spoke, a young muscular man stepped forward. An intense frown knitted his brow above his soft eyes. An older woman of similar expression stepped out of the shadows to stand by him. The young man said, "Helen ordered her kinswomen be summoned from the Western Isles. Are you Antikleia, the one to whom she calls?"

"I am Antikleia's daughter, Ktimene," she said, then shook her head. "But, young man, you must leave the chamber. With my companion and these shrine women, I will attend my kin."

The young man spoke. "I am Father of this child to come. I am a son of a royal house. This is my mother, Aethra, leader of the Troezans. She must stay."

As Kti took in his words, she sensed that his mother knew the Way of the Mother. She turned to Aethra. "Stay. Attend, should you wish, but this is no place for your son."

Two hours passed. Helen, snuggled in a warmed, smoothly woven birthing blanket that all healers keep at hand, had released the shining child—a girl. "The letting go gives me ease. Knowing a divine child enters the world to do work at Demeter's shrine gives me joy."

All the women chanted the birthing ritual Kti and her mother sang, first for the mother, then to welcome her special child.

During the next days at the shrine guest house, Kti comforted and counseled the new mother. After Helen gained strength, Kti entered into frank discussion with her. "Helen, you must think about both your futures."

Helen stared into space. "The child is Demeter's own."

"Then what of your future. Will you follow custom by returning to your family where suitors will come forward to claim you in marriage?"

"So be it if my father wishes," Helen said.

A retinue arrived from Sparta to camp outside the shrine grounds. Among them came Helen's high-spirited brothers. Kti came to meet the group, but before she could speak, Helen's brother, Kastor, stepped on one foot, then the other. "I demand to see the father of the child."

The young chieftain stepped forward. "I fathered the beautiful child."

The brother drew a dagger. His retinue followed his lead.

Kti stepped between the two men. She stretched her arms to separate them and looked from one to the other. "Stay calm. All of us, including Helen, the child's mother, and this young man, the child's father, must meet with the matron of this shrine to decide what the future holds. Let us go into a counsel chamber to discuss the possible solutions."

Agreement came thanks to Kti's adept reasoning. Kti closed the session: "The decisions are final. The child, in three years, will go to Klytemnestra, a matron, by then, in a growing household. Later, the young one can study at Eleusis. Thenceforth, Helen will be named Aunt. Klytemnestra will take on the role of Mother."

At these words, Helen gasped, then her eyes filled with tears. She bit her knuckle but could not suppress a sob. At last her gaze met Ktimene's. "Yes, it will be as you direct."

Ktimene patted her arm, then continued, "The holy women of Eleusis, with the chieftain's mother, will care for the child, while the chieftain will supply all provisions. When the time comes, the father will provide an entourage along with a nurse for the child's safe passage to Agamemnon's citadel at Mycenae. The shrine women will pray to Mother Demeter that the child will return to study with them."

Kti visited with Helen's brothers shortly before their departure. "I hope you have safe passage home. May Tyndareus find a good solution for Helen."

They nodded, then Kastor said, "Before we left, Tyndareus was assembling Helen's kindred to discuss her plight. As you know, we look kindly on women and usually find them a good husband. Your brother will be there, no doubt."

Next Kti visited with the shrine women of Eleusis. "You were kind to offer Helen a place among you, but she cannot stay so near the child. Nor can she ignore her family's wishes to return home She understands your love of the child."

She visited with the child's father. "I know you honored Helen with an offer to stay with you. You were wise to work out the best course for both of you. Your paths, it seems, lead elsewhere."

The young father pressed his palms together. "You were an amazing arbiter on Helen's behalf. She would surely be the best of companions. We see eye-to-eye on how this world should work, but I agree with her that we are young and must go our separate ways."

On the evening before Helen's departure, Kti, alone with her, said, "You and your lover have much in common."

Helen bit her lip. "At first, I ignored, even misread, his attentions. I little thought myself attractive to a man. My studies occupied me. He listened well, even adding his own ideas to mine. When he slipped into little courtesies, I experienced feelings foreign to me. Such attention diverted me. He, no doubt, saw my reaction to him as more than I intended." Helen shook the tassel on her belt. "How can one measure the affair or place blame?"

"You have done well to accept responsibility in the liaison," Kti said, "as you accepted the future arrangements for your child. I know you will love the dear child always."

Kti helped Helen into the litter on the day of the journey to Sparta to learn her future. She watched as Helen took the child in her arms and whispered in the babe's ear, "Farewell, my beloved, my Ipheginia."

Once Helen departed, Kti left for the Western Isles with Freya and Orkemedes, both of whom assisted Kti throughout the negotiations. With guards to protect them, they rode across the badlands to the port and their sea journey to the Western Isles. Once on board, Kti turned to Freya. "Soon, Ody will return with news from Sparta. I wonder what Helen's fate will be."

You will find a treasure. You will know.

Chapter Six

ompleting her practice with Phemios soon after her return from Eleusis, Kti followed his glance to find Ody standing behind her. As she embraced Ody, she gasped when she noticed a tall figure beside him. Finding words, she managed to say, "I did not expect you just yet, dear brother. How long have you been standing there? Who is your companion?"

Ody grinned. "Kti, you were concentrating on your story of the family migrations from Arkadia, named after Arkos, Kallisto's abandoned child who led his people to greatness. You tell it so much better than ever I did. We heard the sequence from the beginning. Phemios signaled us to stay still; otherwise you would have had an audience."

Kti blushed that a stranger heard her perform. She kept her telling private among the three childhood companions.

Ody then turned to the young man. "Kti, do you remember Eurylokhos, our cousin from Sami? Eury serves as my captain, second in command of our local band gathering to contend with renegades coming to threaten these islands and the mainland."

Eury bowed, then studied Kti's face as he stood upright once more.

Ody sighed as he shook his head. "This episode with Helen,

just one of many we heard of when we gathered in Tyndareus's court, foretells warfare. Eury works on Samos Island far to the east where our relatives manage trading ships for the family to support us all. Remember our visit to bid Eury farewell when he was ten years old before he left for Samos to learn the trade?"

"Welcome, Cousin Eurylokhos. I apologize for my forwardness of speech. I had no knowledge that anyone listened. Yes, I remember telling you goodbye. In seven years, much has changed."

Eury, staring at her, stood as if awakened from a trance. "You do the art of telling much justice. I have heard tellers in many ports. They would envy your ability. The art becomes you." Then he raised his eyebrows. "Forgive me for being forward, but you have changed from our last meeting. Then, a playmate of my sister, Erato, now a young woman, you command our praise and gratitude. We heard of your attendance in Eleusis to Helen, who arrived in Sparta to tell of it before we departed."

Kti shrugged. "You praise too much. Regarding the telling, I shall treasure your words. I have spent many hours practicing. I admit the art of telling brings me joy."

She turned toward the doorway. "Now we must join the family to give thanks for your safe arrival and to hear news of Helen. Both of you need refreshment. Afterward, Eurylokhos, you must describe your life on Samos."

Kti stepped in between them to take an arm of each as she nodded a thank you to Phemios. With graceful steps, she guided them to the assembly hall. "Wait here while I arrange for refreshments."

As she left, Kti overheard Eury say, "Cousin, I must admit your sister has turned my head. Is she betrothed or may I hope to claim her?"

All right, brother, Kti thought, as she went about her errand. *You bring your friend to distract me, to turn me from my year of study, but I shall play along to stop other schemes.*

In a short time, Kti approached the men. "Refreshments come. Our parents will bring the household to join us. We shall soon hear your report, dear brother. Later, in private, you must tell me of Helen and Penelope."

Before the gathered household, Antikleia poured libations of thanksgiving and welcomed their guest.

Odysseus rose to his feet. "Helen will marry within the month, quite privately. The lucky man, Menelaos, will join Helen to rule Sparta at the death of Tyndareus, while his brother Agamemnon and Klytemnestra will unite to rule Mycenae. We shall acknowledge Helen's match quietly when we attend their long-planned marriage."

"How did the council reach its decisions?" said Antikleia.

Nodding, Odysseus sat down. "After the shrine women and leaders of Zeus's Olympians blessed the gathering, we began. The gathering was unanimous. All warriors swore protection of Helen, should outsiders decide to take her once again. Some, all outside our kinship circle, make objects of their women, especially those who have been 'used.' No such shame will come to any of our sisters, mothers, wives, or daughters. With that agreed, we discussed Helen's future. At first Tyndareus favored Agamemnon's sending a representative from Mycenae to rule after his death, but wise Phoenix counseled that Helen should carry on the tradition of her mother Leda. The discussion was tense until we agreed that her mate would be Menelaos. That calmed the Mycenaen delegation as they viewed him,

Agamemnon's brother, as their representative in Sparta."

As the family praised the work of the council, Kti relaxed. "I am relieved that the traditions prevail in these changing times."

Kti listened as her father, Laertes, once again summarized for the household. His last words excited her. "We shall soon journey by sea to Pylos where we shall go inland with Nestor and his household to landlocked Sparta for Klytemnestra and Agamemnon's marriage feast and to acknowledge Helen's match with Menelaos in a quiet gathering."

"Well done, both of you," Antikleia said to the young men.

Odysseus raised his glass. "I say we toast the news with this fine wine. Now, Eury, I express our joy that you and your family have agreed to make the journey to the south with us."

Thus, Odysseus helped his parents end the public gathering that settled into a visit of the immediate family circle.

Later Kti and Ody found moments for a visit more personal.

Kti sat next to him on a bench in the family garden. "Were you sorry not to be chosen for Helen?"

"Most of the men may have hoped for Helen's hand. I did not. My heart already turns elsewhere. That likely does not surprise you, dear sister."

Ssmiling, Kti shook her head. "I would have been more surprised if you were sorry."

Ody laughed. "From your first accounts of your two friends, of their hopes and dreams, I reaffirmed Pen as my choice, not Helen. We match well, Kti. I mean to bring Pen as wife to these Isles next year."

"Where will you live?"

"We shall build our home on neighboring Ithaka on lands given to me from Mother's dowry. She inherited the lands from her mother's sister who married into the Palli kindred circle. I put my hopes to Pen at council where she represented her family. We agreed to approach our parents and make arrangements at the wedding festivities in Sparta. You remember, Kti, I first met her at the feast commemorating the boar hunt that tested my manhood."

Kti gave a vigorous nod. "I remember your telling me she visited our grandparents after receiving the rite of womanhood last year when you were wounded."

"Yes, while I healed, she attended me. We talked often. Your coming home this year from Parnassus with praise of her confirmed my first desires."

Kti knew from Pen that her love for Ody matched his for her. "To have Pen nearby, if only she would come, will give me joy, I am happy for you. I know Pen favors you, but her father, Ikarios, wants her near him. Do you think he will allow her to leave?"

Ody spoke in a firm voice. "Independent like you, Kti, she will leave. Besides, her sister Iphthime, betrothed to a prince nearby, will tend to Ikarios."

Still, he has Pen's father to convince. A hard task.

They talked of Helen's giving birth in Eleusis, of Kti's time with Helen, and of the arbitration regarding the child that satisfied all parties.

After a pause, Ody said, "What do you think of Eury?"

Not an easy question to turn aside or to answer, Kti matched her brother's art of strategy. "The trip to the South gives me time to know him better. He will travel with us for many days." Her heart beat faster.

PART THREE

KTIMENE and EURYLOKHOS

THE ISLAND OF SAMOS

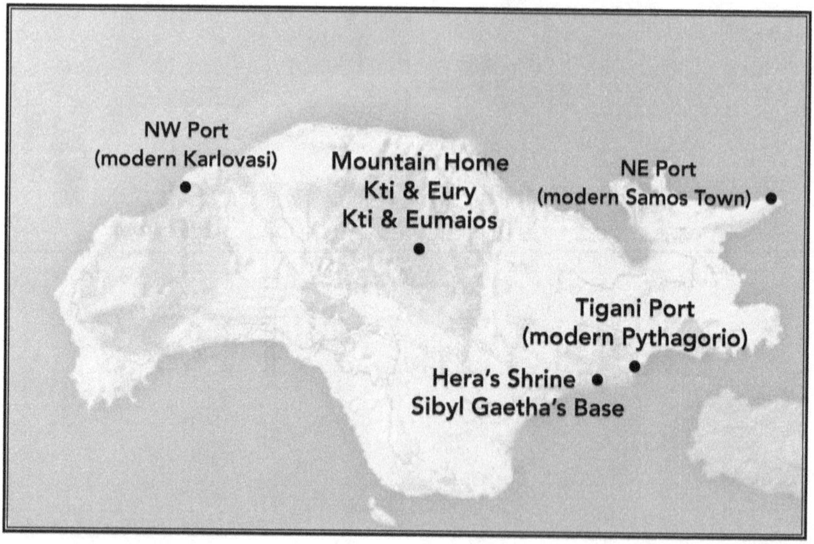

NW Port
(modern Karlovasi)
•

Mountain Home
Kti & Eury
Kti & Eumaios
•

NE Port
(modern Samos Town) •

Tigani Port
(modern Pythagorio)
•

Hera's Shrine •
Sibyl Gaetha's Base

Touching the stars gives you courage to love.

CHAPTER SEVEN

K ti stood next to Eury and Ody at the rail of the family ship and viewed the shore. "How many days must we journey across the land of Nestor?"

"From this port," Ody said, "we traveled inland a day and a night, but we had swift horses to reach the council in time. Now that we have brought wagons for supplies and comfort, our inland journey to Sparta will take longer."

Eury gazed at the sea birds that followed the vessels. "Would that we were birds, we would fly there."

Kti laughed and lunged forward as if to jump. "I am so excited to be going to Sparta, I could swim ashore."

Both men restrained her from the playful jump. They laughed, too.

"At long last, Sparta." Kti leaped from the wagon, stretched, then whirled around to Freya. "After two days of rattling across the mountains and two nights of camping, I am happy to be in Tyndareus' vast citadel where we can settle into quarters with the comfort of bath and bed. But before we see to ourselves, we must attend to Mother. Father's arranging a litter for the last day of her journey helped, but she is weak."

Freya joined Kti in a whirl. "Arriving before high sun gives us time to have a repast with Queen Antikleia and set her to rest Then we shall have until evening to prepare both of you for Helen's evening wedding and supper."

As Kti and her family entered the small gathering for the marriage of Helen and Menelaos, she whispered. "I knew it, Mother. Klytemnestra and her mother are not present. I am glad Tyndareus is here to host, at least."

Antikleia put her finger to her lip. "Hush, child, and think. They are preparing for Klytemnestra's wedding tomorrow."

"At least Agamemnon is here," Kti's whispered.

Kti with Pen chanted the vows with the shrine women. As they ate at the small supper gathering, she turned to her mother. "I enjoyed chanting with the shrine women of Hera, Demeter, and Artemis. Their chants similar to ours in meaning, are cast in words that, I suspect, reflect their regions."

Antikleia nodded, then looked at her plate. "Please take me to my chamber. I am weary."

Upon her return, Kti, with Pen, found Helen. "Oh, Helen," Kti exclaimed as they both embraced her, "I hope you and Menolaos find happiness in this union. Menelaos could not take his eyes from you during the rituals or the dinner. You have captured his heart."

Helen cast her eyes downward. "He is a kind man. I know he is happy with the match. I shall grow to love him."

Kti, took Helen's hand, "You deserve a great love. You will have it." After she and Pen gave Helen more assurances, they left the supper for their chambers.

The next evening, Kti, with her family, witnessed as the priests of the Olympian Gods conducted the magnificent public marriage of the royal Mycenaean couple. She joined the feasting afterward, enjoying most of the dances with Eury "I hope the marriage will be a happy one. I wish Klytemnestra well, but I missed the blessings of the shrine women whose joyous chants rang out in the marriage of Helen and Menelaos."

Eury smiled and took Kti as close as he dared. "I liked Helen's simpler ceremony, but both women deserve happiness."

The next day, Kti with her family met Ikarios and Periboa to arrange the marriage of Odysseus with Penelope.

Later when she was alone with Pen, Kti said, "Our fathers set the marriage contract, but our mothers form the lasting bond in the betrothal ritual when the future couple exchange garlands and jewels."

"Yes, I found most joy in the ceremony of the women. I enjoyed listening to the rituals instead of participating in the chant."

"Ody began your Ithakan home as soon as he returned from the council in Sparta. That showed his confidence in your father's consent. The old ways of inheritance destine me to occupy the citadel at Pronni, a daughter's right, but I relish having you and Ody close. You will love living in the Western Isles, dear Pen."

Pen met her eyes with a measured gaze. "You babble like the nearby stream, Kti. I already love the Isles. Something else, surely, you wish to tell me. Are you concerned about your future studies or some other plan forming?"

"All right, all right," Kti said. "A distraction gives me a turn. Eury and I have declared our love for one another; a 'fine man,' you say. Even Helen, in her enigmatic way, smiles upon him for me. I wonder if marriage can blend with study. I watch Mother and Grandmother Neaira do work of the Great Mother even as they manage households and families. You and Helen will follow that same path. Your examples give me hope that marriage blended with public obligations will still allow a full spiritual life. Few become dedicated sacred teachers who devote themselves solely to the shrines. Before I dedicate myself to a Mother shrine, I must know my deeper heart's needs."

Kti paced a few steps, then turned around to face Pen. "And, yes, Eury excites my passions. As I have come to know him better on this journey, I find we connect with the Great Mother in special ways. He, with his own integrity, frees me to deepen my wholeness. We have talked about a life together. Mostly, in ecstasy, I want to call out for all to hear 'yes, yes, yes.' Then I hear a voice say, 'Wait awhile. Let your heart energy test your inclinations.' If it be 'yes,' I must wait."

Pen squeezed Kti's hand. "You do have time to consider. As we build our home, you will come to the site with us, will you not? I shall enjoy living in your home until the roof goes on ours, and we finish the inner chambers. Your being near gives us time to talk."

Kti knew she and Eury must decide within the year. The time slipped away quickly.

After Pen and Ody married, Eury embarked on a long trading journey. Kti did her mother's work instead of going to Eleusis, an earlier plan. She managed the citadel while her father assisted Ody with building a new home on Ithaka for him and Antikleia. He planted the vineyard and the orchard between their home and the citadel.

Pen stayed at the Pronni citadel after journeys to Ithaka in the early building phase. Besides the fall weather making the sea treacherous from Pronni to Ithaka's wide-mouthed bay, Pen did not venture forth since she expected a child.

Kti relished attending her at Pronni. In due time, she and Freya assisted in the birth of young Telemakhos, whose name marked him a future maker of safe seas.

As spring came, Eury docked his ship. Kti quickened her steps while her heart beat faster. Hand in hand they walked from the port to the citadel and settled on a bench in the grape arbor.

Eury half-grimaced as he twisted his hands "Kti, I know coming to Samos Island with me after marriage adds to our first discussions of union. An even bigger step than our original plan to manage trading affairs from here, the new plan serves us well. I believe we must be close to business interests there. Later we shall return here, but first I want to be sure my younger brother Kephalos takes hold of our business in the trade. We need to establish a firm base for our lives together."

Kti clasped his hand tighter.

In a persuasive tone, Eury rushed on. "When first we talked of marriage, we agreed we wanted many children. If so, we need to assure their future. Aunt and Uncle need us there. They already love you. Pen and Ody will be at hand to help your parents manage your citadel while they develop their own lands."

Kti ducked her head but remained silent.

Catching a breath, Eury said, "Kti, the people of Samos Island need you to work at the shrine much as you do here. Also, you can study at the Samian shrine where the Sibyl Gaetha teaches in the tradition of Hera the Matron. Hera has her own history, well established before Zeus claimed her as consort on Olympus. Visits to the Artemesion on the nearby Eastern mainland can be frequent. That center, a wonder, draws students from all directions. All these reasons add to my deep desire to take you as my own. I hope I build a strong case for our lives together, first there and soon here again."

Kti flinched at the word "take." She knew what he meant, but he had used the language of the warrior. He spent many hours with Ody preparing for what she hoped would never come—possible conflict with those who threatened their way of life or engaged in war. She understood their concerns but saw their military banter in terms of protection and survival, not strategies and acts of violence.

Kti looked into Eury's eyes. "You expect an answer today. You have given me ample time to consider what we discussed last year. The move to Samos Island adds another term, but it cannot bar our marriage. We know our hearts. Our inner lights ache to join. Yes, dear one, we shall meet our destinies together. I happily assent."

After a long embrace, the young couple, their arms entwined, moved toward the main hall of the citadel to set their marriage plans into motion. "I do believe all nature confirms our love as well as our future," Eury said as they gazed at the beauty of the valley and its mellow glow in the late afternoon sun."

Kti looked toward the brambles and weeds that needed tending. *How will I be able to leave this place deserted? Eumaios and his men will come from Ithaka to see after it, but a deserted citadel invites looters.*

Endings spin star stuff to swirl into beginnings.

CHAPTER EIGHT

Preparing for the wedding rituals and feasts filled the time before the wedding day. Kti planned a special good-bye for Eumaios. She arranged to bring him from his work to make final arrangements for the wedding rituals.

She walked along the path from the citadel across the valley past the family tomb where she paid respect at the monument to Kephalos, her ancient ancestor. She prayed at the burial site of Prokris, his wife, and of Pronnus, their son, who had built the citadel, soon to be hers.

Kti thought about tending the lands well. *I shall bring in abundant crops and raise prize livestock. More important, I shall build a port on my western lands to trade beyond the pillars that guard the western end of the Great Sea.*

She jolted her head westward. *I will not disturb the tortoises, a colony that for many generations have come from Zante Isle to nest in the wide bay where I shall build. These dreams, we must postpone for a sojourn on Samos Island.*

She thought of Eumaios' future work. Living near her parents in Ithaka, his main duty would be to oversee their lands and those of Ody and Pen. He would dwell near the well of Aretheusa, the main water source for the herds. The master herder Philoitios would work under Eumaios' guidance to attend her citadel. Eumaios would continue to serve the Mother, extending his work to the hill people of Ithaka.

Eumaios holds positions of trust. He deserves them.

Lost in her thoughts, she little realized the terrain had become more rugged. When she reached the lake in a valley protected by a small hillside, she found Eumaios who had just sent the finest of the herd to the citadel for the wedding feast.

Eumaios greeted her, understood her mission, and prepared to go with her.

As they left the small valley, Kti said, "Let us follow the goat trail over the hill to the beach. On such a warm day, the sea invites us to cool ourselves before we go to the citadel.

They walked in silence.

Kti saw Eumaios' broad smile as they approached the pebbled beach.

"Well, my lady, we soon bid you farewell. Samos calls."

Kti returned his smile. "You speak quite formally today. I must also, I suppose. We have been companions for many years. I know we shall see one another here again before much time passes; still I shall miss you."

Then her voice deepened. "I hope to see you at the feast after the wedding ritual. All the citadel and hill people, our kin along with friends from everywhere, will come."

"I shall dance at your wedding, Kti," Eumaios said, a twinkle in his eye.

Kti said, "Have you the order of the rituals in mind?"

"First I conduct the midnight ritual of the Great Mother. Then at morning's light, I shall assist in the blessings that your mother and grandmother will give to acknowledge your freedom to join in matrimony. I understand sacred women from Parnassus will join women from our Trimetrian shrine, as well as those from the shrines of Hera and Dodona, at a noonday ritual at the Mother's ritual center. Before the feasting, your father will assemble us for the public pronouncement of the vows of Zeus's followers. Splendid rituals will send you into your married life. Is that the order?"

"Yes, you have it right." Kti nodded, then she added with a sigh, "I hope one day the ceremonies can unite into one ritual that will satisfy everyone."

"In time, surely the rituals will unite," Eumaios said.

Kti said, "Your presiding at the midnight and dawn rituals gladdens my heart. For other pairs, you have intoned so movingly the first words of the marriage day. I do not think I could complete the day without that."

By now, the two had reached the long strip of pebbled beach. The turquoise water sparkled in the sunlight throwing gentle wavelets onto the shore. They stripped for the swim, their young bodies shining golden in the sun. For an instant their eyes met. They moved toward one another then stopped, their eyes cast downward to the pebbled beach.

Eumaios knelt and selected a pebble, one with white, red, and black joined by the whipping of the sea. The ancient surface of the stone, now polished by the winds, sea and sun, glistened like a jewel. He stretched his hand toward Kti.

She responded with hers.

Eumaios stared into her eyes. "Take this small stone to remind you of our strong bond. If ever you need me, Kti, send it to me. I shall come to care for you, your husband and your children when they come."

Kti took the stone and gazed into Eumaios's eyes. "O my

Eumaios, my Jamin," she whispered, "I know that you will come to me, should I need you." She paused. "I remember well the first ritual we formed between us. Then I gave you your name, Jamin, that we have always kept as a treasure between us. This stone, another treasure, I shall keep with me always."

Eumaios opened his mouth to speak but instead turned to plunge into the sea. Kti stared after him. She tucked the stone inside her treasure pouch close by and entered the water.

The mountain shadowed the beach as the sun moved lower in the sky. They swam ashore, dried in its final rays, dressed and walked together to the citadel.

Eumaios's last words of the day echoed in her ears. "Kti, I shall see you at midnight as I promised. Remember your promise to call upon me should ever you need me. You abide ever in my heart."

"Yes, I shall remember," she said as they went their separate ways.

In good order, rituals and festivities unfolded. The young couple relished the beauty of the day. Packing completed, Uncle and Aunt sailed first with their many gifts and household goods. Freya accompanied them. She would serve as Kti's main attendant in charge of their household on Samos.

Now the time came for Kti and Eury to depart.

"Hurry, Kti," Eury said with urgency in his tone. "We sail in moments."

Over and over they had said goodbyes to both families. Foremost in his mind, he wanted to take his bride to Samos.

"So soon, so soon, dear child, you leave us," Kti's mother said. "I must hold you for one last embrace."

Kti searched her mother's eyes, then those of the others in

turn. She swallowed hard, gathered resolve from their love-filled faces.

"Be strong," they echoed. "Use the Mother's ways to give you courage."

Kti glided toward her grandfather and father. She planted a kiss on each forehead. No words came to her, but the silence gave her energy from their star points.

Eury stepped forward, swept Kti into his arms and carried her to the ship, with those gathered following close behind. They waved until the shore of Pronni's port disappeared. The ship entered the deep rolling sea and outpaced the land birds that followed them.

"At last, we are alone!" Eury shouted as they walked in close embrace to their sheltered place on the after deck and then their marriage bed.

Kti fell into his embrace. "Ah, my love, our life together has begun. May we treasure this moment and all that are to come."

Lest you forget your journey, star sparks come to earth.

CHAPTER NINE

S mooth sailing gave Eury and Kti time to dally in private. Early evening of the second day brought them to Nestor's port. After refreshing, they joined the household. Nestor had planned a surprise for the young couple. He cleared a pathway for Helen and Menelaos to step out of the shadows.

Kti, eyes wide and smile broad, said, "What a grand surprise. We were saddened when you could not attend the wedding after the birth of your daughter, Hermione."

Kti's outstretched hand remained in Helen's. "Greetings, Kti, maiden no more but matron, and Eury, fortunate cousin, spouse of my dearest friend," Helen's voice resounded in the hall.

Kti looked at Helen, taking in her cascading red-golden hair that framed her face and coiled down around her slim body. "You make a dazzling mother. And you have returned to health quite well."

"Thank you, dear one," Helen said, "Menelaos is the most attentive husband and father."

Kti and Eury embraced all present and thanked a glowing Nestor for his bringing the couple to them. Nestor's good queen presented libations to thank the sacred powers for safe arrivals.

Nestor stood taller. "We are pleased to give you such a wonderful treat. After you refresh and we feast, the young ones of the court will sleep while we visit. Helen and Menelaos tell me they have wedding gifts to present." Kti and Eury followed servants to their quarters.

The conviviality continued in the great hall after the children retired. Their friends turned to two golden chests. Kti felt Helen's hand in hers as Helen led her and Eury to the chests.

Helen swept the air with her graceful arm. "Receive these two chests, your wedding gifts."

Kti clasped her hands together. "They are magnificent. The design is so intricate."

"Our artisans, women of the East," Menelaos said, "designed them."

Eury fingered one of the chests. "They will have a special place in our home."

"Smiling, Menelaos said, "The chest on the left with the red jewel on its top is for lovemaking. Helen will show you ways we enjoy the sacred delights it holds."

"I learned of these arts," Helen said, "from women of the ruling courts of the East. Displaced and disenchanted by conditions brought by invading warriors, our women artisans came to us from caravans, then trading ships They held to the old ways guided by an equal group of Immortals instead of by seven masculine Immortals including a lone feminine Immortal. Some found homes with the Mazdeans along mainland trade routes where their beliefs match those of the people living there."

Kti said, "I have heard of such people from traders who meet the caravans at ports of the eastern Great Sea, but I have never seen them."

Menelaos said, "The women who reside with us in Sparta came because they heard that we honored the feminine way welcoming to their arts."

As she listened, Kti thought, "Helen, her heart awakened, opens more fully. And Menelaos adds softness since the wedding feast. He displays a warrior's manner still, but not the earlier lust. He matches Helen. A powerful energy encompasses them." Setting aside her mind wanderings, Kti joined her arm with Eury's and listened with greater attention.

"Look at the colors of the jewels encircling the life-giving ruby," Helen said. "Our crafters alternated jewels of orange, yellow, green, pale and dark blue, purple, lavender, and rose. The colors come into play as I describe what the Eastern women told us."

Helen swung outward the hinged door. "Inside find perfumed oils for massaging each other's body. Witness the body points that need massage."

At that, she pressed points of her body. "Red matches the lowest point of the torso. Massaging the point stills us while it stirs us. It brings comfort, even balance, to the body, giving us a place in time and space. Orange conducts energy to balance the point just below the body's omphala. It gives us movement, intelligence, and passion. Yellow brings the energy of the sun to the body just here at the lower center of our boney breastplate. When this point achieves harmony, the body heals to enhance creativity, liveliness, and confidence."

Helen paused for each to reflect on her words.

From the hush, Kti sighed. "As you spoke, my body cooperated with each point."

The others nodded.

Helen lowered her eyes. "Each person must balance the first three points before reaching the others. Think on that."

Hush came over the group.

At length. she pointed to the heart. "Green, the mid-point we call the heart, gives us the capacity for compassion as well as centered contentment. Our hearts, free of encumbrances, move us upward. Blue, here at the throat point, passes air for deep breathing throughout our bodies to resonate with our thoughts. Thus, we learn to listen and speak wisely."

As she pinched the upper point above her nose and pressed the spot between her eyes, Helen looked around. "A deeper blue sits between our eyes to form an inner seeing. In it, resides our mother/father sides. The point penetrates to a deep unconsciousness where we gain insight and imagination from dreams and memories. Here, we find our ancestors and gain the vision that places our star in the sky pattern."

Helen patted the top of her head. "The mix of purple, lavender, and rose invites the other colors to our real home in the spacious white prism of the crowning point. Here, resides spiritual connection and unity, not duality. To attain wisdom, we must connect to the spirit, always open to us. Here, the current awakens us, opens us, and frees us."

Kti felt calm in the stillness that encircled her. "What a guide to our well-being the colors give us."

Helen spoke again. "Once we understand that good health of our bodies frees us for broader relationship with our mate, we can expand the bond forever outward like the ripples when we drop a stone into still water of a pond."

Kti lifted her hand to her brow. "That takes more explaining, Helen."

"I speak first of relationship with your mate, the purpose of the contents in the first chest. We handpicked each item in the chest. Here nest wise-eyed peacock feathers, soft dove down, wispy ribbons, and flowing, opaque cloths of many colors. Here are vials of tasty spices and sweet juices to suck from each other's body. These delights will amuse while they heighten the senses. Discover within many other surprises, all intended to perfect the art of lovemaking, the opening of the pathway to a deeper connection to Eros that flashes upward through the body to bring you from there to all forms of love."

As Helen spoke, Kti felt an awakening. She smiled at Eury.

Menelaos broke the silence. "We warriors ignore pleasures as the entrance to our true nature. With practice, we must relearn their benefits."

Helen trembled with excitement. "See what the niches of the door contain."

Menelaos extracted twin objects, one from each niche.

Kti's eyes widened. "I have never seen such things. May I hold one?"

As Kti turned the object over and fingered the latch that opened it, Helen said, "Go ahead open it. Our scribe adapted an object we found in the goods of a caravan master at the port of Ashkelon. Tiny hinges hold together thick wooden covers, inlaid with opalescent mother of pearl. Within the covers, we secured in the one you hold small squares of thinly planed wood tooled with symbols similar to those our scribes use to keep records. Each square illustrates ancient arts of oriental love-making. The other contains inspiring scenes of nature to thrill your yearning to travel. The thin wooden squares record much as clay tablets do. They add to the pleasures that open a couple for their work in the world. When we discovered these wonders, our love deepened and our world expanded."

Kti looked at the piece. "Helen and Menelaos, dear ones, these objects, this chest, will always have a place in our bedchamber. We thank you for such a special gift."

"Use it and you will see how it affects your lives. Now let us look at the second chest."

When Menelaos spoke, the group turned to the second chest, a twin in form to the first but topped with a different central jewel, a flawless, massive emerald. Surrounding it were perfectly cut sapphires, amethysts, and opals that intermixed the colors of the crown point.

Kti put her hands to her mouth as Helen opened the hinged arms to reveal three striking figures. "What a stunning tableau."

Helen's fluid words moved Kti to look closely at the figures. "These three figures blend the Eastern immortal sisters with characteristics of our Great Mother's forms of maiden, matron, and wise elder. The Eastern women designed them well. Much like our Mother Gaia, the Eastern women say one of the feminine immortals, whom the Mazdeans call Spenta Armaiti, came to earth to bring us wisdom and expose us to the wonders of the world. They say her body forms our earth to replicate here the pattern of the universe. Although she tends us, she constantly desires that we dwell with the Immortals. When all of us return to our source, she will go back to her place: a realm that forms the larger world beyond ours. These complicated ideas need much reflection. They shed light on how our ideas have evolved in the West."

Kti sighed. "I see the connection. I gain reassurance from knowing our Mother Gaia has kindred spirits in the Eastern world."

Helen pointed her delicate finger to the figure in the niche of the left door. "This figure depicts a female in the greening time of life. Carved from polished green jade, a rare find, she wears a flowing gown, bedecked with jaunty ribbons that hold their place, as if gentle breezes set them into motion to remind us of her vitality. The just-opening lotus blossom adorning the garment over her heart, suggests that her heart gathers scattered resources to move her into the next phase of her life. In our tradition, we call her a kore, a youth or a maiden who prepares for the ritual of adulthood."

Kti's words burst forth. "Everyday, I also see her male counterpart. She is springtime."

"Look, now, to the niche in the right door," Helen continued. "Its niche contains a matron with a face of ivory. Her gently flowing lapis gown of deep blue indicates that she builds a full life here. Through life's experiences, she knows the business of the world, but she also knows that more exists. Note her fully-opened lotus broach, her settled ribbons, both emblems of her calm nature and her steady heart. Spend time examining her surroundings. Lush trees line the shores of the gentle streams. Beyond them, waterfalls pour forth from the jutting, misty mountains where the tall, wild trees create chaos that stirs our more settled world. As the scene integrates, so her nature moves to the deeps of her inner eye, then upward to her crown."

Kti shook her head. "Yes, yes, I see my mother, all the mothers."

Eury said, "Fathers, too."

"Feast your eyes on these two figures before we look at the figure deep in the middle chamber," Menelaos said. "The young woman stands free, with no attachments, but vulnerable as she faces life's experiences. The serene matron, after tending to the world's affairs, shows readiness for a deeper existence. Both manifest our human nature that echoes that of the Great Mother. Men and women learn from their life experiences and know well that they journey here to prepare for a place in the immortal realm."

For some moments Kti gazed at the two small figures. She sensed the warmth of Eury's body standing next to her.

Then Helen pointed to the central chamber. "This figure forms an elder carved from a piece of rare stark-white jade with edges of pale pinks and violets. She comes forth from the stone to manifest wisdom gathered from the spirit stuff, a part of our finite being already joined to the infinite. Having fully integrated her experiences, she reaches the still point within. Mature in her all knowing, she belongs in the realms beyond."

"All of us, female or male, become her in one way or another," Menelaos added. "Some make the journey smoothly. Most find byways and opportunities to begin again. We must choose our path."

"The small pieces will fit in your treasure pouch. As you study these Immortals, our Great Mother will renew you." Helen closed the chest. In deep silence, all moved from the great hall to their bed chambers for restful sleep.

The next morning amidst farewells, Kti embraced Helen and took her hand. "We discussed the effect on you both of what you have learned. It is a wonder, and we are glad. May the chests be a reminder to us of what we can achieve. Thank you, dear friend."

As Menelaos helped her aboard the awaiting travel wagon, Helen said, "I know your next port brings you to Mycenae. If

Iphigenia has arrived, give her an embrace from her Aunt."

Kti plumbed Helen's face as she released her hand, then took Eury's arm. "I shall seek out Iphigenia if she has come to Klytemnestra. In turn, please hug Hermione, your newborn, for us."

Kti walked with Eury to their ship. "Oh, Eury, I wonder how Klytemnestra will receive us. I wonder, too, what the future holds for Iphigenia."

Starry skyways guide you.

Chapter Ten

As they were under way to Mycenae, Helen called to them across the deep waters, "Go with the Gaia's blessing. May the winds blow you to safe ports. Farewell, dear ones."

Smooth waters brought Kti and Eury around the Peloponnese to Naphali, the southern port of Mycenae. Klytemnestra and Agamemnon missed their wedding, a difficult birth of Orestes keeping them home. Kti scanned the dock for the royal couple. She turned to Eury. "I hope Klytemnestra has recovered enough to see us."

As she spoke, a messenger from the citadel approached. "Queen Klytemnestra sends her greetings, as does King Agamemnon. The King stays by her side. They send assurances that the queen's health returns and that the young Prince grows heartier each day. They offer wishes for a safe journey."

Kti glanced at Eury. "Tell the King and Queen that we hope for the queen's speedy recovery."

They sent gifts to the royal family, received some in exchange, and caught the evening winds for night sailing toward Krete, now a Greek colony long-divided among the chieftains of Athens, Korinth, and Mycenae, the latter including an alliance with Argos, Sparta, Pylos and the Western Isles. Before falling asleep, Kti said, "The messenger would know little of household affairs. We must wait to learn of Iphigenia."

Two days later, they spied their destination, a small southwestern port run by Klamakis, whose wife, Eurynome, was kin to Klytemnestra.

"Eury, we must tread with light steps as we visit and trade here. Long-standing tension stirs between Eurynome's brother, Aigisthos, and Agamemnon."

"I know little of the strife between them," Eury said. "Krete has not been one of my trading stops until now."

"You are fortunate. I thought the traders exchanged as many stories as our tellers."

"This is one I have missed."

Kti chuckled. "Well, you should know a bit of it before we meet the family. Certainly, before you trade. Until her marriage, Eurynome lived with her mother and brother, Aigisthos, near Argos, their family home. They are heirs of Thyestes who lost the rule of Mycenae to his brother Atreus, Agamemnon's father. Some say treachery between Thyestes and Atreus caused the feud. Each side has followers who tell dark stories about the outcome, but Agamemnon won."

Eury said, "That would make Aigisthos and Eurynome first cousins to Agamemnon. No wonder Agamemnon and Aigisthos are rivals."

"True," said Kti, "But that Klytemnestra's grandmother married into the line of Eurynome complicates matters more since her dowry brought land into the Argos holdings."

Eury gave Kti a wry smile. "How do you know these things, Kti? I thought I kept my ears open for stories."

"Phemios heard it from an Athenian teller and sings it often in our great hall."

Eury shook his head. "I am glad I know this before I trade here."

"You listen well and use good judgment, but it is good you know," Kti said. "We are determined to rise above family feuds and visit all the kin."

Eury nodded. "We are rooted in the customs of Arkadians and the Western Isles. Our tribal role has always been to maintain family peace."

As they disembarked, a polyglot of faces reminded Kti that the region blended the tribes of the Myceneans with her tribe, the Pelasgians.

Kti looked around. *Truly all of us live now as one family.*

Traders of varied skin color and dress, many that she could not place, passed her at the dock. "I shall ask my cousin to shed light on this cross section of people from many trade routes."

Near a gateway, in a shaded nook of the wall of limestone that protected the upper city, stood an elegantly dressed group. Among them a statuesque woman replicated the features of Klytemnestra.

Kti pointed toward the woman. "Eury, I see Eurynome. The entourage has likely come to greet us."

A young man broke away from the group. He joined the couple as soon as they reached shore.

A cloying voice made the hairs of her arm stand on end. "Welcome, Eury and Kti, we come to meet you. I am Aigisthos, Klytemnestra's cousin. My sister, Eurynome, and some of her household have joined me to welcome you. I will help you with your luggage and take you to them."

Kti waved toward the group and, with eyes wide, took

Eury's arm. "Eury, meet Aigisthos of Argos. He will assist us by taking us to his sister."

The men shook hands.

Aigisthos said, "Eurynome's husband, Klamakis, detained on business inside the gated city, asked me to greet you on his behalf. I, too, am a visitor."

"Really?" said Kti. "How long are you here?"

"Soon I will return to our Argive lands north of Mycenae. I understand Klytemnestra, unable to greet you in our southern port, sent an emissary in her stead. She asked me to deliver special greetings on her behalf."

Kti averted her eyes. *I wonder why Aigisthos brought this message.*

Aigisthos shifted from side to side. "Although I oversee our ancestral home with my mother near Argos outside the walls of Mycenae, I see Klytemnestra and her growing family then and again. Her family married into ours to make her a cousin. Klytemnestra recovers from the birth of her son. Recently her eldest daughter, Iphigenia, who lived away, joined them. Iphigenia thrives as do the other young ones." He looked directly at Kti as he mentioned Iphigenia. "Klytemnestra wanted me to tell you of the child's arrival at Mycenae and of her wellbeing."

Discomfited by the personal manner of this intense young man whom she had never met, Kti managed a polite smile that acknowledged his greeting. For an instant, she returned to earlier times when she had assisted at Helen's birthing of the young girl.

So, Iphigenia is with Klytemnestra as planned. I hardly believed her chieftain father or the shrine women of Demeter would let the child go. I wonder if the arrangement well serves the young one, now that Klytemnestra has three of her own.

Eury, less aware of all the nuances of Aigisthos' words, greeted Aigisthos. "Your kind welcome on behalf of your family makes us eager to visit."

Aigisthos seemed relieved to direct his gaze to Eury. "Allow me to take you to my sister, just there in the shade of the wall."

Smiling, Eury said, "Ktimene will join them. I shall come directly, but first I must settle our ships and bring ashore our necessities."

"Of course, of course." Aigisthos said. "I shall send a servant to transport your belongings to Eurynome's villa in the hills beyond the town. He will guide you to the city house within the walls where we shall await you."

Taking Kti's arm, Aigisthos led her to the family group. Kti felt relief when Aigisthos released her. Each greeted her with sincere warmth. She and Eurynome embraced. Then the entourage moved into the city.

As they walked, Kti and Eurynome held hands. "From here, we will journey inland along a broad ancient road built in the time the Minoans reigned on the island," Eurynome said. "You will find it a better road than any I have seen in Argos."

"Thank you for your warm welcome. Eury will be along shortly. Someday, perhaps I shall visit Argos." Kti did not miss Eurynome's using Argos, the more ancient name for the homeland that signaled a time when her family line ruled the kingdom citadel now called Mycenae.

Soon Eury and Klamakis joined them. The entourage set off toward the hillside home.

Kti listened to Klamakis' account as they walked along. "This broad road connects the port and town here with our home that is fashioned within the summer home of the ancient Minos of the West who ruled the region long ago. When not detained in the main citadel of Phaistos, the ruler enjoyed the green hillside, the sea breezes cooling him at his country retreat, now our home.'

Kti said, "Does the road stop at Phaistos?"

"The road leads to the citadel of the great Minos at Knossos, a center that dominates the northern shores. That stately palace belongs to Ideomenus of Athens, the most powerful ruler of the island. Before Ideomenus, a series of ancient Minoan rulers conducted public business there on behalf of their daughters who themselves oversaw rituals of their Mother Goddess."

"Interesting," Kti said. "Is the ritual still alive here?"

"Oh no. When the early Hellenes took over the lands, they took the earlier ruling peoples to the citadels of Hellas or eradicated them. A few of the native people escaped, but some our ancestors here kept as servants. My family came from the Peloponnese to build our vast trading network. We brought our own religion, too."

"Very soon, dear Kti," Eurynome said, "while Eury conducts business, you must see lofty Phaistos that overlooks the southern valley of our region. Now in ruins, the citadel contains many mysteries, I am told. First, you must enjoy our greener, more inviting home."

As they approached the villa, Kti marveled at the setting among the vegetation, by far the greenest spot they had seen on their journey. Nestled among the trees and lush undergrowth, the home took full advantage of the ancient walls to capture wafting sea breezes and shade of the terraced greenery.

In its present state, it integrated the walkways and terraces into livable interior spaces. Mosaics depicted graceful swimming sea creatures and landscape scenes with fields of lilies whose stamens still yielded a rare cooking spice and equally rare dyes for making cloth bright yellow or orange.

"What lovely mosaics these are. Did your artisans prepare them?"

"They were here when we redesigned the villa," Eurynome said. "The lilies have secrets lost to us, but some of the servants remember them, if only they would tell."

Farther on, walls with images of blue monkeys swinging from tree limbs prompted Eurynome to say, "What, we wonder, are the origin and meaning of these odd creatures?"

They entered the central room, spaciously extended onto a terrace. Kti directed her gaze to a stone sarcophagus, the prominent decorative piece of the great hall. She moved closer to inspect it. *Perhaps the vessel portrays a ritual of the Great Mother. If so, the women who are carved and painted on it carry libations and gifts to honor the deceased one whose ashes the vessel once held.*

Kti turned to Eurynome. "How interesting this piece is. The women on the piece must reflect the history of the island."

She inspected them more closely. "They wear free flowing skirts, their bare breasts gracefully erect, their black hair pulled back to fall into long coiled ringlets alongside faces accented by rouged cheeks above which shine wide dark eyes heavily made up with white and black paints, no doubt reflective of their time." Kti glanced at Eurynome. "The family who viewed the scene on the vessel commemorating their loved one surely received great comfort."

"I suppose so. I had never realized exactly what it was. I just liked the decoration."

Kti and Eury presented Eurynome and Klamakis gifts, chief among them elegant drinking cups depicting scenes of home. They also presented vintage wines in elaborate kraters. Kti said, "Enjoy these reminders of home decorated in the ancient Minoan tradition by Kretan artisans, descendants of Minoan slaves."

"Thank you, dear ones," Eurynome said, "for a beautiful touch of home."

"We understand the indigenous palace people of Minos who remain on the island have lost the ancient arts," Kti said. "When I was a child, my father told me of the dispersal of many Minoans after a great quake to the north on Thera Island that tipped and flooded Krete when a sunami came, destroying its palaces, marring the land. He said many scrambled to the mountains, but others took to ships that came to our shores. A few of the women among them were weavers or potters whose ancestors create useful wares. The Minoans who remained on Krete built even stronger palaces that could not withstand the next quakes and the invasion of the Athenians, too soon coming after their rebuilding."

Eurynome said, "That explains the beauty of your gifts."

"Yes, my ancestors, along with those of Peloponnesian strongholds, brought to our lands many other talented women and their children," Kti said. "Some joined our small band of craftsmen. Now their ancestors carry on the crafting tradition."

"Here, our servants have lost their vision so evident in their earlier accomplishments," Eurynome said.

The gifts Kti and Eury presented brought tears to Eurynome's eyes. "I yearn for home. These treasures will help me remember."

One day as Kti sat in the garden with Eury, she said,

"Mother viewed the external forces that destroyed the Minoans as Gaia's punishment for their loss of vision. She disagreed with Phemios who sang in our hall of the Sky God's punishing those who did not recognize Zeus. Such a telling, Phemios claimed, firmed Zeus' claim on Krete."

"Our teller in Sami," Eury said, "depicted Krete as the site of his birthing cave."

"I learned from a skeptical servant that two different caves vied for the site of Zeus's birth. I do not plan to see either of them snd I am ready to sail on as soon as you are."

"After our ships trade to the south, we shall continue our journey," Eury said. "When the ships dock here again, we shall trade in the north and see ancient Knossos."

"While you are gone, I shall go to the ruins of Phaistos, the citadel of the Minos of the West. I wonder what I shall find there."

Know more deeply my displacement.
Understand I spark forth still.

Chapter Eleven

Kti climbed the winding path to the gateway into Phaistos, its two lions guarding the city from the stone arch. "I see here the last Kretan stronghold of the west. What sad tumbled rocks. Do you know of the days when the Kretans held the lands?"

Slowly her guide Phaedra, a young serving girl, answered. "Early, the palace thrived in the hands of the people. Women governed and conducted rituals in its public spaces." She leveled her eyes. "My ancestors once ruled the area."

Their footsteps echoed on the massive stones as they wandered among the ghostly ruins, the inner chambers and outer walls.

"I hope you have some artifacts that tell your history," Kti said.

"Long ago, both fleeing Kretans and invading Hellenes stripped the citadel," said her guide.

With the winds whipping their garments, they stood on the ramparts of the barren ruins. "I feel the presence of those who lived here," Kti said.

"Strange that you say that. I often come here to speak with my ancestors," Phaedra said. They overlooked a rich valley that sloped southward to the sea. "Another port with beaches and caves lines the south shores. Long ago, that port served all the region."

The young girl, just before they departed the grounds, led Kti to an inner niche.

"Where are you taking me?" Kti said.

"Before the invaders came and after the great earth-shaking toppled many of these stones," Phaedra said, "my people removed vast treasures, among them clay discs that recorded our history. Many discs remain hidden in our mountain retreats. Here, you will find one."

As she spoke, from a deep crevice she took a small circular stone imprinted with a swirling text of figures Kti did not recognize. With pride in her voice, the young girl stumbled over the words, for she had lost her people's full power of reading. She related the story of a peace-loving woman who took grain and planting tools to a dark region where a hunting tribe knew only violence for gaining their food and shelter.

Abandoning her reading, she said, "The woman sought the hunters and their mastiffs to show them another way to live. I wish for the time of her coming again on this island."

Smiling, Kti nodded. "Yes, peaceful times nurture us all."

The young woman held out the disc. "Take this to remind you of our hope for better days. You alone of the many visitors walk in rhythm with us."

Kti held up her palm. "No, I cannot take the disc. Instead, let us place it deep into the niche. Someday, found there, it will serve as a record of your people."

The young woman bowed. Then they stowed the disc. In thoughtful silence, they returned to the villa.

Kti sat with Phaedra one day in a shaded nook near a field of lilies beyond the outer arches of the villa. "Do you know the story of the coming of Theseus in the ancient time of the second quakes?"

"Not only do the stories we overhear from our overlords exaggerate the role of Theseus, son of their chieftain Aegeus," Phaedra said with a clenched jaw, "but they diminish the role of Ariadne, a powerful heir to the rule of Krete in the old way of the Mother religion."

"The Athenians diminish ancient Athena, too," Kti said, "by adopting her as the patron of Athens and subservient daughter of Zeus, born out of Zeus' head with no mother—a story no one believes. They also reduce many of our other mother figures, for instance, Medea of Kalkis whom they call a betrayer of her people and a scheming enchantress."

Kti turned to Phaedra, "Please tell me how that same Greek tribe puffed up its power at the expense of Ariadne."

"According to our custom, Ariadne, the daughter of our consort and Pasiphae, would inherit from her mother the rule and leadership of the shrine women. They had lost their first son in a skirmish with Athenian warriors on a trading journey; thus, we demanded tribute of the Athenians. But in the exchange, Pasiphae's consort listened to the description of how, in Athens, they overcame the shrine women and their wives and daughters by shifting the inheritance rights to the son. When Ariadne's second brother was born, the Minos, as the Hellenes later named the consort, schemed to undermine his women and set up the same system on Krete, but the Hellenes betrayed the greedy man. They sent Theseus, the son of the Athenian ruler, with his men to kill the son and made the consort their puppet. They killed their so-called Minos as soon as he quieted the people. Before long, they killed Queen Pasiphae; married Phaedra, a second daughter, to an Athenian overlord; and took Ariadne, with many other women and children, with them. Other Athenians invaded our palaces. More earthquakes came. Weakened already, we were subdued. Those not captured hid in the mountains."

"Have you heard how the Athenians depicted Ariadne as an accomplice to Theseus? For love, she helped Theseus kill her brother the male heir, weaken her father's power and betray her mother."

"No," said Phaedra, "I have never heard that story, but I can tell you that Phaedra, whose name I proudly bear, was no submissive wife to the overlord forced upon her. She helped my ancestors hide, she hid treasures, she fed us and she kept our ways alive by training women who passed on the old ways in secret to this day."

"The Athenian version, now a firm legend in most courts of the mainland and islands of our land, made much of Ariadne's guiding Theseus in and out of a labyrinth that the Minoan master architect Daedalus contrived to contain her brother because he was deranged."

Kti paused so Phaedra could take in the story. "All fabricated by the tellers of the victorious Athenians, the story grew. The murder of the brother, of course, paved the way to remove the roadblock for Theseus' takeover."

"I see how legends slant the truth." Phaedra shook her head.

Kti took Phaedra's hand. "My teachers on Parnassus claimed Ariadne would view Theseus' stepping forward as a proposal that he replace her consort brother and take her to a shrine for purification before they returned for her to rule, the tradition of the old way. Ariadne misunderstood Theseus's motives. He took Ariadne to the holy women of Artemis on the island Naxos for the purging, but he left her. The Parnassian women say Ariadne became a shrine teacher on the Eastern mainland, but most tellers suggest she became the mate to another god they created, Dionysius, who honored her with a starry place in the heavens. Is not that an interesting way of bringing another strong woman to subservience."

"I prefer to think with the teachers that Ariadne continued the work of our Great Goddess," Phaedra said. "Better still, I would like to think she made it back to those who were hiding in our mountains, but we have no such story in our history,"

"The traditional teller's song," Kti said, "simply bragged of the winners' invasion of the Kretan people already weakened by changing mores, also by nature's random acts of quakes and waves that destroyed everything in their wake. The tale, in any form, carries the hurts of displacement, but why must such violent displacement exist?"

"In a very short time," Phaedra said, "the Athenians diminished Ariadne, a strong Mother figure. I fear the truth about the fall of Krete will never be told correctly."

"Dear friend," Kti said as she left Phaedra, "you have helped me see the truth. I shall tell it in my history."

In days of leisure thereafter, Kti thought of the differences between the servants' accounts and those of Phemios' songs of the fall from power long ago of the Minos. Phemios' lore came from the Athenian school of tellers. She realized that beyond the Mycenean and Korinthian trading empires, Athens had ascended rapidly as a trading power and as a disseminator of

Olympian Zeus that threatened to displace the Mother Gaia. None of her kin on Krete had asked of the early days on the island. *I vow to correct the record in my telling*.

Some days later, Kti and Eury left their kin. They journeyed northward with their other trading ships. Some of the ships traded at Kydonia in northwestern Krete and in eastern Zakros. Kti and Eury sailed to Mallia and Heraklion, the central ports of the island. There they went inland to Knossos, the palace of ancient Minos, now restored. The couple visited Ideomeneus, the Athenian overlord to whom all others from the mainland turned for governing support. He greeted them with ceremony, thanking them for their gifts. In return, he gave them a mosaic of dolphins uncovered in the ruins of the palace.

Kti saw Knossos, its ruined splendor now restored, as a triumph of a dominant culture. She wondered how long Mycenae, Korinth, and Athens would hold sway before another culture toppled them. A single question formed: *How many times would such a pattern recur?*

The ships turned toward Samos Island. The young bride, two months at sea, viewed the island of Ikarios so near the welcoming port of her future home.

Eury told her the story of the island's naming. "The island bears the name the son of the Minoan architect, Daedalus. Here, Ikarios fell into the sea when he did not heed his father's warning and melted his wings when he flew too close to the sun. The wily architect must have invented waxy wings to fly away from Krete to escape the wrath of the Minos after he aided Ariadne and Theseus."

Kti's lips twitched but she said nothing.

As they sailed into the harbor, Eury embraced her. "Kti, you now land in the Tigani port of Samos and your future home."

"Can it be true that this bustling, beautiful place will be our home? I see trading ships at dock for unloading next to fishing boats with nets ready. Such activity promises good profits and even better eating. The surrounding hills are brightened with the green of springtime. I can hardly wait to see Aunt and Uncle, our new home, and Freya."

What weeds lie hidden in this green land? How will I fit in? Will I ever return to my home?

See with your heart.

Chapter Twelve

Kti and Eury walked along the sacred path of Hera's Samian shrine. The primitive dirt path, bounded by sea plants, an occasional seashell, and wooden stakes, took them from the shore to a wood-framed image of Hera. Her simple beauty welcomed the young travelers. Behind them islanders followed to offer thanks for their safe arrival on Samos Island.

The young couple approached the wooden form. Around Mother Hera gathered the robed shrine women and Aunt Penthenia and Uncle Aglaeus. All welcomed them with outstretched arms. A bearer presented gifts of wheat, honey, and olive branches.

For a time Kti gazed upon the weathered wooden image whose annual ritual washing in the sea brought favorable trading and harvesting. The welcoming form, so natural and peaceful, shone in the beams of the morning sun. *Here,* Kti thought, *I shall gain solace when I miss my ritual space dedicated to Mother Trimetria. Now, I shall call her Mother Hera.*

To end the ceremony, Kti and Eury placed before Hera emblems of their household from Sami and Pronni. Their treasures would remain among those of the others as long as they lived on the island.

As they departed the sacred space, the villagers filed past the altar upon which the couple had placed two carved dolphins to represent their harbors of Poros and Sami and two cones from the mighty pines of Mount Aenos that loomed above both of their citadels to reflect their land holdings.

The sacred ceremony erupted into joyous chants of their new neighbor. Kti and Eury linked arms with Aunt and Uncle. The sacred women led the procession from the shrine grounds to the family's port home nestled among citrus and olive trees and grape vines. Those gathered partook of sacred wheat from the village cauldron, honey cakes and juices from the orange and lemon groves.

When the guests departed, Penthenia and Aglaeus and their children gathered Kti and Eury into their arms for a family welcome. They enjoyed more intimate visits with their cousins, Penthenia and Aglaeus's boys, Glaeus, the eldest; Maki, next in line; and Theodoros, the youngest. The two men managed the northern ports while Theodoros, still a lad, remained at home to learn the trade.

Kti noticed that Theo watched the festivities from a distance. She patted his hand, eliciting a smile. "I hope we shall be great friends since we shall be living close."

Above the mountains that sheltered the rich valley, the noonday sun lit the fragile green of new growth mixed with the yellow and white blossoms of late spring flowers.

"The springtime here must bring joy to you each day," Kti said as she took Aunt Penthenia's hand.

Nodding, Aunt Penthenia clasped Kti's other hand. "You have come as the island greens to its most beautiful, but the noon sun's blaze moves us indoors behind thick, cool walls."

Once they settled inside, Kti addressed her uncle. "How have you progressed with our hillside home?"

Aglaeus chuckled. "Eury, in his wanderings, found the perfect location with a view that sweeps the sea from west to east, just as your favorite spot on the terrace of the Pronni citadel. When you both asked me to oversee the construction, I had my doubts of its completion. It follows exactly the plan you two laid out at your wedding. Your trading journey has given us time to complete the unusual plan. When your remaining household goods and gifts come ashore from your ships, Freya, your efficient companion, will manage the last stages of the move. What excellent help she has been."

Kti embraced him. "How good you are, Uncle, to manage the homebuilding so quickly. I am most anxious to see it." She smiled as she looked at each in turn. "All of you have made me feel so welcome. Thank you for such warm hospitality."

Uncle grinned at her "It was a joy to work on your new home. You and Eury will go up the hillside very soon, but first, let us talk a bit of business. To have you safely here cheers us all. I must be honest. We need your help. The business thrives. My sons and I find it hard to manage the family interests here in the East. Having Eury tend to the interests of your families relieves us greatly. Eury, until your brother Kephalos takes hold, we are blessed that you both have agreed to reside here."

After a rest, Kti joined her husband to tour the home and a nearby smaller port where the family entered into the daily life of the community.

"Near the main port of Tigani, the family stays here most of the time, to conduct business while they do their work at the ritual center," he said. "This port home, more modest than the more spacious main home up toward ours, serves them well."

They settled on a shaded garden bench.

"Remind me, Eury, of Uncle's connection to this place."

"Aglaeus comes from many generations of seamen, every first son bearing the name of their great ancestor. The first Aglaeus built strong ships, allowing them to trade in many ports. As then, our ships sail northward, deep into the Dark Sea to bring home ores, amber, exotic furs, sometimes even the golden fleece of a rare breed of sheep. The ancient story of the Argonauts's feats comes from the lore of bringing home golden sheep hides."

"Ah, yes, I know that story from Phemios."

Kti followed Eury's lead and stood. As they strolled toward the cool house for an early supper with the family, Eury said, "We shall tour the Tigani port with Uncle when early evening breezes come to send Glaeus and Maki home with their families. Then we rest for our journey at morning's light to see our Samian home."

At the port, Kti and Eury waved with vigor as the two families from the northern ports of the island sailed away. Kti sent a cheerful message when they embarked. "I look forward to seeing you soon at your own homes as we tour the island."

Turning to face Aglaeus, Kti said, "Eury told me of our trade in the Dark Sea. Please tell me of our other ports of call."

"We travel southward to thriving ports of Cyprus Island or the nearby mainland of the Anatolians and Hittites, still farther south still to thriving ports of Ugarit of the Assyrians, Ashkelon of the Canaanites, and Lower Egypt, the land of the great pharaoh. We meet caravans and vessels from as far as the Indus River to barter for wares native to all the lands they visit."

Kti's gaze followed where Aglaeus pointed. "What items

come here as part of the trading agreements?"

"Out of Egypt, from traders who sail their swift felukkas deep into the dark continent or move their caravans across the desert to meet traders who barter ivory tusks from great lumbering beasts; rare skins of panthers, leopards, and other strange creatures, plus sparkling stones from deep within the earth which brought high sums at market."

"Trade from Egypt alone must keep the port humming," Kti said, "but you tell me you trade in the ports along the Eastern Mainland."

"Yes, others travel to the East to meet overland donkey caravans that bring fine ores for bronze tools or weapons, and turquoise, resins, exotic loomed rugs, spun cloths, along with other goods from far inland among high mountain passes, the lands between a second sea that flowed far beyond and the coastal lands of the Dark Sea."

"I can see why you need help."

Aglaeus pointed next to the harbor. "We account for all of the goods on board or on the dock. Then we sell them in the centers of all the islands and other mainland ports. Already, exploring vessels move beyond the great rock that guards the farthest western reaches of our present routes. There we meet Northern traders who bring goods from ports as far as Freya's land. We need more ships to sustain and expand our business, so we welcome the newest vessels you have brought built from the tall pines of Mount Aenos. Those sleek ships outpace the slower, rounded ones built on the eastern mainland from the cedars growing there."

"How do you find time to work at the shrine?" .

"Ah," said Aglaeus, "We enjoy our work there. Also, we find

gratification from solving governing matters and arbitrating public disputes. The shrine women ask for our assistance more than we can give it. Eury's help will free some of our time for community work."

A thought came to Kti. *Soon I shall have my part to play.*

At sunrise the next day, Kti and Eury set out for their mountain home. They left alone, taking only a few treasures. Under Freya's supervision, three days hence, the mule caravan that bore household goods and the builders' finishing crew would come.

Kti took Eury's hand. "I look forward to Freya's coming and to our home being settled, but I know I shall enjoy a few days alone."

Eury sighed. "Alone with you, yes, my dear, what a pleasure."

Kti wrapped her arms around Eury's neck. "Would that time stand still, Freya be delayed, so we could be alone for days. Still, having our household up and running would give us greater protection should intruders come."

Home treasures duplicate star treasures.

Chapter Thirteen

Aglaeus' word "unusual" described the home well. Kti marveled at the site. "Just as we intended, I see no home at all."

"Yes, our plan to integrate our home into the mountainside has been carried out perfectly." Eury opened the massive, hinged arms of the home.

They walked hand in hand into the space. The major living area, at first hidden in the enormous inner mountainside cave, contained the main hearth surrounded with comfortable seating. Near it, the dining area awaited the rest of their gifts.

"Just right for receiving our guests," Kti said.

They went deeper into the cave. Hidden behind double walls, their treasure room opened before them.

"The private ritual center next to work area will serve me well here," Kti said. "Also, I can script the family history as I practice my telling."

Eury hugged her close to his side. "Here we shall hide away chosen treasures, should we ever need to evacuate our home."

They inspected three nearby caves for cooking, storage, and bathing. They walked the small village along an inviting stream with housing for their attendants. A casual observer would overlook the site, once everything disappeared within the caves and among the undergrowth. Strategic clearing did little to disrupt the trees, the undergrowth, and the rock formations.

They next entered the sides of the main house after they secured the spacious wings to the mountainside. Each wing, angled and vented to receive the breezes, was enclosed enough to retain heat in winter and coolness in summer. Each folded inward, disappearing from sight to hug the central area and the mountainside.

"Again, just right!" Kti swirled around in the chambers. "See how this space catches the rising sun. What a wonderful treat for our guests!"

Eury grinned. "Now let us see the chambers for our sleeping and private bathing."

Kti caught her breath as she entered the space that would be their private retreat. "This space will catch the glow of the evening sun and sunset."

Eury wrapped his arms around Kti and pointed. "This small niche is for the nursery."

Kti snuggled into Eury's arms. "Yes, we shall spend time with newborns here, while the niches beyond are for older children as they grow."

Kti held her breath as Eury placed Helen and Menelaos' red-topped chest near their bedside. They stopped and stared. Kti glanced at Eury from the corner of her eye. Eury undid the clasp of the chest, took Kti by the shoulders, and eased her to the bed. Kti's languid hand stretched to withdraw a feather; Eury took massaging oil.

Much later the young couple arose, took sustenance from the large basket of food prepared in Aunt's kitchen, but stayed in their chamber until the next morning's light.

"Birdsongs and gentle breezes awaken us." Kti sighed as she stretched.

"Yes, my love, what a fine habit to nurture." Eury's mouth twitched as he twisted a ringlet of Kti's raven hair.

Kti tickled Eury's ribs, then placed the feather in the chest. "How uncannily the structure of chest anticipates the structure of our home. Both, rounded and hinged, close upon themselves to form a circle."

Kti followed while Eury placed the other chest deep within the hidden inner cave as the centerpiece of their private altar. "Hidden from the world, this cave already gives me the peace of Mother Gaia's presence."

Kti opened the chest to gaze in reverence at the three statues. Eury joined her and together they chanted the prayer of home-coming: "Ancient Mother…" to bless the chamber.

"Should we ever have to leave in haste," Kti said, "I hope to return to claim treasures. Even so, exploration of the Kretan palaces tells me they might be left for others."

The days passed. Freya arrived with the caravans and the workers. All was made ready for the blessing of the home.

At week's end, the family, the shrine women, and the villagers bought forth the first foods and smaller furnishings, a part of the ritual of the blessing. They placed hand woven and decorated linens, some made by Kti or her mother. They laid elegant rugs loomed of fine wool. Next came the blessing of the bed dressed in finely loomed bed clothing stitched with designs of fragile olive branches, birds in flight, palm fronds, and lotus blooms, a mix of East and West.

To the dining and kitchen areas they carried cooking and

eating vessels shaped on the wheel of Kti's Pronni potters or cast in bronze by the metal artisans. Around the rims of their dining platter spirals of inner and outer journeys of life, emblems of the ritual feast of the Great Gaia, reminded them that the partaking of food signified communing in the Great Mother's own feast.

Each piece intermixed emblems of Pronni's own Trimetria, Arkadia's Artemis, and the Samian and Argive Hera: wheat shafts and heads, the great egg, and the all-seeing eye dominated the designs. Golden wine goblets from Kti's parents, and magnificent silver and gold serving dishes from Eury's parents, found places in a special niche.

Bronze cauldrons, pans, and deep pots with attendant tongs and ladles completed the kitchen. Nearby in a storage area, they placed amphora full of grains, oils, wines, herbs, and other necessities. Torches and clay lamps found places in all the rooms in brackets already fastened to walls or on lamp pedestals. The young couple lacked nothing.

The shrine women, in rhythmic procession, chanted the house blessing. As they moved from place to place, designated guests preceded them to show the way. The holy women gave first light to the chamber torches treated with nard and rosemary.

At last, everyone gathered around the fire pit of the great hall for the final blessing. All that night, they feasted to commemorate the magnificent home. Still dark, the young couple said goodbyes to their guests.

Eury took Kti by the hand and led her to a great boulder that fronted the property. "From here we can follow the procession, their torches alight as they descend."

He drew Kti close. "Then we shall explore the island. I want you to see the full beauty of the island."

"I look forward to exploring the island," Kti said. "But will I be able to find my place here as well as I knew it at home?"

Vast expanses of Mother Earth tell us,
as one great whole, we pattern star stuff.

Chapter Fourteen

Standing on the boulder, Kti watched as the last torch was extinguished. "Our guests are safely home. Already lights shine in the houses of the awakening valley. Overhead, the starry sky is showing its last radiance."

"Look to the east to see the contours of Tigani showered with the oncoming sun."

"Oh, Eury, from here I have the best view of the sweep from east to west just like my view at home."

Eury took Kti's arm to help her descend the boulder. "Now is the time for us to explore the island."

Kti tied her sandals tighter, while Eury shouldered a small pouch of supplies. With sturdy walking sticks in hand, the young couple ascended the central mountain range.

As they climbed, Eury said, "The most verdant of the island, this range has thick undergrowth beneath evergreens, some so stately that they serve as masts of the long ships. Here wild turkeys and deer roam, while hare and nutria scamper. We shall hike along the animal trails until late morning."

At the highest peak, Eury stopped to give Kti her first look of the north. He pointed to valleys interspersed with lower peaks that stopped at the blue waters of the northern coast.

"The winter rains have nourished the lands and fed the mountain streams."

Kti took a deep breath. "The winter activity has created spring blossoms as far as the eye can see. Wild orchids, rhododendrons, iris, yellow and white daisies mix with deep red wine cups, pale pink primroses, and deep purple verbenas. What a magnificent vista."

Pointing to the east, Eury said, "The islanders say that long ago the island connected to the eastern mainland. When the earth quaked, herds of massive creatures, with smaller ones following, came running to the valleys of this land mass. Trapped here when the land broke away, they died once they depleted the food supply. Their bones fill an immense burial ground, now considered sacred. Soon, we shall travel to that inner valley."

Kti clasped Eury's hand. "Yes, some day we must go there to see nature's work."

When the sun reached its highest point, they stopped at a nearby shaded stream. Warm but not too hot, sunlight filtered through the overhanging trees.

"Here we shall rest before our midday meal," Eury said.

Kti listened to the babbling water and the sounds of birds and insects. She sighed in contentment.

"I have dreamed of you here, my love." Eury settled beside her on the soft, mossy ground. The sound of his voice played like a mellow lute in tune with the fluted returns of the stream.

Kti bent to his mood. She entwined his golden hair around her fingers and peered into his eyes. "You knew I would love this place."

Neither words nor thought of food interrupted their feast

of each other's body. Then they slept. Kti awakened to Eury's preparation of their meal. After they ate, they plunged into the first northern valley.

They reached the sea, the sight of it teasing them from the heights. Sunlight played on the northern waters, showing blues and greens over the white rocks of the shallows near the shore. In a small inlet, they caught fish for an evening meal and gathered twigs and limbs from nearby woods. Eury lit the fire in a circle of stones. Their simple evening meal finished, they slept under the stars until dawn.

At first light, Eury uncovered a small sailing skiff he kept in the inlet. "We shall travel west to our port in the hands of Cousin Maki. He and his wife Prokris expect us today."

"I look forward to the visit."

They arrived at the northwestern port as the sun descended into the western sea. In the dusky light, Maki unloaded goods from a trading ship docked in the snug harbor sheltered against a craggy mountain wall.

Maki smiled a welcome as he kissed Kti's cheeks. "Prokris expects you at home. Please settle in with her and the children. I shall join you as soon as I visit with the captain."

To them both he said, "I know you plan to travel next to the east, to the port of Old Vathy. Shall I arrange your passage with the captain or can you stay a week when we expect another trader?"

"We stay only briefly this time," Eury said. "Do speak to the captain. I know the way, Maki. I shall take Kti and return to assist you."

"Good, good," Maki said, as he turned to his work.

The visit showed Kti the pleasures of family life on the

island. "Prokris, how skillfully you use the herbs of the island. The blend of mountain oregano and rosemary with the lamb smells wonderful."

As if dancing, Prokris shifted her weight while she mixed the greens.

"How may I help?" Kti said.

"Why not play a game with the children?"

The competitive brood took out slender sticks, all the same size, but with colored tips of red, green, or black.

"What is the game?" Kti said.

The eldest held up the one black stick. "Each in turn will pick up sticks without moving another. If you move one, you lose. Try for the black which counts the most. Green counts next, then red. The one with the most count wins the game."

With eyes wide, the youngest said, "Father made these sticks, but we helped. I painted some of the red ones. You go first."

Everyone watched the throw. Kti stayed in for two rounds. The middle boy lasted the longest with the highest count.

"What fun!" Kti clasped her hands together. She then watched the children stack squared pieces of wood. "I never thought of smoothing wood chunks from nearby trees for stacking. You can build walls, fortifications—all sorts of things."

When the men returned, they enjoyed a good meal. As the moon rose, they retired.

Settling into the bed Maki had hand-carved and assembled, with her eyelids drooping, Kti said, "After sleeping in such comfort under these soft hand loomed blankets, at dawn, I shall wake up refreshed to sail east. What a lovely day I have had."

The next morning, they traveled toward Vathy. Along the

way, Eury pointed to vistas at the edge of the northern shore. Passing one spot, he said, "There is where we camped."

Later, Kti in excitement pointed ashore. "I see a beach perfect for future swimming."

Eury pointed to an inlet where he had fished, swum, and camped. "At last we reach our destination."

Eyes wide, Kti said, "What a deep-grooved harbor."

"It is the largest port on the island."

As the ship docked, Eury signaled to a youth, the very image of himself. Indeed, his younger brother Kephalos welcomed them. Kti gave him a quick embrace. "I have not seen you, Kephalos, since the wedding."

"I was sorry I could not greet you when you arrived, but I tended the harbor so that Glaeus could bring his family."

"I am glad you are taking hold of our interests very well," Kti said. "That assures of our returning soon to Pronni to supervise the trade from Kephallenia."

Before Eury assisted the men, he asked Kti to stay at dockside to observe the operation of the port. "Look especially at the record-keeping while the crew checks and disburses inventory. See how your scribing methods might make them more efficient."

Although most of the men ignored her, some cast their eyes toward the striking young woman. Others stared in bemusement.

They did not see Cousin Glaeus, who seldom had leisure. Kephalos' coming had given Glaeus time to holiday with his family on a nearby island.

Good, very good. Kti considered returning to her homeland and developing her own ports.

Two days later, the couple sailed homeward around the northeastern end of the island. Kti lounged with Eury on deck while he pointed to a mountain range that came to the sea rim.

"Soon," he said, "we shall visit the inviting hidden beaches of this eastern edge, some of the most beautiful on the island. We shall also visit Great Kirkus, the farthest to the west, known as the most formidable mountain of the island. North of Great Kirkus, we shall visit the nesting ground of sea creatures rare to these waters. Some say the old man of the sea takes his noonday nap among them."

Kti nodded. "Prokris mentioned the creatures that are not far from them. She said that Protea, not Old Proteus, leads the nymphs, keeping them and the seaways safe. In other breeding regions, including one far to the south in our own Samian lands, you call Proteus by the name of Neairus."

Eury laughed.

"And the women of the western isles say that Neaira, not Neairus, and her nymphs guard the creatures. Freya says Selje also have a female tending them."

Eury sighed. "All tales have a twist; still they have a sameness." Then he added, "I hope you have enjoyed the journey. I promised you beautiful vistas along with sunny beaches. I hope I have made my Samos yours."

"I love our home. I feel at ease. I shall know your whereabouts when you travel to the ports. I look forward to our swims in the waters of the coves."

She added with a teasing twinkle in her eyes, "You know that I can swim these warmer, southern waters more easily than the colder waters of Pronni or Sami."

Then she snuggled closer to her proud husband. "Dearest

one," she said, "the journey pleased me very much. I am a Samian by adoption now."

As they entered the port, Kti thought of their mountain home. Once there, Freya saw to their privacy as they lost themselves in happy homecoming.

During the early days of their living atop the mountain, Eury left before dawn for the hour's walk to the harbor. The evening climb eased in his eager anticipation of being with Kti.

In the third month of their marriage, Kti told Eury of her body's changes. As they enhanced their lovemaking with the contents of the golden chest, she pointed to a firming of her breasts, a slight thickening of her waist. "I am ravenous for unpredictable foods at strange times. But not more so than I am ravenous for you," she added in a playful tone.

One more embrace, she said, "Seriously, my love, I believe we will be parents before the winter solstice."

Eury grabbed her shoulders, then eased his hands as if Kti might break. "My dearest one, we shall be the best of parents."

Kti took his hand. "Yes, love, we shall." She patted her belly. "The family we have wanted has begun to form."

From that day on, Kti relished seeing Eury rush up the hill to their mountain retreat to be with her. Soon she went with him to observe the moving cargo to or from the docks. "Might I suggest that efficient record-keeping on clay tablets will do much to speed the operation."

They planned her walk to port so that the exercise once or twice a week would make her healthier and stronger for the delivery of their child. At first the men looked askance at her working in the trade. Soon, however, they saw the results of smoother landing, unloading, and loading. Even the distribution of goods was carried out with less effort.

Kti trained a staff of scribes. Together they won support of everyone.

As the child grew larger within her belly, she rested at the home of Aunt and Uncle for a few hours each day. Three moons went through cycles.

One day, her aunt greeted Kti with guests. "I bring you a treat. You have heard these good women intone the rituals at Hera's sanctuary. Your work has kept you from knowing them better. Now, you will connect with them in friendship."

Kti recognized and acknowledged Gaetha, the eldest teacher, called by some the Samian Sibyl, or wise one.

Gaetha waved a hand toward her companions. "I present Aglaia, Sophia, Erato, Klio, and Vergine—all your peers, Kti."

As they gathered around the table for a meal, Gaetha said, "Kti, before you know it, you will go to the birthing cave. I would say, from the look of you, in fewer than three moon spans. You will birth a boy child; the birth will warm the hearts of the Sky Gods of our warriors as well as Mother Hera, a guiding force for all of us."

She paused, then swept her arm into a wide arc. "You have done wonders since you arrived. Penthenia tells us of your ordered household and of that same order to the family trade. Now, you retreat with us to refresh yourself and to reconnect with your studies of the Mother. You will learn more of our ways here while you prepare for your birthing ritual. As our first step, we will take you to the eastern mainland for a great gathering at the Artemision. There, we will join groups from other Mother shrines to discuss the status of the Mother."

Her mouth gaped, but before Kti could speak, Aunt said,

"With Eury going on the next long trading trip to the Western Isles, the last he plans to make before the birth, you will have a month to refresh and study. Thanks to you, work goes smoothly at all the island ports. Your best scribes can see to the work. I can manage household needs. Freya will travel with you. She and these able women will attend you should your time come early."

Kti's eyes grew wide at the thought of such a journey of which she had long dreamed. "Aunt, you have anticipated my every need," she said. "I know I must prepare for the coming birth. I have long desired to visit the Artemision. What a generous offer. Of course, I must consult Eury."

Her last statement, she noted, brought smiles to all of them. She knew the women had prepared for his assent. Thus, when the young couple talked later that evening, Eury agreed with her that she should go.

Earth and sky reveal connections.

CHAPTER FIFTEEN

Kti journeyed east to the Artemision when Eury sailed west to Kephallenia Island. She traveled homeward in her mind with Eury. She settled on deck of Algaeus' ship. "I need to refresh my knowledge of the Mother rituals gain a deeper understanding of larger concerns of the Mother. I have much to remember, even more to learn."

"Never before, not in my memory at least," Sibyl Gaetha said, "have so many women of the Mother shrines gathered. Discussing the changing Way of the Mother seems to loom larger each day."

Sophia turned to Kti. "Each of our cultures describes Her in different forms, by different names, but the variations should not hamper us. We thrive on the similarities of the star pattern that came to earth to become the Mother. The Mother has guided us for many eons, but the warrior rituals take hold to threaten our Way."

Erato moved her hands forward, palms up. "We espouse equal roles for men and women." She dropped one hand down. "The warriors install power solely in men. Such unevenness threatens the balance of the cosmos. We must restore the harmony."

Sophia leaned forward. "Shrines related to Great Gaia, like ours, already prepare rituals together. Our Heraion communicates often with two other Heraions, one to the north in Thessaly, another to the west in Argos; with the shrine women of ancient Athena, Metis's child; with Demeter who comes from Metis and with Artemis who incorporates eastern aspects of the center where we are gathering and of Arkadia where Amphito, the Sibyl of Lusi, resides."

Kti nodded. "Amphito was my mother's first teacher. I hope to meet her if she comes."

Klio stretched her arms wide open, as if pointing to different lands. "In her oldest form, shining Aphrodite, who reflects the compassion of her sister Hera, travels over the ocean waves to reside in many shrines. Her shrine sisters will come from an island off the southern coast of the Peloponnese. Followers of Themis and Dione, the Titan sisters who prevail still at Dodona, will come. Some of the followers of Medea who retreated to Hera's Shrine in Thessaly from the dark sea regions of Kalkis may come. We hope that Medea's followers who went to the eastern mainland will come, too."

Erato's melodic voice held the group in thrall. "Medea came to our shrine at Thessaly to evade the Argonauts who maurauded her homeland of Kalkis. She taught our northern sisters until the lands beyond the Dark Sea called her. There, restless nomadic people settle, produce grains, and domesticate animals. Medea and her travel companions helped them thrive."

"Can she still be alive?" Kti said.

Gaetha gave an expansive gesture of her hands. "She lives in rituals she pronounced, if not in flesh. Most of the Mother shrines fend off threats of extinction. We hope they will share how they stay vital. Those who follow the teachings of Medusa and Kirke are in serious danger of extinction. We hope to hear from those who keep in their rituals Hekate, the wise crone of our tradition who guides us to our place beyond the limits to Kalypso who incubates us, stills us, gives us our dreams as she renews and transforms us in the world between waking and sleeping. Even more exciting, we shall have more contact with Eileithia, Kybele, Tiamet, Ishtar, Astarte, Inanna, Ashtoreth, among others from the Eastern traditions."

"A traveling sister told me," said Klio in a breathless voice, "that she crossed paths with teachers from the South of Egypt and to the Northeast of the Balkan steppes who were heading to the Artemision. Imagine how excited we will be, should some come from as far as the Indus River and Chen. Our sharing of rituals, histories, and customs will make us a stronger force in these times."

"Perhaps we should abandon the Way the Olympians have toppled." Vergine's voice turned edgy. "We can always begin anew. We can change from within their system. I, for one, want radical change."

"Our Mother serves in many places," said Aglaia, as she jabbed her needle back and forth through the cloth of the ritual garment she repaired. "We should engage the usurpers of the Mother's realm, retake the territories we have lost, join the bullies at their own game until we overpower them."

"Change will tear us apart and destroy us or unite us and help us survive," Erato said. "I take the long view. I see a time when we conduct our rites behind the scenes—in the women's quarters or in chants we sing to influence while we entertain. We would encrypt only for our initiates to know the code. In some centers, we do shadow rituals already. At all costs, we must preserve a civil society." Then Erato looked directly at Kti. "You, Kti, might help with encrypting. You bring the arts of scripting and telling to us."

Before Kti could respond, ever-restless Aglaia dropped her mending as she leaned against a nearby rail. "Sophia, you hold the wisdom of our rituals and instruct us, lest we forget. What do you think about scribing written records?"

Sophia calmed the tenor of the question, then turned it to Kti. "I see merit as well as shortcomings in scripting. How do you see it, Kti?"

Kti kept a tone of caution in her voice. "I preserve the earlier versions of the myths, legends, and tales that reflect the Mother's Way. I interject the Way into the dominant voices of the tellers' set formulas. The tellers favor the warriors all across the Great Sea. On our island of Kephallenia, Phemios, who learned from the Athenian tellers, regales us. I learned the telling art from him. I have often heard others in our court. They gather their stories from many ports of our vast trading territory. All these tellers threaten our way of life."

Sophia raised her eyebrows. "Kti, have you found other versions to counteract their distortions?"

Kti shrugged. "I have heard other perspectives of the same event from my mother and grandmother as well as from the shrine women of Parnassus. Their memories reflect different views of the waning truths of our ancestors' histories. I preserve our family history in the tales, a history told from the memories of women often not heard in the public songsters of warriors' feats. I relax those versions into a formula of 'Some say this, but others say that.'"

Vergine paced the deck. "That will not work always. Integrating indirectly can be less effective than using direct confrontation."

"I remain kinder when I speak of the Sky Gods than do some of the male tellers who interject caustic versions of the Mother figures. I include the Mother's wisdom. I use a calmer tone that appeals to both men and women." Kti gazed toward the waves the ship formed as it cut through the water. "I admire a person who takes a stand. For years, I wanted to use the male tactic of belittling invective, but recently I have lessened my strident tone and try to forward the Mother's Way in a positive light. What I do reflects only one way to integrate the Mother into the telling tradition, but I hope I can help us survive."

Gaetha shook her head. "Kti, you give us insights about the telling world that I, for one, have not considered. I remain conflicted about recording the direct words of our rituals. We have kept them in the language of the chant, on the lips of our teachers or in the signs and art we use in our vessels, our gravesites and our shrines. The fluidity of our oral language keeps the Way alive. Scripted words might lead to rigid interpretation and destroy us."

"On the other hand, if we do not record, our way of knowing may disappear," said Klio, in an eager tone. "Some shrines already make their rites sensational. They say sensation attracts others who find the Way too inward and reflective."

"No doubt we shall discuss recording our rituals at the Artemision," Gaetha said.

"I am ever ready to use all methods of keeping clear records," Klio said, "but brute force, rape, pillage, and death of the people who roam the lands and sail the seas call for desperate action.

Recording our history and our rituals will preserve our way better than any other means."

Sophia nodded. "We must be sure not to impose our way as the only way. A written record can strengthen all of us because it gives us a strong unified voice."

"If we rely on memory of teachers who pass on everything orally and never record or encrypt," Erato said as she tapped her forehead, "we will lose our voices in the ever-changing times. The past shows us that we thrive when we practice ways fair to all of us. Whether we come from the North, East, South or West, we must cooperate. We must choose carefully those issues we need to address to keep the balance."

Gaetha looked at each member in the group. "We have much work to do at the conclave. I know diverse views will come out. This gathering should be an interesting beginning to a longer debate which should surely lead to some action."

Silence set in among the women as the ship approached the harbor where they would disembark to make their way to the Artemision. Kti hoped the days ahead would clarify her role in keeping the Way of the Mother alive. If the views at the conference reflected the same diversity as theirs, she would gain many insights from the meeting. But avoiding conflict would be a challenge.

Dance your life, my love.
You flow in the rhythm of change.

CHAPTER SIXTEEN

Kti and Sophia claimed a chamber together, as did Freya with Erato, and Klio with Aglaia. Vergine joined a friend from the Argive Heraion. Gaetha stayed alone to give private counsel.

First came a gathering for developing friendships. Kti visited shrine women from Kephallenia, Eleusis, Parnassus, and Dodona. She met others from the Heraion at Argos and from the Mount Kyllene hillside shrines of Artemis.

To Kti's disappointment, Sibyl Amphito remained in Lusi. From Parnassus, Kti found those who practiced Athena's Way in the tradition of her mother Metis, not Zeus, who claimed he birthed her out of his head. The Athenians lived at Parnassus among the Parnassian Gaians. She saw her first advisor, Pythia, the honored Delphic Sibyl who with Gaetha and the other Sibyls formed the High Council of Elders.

Kti agreed to visit Pythia the next day. Times for visiting, interspersed among the general meetings, particularly pleased her.

The first ritual, guided by history, featured dancers who chanted of an early time when Mother and Father, just out of the egg, were one in partnership with all Nature. Mother and Father combined equally as progenitors who perpetuated knowledge. Harmony provided balance to guide their lives.

Afterward, the discussion centered on ritual. The opening ritual reminded the women that ancient wisdom, commonly called Sophia, brought first light. Sophia existed before sunlight, before the moon glow, in its waxing and waning. She gave rhythm to procreative cycles of not only plants, but also animals, to replenish the earth, the great oceans, and the skies. Her light guided all forms of life to star families, the divine union with the One, the unified Mother and Father, both below and above. In that season, all nature had freedom. No form dominated any other. The human animal lived in rhythmic harmony, dancing in unity with all nature to the joyous music.

Kti was caught up in the rhythmic dance, relishing a sense of renewal. But she also realized the difficulty of invoking a common language. *I see a Mother-Father form that split many eons ago. Thenceforth, the eternal egg cracked apart. Now we must gather the shattered parts to regain sacred unity. That is my mission. I see it with clarity. Will my words ever work to mend the duality that resulted from the split? The gap seems wider than ever.*

Then the first public voice of the conclave interrupted her thoughts. "The mood that unifies us still dominates our Mother ritual."

Many voices agreed. Then someone called out, "How can we keep the rhythm alive?"

Before the question could be answered, some countered the positive mood to complain of the temper of the times.

"Men have taken our roles in public ritual," said a strident voice.

Another shouted, "They focus on the male rites of passage

in the hunt and debase the female rites."

"They leave to women few ritual tasks at all," voiced one more.

Still came others. "We have been shoved into women's quarters or brothels. Men, who now inherit everything, consider us property. We never know who will own us. Will it be father, husband, male ritual leader, or slave owner? Who?"

In swift succession came many more complaints.

"Free one day, the next, taken in war, we are slaves. Wars make us pawns of the winners. As losers, we die or serve masters, our history erased. We do not have the right to help other women with their marriage rituals, their birthing times, their household organization, their healing and burial, their public roles, their transitions to the wisdom of old age. Where does wise counsel of our children exist? Wars as much as feuds make us unwilling victims. We no longer create the cloth, the pottery, the jewels, the farming tools."

Questions and observations created chaos in the conclave.

Amidst the venting came tempered voices. "We lose sight of what we have in common, of the power we do have, of our capacity to keep our equal place in the shift to male dominance."

Other positive voices followed.

"What can we do to restore partnership? Have we contributed by becoming complacent or even complicit, irresponsible or abusive? Let us hold the ground we have. How can we once again integrate our voices into the public rituals? Where I live, we still have a say, yet we draw in our collective breaths in fear of invasion and eradication of the Mother's voice. What can we share that works?"

As the positive voices prevailed, the group turned to the

order of the next days' work. The role of leader, they agreed, would shift each day. The first leader would come from the Artemision itself.

Sibyl Admetus, who came from the tribe of Pelops and carried the name of her ancestor, the daughter of Eurytheus, took charge. She negotiated an agreement on the process. A speaker would never criticize without following the complaint with solutions. Two questions would frame their comments. "What could sustain or bring harmony and balance once again?" and "Where do we find the successes that have kept the balance?"

Then the leader turned to a keeper of the comments. "From your recording, have you gleaned threads that might order our discussion?"

The recorder presented a sampling of the scattered litany, then added, "The rest of the first day could be spent discussing our role in public ceremony; the second, our role in internal governance of shrine life; the third, our role in community matters; finally the fourth, our role in the education of all children and of adults. If all goes well, we shall have much to take back to our shrine centers."

Consensus came. The proceedings began in earnest.

To keep her thoughts straight, Kti scribed key words on clay tablets. When she reviewed the first four days, she saw the benefits of a positive spirit in the gathering.

Under public ceremonies such words as "flexible" and "inclusive" encouraged her.

Under internal and social governance, she noted, "do consistent good within or outside the shrine itself"…"be an example"… "consult everyone, both men and women"…

"communicate"… "counsel wisely"… "assert with a firm voice"… "use everyone's talents and experience"… "balance to unify."

Controversy erupted during the discussion of how to educate the young. Voices rang out with, "Study together or separately? Who would teach: shrine teachers, parents, both? A joint effort?"

The discussion elicited such words on her tablet as "separate"… "together"… "same needs"… "different needs" women warriors"… "men warriors"… "change all to spiritual warriors"… "need a common language for all"… "men and women speak different languages"… "script rituals"… "script and tell"… "oral only."

Dichotomies existed, but underneath came a voice encouraging unity. The women agreed to start the next conclave, in two years, with effective models of education. All consented to keep shrine centers involved in society while they kept their sacred integrity. The last morning ended with a final friendship gathering.

As time came to leave, a young girl and three older women approached Kti. They had just arrived from Aulis, although she recognized their dress from the Eleusinian shrine.

The eldest spoke to Kti. "I assisted you to bring the child with us into this world."

Kti peered at the speaker. "Lefteria, I remember you."

She embraced the young traveler. "Dear Iphigenia, I am your cousin, Ktimene. I greet you most warmly."

The child smiled as she embraced her newfound relative.

Then Kti said to Lefteria, "How can Iphigenia be here instead of with Klytemnestra?"

"Time comes for her to receive more teachings, first here, then with us at Eleusis," Lefteria said. "We knew at her birth at Eleusis that she might one day study with us should she choose."

At that, Lefteria signaled her traveling companion to take their young charge to her quarters.

Kti again embraced the child. "Iphigenia, if you send for me, I shall come. I live close by on an island just across these waters."

After the child disappeared, Kti again turned to Lefteria. "What has happened, Lefteria?"

Lefteria sighed. "The world has changed. A call came to us that we participate at Aulis in Iphigenia's betrothal to Akhilles, most natural since she had stayed with us after Helen gave birth to her. But quickly the call turned into something else. We did not know that Helen's kindred from Truva, a trading port at the entry of the Dark Sea, had abducted Helen, nor did Klytemnestra know. We thought we awaited Helen's arrival to begin the ceremony. Then the truth came out. Helen would not arrive. She had sailed, we learned, on a vessel captained by Hektor, the son of Priam, ruler of Truva."

Gasping, Kti held her hand over her mouth. "How could such a thing happen?"

"Hektor stopped at Mycenae to trade in the Great Sea. As they conversed, Hektor told Menelaos, who, with Helen, came to Mycenae from Sparta, that he planned trade in Egypt. Thus, when news came that Menelaos must attend the burial rites of their Kretan relative, Menelaos asked Hektor to take Helen to Egypt ahead of him so that she could negotiate a trading agreement between Sparta and Egypt."

"Sensible enough, I am sure." Kti shook her head. "What

happened then?"

"One of the Mycenean heralds reported to Agamemnon what he had overheard. Hektor's young brother, Paris, would take Helen as bride. Some said that he seduced her; others, that he forced his attention on her; still others, that she returned his affections. Whatever the case, in Ilium, the place of Priam's citadel, the custom prevailed that a man may take any woman as wife. Thus, he claimed her. He insisted that Aphrodite mandated it. The sons of Atreus amassed a great fleet to bring her home. But the winds had stalled them, and Apollo's representative mandated the sacrifice of a royal maiden."

Lefteria shrugged. "Agamemnon needed to assure fair sailing. Our duty, we learned, was to participate not in a betrothal, but in a ritual sacrifice of the royal child. The seer of Apollo called for it after detecting omens in his reading of bird's innards. Appalled, we delayed by claiming that a prize deer be sacrificed to Artemis before the maiden could be offered up. We argued we must follow our way, mandated by Artemis herself. In the meantime, we insisted that Iphigenia stay with us for preparation."

A small frown wrinkled her brow. "We believe Artemis inspired us, for the winds came and the fleet sailed without our committing the foul deed of human sacrifice so counter to our beliefs. We have never subscribed to animal sacrifice of any kind, but our plight called for desperate measures. The callous warriors thought little of sacrificing a maiden, but Queen Klytemnestra, incensed and distraught, helped us. She agreed that the child's coming with us to study kept her safe. Iphigenia, destined to be with us one day, should come now."

Kti jumped, startled as if someone had pushed her. She

knew that Iphigenia's presence and the events surrounding Helen would stir furor throughout the seaways. "The dear child," she said, "so young to have such an abrupt uprooting surely needs a safe haven. From nearby, I shall visit her. I can imagine my brother Ody and our many kin brought ships to join the fleet. That means that my husband Eury, who traded in the Western Isles, came as Ody's first mate. Were they among those assembled?"

Lefteria nodded. "Your brother commanded a large fleet from the Western Isles. Your husband captained a ship of his own fleet. I remember him well from your wedding."

Lefteria's account rang in Kti's ears. When the call came for her to leave for Samos Island, Kti covered her mouth as tears formed. "My Eury," she said, her thoughts whirling, "my own dear one, where are you?"

Stars come to earth at birthing time.

Chapter Seventeen

Kti needed more information. Foremost in her thoughts, Eury's ship traveled with the fleet to Truva. Could Helen have done such a thing as to go willingly? She did not believe it. Helen showed no signs of unhappiness when they saw her at Pylos.

Kti arrived home from the Artemision in shock. She must delay her reflections with the shrine women. She must collect herself to await word of Eury from traders whom she expected in port any day.

Soon ships docked. One captain came to her right away. To her question of Eury's whereabouts, the captain said, "Yes, my lady, your husband, second in command, joins your brother. His vessel, along with two others, joined the fleet of the Western lands. Under the command of your brother, ten strong ships from the West headed to Aulis to meet the Atride brothers and their many allies. Your husband will come to port soon to run supplies to Truva. Now our ships, with those at our other Samian ports, must take much needed supplies."

Kti released a long sigh of relief.

He continued, "Captain Eurylokhos sent you these tablets. They contain the list of the supplies we deliver to Truva."

Kti read the top tablet. "Kti, dearest, Ody leads the fleet of the West to Ilium with my vessels and others as support. Our kindred there will see the rightness of returning Helen. Please amass supplies quickly. Take care of yourself, the child to come, and all Samians."

Kti looked up at the captain. "Were there other stated messages?"

"Yes, my lady, he asked that you pray for us at Hera's shrine." He delivered the message in one breath, as he shifted his weight from one foot to the other.

By dusk, Penthenia, Kti, and Freya bade farewell to crews of two laden vessels.

Aglaeus insisted on accompanying the supply ships. "I know the uncharted coastlines, the harbors, the treacherous tides, especially the conditions around Truva itself. Those crafty men of Ilium—our ancestors, mind you—have become wealthy as collectors of fees each time we use their harbors or seek safe passage into the Dark Sea to connect with the trade routes to the East."

After the ships sailed, Kti went with the household women to offer prayers at the shrine. As they left the grounds, Gaetha took Kti aside. "Kti, you must rest now. Calm your body with the breathing techniques we used at the Artimesion. We will continue through the night to pray for good news from Ilium. No matter what happens, you must prepare yourself for motherhood."

When Aglaeus returned, his first words made clear the extent of the fleets supporting Agamemnon and Menelaos. "Never have I seen such a gathering of ships. The tribes of the Great Sea will succeed if it comes to war. If necessary, they will topple the walls. Old Priam must see reason or die. As I left, Odysseus, Menelaos, Agamemnon, Phoenix, and Nestor went to consult with Priam."

Aglaeus studied Kti's anxious face. "I assure you Eury remains safe. He will arrive with the full moon. He plans to stay until the young babe arrives. Your brother, although in the thick of it, also stays safe. By the time the moon waxes, this ridiculous incident will end."

Kti awoke from restless sleep. Each sound meant Eury had arrived. Late one night, she appeared with Freya at Penthenia's door. She could not speak as tears formed, streaking her face. *How unlike me, these tears.* She sat silent.

Freya rubbed Kti's hands and massaged her shoulders. "We thought it best to await Eury here."

Nodding, Penthenia embraced each of them. "I shall prepare a warm drink for you both. Then you must sleep. Eury will come soon."

Eury did not come, but the day came for the birthing. Kti made her way to the birthing cave with the two women. The sacred women, summoned when labor began, came in haste.

With the sacred women, Kti descended into the cave. The smooth damp stones gave comfort to her feet. Soft light of the torches guided her way.

Kti relaxed a bit at the sound of Sophia's soothing voice. "Kti, I direct your birthing time. We have helped many mothers bring forth life. Peace resides here. You have chosen a water birth in our underground lake. Be prepared to place your feet, then your legs, finally your whole body into the cool inviting pool."

Kti's eyes adjusted to the torchlight. The sound of rushing waters surrounded her. The supporting presence of Penthenia,

Freya, and the holy women were a comfort to her.

Kti slipped her loose garment from her body. Inch by inch, she let herself into the water. Although the women assisted, she knew she must descend alone.

Her mother's voice came to her. "I shall abide with you at your birthing as will all the mothers who lived before you, even Kallisto, your star guide."

Sophia chanted the first words of the birthing ritual. "In the water, the source of life, many eons ago Mother Gaia and Father Ouranus formed us to live in the sea. Birth in the water came first to all creatures."

The chant lulled Kti into a peaceful trance. The next words awakened her. "Your boy child, newborn into his earthly life, swims forth from the life-giving water. He takes his first breath from the nurturing air of the cave. We call you, dear Kti, to name him. What do you call him?"

Surely, only seconds passed after my watery descent to slip this child from my body into the pool.

"I name him Autolykos after my dear grandfather," she said.

Chants of welcome bearing his name echoed around the cave. The women wrapped the warm soft birthing sheet around Kti's body. She stared in wonder at the small infant beside her. Ample milk filled her breasts. She took the child to her nipple. The thriving boy latched and nursed with vigor.

One moon span after she returned from the birthing cave to her mountain home, Eury appeared at her side. He gazed with love into her eyes, then looked at her from head to foot. "Motherhood becomes you, my love."

He held her in long embrace before he turned again to the tiny child. "I came as soon as I received the news of our child's early arrival. Our little Lykos, how wondrous he is. I lamented not being here for the birth. I hope overwork at the port or anxiety about Truva did not cause your early birthing time."

"Ah, my love, these things happen. I flourish. Our son thrives. You have come. What else matters?"

His worried look changed into a broad smile. Again, they embraced.

They had only a few hours while the ships loaded. "We have so much to say, so much to do," she said.

They receded into the language of love, hungry for each other's full embrace. As Eury came down on her, she felt in him a hardness that did not reflect his usual temper. She brought his intensity to her gentler rhythm. The tension left his body as he returned to his natural softness. The long aches of absence subsiding, they slept for a time.

Soon Eury arose to coo at Lykos. He once more enfolded Kti into his arms. "I am lucky," he said. "When I come for supplies, I shall see my true love and our dear child. Far away from loved ones. the others, restless and anxious, await the end of this senseless strife."

Knowing her own impatience for the resolution of the dispute, Kti said, "The end must come soon. Have we tried all means to resolve it?"

"Many times, we have parlayed, but each discussion ends with issues unresolved. They have Helen of her own free will, they say. Still, they do not allow us to see her. The lines of disagreement grow more hardened. I shall be back soon, my dear. Stay well. Keep your prayers strong for an end of the bitter strife. I hope we need no violent action."

Eury's words, "I shall return soon," echoed in Kti's ears

through the long months that followed. Eury had sent many scribed tablets, often adding, "I cannot come, but soon, soon." Even her news that she would deliver their second child did not bring him.

As birthing time drew near, again Kti and Freya stayed with Penthenia. One night, awakening with a start, Kti said, "We have no time to move up the mountain to enter the water of the cave. Call the shrine women to come here now."

Freya left to summon the women. Penthenia made quick preparation for the birth. She spread the bed with clean tanned skins overlaid with soft woven blankets, then an outer, softer hide to catch the fluid of the birth.

Kti lay still. Her breath merged once more with the movement inside her body. She imagined herself on the earlier journey into the water. To her amazement, she transported her body there. The efficient bustle around her led to the beginning of the chant, "In the water, the source of life…" intermixed with her mother's clear voice, "…all mothers abide with you."

As the infant girl emerged, the voices of those present chanted the joyous news. This time Kti sang with them. She filled into the naming space "Neaira."

"Dearest Neaira, namesake of my grandmother," Kti whispered over the small body as Neaira received the ritual washing and wrapping. Gentle hands cleansed her body. Soon they wrapped her in a soft, warm wool blanket. "I went to the birthing pool," she murmured as she slipped into sleep.

Still Eury did not come. Many moons passed. Lykos and Neaira gave her great comfort as she watched them grow. Kti filled her hours at the port, at home, at the shrine, at the side of the children, and again at her scribing table where she added to the family lore. She, Aglaeus, and Penthenia kept the trading and supply lines open. Aglaeus' sons and Kephalos, Eury's brother, plied the waters, often staying for a time with other men of Samos to swell the warriors' ranks.

Kti went the shrine to counsel those whose husbands had gone to Truva. The families turned to her as she shared their concerns. Eury's spirit hovered over the rhythms of her days.

Still he did not come. Kti scanned the ships each day. Often, she thought those who knew of him kept secrets. Had Eury been lost in battle or on a mission?

How can I bear this waiting? Yet I must.

Stars birth, spark, swerve, struggle toward solace,
then shoot forth again from the source within.

Chapter Eighteen

"Kti, I wonder at your decision." Eury's voice accompanied his presence, as he embraced her. Lykos, at seven, and Neaira, at six, warmed to him. Kti had kept him alive in their young hearts.

Kti smiled. "This time, I shall accompany you to Truva. I have planned my disguise. I go as your personal attendant, an apprentice to learn the trade. Young Mentes, grandson of the great Mentor of Ithaka, at your service, sir."

Shaking her head, Freya led the children to their naps. Kti had often talked with her about a plan to travel to Truva to surprise Eury or to accompany him, should he ever make the trading run himself. So far, her work, coupled with caring for the children, had held her on Samos Island, but Kti kept the scheme alive.

"Kti, no one, not even I, can stop you when you make up your mind." Eury spoke these words with admiration. "You have the children to see after. For their sake, we must be sure one of us survives this war. You have duties at port. The shrine women need you. We do not practice peace on the battlefield. I forbid your coming into so much danger."

To each argument, Kti offered a counter one. "Freya, along

with their tutors and attendants, will care for them. We have family to see after our children, should we not survive. I shall stay out of harm's way in your quarters. No safer place on the battle field than officers' quarters, you often assure me."

"But, Kti, you are needed at port."

"Penthenia, Aglaeus, and my assistant scribes know the port business. Aunt and Uncle approve my going."

"What of your work at the shrine?"

"The shrine women believe the experience will help me counsel the others."

"You cannot come. It is too dangerous."

"We never deny each other. Our way gives us both the right to make our own choices. Eury, I will not disrupt the troops. I go to Truva to learn, to experience, to try to understand. Besides, now that you have a spare crew, you need an extra hand."

"You will never fool Ody even if your disguise keeps your identity hidden from the rest."

Kti laughed. "I do not plan to deceive my brother. If he recognizes me, he will be amused. Plus, I need to work out the details of his coming soon with you to Samos Island. You know I have arranged for Eumaios to bring Pen here for a visit."

"I could take that message."

"I have one more reason to go. I must have better information about a rumor that Helen never traveled to Truva. Traders often bring the rumor. As one wizened traveler told me, 'The war is not being waged to rescue Helen. The Queen of Sparta resides, not there, but in Egypt. The real reason for the standoff at Truva centers in all traders' desires to open the Dark Sea, free to everyone. Greed drives Old Priam'."

Eury nodded. "We must explore the rumor with Ody."

Within two days, captain and his new apprentice stowed their gear on the aft deck where Eury had makeshift quarters. "Nothing unusual," they agreed.

They sailed from Tigani port, heading east, then north to the busy northern port for more supplies. They docked at Kios and Mytilini, friendly islands, where they took on weapons along with food supplies.

At the latter, the crew took rest to renew their bodies at the thermal springs, a tricky maneuver for Kti, whose nude body would give away her feminine figure. As luck would have it, the captain claimed privacy with only the company of his young aide. "What would my wife think of that?" He threw the words over his shoulder.

Kti turned aside, but not before she caught a glimpse of their knowing smiles.

The final push toward Truva's port, now in the Argive hands, would prove more difficult. So far, fair weather and safe ports blessed their journey. Lookouts had sighted no unfriendly sympathizers of Priam.

As they neared Truva, Kti, witnessed the end of a peaceful journey. When two barrages of boulders, fireballs and arrows, thrown in quick succession from allies of Truva, Kti cheered with the crew when the enemy missed. She cheered again when they evaded the attacks or dispatched into the sea all flying objects, suffering no casualties and little damage.

Kti spotted Eury nearby. She went about her duties. *I am comforted with Eury near, but I know he cannot come to me or reveal who I am.*

Near journey's end, she said in a low voice to Eury, "I dread these tides and currents as more treacherous than the hostile villagers along the shore. Aglaeus told tales of winter delays in the port at Truva to await passage into the Black Sea when the waters turned menacing.'

The trading ships eased their way among the Argive fleets. Kti recognized friendly banners, first Pylian Nestor's, then those of Idomeneus' Kretans, Menelaos' Spartans, Agamemnon's Myceneans, and Diomedes' Argives, and Tiryrans. One, a mermaid emblazoned upon it, she did not recognize.

"That banner," Eury said, "the emblem of the Myrmidons' leader Akhilleus, son of Peleus, reflects his lineage. The sea nymph, Thetis, according to some, mothered him. Although young, brash, and easily angered, he stands as our bravest fighter, most valued of our allies."

At last, Ody's banner bearing an eagle subduing a boar fluttered before them, along with attendant banners of the other western peoples: the dolphin of Palli; the olive branch of Kranni; the giant tortoises of Zante; the stately pine of her own Pronni; and the bull of Eury's Sami. The wind rippled many other banners of the western mainland, including the wolf of her grandfather Autolykos.

A formidable gathering welcomed the vessel of the supply master. Long away, the men looked forward to receiving news delivered with packets from home. Then unloading began.

Ody made his way toward Eury, but stopped to stare at Kti.

Eury tried the ruse. "Meet young Mentes, grandson of Mentor, our Kephallenian adventurer of the seas. He learns the ways of supply officers as my apprentice."

While playing along, Kti busied herself with the unloading. She kept clear of her brother's direct gaze.

"Not bearded yet, young man?" Ody said. "I do not

remember your birth time, but you look to be about the age of my sister, Ktimene. Did you ever meet her? I would like to see her. I miss her."

Kti burst out laughing. "Oh, Ody, ever Lykos, son of Laertes, grandson of wolfish Autolykos, you knew me right away. What gave me away?"

"You have the likeness of our mother, her beauty, her stature. Still I see our father in your walk." His tone turned tense. "Why did you come? Great danger abides here. We must house you at a distance among the cooks and followers."

"Now, Ody, I did not come to be shut away. I shall do my work while I live in Eury's quarters. You have talked of war strategies often enough in my presence for me to know that officers live more safely than the cooks."

"Welcome, young Mentes, I shall see you with your captain tonight at supper." Ody walked away without another word.

Kti turned to Eury. "I look forward to this evening. I have so much to discuss with Ody; especially do I want to know of Helen. But Ody had the look of a schemer when he left. He knows something."

Recognize what appears before you.

CHAPTER NINETEEN

That evening, their work completed, Eury and Kti joined Ody. The table, set with military fare, bore skewered mutton, beef, and pork. More sizzled on a nearby pit. Kneaded breads completed the main course. Kephallenian wines, a treat for everyone, enhanced the meal.

Ody studied a chart sketched with ash and ochre on a tanned skin.

"Tell me what I see on the skin," Kti said.

"It lays out the walls of the city along with an inner schema of barricaded Truva. We camp here, near the south gate, the public entry to the citadel. The strongest part of the wall, the gate, gives access to the sea to the force that controls it. For years, this point has been ours, as has this port and the one to the west that you passed before you turned to come into this harbor."

"I see, but what are the black marks sprinkled all around?"

"The marks designate our strongholds. We now ring the city except to the northeast, the only supply route. There, we regularly intercept their suppliers, a good way to add to our own larder. Truvans from beyond the walls flee into the city, die at our hands, escape to other lands, or defect to us. We have many slaves, allies, and some informers. Soon we shall starve them out."

"What else can you do while you wait?"

"We spend much of our time sailing armed trading ships into the Dark Sea to barter among many willing Eastern traders." Ody pointed across the table. "Thanks to Eury's efforts, our contacts multiply. You have seen at Samos Island the stores we send of precious ores. We find rare purple stones or jade slabs for decoration along with much-desired hard metals to make weapons."

He held out a purple stone. "Here, Kti, take this fine piece. Found only in the mountains beyond the Dark Sea, the purple gemstone makes fine jewelry."

Kti's eyed widened. "What a beautiful brooch I see being formed from it."

"We have consulted shamans, both holy women and men, who preside deep into the frozen land. Their shrines, they say, surround a vast inland lake of such depth no one can plumb it. From there, hunters bring the best hides we have ever seen. Kti, you have received white ermine from there as gift for covering your newborns."

"How do you know this, Ody? Have you been there?"

"I have gone there in my dreams, but Eury has collected valuable information from traders about the vast eastern expanses of mountain and desert that end at a sea far to the east."

"Wide-eyed people live there," Eury said. "In the Samian ports, you likely have seen a few of them who join our crews. They work on our ships while their women help in our households."

Ody added, "Or they perform other acts of which you need

not hear. Once we secure this place and rescue Helen, I hope to go there."

Eury nodded. "I shall go with you, dear brother."

"No more idle talk." Ody cleared his throat. "Let us discuss your presence, Kti."

Kti laid her hand on her brother's arm. "Ody, I sojourn here for a time. Then, I hope you will come to Samos Island. I plan as a lure, visitors from the Western Isles. In the dark of the moon just before its waxing, Eumaios will bring Pen, perhaps Telemakhos. That should entice you."

"Ah, sister, ever the arranger of miracles, you know I will come if only I can." As Ody delivered these words, longing filled his eyes. "Since our coming here, I have visited the thermal spring of Mytilini once. I enjoyed a brief rest there followed by one journey into the Dark Sea as far as Kalkis. As you know, our distant ancestors traveled to Kalkis with fabled Jason on the ship that carried many adventurers."

"Yes. I laugh to think how tellers, to enhance their tales, expand the list of warriors who took the journey. Our own father supposedly served as navigator, but we know his distant ancestor went instead. Father, slippery in the telling of the tale, makes me wonder what he or another ancestor saw to haunt him. Whatever he saw or heard about has turned Father from the sea. A visiting teller, you may remember from our child-hood, regaled us once with the tale of the Argonauts' voyage."

"I recall that Father stopped the teller, told him he had it wrong," Ody said, "but never afterward would say more. Even Phemios dismissed us when we asked if he would explain why Father silenced the teller. Someday perhaps we shall journey to places where the tellers sing the true story."

Kti added, "I heard nothing of Kalkis at the Artemision when I went there with the shrine women of Samos Island. I had hoped to see their shrine teachers because they follow Medea who has served as revered leader of the shrines in remote regions in the East. For some, she has achieved the status of Great Mother. Such a gathering at the Artemision, I had never seen of those who still practice the Mother's Ways. As I left, Iphigenia arrived with the women from Eleusis."

"You no doubt learned of our skirmish here from those canny sisters who bested Agamemnon's priest who would have sacrificed Iphigenia. I am glad she was with them."

"Through them, I learned of Helen's supposed arrival at this remote spot. Since then, dear brother, many rumors come to us about that act. Most persistently, we hear that Helen resides, not here, but in Egypt. What do you know of that? Believe me, your answer responds to a major reason I came. When I posed the question to Eury, he said to ask you."

Kti turned to Ody, expecting an answer.

"Just recently Diomedes and I scouted the walls to the north. We saw Athena's shrine where the women of Priam's household make offerings and pray. At the right time, we plan to take the statue of Athena from the shrine. Whoever holds that image, we believe, prevails."

Pausing, Ody stared at Kti. "Yes, the rumor persists here, but no one believes it. Each time we visited the shrine, a woman of Helen's features prayed among them. The same woman walks on the ramparts of the citadel. Menelaos remains convinced of his Helen's presence."

"Oh, poor dear Menelaos, he wants Helen back at any cost, does he not?"

Ody tapped his head as if struck by lightning. "Kti, you know Helen best of all of us. I propose you go with Diomedes and me on our next scouting trip tomorrow before dawn. That way, perhaps we can dispel or confirm the rumor."

Ody's proposal, Kti sensed, may have already formed when he saw her at the dock.

They debated the safety of the mission. At last, Kti concluded, "Even though our discussion resembles the makings of a tale Phemios would spin, I see the logic of the mission. You have good intuition, Ody."

She glanced from Eury to Ody. "If you two agree, I will go with you."

A nod from both was all she needed. Before first light, she and Ody left with Diomedes, who was told that, because young Mentes knew Helen well, he wanted to see her.

During the mission, Kti kept silent, followed pre-arranged signals, and remained out of the way. Soon the siblings returned to quarters where Eury paced as he awaited them.

"I did not see Helen there," said Kti. "When you pointed to the veiled, bejeweled woman in purple who had Helen's characteristics, you had, of course, singled her out as Helen, correct?"

Ody nodded.

In a firm voice, Kti said, "Well, another, not my Helen, prayed with the women. But still Helen could reside within the walls. They may have sent a double, hoping you might attempt a rescue. They might believe Helen faced danger at the shrine."

"Since you do not identify the woman as Helen, my dear Kti, you present me a puzzle. Next, I plan to enter the city in disguise to seek the woman out."

"When will you go on that dangerous mission?"

"You," said Ody, "will have returned home to safety before I go."

"I hope solving the mystery of Helen and taking the image of ancient Athena from the shrine will end the siege."

Silently, Kti prayed to Gaia, *Bring forth such deeds with little bloodshed.*

To the two men she said, "The women showed much courage to come to the shrine. You told me Queen Hekuba, Priam's major wife, and her daughter Kassandra have always been among the praying women. I hope one day to visit with Kassandra. I identified her as the officiating leader of the followers of Athena."

"Correct on both counts, Kti, but no one believes Kassandra has any power. She has beauty enough that Agamemnon wants to take her home as a slave when this is over."

"I learned at the Artemision that Kassandra has studied there as well as at the Samian shrine. She devotes her life to ancient Athena. The holy women laugh at the tale that she foresees the future, a supposed gift of that upstart, Apollo. The legend goes that he gave her the power, then altered it so she would not be believed, a penalty for her not agreeing to a tryst. All untrue, the holy teachers say. They assure me she has much intelligence that engenders good insights about the inner workings of our sacred alphabet."

Kti again asserted that Helen did not pray at the shrine.

Ody smirked.

At week's end, Aglaeus delivered supplies and took on board young Mentes, a disguise Kti wore now with ease. Kti had much to ponder. Mystery surrounded Helen's whereabouts.

Once home, she continued her work at the shrine as she

awaited the visit of Pen. Kti hoped Ody would come with her own beloved Eury to relieve her loneliness and to protect him from the senseless bloodiness of the warring plains of Truva.

Stars shine everywhere. Absorb their energy.

CHAPTER TWENTY

"Helen." Kti looked up, eyebrows raised as she threw a ball of wool to Neaira. "You are here, not in Truva? When did you come? Just now?"

Kti had returned to her mountain home after working at the port. Only a week home from Ilium, she lost herself in her children's play. She shook her head. Was she ensnared in a spell or a dream?

"I never traveled to Truva at all." Helen embraced her dear friend, then ruffled Neaira's hair. "The shrine women of Hera's Way brought me to you. I arrived at the shrine on one of Pharaoh's swift crafts after you left the port. Pharaoh's sacred women, who practice the rites of the Mother of the Sky, Nut, and her daughters, Isis and Nephys, accompanied me from Egypt."

Kti took in those with Helen and sent Neaira to request refreshments. She welcomed three Egyptian holy women and her Samian Heraion friends: Gaetha, Sophia, Klio, and Erato. Kti served refreshing juices and sweets. "What brings you here?"

"I came to consult Sybil Gaetha and her holy ones. I shall go on to the Artemision. I hear Iphigenia resides there, an added incentive. I could not leave without including you in the conversation. We have no secrets, we two."

"Not much escapes you, Helen. I suppose you know I traveled to Truva where, with Ody, I confirmed, not you, but one very like you, prayed to Athena with Priam's wife Hekuba, their many daughters, and the household women."

With a shrug, Helen half-smiled. "Quite clever, we thought, our sending one of my likeness with Paris, so ardent I could not fend off his advances. Pharaoh requested his holy women to conjure the scheme. He gave me refuge after Hektor brought me ashore those many years ago. The boy had roughly handled me. We tutored my double but had little time. Courtly Hektor had despaired of resolving the unseemly behavior of his younger brother, who kept muttering that Aphrodite had ordained our bonding. Well, we had bonded, all right! Hektor agreed the ruse was the best solution."

Kti laughed, but then her expression turned serious. "The decision stirred the cauldron of the Great Sea beyond your intentions. I learned of your being taken from Lefteria, a shrine woman of Eleusis who brought Iphigenia to the Artemision after she barely escaped being sacrificed to start the winds that sent the great fleets to bring you home from Truva."

After a pause, a wry smile engulfed Kti's face. "But why not wait here a few days? I expect a visit from Pen. We hope Ody will come with my own Eury. We can have a family gathering, dear cousin."

"That would be a visit, indeed," said Helen, "but I shall be absent. You must have guessed, that shortly after your visit to Truva, inquiries came to the Pharaoh from Menelaos. Ody had confronted Menelaos after a foray into the city in disguise that confirmed my absence. Menelaos could not believe it to be true.

Now he knows. They will end the skirmish by attacking the city. I think, however, that they will not tell the troops of my absence. I am a battle cry for victory, I hear."

Kti shook her head. "You keep a powerful secret. All of you, caught in a net of lies, surely see the consequences of your decision. How has Hektor saved face? He never told anyone in Truva of the deception, surely."

"No, I understand he did not. Akhilleus killed Hektor in a hand-to-hand challenge. The dilemma of how to untangle this knot, I have discussed with these Heraion women on our way here."

Helen's mouth twisted into a grimace, as her eyes grew moist. "One other thing you must know, Kti, Paris left me with child. The pregnancy ended in miscarriage. I cannot be persuaded that the child's life ended naturally. The Pharaoh's women nurtured me during my healing time. I had been badly mauled when I resisted Paris's ardor. I may never know if herbs took the child or if my body rejected the dear one. I grieve the loss still."

Kti stared at her, eyes wide. "Helen, whatever am I to do with this knowledge?"

"Promise me, Kti, that you will script the story, for now, in secret. Tell it in years to come, perhaps, but now, with so many alive who will suffer at its telling, let it lie hidden. I have discussed my reasoning with these good women and with the holy women of Pharaoh. They insisted we must keep silent. Gaetha urged me to tell you the truth but agreed the world must wait to know."

Kti searched Gaetha's eyes to read her thoughts, but the woman gave no signal to contradict Helen's words.

"For now, I promise, Helen," said Kti. "After the skirmish

ends and all arrive safely home, we must talk again."

With those words, the entourage took its leave. Kti sat for some time as she watched the procession descend the hill.

"One day, I must reveal the truth," she said aloud to no one, "but as Hektor must have known, and as Menelaos, Ody, and the inner circle attacking Priam's citadel must now realize, like Kassandra's predictions, my telling of the truth will not be believed."

Be sure of the deep bounds.

CHAPTER TWENTY-ONE

As she walked the trail, Kti reflected on how quickly the Truvan fiasco ended. Already the Samian warriors trickled home. They confirmed the taking of Truva. With nerves on edge, Kti awaited the homecoming of Eury. Perhaps Ody would come with him as he expected Pen to be there.

"Kti, we must leave immediately. I have come to take you to safety."

At the sound of his words, Kti jumped as Eumaios appeared before her, blocking her path. She searched Eumaios's eyes. "What causes such urgency? Did Pen come?"

Eumaios squinted, then widened his eyes. "Did you not receive the news from our messenger? Raiders pillage Ithaka and Kephallenia. The households of Pen and Antikleia fled from Ithaka, as have the households from Pronni, Palli, Sami, and Kranni. They find refuge in the mainland stronghold of Autolykos and Neaira."

"Oh, Eumaios. I heard nothing of this."

"Pen and I had just boarded ship, ready to embark on our journey to you, when an island lookout rushed to the port. He had rallied the household to come to the harbor and sent messengers on swift skiffs to other ports on the Island. At

some distance, a fleet bearing the banners of known despera-
does approached. We collected everyone on board and sailed to
Parnassus. Immediately, I came to assure your safety."

"But Eumaios, I must wait for Eury."

With a vigorous nod, Eumaios said, "To Parnassus, you
may go, or you may join the people here who will retreat to the
mountains. We have had little time to absorb the good news of
Truva's fall but know that some of the adventurers from there
join the marauders, even though most of them return to their
homes. The hordes plan to sweep on to Egypt, but they will
surely include this port, a natural launching place for skirmishes
nearby."

Grasping Eumaios' words and her choices, Kti said, "I have
heard only the joyous news from Truva. Menelaos came briefly
to take on supplies. He confirmed our victory and sailed to
Egypt without disembarking his troops. There he completes a
trading mission, then returns to Sparta."

She did not add, but thought, *He told me he would rendez-
vous in Pharaoh's court with Helen and leave in Egypt her beautiful
double, whom he rescued from the melee at Truva.*

"You must make haste to close your home and make your
decision."

"Yes, my Eumaios. Come with me to summon the
household."

As they walked, Kti spoke more of Menelaos' visit. "Menelaos
told me Agamemnon hurried home along a northern route to
see his family. He also said Ody and Eury headed back into
Truva where they would complete plans for the new city to rise
out of the ashes of the old one. Already ships freely enter to
trade in the Dark Sea. 'We will build our outpost upon the

ruins,' he told me. He left his master architect with a contingent of able men to do the work. Eury had assured them he would support their efforts from Samos Island. That must be delayed, of course, while we settle this crisis."

Eumaios knitted his brow. "That means those who stayed in Truva know nothing of the unrest."

Kti sent him a reassuring glance. "Ody, who keeps in Truva a portion of the western fleet—six ships, I think—intends to come here as soon as they complete plans for the new Truva. I expect the fleet any day."

"As you have told me of the news from Truva, I know you consider your choices. Be aware that the council of western islanders has convened at Parnassus. If the past pattern holds, the marauders will pick us clean of livestock, taking all the larder they can carry. Usually they move on quickly. Work crews from all the citadels will, in turn, help each other rebuild. The council will establish the order of rebuilding by lot, yours among them."

Kti caught sight of Freya in the courtyard. "Freya, I have news for the household. Please assemble them here under the plane tree."

Eumaios shook his head. "If you stay, the marauders may keep you in the mountains and occupy these ports for some time. The sea people, their ranks swollen by other restless people, plan to take the Nile delta so they can use its grain bins for food while they make it a base for trading. The refugees, exiles, and adventurers all hunger for a homeland."

"I think you told me that you saw Aunt and Uncle on your way here. Right?"

"They arrive soon to learn your decision. If you sail with me, they will send Eury to you, should he come. He might join us as we sail on to Parnassus. I understand the shrine teachers will come, except one or two who will stay at the hillside cave above Tigani. I posted our fleet to the northern port. Armed and ready, they await us if you decide to leave."

Kti considered Eumaios' urgent words as she formed in her mind the route of the invaders. When they rounded the land of Pelops, they would stop to wipe clean the inhabited islands east of the mainland before they swept on to Krete. All these places serve as watering stops. Perhaps Eumaios could guide the Kephallenian ships past Krete and Thera before the marauders arrived there.

"I will have my decision by the time the household assembles," Kti said. "Thank you for your thoughtful advice and for being here."

Eumaios looked at her from head to foot, pausing to assess the bulge at her middle. "Can you travel safely?"

"I believe I shall deliver a child within two moon cycles," Kti said. "We have ample time to reach the Parnassian retreat, perhaps even my own citadel at Pronni."

Before proceeding, Kti pulled Eumaios aside. "Eumaios, my wise advisor, I cannot keep secrets from you. I did not tell you of an earlier visit here of Helen. What I now reveal must stay between us."

She paced away, then whirled to face him. "Menelaos had another motive for going to Egypt. He wanted to leave a double of Helen and fetch the original who never went to Truva but was left in Egypt by Hektor when his brother Paris badly used her."

Eumaios gasped. "How am I to take in such a thing?"

Kti shrugged. "Helen has an uncanny way of stirring the

souls of us all. She and Hektor, with the help of the Pharaoh joined by his holy women, formed a plot that cost many lives. She did not know until she received emissaries from Menelaos seeking the truth of her presence in Egypt what carnage they caused. But she asked me to keep the truth to myself."

Eumaios nodded. "Menelaos and Helen must tell of her true role in the long years of raids. For my part, I will say nothing publicly of the information. Keep silent, script it though you may."

"You always give good counsel, dear Eumaios," Kti said. "Still, others may spread the truth too soon. I hope not."

"Let us hurry now to the assembled household."

"Yes, time rushes forward. Will I stay or sail? Oh, where is Eury?"

She sighed, then said, "Great Gaia, guide my steps."

Travel again. Remain secure in your heart.

Chapter Twenty-Two

Kti walked toward the gathering but stopped when her eldest son, Lykos, approached. "Lykos, I present to you Eumaios, our family friend. As you know, Eumaios planned to bring Aunt Pen to visit from Ithaka. Instead, because of trouble heading our way, he has come to warn us."

The young man shook hands with Eumaios.

"He will help us close the house, then escort us to safety either with Aunt and Uncle deeper into the mountains or with his fleet to Kephallenia. If we go back, we will trade from there while we rebuild our citadel that raiding scoundrels will have left in ruin. Should we go west, your father, with your Uncle Ody, may merge with us at sea. Long ago we planned a retreat from here. Your father will know to find us either in the mountains or at our home citadel of Pronni.

She paused to give him a reassuring pat on the arm. "Meanwhile, Lykos, I shall depend on you, to assist me as we prepare for departure."

"Mother," Lykos said, his eyes glowing, "I just arrived from the port. There Vagelis, Lefthis, and I watched sleek ships arrive. They had the tallest masts, the longest undergirding, and the most pointed prows I have ever seen. I learned the shipbuilders made them from tall trees of Mount Aenos, just above your homeland. A dolphin decorates the bow of each ship, but the head of each dolphin takes the shape of the wide-eyed nymph, Protea."

"Lykos," Kti said, "we must make haste. Eumaios has ships in our northern port to meet us to take us to our land of the tall trees."

"Eumaios," Lykos said, "I have heard much of your support to our family. Sailing with you on one of the swift ships will bring us to our western citadel which I have yearned to see."

Kti took an arm of each to walk between them toward the assembled household.

She stood in front of those gathered. "Good friends, my loyal household companions, I speak directly. A large marauding fleet comes upon us with great speed. We must close the house and leave immediately. The harbor villagers, already alerted, will take refuge in the mountains. They leave little behind, just enough to satisfy the greed of the coming hordes. To deter anyone from making inroads into our mountains, our traders have long spread tales of our treacherous inlands haunted by the ghosts of great monsters."

Kti turned to her left. "Freya and I will guide your work. Once we secure the household, pack one small pouch of necessities each. You must choose between two destinations. The first one, you may join the villagers in the mountains until I return or send for you. If you stay, you will be living in hideaways until the raiders leave. Their stay, long or short, you must endure with patience. Life will be lean and rugged but safe if everyone pulls together to support the community. The villagers welcome your stay as long as you conform to their customs, in reality, the same customs we follow."

Watching for any sign of panic Kti paused. "Your other choice, you may depart with me on the tall ships from the Western Isles to travel back with this loyal friend, Eumaios, to my home citadel at Pronni after a sojourn on Mount Parnassus. There, among the people of my mother, Queen Antikleia, your own shrine leader, we reach safety. Our Pronni hill people, with others of Kephallenia Island, find shelter, already, in the Parnassian citadel of Queen Neaira, my grandmother, because the marauders heading here have already devastated our Kephallenian citadels. Some of you will help others in the West rebuild the citadels of Kephallenia and Ithaka once we know the invaders have moved on. If you stay here, once the raiders leave, you will rebuild here."

The household buzzed with chatter, as people weighed their options. After a few moments, the noisy exchanges died down.

"Either choice requires hard work. In both places, you face dangers. With young Lykos, who has trekked with me many times over these mountains, and this brave man, I shall lead those who go to the ships. Aglaeus and Penthenia will be here soon to take to the mountain retreats those who stay. Some of you, I know, have family among the village people. I bear no ill will toward you, should you stay. I cannot promise safety to either group, but fighting men swell the ships' crews as well as the ranks who go to the mountains"

Amidst voices of "I'll stay" or "I'll go," Kti raised her palm for silence. "So far, we have avoided the wanderers of the seaways. Their number grows as displaced people join them. I understand they head to Egypt, but the rim of this island, well known for its ports, will attract them for a time. Think as you work. Be ready with your choice by sundown."

Kti took the filled wine cup, offered libations and prayed, "Oh Great Mother and Consort Gods of the Sky, give us secure places for shelter, fair winds for sailing, safe home comings. Abide with us these many days."

Soon each member of the household carried out assigned tasks. Kti worked in the inner cave room with Eumaios.

"You chose well, Kti," he said. "Worn, yes even worried, but stately still, your parents need you. If, for now, all of the family cannot come home, you, with your children, will break the gloom with your happy, wise ways."

Kti thought of her home and her parents. To keep back tears, she busied herself with sorting scripted tiles. She placed them in carved out niches, soon secured behind stones to form a part of the wall of the cave. If anyone penetrated the cave to plunder, they would, she hoped, overlook them.

The lovely chests, gifts of their friends, had hiding places, but from the shrine chest, she dropped into her treasure pouch the tiny figures of green jade, blue lapis, and white jade. She remembered Helen's wise counsel to keep them close for guidance.

Freya, with two trusted servants, brought other treasures of the household. All stowed, they closed the stone entry to the inner cave.

Taking only a few moments, Kti gathered one change of clothes, her special spindle, and two cloaks, along with small necessities. All secured within, they snapped the side chambers of their home into place for one great hug of the mountain. Others hid the outer areas. The home site disappeared. Nature returned to the hilltop.

As evening twilight came, the household assembled at the trail where the weary villagers met them. Kti, Lykos, her young daughter Neaira, and her attendants led one group over the mountain to the northern port to board the ships. About half of the household, twenty strong, joined them. Eumaios and Freya stayed at the rear of the procession to assist the travelers and to see that all remained secure.

With sober reserve, the rest joined the villagers. Aunt and Uncle's eldest sons would bring their households from the northern ports. Young son Theo led their household and the local villagers. Kti learned that Gaetha and Sophia stayed behind at the cave above Tigani.

After brief embraces, they parted. Each prayed for the others' safety until they met again.

Kti uttered last words to the family, "Tell Eury, should he come here, that we make our way to Parnassus, then to Pronni. Wish him the safety of the Great Mother and the Sky Gods as he makes his way to us."

Oh, Mother Gaia, without your strength, I cannot face the days to come. I know I shall not be alone as we travel these treacherous waters. Still, I must, for the children's sake, for the sake of those who journey with us, stay brave. May Eury find us and travel with us. May Ody avoid any harm. Bless us all with a safe journey.

Starry woman, return brings a safe haven.

Chapter Twenty-Three

T he trim ships entered the Parnassian port just as Kti's belly contracted with pangs of labor. Freya had prepared for the delivery on board, but Eumaios docked and a litter carried Kti to the Pythian shrine grounds. In the stone circle near the springs that fed the sacred pool, Kti gave birth.

As Kti awakened, Pen said in a soothing tone, "The healthy twins are here, dear Kti."

In the twilight state of her birth trance, Kti had entered the waters of the Samian cave accompanied by voices of the holy shrine women of Samos Island. Their voices blended with those of her mother, her grandmother, and the Parnassian chanters of Gaia.

Kti moved her body, now enwrapped in the soft, warm woolen birthing blanket. "What a beautiful birth, Pen."

Summoned from the citadel, Antikleia and Neaira, mother and grandmother; Antipe, Eury's mother; Erato, his sister; and Pen, her dearest friend, had attended the birth and now joined in the chanting of the shrine women. One of their own had come home to bring forth new life.

Relieved to make shore before the birth, Eumaios and the crews of the two ships had joined the men gathered on the rim of the sacred grounds to await the birth. With them, Autolykos, Laertes, and Eury's father, Kephalos, awaited the coming of the babes. Elated to hear of the safe delivery, all awaited their naming.

The women chanted to the now-awake mother, "Great Mother welcomes these newborn little ones who bear the names…"

"Antikleia and Laertes," Kti said.

Kti chanted with the others. She then turned to Pen and whispered, "Mother and Father now have namesakes. These newborn wondrous ones join me, Lykos, and Neaira to complete the naming line of my fmaily. Will Eury, I wonder, come to start the naming line of his family?"

Nodding, Pen half-smiled. "Eury and Ody will come."

The chant climaxed with the Great Blessing given to Mother and her newborns. The rhythms now included the men's voices. Never had such a welcome occurred.

"The birth of these wondrous twins gives me great satisfaction," said Antikleia, as Kti beamed at her. "How could I have imagined such a thing? Having to hold so many of you, so far away, in my heart all these years has taken its toll. Your arrival signals that both your husbands will soon return."

Antikleia clasped her hands together and raised them to her chest. "Having two lovely wives here, both young mothers, along with their thriving children, warms my heart."

Pen tilted her head at the comforting mother. "Eumaios may not have hazarded such a voyage had he known how soon these babes would arrive. Just think, they were born in the very circle where you received your name not so long ago, Kti"

Kti squeezed Pen's hand. "Please bring Father and

Grandfather Autolykos to me."

Antikleia fussed over Kti, doted on the newborns, all the while showering loving attention upon young Lykos and Neaira. "Will we call my young namesake 'Kleia,' as I am called in more familiar settings?"

"Ah, Mother, you lead the way. How good I feel to experience your touch, to hear your real voice blend with the voice I heard at the other births. Always, you filled my waking hours and my dream times. You remained an illusion until I touched your arms, felt your embrace. Now I relish your presence. Kleia, yes, let us call her Kleia, but as for Laertes, I prefer it all. Did Father have a pet name in his youth, do you know?"

"You might ask him," Antikleia said, as her husband approached.

"What do you ask? Did I have another name? Of course, I did, my child. As grandson of Askanius, I received his name. I treasured being called 'Aski,' my mother's pet name." Laertes beamed as he caressed his namesake.

Grandmother Neaira brought Kti's first-born children, Lykos and Neaira, to gaze at the babes. Then she ushered them out, saying as she left, "What a wondrous day of welcoming these four loving children to our home."

Autolykos took Kti's hand. "Dear Grandchild, Kti, our own Kalli, the name given you in childhood to remind us of your deep roots in golden Arkadia, my loving wife's homeland, I welcome these special children. Truly double blessings, gifts of the Mother and the Sky Gods, their births bode well for the future of the West. The interlopers may come, but we endure. Stay with us as long as you can. Your safe homecoming gives us heart that Odysseus and your own Eurylokhos will come soon."

Tears welled in his eyes, a sight Kti had never seen.

Squeezing his great hand, Kti shed her own tears of joy mixed with those of apprehension. "We abide now in a safe haven. Thank you, Grandfather." Then she slept.

Kti would discover later that Autolykos held back telling her of the bloody murder of Agamemnon. She would learn that the commander received a grim welcome home, among rumors that flew to them after the foul deed. Some said Klytemnestra, grown used to ruling in his absence, still chaffed over the near sacrifice of Iphigenia, so she murdered Agamemnon in his ritual welcoming bath. Others said Aigisthos, as heir of Thyestes, ambushed him on his way to Mycenae so that he could take over the ruling line. Some reported that Klytemnestra wished to establish a matrilineal line. After her, her daughter Elektra, who followed the Way of the Great Mother, would rule.

Such a rumor would threaten the shrine of Hera at nearby Argos where Elektra served. The warriors, if Klytemnestra took hold, would surely retaliate. The Great Mother, others countered, would not condone such a plan. No one would support Klytemnestra if she shared a part in Agamemnon's death.

The coming of the babes kept Kti in high spirits. "Just what we wanted, a household full of little ones," she repeated to those who offered their good wishes. Often, she added, "To have Eury come to welcome these dear ones will warm our hearts."

Being at Parnassus rallied her. She joined the business of the household. Everyone celebrated the homecoming of a daughter away so long. The spirits of the community soared at the news of the double birth, an omen for future good fortune.

Before fall rains came, Pen, Telemakhos, and her household departed for Ithaka. Work on their citadel neared completion.

Pen learned that the great hall she and Ody had built before he left withstood the recent incursion. They set to work to replenish their flocks, their granaries, their wine craters and oil jars the raiders depleted.

Those who rebuilt the citadel had moved to Sami, Erato's land, the childhood home of Eury. Next, they would begin work on her nearby citadel to the south, at Pronni.

"By late spring, when the twins reach the age of one," Kti said, "I shall go to Erato's finished citadel to stay with Eury's family. From there, I shall see to the last phase of rebuilding my Pronni citadel."

Early spring rains kept her at Sami until summer. One day, with her daughter Neaira, Kti stood on the edge of her Pronni lands to view the seas below. "Our recent trials have shattered much of your childhood, Neaira. Even so, these beautiful lands will restore your spirits. You, at only ten, and Lykos, just eleven, have been my support for many years. Soon we shall open our port for trade. Completing the work before your father arrives will bring a great comfort to a war-weary man so long away."

"We have looked forward to coming to our renewed home, our own citadel. We shall help all we can. Lykos, with Philoitios and Eumaios, will oversee the farms along with the ports. You have shown me how to run the household."

"You do all of that so well, as you are already quite practical. Have you other plans?"

"I plan to use the scribing you taught me to help at the port. Just think, Mother, in two years we shall journey again to Parnassus to complete my studies. Then I shall receive rites that officially begin my adult life. Before we know it, Kleia will go to Parnassus for her name. Perhaps Father will arrive to take Lykos for his naming."

"Neaira, you are wiser than your years. I have counted on you and Lykos as though you were already adults, but I look forward to welcoming you both to official adulthood."

Taking her mother's hand, Neaira bowed her head. "I will receive the rite with great joy."

"For the next years, though, I hope you will drink in the beauty as well as the joy of this place," Kti said. "I want you to have moments to explore the grounds and the valleys beyond, to learn the hideaways and the beaches that gave me so much pleasure in my youth. These years should include some time for just you. Soon enough, you will enter fully into helping the villagers know well the Way of the Mother. If you wish, young Ariel, our teller, well trained by Phemios, will acquaint you with the telling art. Telling gave me pleasure in my childhood. I enjoy it still, as I scribe the stories of our family."

"For whatever comes, Mother, you know you have our support." As she raised her head, Neaira's eyes met Kti's.

In short order, the citadel took shape. The family occupied it by mid summer. They thrived in their renewed home. But without Eury, Kti found herself fending off suitors who were convinced Eury was lost. "I am still wife," she said as they, daring not defy her, skulked away.

Often in her bed at night, she clinched her bedclothes. "Oh, Mother Gaia, bring Eury back to us."

Search and confirm. Leave nothing to chance.

Chapter Twenty-Four

In the second year at Pronni, Lykos, free of duties, took his mother by the hand. "Come with me."

Kti left her loom where she prepared a magnificent cloak for Eury's homecoming. They reached the upper rim of the citadel grounds, her favorite spot enhanced by the view the three waterways. Her work seldom allowed visits there.

"This place brings me peace," Lykos said, "a true retreat. Here, I pray often for Father's safe return. Below, I found a small cave where I come before dawn or in the dark of night. I have slipped from my bed to sleep there. Did you know that, Mother?"

Kti shook her head. "We must all find special places, Lykos. You honor me by telling me."

"Soon, Mother, I shall travel to Parnassus for the hunt that marks my manhood. But I have so long done manly things that I secretly gave myself a name to carry to Parnassus. If Grandfather and Father, for he will have returned by next spring, will allow it, I would like that as my adult name. May I choose my name?"

Kti gasped, then admitted she did not know. "I cannot speak for the men, but Lykos, another ritual, that of the Great Mother, names boys at manhood. In that ritual, initiates can choose their name or be given one. As we stand here above your cave, let me guess the name you choose. I say Arkos, the name of our great ancestor. Have I guessed correctly?"

"Wise Mother, you know me well. Yes, I feel at home with that name," Lykos said. "The warriors may give me another name. Still I choose Arkos."

Kti intoned the rite she said long ago when she gave Eumaios his name. As she said the final words "…and this man goes forth Arkos, now and evermore," she smiled at her son. "Arkos, whatever happens at Parnassus, know that the Great Mother has affirmed your choice. Henceforth, I shall call you Arkos. Wear the name proudly."

"I shall, Mother."

As the sun sent forth a burst of rays signaling its descent, the family settled on the terrace for the evening meal.

"Neaira," Kti said, "tonight we enjoy a feast of celebration. Today, I gave Lykos his adult name according to the Mother rite. He chose Arkos."

"What an appropriate name you gave my dear brother, who often gives me hugs as I imagine a friendly bear might." Neaira took a step toward him. "Now Arkos, you may hug me."

Arkos laughed as he reached for Neaira's outstretched hand and pulled her into a gentle embrace.

Soon the star points of ancient Kallisto and Arkos appeared in the night sky. Kti said, "Look up, children, our ancestors Kallisto, the great bear, and Arkos, the little bear, bless the naming."

Kti continued to look for the remnant of the western fleet, Ody's last vessel and Eury's supply vessels. Often she said, "I know they still struggle to reach home."

In due time, Kti visited at the stronghold while Arkos hunted with the warriors to receive the rite of manhood. They confirmed his name, Arkos. Neaira's time to go to Parnassus came. She received the name Protea, another form of her own name, but chose to keep Neaira.

"What difference does it make which I am called? Either confirms that I shall be involved with the seaways. I shall marry a trader."

As if she pronounced a truth, Theo, Aunt and Uncle's youngest son, came with a trading ship from Samos Island. Kti received him.

"I have watched Neaira grow into a lovely woman with whom I feel much affinity," said Theo. "We worked side by side in the ports of Samos Island and when I came with other islanders of Samos to help kin of the Western Isles restore lands, homes and ports, our friendship grew. Now, I come again to ask her to return to Samos Island as my wife. With your assent, I shall approach her."

Smiling, Kti bowed her head, then lifted it. "Ah, Theo, you have my assent, even though I do not relish having her so far away." She stood, took his arm, and led him to an arbor where Neaira sat mending a fishing net. "Now you must win her."

Kti made ready the citadel for a festive marriage. She chanted the marriage rite, then took her place at the feast beside Arkos. "I miss Aglaeus and Penthenia, Theo's parents, now bound mostly to home on Samos Island." With a tear rolling down her check, she said, "But the greatest void, your father is not here to see his glowing daughter begin her new life."

Arkos took his mother's hand in his. "Father and Uncle, both sturdy, sensible warriors, will come home."

After the ceremony, Kti sought Pen and melted into her arms. "Oh, Pen, you above all know the sorrow of Eury's absence. How can we bear the pain of not knowing much longer?"

Pen leaned into the embrace. "My dear friend, I know today without Eury was unbearable. Sorrow breaks my heart daily. That grief hollows your heart, too. The waiting wears us down."

Kti looked into the distance. "I cannot endure the separation much longer."

Pen nodded. "Nor can I."

The painful silence hung in the air between them.

In the seasons that followed, Arkos and Kti looked east and west for trading opportunities. A connecting port to the west for the Eastern traders, the activity at their Poros harbor increased. They opened a small port for their western operation that Kti and Eury planned long ago south of the mating grounds where the massive turtles from Zante Island churned ashore for nesting.

In time, Kti received Pen's summons to Ithaka. Antikleia, her heart breaking, died as she yearned for the return of her son. Hekate, the wise elder who opens the gateway beyond the limits, led her forth to catch the winds to her star.

That evening Kti walked on the terrace with her father. "Look up, Father, a new star shines brightly. Mother enjoys the company of our ancestor, Kallisto, the Great Bear."

Kti put her arms around her father, noting his bones lacked the flesh he had before. "Father, come from Ithaka to the Pronni with me to take Mother's bones.

Laertes shook his head. "I send the ashen bones of my loving and loyal Antikleia to their burial tomb in the valley below the Pronni. I shall come in the spring to pay homage."

Right before Kti left Ithaka, Pen confided to her that many suitors came to urge her to marry. They seemed convinced that Ody would not return.

"Hold fast to our belief that our husbands will return," said Kti. "Those not at your door in Ithaka came to my door in Pronni. Some come to both. When Ody and Eury come, we will disburse them all."

In the tenth year after the fall of Truva, Arkos and Telemakhos, now considered men, grew unsettled by their mothers' harassment that depleted the households and the heritage of their children, so they decided to search for their fathers. In Pylos, the first stop on their journey, they visited Nestor. At Sparta, they consulted Menelaos and Helen. Strange words of Menelaos recounted what the Old Man of the Sea had told him in a dream. His tale convinced Telemakhos that his father already returned. He left immediately for Ithaka.

Arkos would not accept Menelaos' words that Eury was among those who lost their lives at sea. "I will search for my father along the rough shores of Truva, including the surrounding areas, and, if need be, travel beyond the Dark Sea."

Telemakhos carried Arkos' parting message: "Tell Mother I love her and I shall return with good news."

Kti met Telemakhos at the port when she saw his ship dock and heard his account. "I, like Arkos, do not accept Eury's death. He will come with Ody. I shall see him soon."

Several days passed. She had word from Ithaka that Ody had returned. She learned that Ody, Telemakhos, Eumaios, and other loyal followers purged the Ithakan citadel of Pen's suitors. Ody reclaimed his queen, his son's heritage, and his lands.

Kti sat at her loom when she heard footsteps. Jumping up,

she turned to face Ody. Her eyes searched beyond him for she believed Eury stood just behind him. "My own brother, at last you have come. And…"

Ody folded her in his arms. "My dearest sister, a storm took your Eury with the other crew. I found him among the bodies that washed upon the land where we earlier had taken on supplies. I performed the rites to give all of them passage to the underworld. I burned the body of each man on his own great pyre, then gathered burned ashen bones. Except for a small portion that I brought home in pouches for burial in the home tomb of each, I buried the bones in a stone tomb that took many days to build."

He placed in Kti's hands a pouch that contained the token remnant of Eury. "He was a good man, a leader… a stalwart warrior to the end."

Kti pushed away from Ody and shook her head as if trying to free it from a tangle of branches. "I hear what you say, but you are wrong. I do not accept that Eury will not come." She grabbed Ody and pounded on his chest. "No, No, No! Arkos will find him. Telemakhos found you, so it must be that Arkos will find Eury."

Pen stood nearby. "Kti, Kti, please try to understand. I beg you not to retreat into your inner core. Such shock needs tempering, but stay with us so we may comfort you."

Even so, Kti shielded the rawness of Ody's words with numbness. Denying them, denying Eury's death, gave her space in which to live. She went through the burial ritual with Pen, Eumaios and Freya's intoning of the words that seemed only a distant hum.

"The bones of whoever came back with Ody deserves

respect," she said in a voice raw with emotion. "The pouch can rest temporarily in the tomb. No harm would come of that."

For days nothing stirred her.

Each day, Freya brought to her the young twins, Kleia and Laertes, now nine so she could enfold them in her arms. Her mind told her she must allay their grief. "I will resume my duties as your mother, as the reasonable matron of this household."

Her heart, instead, took her to a still place deep inside. There, with the Great Mother's help, she must heal. "Gaia, initiator of us all," she said, "why have you given me this trial?"

"You are strong, my child. Have courage."

Kti's head spun toward the voice, but no one was there, only darkness.

Once more you journey.

CHAPTER TWENTY-FIVE

After hearing of Eury's death in the stormy shipwreck, Kti alternately felt numbness, followed by sorrow, then anger. In her distress, she questioned the Great Mother herself. Over and over, she asked to hear from Ody the details of the storm. Then she repeated to others what he told her, as if she had been there herself:

"We suffered many trials together."

"Eurylokhos kept us going."

"We fell short of rations."

"Skin alone covered our bones."

"We at last found food and water."

"I cautioned no eating of the herds as they belonged to someone."

"I would barter for some of the cattle."

"We must fish."

"We must hunt wild animals."

"I returned from a hunt to find disaster."

"With no sanction, the crew slaughtered kine."

"They ate ravenously."

"Sustained, we moved on."

"Great Helios, whose daughters tended all our cattle, hid

his rays."

"Poseidon, to avenge my killing his one-eyed son, stirred a great storm."

"Zeus sent lightning to the stormy seas that Aeolus' winds stirred."

"How else can I tell it?"

"Overturned, afire, we sank."

"I found bodies."

"I performed rites to give proper passage."

"I gathered sacred bones."

"The men's souls, released, I yearned for home."

At other times, she cried out, "You tell me lies to create the words of a teller. Why? The words bring no comfort."

At times she pounded her brother's body. "You killed my husband. You create your tale to free yourself from guilt. Commanders bring their men home."

Sometimes she just muttered, "Great Mother, you should have contended with the Sky Gods."

Days turned to weeks before Kti returned from her deep place. She discovered she had, in her state of waking sleep, tended to daily duties. Ody, much at her side, went twice to Ithaka to consult elders of the island. He comforted the grieving families whose ashes he had returned.

Seldom did Pen and Freya leave her to herself. In the fourth week of her dark gloom, Ody entered her great hall. With him, he brought their father, Laertes, and his son, Telemakhos.

Kti smiled her first smile since Ody came to her. "I have been lost. In the depths, the Great Mother called me to healing. I have communed with Eury. He came to me in the realm where I go for solace."

From that day, she opened her heart's eye to the beauty of her family. Often her twins came to her side. Whole again, but changed, Kti called them "my blessings."

With Arkos gone, Kti guided the trade and the household. Approaching their maturity, Laertes and Kleia assisted their mother. Her ports of Poros and Skala thrived. Her traders plied the water to Samos Island onward into Byblos, Ugarit, and other southern ports that stretched all the way to Egypt. Some went into the Dark Sea to the North.

She expanded the western port where traders from the long span of the Western Sea and beyond the great rock barrier docked to barter. Earlier, Freya had dispelled the myths about sea monsters, hyperboreans, and mysterious feys of the northern seas, even the tales of her homeland farther north. One striking northern group, the redheaded, green-eyed, fair tribe that some called Kelts, stood out starkly from the dark-haired, bronze-skinned traders of the southern seas.

In the third year after Ody's return, Eumaios greeted the family. "I have come to bring you to Ithaka to visit your father. Waning in strength, Laertes needs you."

Kti spent many weeks in Ithaka with her father as he wandered among his orchard trees and reminisced to the songs of old Phemios. One early morning, she found Laertes very weak.

"Call the family to my side," he whispered. "I must give them my final blessing."

All that day Kti nestled him in her arms, while the others surrounded him. The household and friends said their farewells and received his blessings. As sunset brought cooler evening breezes, he took his last breath. Peaceful release sent him on his final journey.

Kti, Pen, and the household women prepared his frail body, still kingly. Honored among the islanders along with many of the mainlanders, they laid him upon a massive pyre for rites of the Great Mother that assured his place in the star dance of the universe.

The followers of Parnassian Apollo and Dodonian Zeus accompanied his body to the entry of the warriors' field, Hades' domain. The men imagined Hermes and the women Hekate leading the procession from the burning ceremony at the great pyre to his appointed place. They placed Laertes in the hero's domain; the women, in his star yard where Antikleia welcomed him.

Then Kti joined the family south to Pronni where they placed his bones beside Antikleia's in the grave below the citadel. Shrine women of Palli, Eleusis, Delphi, Dodona, Lusi, Argos, and Troezen joined them. All the Powers honored him, for he, in life, had honored them.

Before she returned to Parnassus, Kti visited Pythia, the Delphic Sibyl. "I remember the day we named you and the day we birthed these two thriving children. Perhaps, with your vast experience, you will join us to teach below the mount. We need to bring along our people."

"I am honored by your request." Kti had already thanked Gaetha, her wise Samian Sibyl, who likewise sought her at the shrine of Hera on Samos. She said to Pythia, as to Gaetha, "When the twins reach adulthood, perhaps, I shall come."

Nodding, Pythia closed her eyes as if in prayer.

Some weeks later, caught by surprise, Kti met the eyes of Eumaios, wondering at his concerned look.

"What has happened, Eumaios?"

"Raiders from the north threaten us again. Pen and Ody left Ithaka for Pen's Arkadian citadel. After the deaths of her family members in last winter's cold, Pen will lead the people there until she can pass the citadel to her daughter, should she bear a girl, or to her sister's daughter. Neaira, along with her husband Theo, would welcome you on Samos Island. They face no threats this time. With their urgent departure, you realize the danger of staying. I come to help you prepare for the journey."

Gazing at the window as if watching a visitor approach, Kti nodded.

"As you know," Eumaios continued, "Laertes, at his death, freed me to seek my own destiny. I shall seek my parents. I must know if they still live. From Laertes, I received a fleet, as well as the lands and their house on Ithaka. Later I plan to come back to work my land and trade, but now I must go."

Kti, taking in all he had said, addressed his last news of his freedom first. "My Eumaios, my Jamin, many years ago, we hoped that you might br free to go claim your birthright. My heart leaps with joy that my father treated you fairly for your many acts of kindness rendered to our family. If I must once again leave my citadel, I have one more choice. We can go with you."

Her eyes twinkled as she delivered her last words. "Of course, that would be going into the unknown."

How brash I am.

Then she said, "Yes, Eumaios, I have many choices. Just now, I think I shall join Neaira and Theo. Samos Island, a good place to attend to our trading interests, gives me opportunities to serve the holy women of Hera. Thank you, dear friend, for coming to help us."

"I am encouraged by your words that we might meet again," he said in a soft voice, leaning his head toward hers.

For a time, they talked of her plans and of his. Eumaios would leave before week's end. With her household, along with Erato and her household from neighboring Sami, Kti would depart shortly after for Samos Island.

As Freya prepared the household, young Kleia helped her pack. To prevent desecration, Eumaios buried ritual articles at the valley shrine. Then he covered the valley tombs. With young Laertes, Kti organized the ports for the move.

Eumaios sailed when fair winds of the fourth day invited his travel west. At their goodbyes, he said to Kti, "You have the pebble I gave you long ago to call me for help."

Then he cast his eyes westward. He wondered aloud, "Shall I find my parents well? How will they receive me?"

He gazed at Kti. Finally, the strong, reticent man strode toward his ship. "Send for me if you need me, Kti."

Kti planned to spend one more night in her own bed. Only her children, Freya, and one more servant, Panthea, stayed with them. Kti planned to take her fleet to the East at dawn.

Later that night, startled from a deep sleep, Kti awoke.

"What a fine prize you will make, my dear," snarled a voice thick with a different accent.

At once alert, Kti freed herself from the grasping man. She grabbed the dagger beneath her pillow and plunged it into his heart. Then she and Freya gathered the children into their arms. Kti searched for Panthea, only to find her lifeless body at their feet. In front of her stood a towering figure, whose piercing green eyes sparkled in the torchlight. He held her in a grip she could not break. Others held Freya and the children.

Pushing Kti into a chair, her captor said, "You are a strong woman. You killed one of my men. I should kill you at once, but I will not kill a woman who has protected herself and her own."

Kti barely heeded his words. She darted protective eyes toward her children, then toward Freya. Freya's eyes signaled her to stay calm.

"Ah," he said, "you look to the young ones and your companion. I assure you and them safety as long as you do not try anything else."

As he spoke, Kti realized he spoke her language, but with the accent belonging to the western traders, the Kelts. His red hair and green eyes confirmed his origin. His tone told her they might survive, perhaps even break free.

He spoke to two of his men. "Guard her. Keep the others here with her. We cannot risk leaving them behind, as we killed one of the women. We shall look around for food and whatever else we might find."

He turned to face Kti. "I had not planned to depart so soon. We believed this citadel would serve well as our future port. I have plied your waters, then docked at your western port for many days of trading while also exploring. I saw you many times there. I admired your industry."

Kti stared at her captor with unrelenting eyes as she absorbed his words.

The Kelt said to his men, "Free your hold."

To her he said, "You want no trouble. Just sit still. I heard you had departed for your Samos Island ports to seek safety from oncoming hordes from the North, some, likely my tribal brothers."

Kti nodded.

"Many come, but most will pass this place. I plan to fight for the right to stay here. Having you out of the way serves my intentions well. Reassure everyone I shall not harm you or them. We leave within the hour."

Kti felt foolish for her whim to stay at the unguarded citadel that left them in such danger. She wondered if they would ever see their home again.

Stay calm. Cooperate. Watch for chances to signal for help or to escape. These phrases echoed in her mind.

"Thank you, Great Mother," she muttered. "We still live."

PART FOUR

KTIMENE AND CONN

SPAIN, GAUL, HYPERBOREA
(The Green Isle and Denmark)

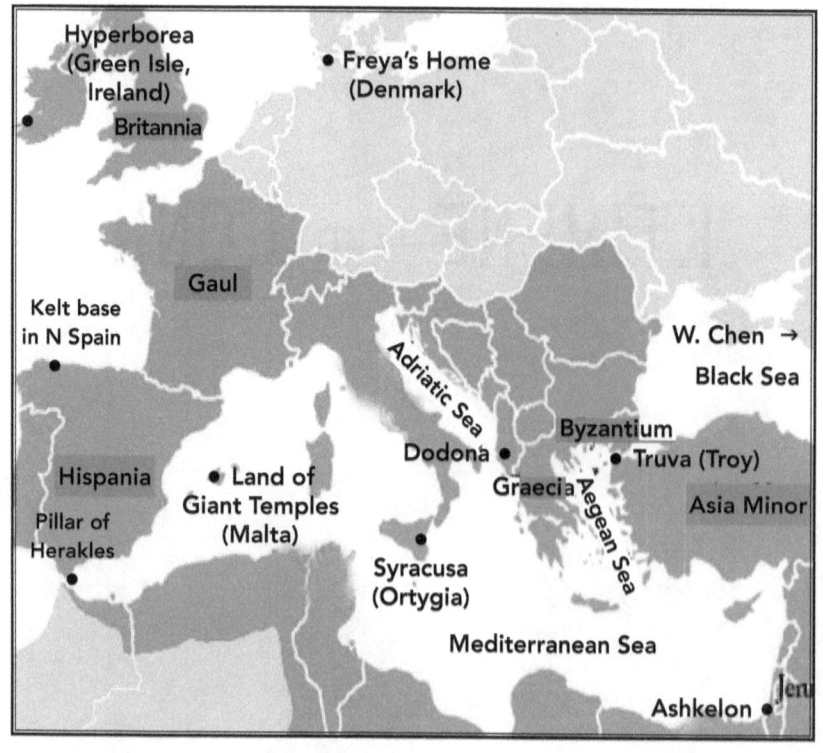

Hyperborea
(Green Isle,
Ireland)

Britannia

Freya's Home
(Denmark)

Gaul

Kelt base
in N Spain

W. Chen →

Black Sea

Adriatic Sea

Hispania

Pillar of
Herakles

Land of
Giant Temples
(Malta)

Dodona

Byzantium

Truva (Troy)

Graecia

Aegean Sea

Asia Minor

Syracusa
(Ortygia)

Mediterranean Sea

Ashkelon

Jeru

I have points in the North.
Go there to complete another part of you.

Chapter Twenty-Six

With her children and Freya beside her, Kti huddled aboard ship in a small space. She wondered why the enigmatic man had not killed them on the spot. Yes, Laertes and Kleia would bring good prices on the slave market, and she and Freya might. She hoped for rescue until the ship slipped from port. Night must turn to dawn before they would be missed.

For two days, while the ship caught the rapid west winds, the small retinue kept to its allotted space. They received food without a word from anyone. The dagger, no longer among Kti's belongings, left the small family no protection. Only physical strength could Kti use as her weapon. Slaves came to their ports unharmed. She and Freya assured her children they would be safe.

They sailed for three days and two nights more. On the evening of the fifth day, the small retinue was allowed to wander the deck.

When the others returned to their space, Kti was summoned to dine with her captor. He treated her as an honored guest. Still, she knew her plight as well as her place. Not once did he touch her as if to harm her or to bed her. He often stared over the waters to the west as if in anticipation of some sign. Mostly he directed her to eat.

He spoke only once. "The ship is close to shore. We dock for supplies in the morning. With two strong mates, you and your daughter will be allowed to walk the port. We shall show you off to great advantage. Holding your attendant and your son assures your cooperation."

Kti stood up and turned toward the doorway.

As she left, he said, "If we do not leave you here, I shall summon you to my table henceforth."

The next day she and Kleia strolled along the dock but found no one to signal for help. Although two leering men inspected them, pawing them from head to toe, their captors could not agree on a price.

During her visits with the captain, Kti discovered that he journeyed to the north past the massive rock that guarded the sea of her home waters. After rounding the land mass beyond the mouth of the sea to reach the northern shores, he would join his family, many of his tribe, and other branches of his kindred. Years ago, his tribe had traveled overland from the far eastern steppes above the Eastern trade routes. Fast changing to settled farming, their nomadic ways caused them to vie for land space, already in short supply.

She learned he had married a woman of his tribe, from an island in a fertile green landmass farther north. He led his tribe from their peaceful river home to search for southern trading ports. A seafarer by trade, he extended trade with the ships in his wife's dowry.

"When we use your citadel, we will expand trade. We have no fear of the marauders who threaten you. Do we foreigners really strike fear in your people?"

The last question, he delivered with an incredulous smile. "We come in peace, but you eastern sea dwellers have taught us a trick or two about treachery as well as war. Before we learned of your slave bartering, we murdered captured men but kept the women and children as servants or married them into the tribe."

He gazed out over the water. "We sail toward the entry of a far larger sea."

Kti said, "My people call the rock that guards our sea the 'Gate of Herakles'."

He laughed. "Your small world will enlarge on this journey, should you still be with us as we make the turn to the north. But I plan to barter you long before we leave your sea. We pass many princely lands still."

Encouraged by the talks, Kti reported to the others that no harm awaited them as long as they cooperated. But Laertes, mature beyond his twelve years, resisted their advice. "I shall jump ship to seek help."

Storms kept them from port for three days. Each day, her captor Conn lamented running out of places with occupants who would enjoy her and her attendant's genteel manners. Storms blew them past the tip of the lands of people he called Etruscans and Latiums.

Then he anchored near a beach. With guards, they enjoyed swimming in the waters and feasting with the crew on the smaller offshore island that faced a larger one.

"There is no escaping here. Swimming the stretch to the landmass close by to the north, if one succeeded in making it ashore, would land the weary swimmer on a ghost island. Should he survive the rocks, a swimmer would find himself among strangely shaped stone ruins. No one can survive there." He delivered these words gazing at young Laertes.

After the outing, everyone returned to the vessel. All of a sudden, Laertes darted forward, shouting his farewells, and disappeared overboard. Conn ordered two of his best swimmers to pursue him, but just as they were about to jump, he called them back. Then he ordered the ship to hoist anchor, furl the sails, and head west.

Kti tried to plunge into the sea after Laertes, but Conn held her. "You cannot go."

Perhaps this plucky boy, so much his father's son, will make it to shore and onward to a port to find help.

For two days more, they sailed before Conn ordered taking on supplies. He traded among the people of what he called their small sea.

At first, Kti and Conn exchanged few words. He realized she knew enough of his language as well as his destination to communicate information to the other sea people. Leaving her at any port endangered him, his crew, and his family.

One evening as they dined, Conn said, "I must ask you a question I have formed in my mind many times."

Kti stared at him and waited.

"How could your husband allow you the freedom of occupying your citadel alone?"

"I am my own keeper. My husband died in a recent war."

Conn looked her up and down. "How did you learn the ways of the sea and come to live alone? Surely your parents wanted to arrange another husband for you. Still young, you would have more children to carry on your kingdom's work."

Kti sat in silence as she pondered his personal question,

along with her careful reply. "I admit it; many tried to convince me to re-marry, but I delayed while I became more independent. My children needed me. Besides I knew trading since I engaged most actively in it when my husband went to war. Supply officer to my brother's fleet, my husband often arrived home to take on supplies. He always yearned to see us."

"You have other children, then, and family?" Conn said. "They always give us a stable port in this unstable world,"

Kti nodded. "My life, most blessed except for dear Eury's death and this recent setback, has taught me much. Wars and unrest may be inevitable, but the Great Mother teaches us that peace brings greater harmony."

Until now, she had inwardly called the Mother's name, but she sensed that the man before her knew the Mother, perhaps in another of Her many forms. While she had watched him staring out to sea in deep thought, she could not fathom that he would not know the Mother's Way.

Our Mother sees after the seasons, the weather, and our inner needs," Conn said. "She tends to our births, heals us, and takes us in death to join our ancestors. She lives within our hearts but seems strangely absent of late. We have had difficulty with some of our tribe who joined renegade warriors of other tribes. These pariahs steal our land and our women, and murder us as we live in peace. Mother Maeve and Mother Bridge may be punishing us with sickness, even famine. I wanted a better place for us to settle."

Kti sighed. A man of peace, this captain wanted to lead his people to a better place. "Surely all of you will find a good place to fulfill your destiny, but I would not settle on Kephallenia. Despite what you say, the island remains unsafe. We know the ways of the pirates who sweep down from the north. Be assured, my own family will return to do battle with you for their rights."

"My wife, along with our two sons and my wife's mother, are my deepest concern," Conn said. "But I have a large group of others to watch over. If we do not establish ourselves in your land, we must find a safe home elsewhere."

"I pray you do find a safe place to settle," Kti whispered.

"I must take on supplies for a long two days at sea to our current home." He rested his hands upon his hips. "I have decided you will be a companion to my wife and good help in our household. Perhaps one day you will marry again. I will see to it that your attendant has a good husband. When she is grown, your child will marry well." With a smile, he turned to the doorway to leave for the night.

Kti shook her head. "We shall see what the Great Mother has in store." She walked to her quarters, thinking, *Laertes will come for us. Gaia, I pray you bring him to us with many rescue ships.*

To the edges of the earth you travel.

Chapter Twenty-Seven

Kti followed Conn into the clearing where he left his family and followers. Scorched earth still smoldered. No one greeted them.

A crazed Conn ran from spot to spot overturning debris. Just then, he stopped, knelt slowly to sift the ashes, and wept. With loving care, he and his companions pronounced rites over the charred bodies of those found among the ashes. Conn tended to the preparation of the bodies of his wife, his wife's mother, and one son.

For many days, the tribe keened. The entire ship's crew searched in all directions for survivors. Conn hoped to find O'Conn, his eldest son.

Kti stayed close to Conn to see that he ate. "What will you do next?"

"We shall journey far north to the green isles. There near the stone circle, I shall place my departed ones in the family burial space below a balanced boulder."

Kti set down her cup. "Our burial rituals differ. We place the dried bones of our loved ones in a stone-lined shaft to rest upon benches in special niches."

Conn stirred the embers to keep the flame alive. "Ours tarry a short while in the wintering time before a sun ray takes them to their sky home."

"Ours settle in the star yard of our ancestors." Kti spoke in a hushed tone as she stood beside him, reaching her palms forward to warm her hands. Then she put Kleia to sleep near her own bed, one she shared with Freya.

Most of the others chose to bury their loved ones in a site near the shore. They found evidence that some renegades of their own tribe had joined the invading tribe.

Word came that searchers found O'Conn, unconscious and delirious. Conn carried his son into his temporary shelter. Then he collapsed.

Kti, Kleia, and Freya tended them. "The poor man kept his courage and his strength until they found O'Conn," Kti said. "Now he succumbs to his time of grief."

For days Kti nurtured Conn. Revived, he stayed by his son's side. Only two of the crew tracked down their wives. Another found a son; another, a daughter. Some talked of revenge.

Kleia spoke in soothing tones to the delirious O'Conn as she administered healing balm to his burns. One day, she reported to Kti and Freya that her visits with the surviving families revealed a plot to pursue the invaders. In a soft low voice, Kti informed Conn. He took in the information without moving away from his son.

O'Conn roused. "Father, you must stop the pursuit. The invading tribe will fight, should we find them. We will lose more people. I can travel. Let us go north in this greening time. The Mother Maeve rights wrongs. We must live on."

"I see the wisdom of your words, my son."

The two men, now stronger, joined the discussion at council.

The remnant made preparations for the journey north.

Kti strolled by the sea with Conn. "You grieve still, but calm comes as the spring greening brings beckoning sea breezes. You move among the people, the true leader that you are."

They sat on a grassy knoll above the water. Conn took her hand. "Thanks to all of you, we have returned to health."

Kti shook her head. "Young O'Conn improves daily. His burn scars hardly show. Everyone rallies as you prepare for the journey north."

On a day close to the time of leave-taking, in a moment alone with Kti, Conn said, "Kti, you could have left me to the care of others. Why did you not?"

Kti turned her head and peered into his questioning eyes. "You needed me."

That night they walked into the deep woods, communed with the Mother, and entered the marriage chamber.

The next day, Conn turned to Kti. "We go north, my dear Kti. I know you would rather return to the southern sea, but first we must honor my promise to my departed wife. She and her kinswoman and our son must make their passage from their ancestral grounds.'

Kti nodded. "The time will come when we shall return to the southern sea, my homeland, and reunite with my family."

"In the North, I predict, you shall bear our little one." With a grin, Conn patted her belly.

Kti laughed at the rough-hewn, gentle man, her dear spouse. "I can wait to go south. My household has gathered on Samos Island safe with Neaira and Theo. Laertes, I sense, has joined them to tell them of our route, for he heard enough of your plans."

To her relief, Conn said, "We shall send a ship with word of your safety, of your queenly status among my people, and of our plan to travel south soon."

"After the burial journey, we shall continue to develop the trading center at my home ports."

On a sunny spring day, three ships left the tribal grounds. They sailed northward up the mainland coast for several days. Kti noted Kleia and O'Conn, protective of one another, developed a close relationship as siblings. She relished Freya's finding a comely companion among the sailors, a lusty captain who approached her with marriage terms.

Kti smiled when Freya said, "I have always thought I would travel home. Now I have the means for the journey. I hope to find my mother and to make peace with my brother. Besides I favor this fair man." She added with a wistful sigh, "Perhaps even my father and uncle will welcome me."

Kti and Kleia planned a festive wedding for Freya to marry her captain. On the day before the ships crossed a massive westward expanse of water, the most turbulent of the journey, the three ships anchored in a small inlet. The captain boarded Conn's ship to claim his bride. Conn, the tribal chieftain blessed the marriage. Then Kti, the only one present except Freya who knew the rites of the Great Mother, pronounced the marriage ceremony. Cheers from all the ships echoed across the water as she said, "…and this couple goes forth in married bliss." Afterward the newlyweds returned to their ship.

At dawn, they sailed west. On the third day, the turbulence of the sea moved Kti to her bed. Kleia attended her. Kti said, "I did not realize how weak my body had become."

"Rest now, dear Mother. For many days, you administered

to others. Your turn for help presents itself. Keep your food down in these rough seas, so you can return to health very soon."

That night Kti awoke from a feverish slumber and grabbed her abdomen in pain. "I am too weak to help myself. I must let go."

Both Conn and Kleia held her as she disgorged a mass of blood.

She looked at each in desperation. "I have lost our dear child." She groaned as tears rolled down her cheeks. "It was a lad, I know."

Turning aside, Conn wiped a tear from his cheek, then he patted her hand. "The sea was rough; you are strong. You must slow down until you are mended ."

Kleia moved the bereft Conn to the door. "Take my bunk and I shall see to Mother. Come later to see her."

The next morning the ships rounded the green landmass to the north. The roiling seas calmed in an inlet bay. Kti held out her arms to welcome Conn to the chamber. "I am better, my love, but I have failed us. Our boy is gone."

The gentle man took her cheeks between his hands. "Do not fret, dear love. You will never fail us. When you are able, we can slip the dear lad into the sea, a fitting place for a seaman that he would have been."

Kti shifted to one side and drifted into sleep. She felt grateful he stayed by her side until she grew stronger. The next evening, they gave their babe a sea burial. Freya and her captain came aboard so that Freya could pronounce the ritual.

We must be patient while we heal, Kti thought as they walked slowly to their quarters. We both enter a fragile time, and we need each other even more now.

"We must stay strong," Kti told Kleia that evening while Conn checked the ship. "Conn thinks the same as I, even though he does not speak it. We shall find our way together."

Nodding, Kleia hugged her mother good night. Then she slipped from the room, giving the returning Conn a squeeze as she passed him outside the doorway. "Yes, dear parents, time will heal."

Learn anew. Heal.

CHAPTER TWENTY-EIGHT

The next day, the three ships turned into a bay that met the wide mouth of a deep river. They made their way to a nearby dock where other rough-hewn boats awaited them. Kti and Kleia received a warm welcome when the villagers learned of the disaster, especially their part in nurturing the survivors of the massacre. They keened as the bodies came ashore, but their laments mixed with happy shouts when they learned their headman had found a new mate. They cast their lot with Conn and Kti as their leaders. Kti gave Conn a questioning look.

With a shrug, Conn wrapped his arms around Kti. "That is our way. Life must go on, my mate. Soon you will have a new name to suit your role."

While Conn stayed longer with the men to discuss what the tribe must do to survive, Kti helped the women prepare the dead for burial. "Kleia, we will walk with Conn and O'Conn to the ancestral grounds."

At the burial site, a large contingent gathered. Kti told Kleia why they acted in haste. "The onset of the summer sun is the time for the burial rituals to begin so that the souls will be ready to follow the beam of the winter sun to their home in the skies."

The welcoming summer days regenerated the tribe. Kti mingled among them, absorbing their ways of ease. She enjoyed the beauty of the river valley, its lush green grass dotted with flowers. The weather invited the people out into the energizing sun. She learned their rituals, now hers, as she shared her skills of the south.

Kti and the holy women among them helped the others stay connected to the Great Mother. She and Freya instructed Kleia, for soon she would be a woman in her own right. They celebrated when Conn's son received the Mother rite of manhood. The Mother, strong among O'Conn's people in the forms of Bridge, Maeve, and others, gave the tribe wise guidance. The holy women of the north in council gave Kti her name, a most revered one, Bridge.

The tribe rekindled its gentle nature attuning it with the rhythms of the earth. Most of the men remarried.

Some moons later in deep summer, Kti sat amidst the green land, Conn beside her. He fondled a ringlet of her ebony hair and looked at her with expectant hesitation.

Kti nestled closer to him. "Conn, dear one, you have come back to me."

Happiness and fecundity reigned in the village. Nine moons later, Kti bore a fair son whom they called Lykaon after the ancient mate of Nonakris who had nurtured her only daughter Kallisto and, after her disappearance, her son Arkos.

Kleia, at her first blood, took the name Maeve. She and O'Conn no longer could be considered siblings, as their deep love led to marriage. As his father's heir, O'Conn would lead the tribe and join the council of tribes on the sacred hill far to the east of their village.

Kti designed their spacious home mostly integrated into the high hill above the river. Around it the tribal community built a thriving city along with other homes of the same style.

One bright late spring day in their fourth year, Conn said, "We must journey south to your lands so we can open the ports. Wisdom tells me to leave the village in the hands of O'Conn and Maeve. We shall enjoy them and their newborn child for the rest of this year's cycle. By next spring, our own hearty one will be old enough for us to travel. What do you think?"

"Your plan is perfect," Kti said. "All goes well here. We should connect with my citadel and my family."

The harsh winter brought illness to the village. Kti and Conn administered to the people, as did all who were well enough to help. One blustery night Conn came home from a food delivery. His cough was deep, his face flushed, his brow feverish.

"To bed with you," Kti said as she covered him with warm blankets to counter his chilled body. She administered hot compresses, salves, herbs, and nourishing soup when he could swallow.

Kti sat by him all night. When Maeve came the next morning, Kti felt a wave of relief, but she sent her away. "Dear daughter, you must stay well for your family."

Conn declined no matter what Kti tried. Before three days passed, he died. His last words came softly, "Live and love again, dearest."

Kti, gasped, then shrieked, "No, No, No!"

The next morning Maeve found her mother lying over Conn's cold body. Lykaon's skin felt feverish. "Mother, I must take you both home with me."

Kti shouted as she turned a shoulder to her. "Go home. I will prepare Conn's body for burial. O'Conn is in charge now. You both must stave off this plague."

O'Conn called a council to discuss ways to quash the disease. They agreed they could not wait for the thaw or the customary summer ritual to place the bodies in the cairn under the massive boulder for their journey to their sky home. The bodies must go into the grave before the upcoming winter solstice.

The bones of Conn, along with their young son who followed him in death, were placed among the many charred bones in the cairn under the massive boulder. A stoic Kti joined the mourners who trudged to the tomb, where Maeve conducted the ceremonial goodbye.

Kti received tender solicitude from Freya and Maeve. Another cycle of twelve moons passed, then another. When she helped birth Maeve's second son, Kti saw how much he favored dear Conn. Still she seldom stirred from her home.

One day, as Kti played with her grandchildren, a voice came from behind her, "Kti, you would not come to us. I have come to you."

There stood Eumaios, whose words stirred her. As he placed her pebble into her hand, she looked at the stone, then at him, her eyes wide. "Did Kleia find it in my pouch and send it to you?"

"A ship's captain found me at my home on Ithaka Island. He placed the stone in my hand as he told me of your sojourn in the north."

"O my Eumaios, my Jamin," she wept as she fell into his embrace.

He wrapped his arms around her, pressed her closed to his

chest, stroking her hair as her tears fell on his strong arms.

After a few moments, Kti raised her face to him. "I must go home. My people here have been good to me. Still, I yearn to see my home."

PART FIVE

KTIMENE AND
EUMAIOS

THE ISLAND OF SAMOS

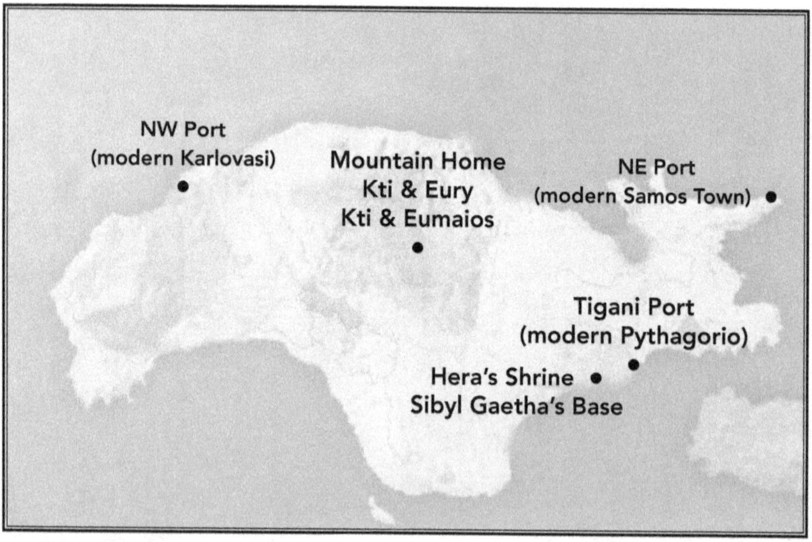

NW Port
(modern Karlovasi)
•

Mountain Home
Kti & Eury
Kti & Eumaios
•

NE Port
(modern Samos Town) •

Tigani Port
(modern Pythagorio)
•

Hera's Shrine •
Sibyl Gaetha's Base

You leave stardust in the North.

CHAPTER TWENTY-NINE

Some days passed. Kti sat with Eumaios near the fireside, gazing at him, then relaxed for the first time in days. "Your coming surprises and delights me. We both have aged, I see."

"I do not accept your aging refrain," said Eumaios with a wink. "We all adventure on in this world. Queenly Pen enjoys her young daughter, who keeps them company in her lands below Mount Kyllene. Helen just returned from deepest Egypt and the shrine of Isis, but mostly stays with Menelaos in Sparta. You, my friend, have pushed beyond any of us to this isle so green and lush, this fabled land of the winds. These adventures do not suggest aging to me. We can scarce guess where the next generations will go."

"Speaking of the next generation, tell me of my children."

"With Neaira and Theo in charge, the trade thrives on Samos Island. They speak of expanding your ports at Pronni. The trade stretches beyond Truva into the farthest coasts of the Dark Sea along to the south among the Assyrians, the Canaanites, and the Egyptians. Laertes made it back to let us know your captor headed to lands beyond the Pillar. He has searched for you over these several years. Now he ventures to the East to trade. We lost track of him, but rest assured he is out there somewhere and will make it back to us. We seek him, as we do for Arkos."

"Must I add Laertes to my concerns?" Kti said, as she stared beyond the horizon. "The time has come for me to help find them. Kleia and O'Conn lead well these gentle people. Their Great Mother brings them deep insights, much as our Mother Gaia. Now, yes, I must go home."

She shifted in her chair. "Tell me of your own journeys. Have you found your family? Have you developed your lands on Ithaka that my parents left you? Do your ships ply the trade routes?"

"Always the questioner, you are. But first I must tell you how pleased I am to find you well. Please forgive my forwardness in coming to you. We learned from the ship's captain of your Conn's death, of the deaths of your progeny, and of your illness. I knew when he gave me the pebble you needed me."

"Yes, my friend," Kti said, "I went through deep grieving. I still have days of sadness, but more of consolation. Again, as when Eury died, Mother Gaia moved me through the moon changes. Now speak of your family."

"I bring good news from my home of Ortygia," Eumaios said. "My parents still thrive. They always hoped to find me." He sat in a chair across from Kti.

Kti reached out her hand to touch his. "What good news that they live!"

Eumaios shrugged. "Not surprised that I had rendered faithful service, they praised your parents for recognizing my abilities. As the only living child, I inherit their kingdom. I urged them to name a cousin as heir. Still they persisted. I will not face duties there for some time, I hope."

He stood up again. "That I served as a shrine servant of the Mother among your people pleased them."

"I am glad to hear it."

"I spent hours with their shrine leaders. They blend well the Mother's Way with that of the warriors who, in turn, influence their rituals. I have learned their style of governance, but for now I reside on my Ithakan land. There I see after my lands and herds and send out my trading ships. I work with Telemakhos, who continues to lead the people of Ithaka while he lives at the Parnassian citadel."

"Have you visited my citadel?"

"Your citadel needs rebuilding, but we keep your herds in check, while Neaira and Theo use your ports. Busy on Samos Island, they hardly have time to tend the ports. They approached me to take over the operation on your behalf, but when we received word of you, they hoped you would come home to take charge."

Eumaios leaned against the back of the chair, resting his muscular arms along the side. "Now, I must be forward. In my own right as an heir to a kingdom, I ask you to become my wife. Long ago you began to speak of it, but I stopped you. The time was not right then. But now, I come with my own lands and many gifts to ask you to join with me. I come with the same commitment I wish I could have forwarded then. You have been, are... will forever be my love. I may be free, but I will always be yours."

These last words rushed from Eumaios' lips as though he must complete them all at once. He shifted to face her, an impish grin across his face.

His intensity brought a glowing smile to Kti. "You deserve

a fresh virgin. I remember my words of long ago, but surely you would release me from them. Two times a wife and six times a mother, what kind of bride would I be? Besides, I have no parents to arrange our bonds. I do not think the Great Gaia will appear to do it."

Eumaios, at first downcast, looked up to see Kti's bright eyes. "You would trifle with me now after all these years, my beloved?" He swept her into his arms for a long embrace. "I have waited many years for this moment."

They planned to sail right away. The tribe joined Maeve, O'Conn, and Freya to send their Queen southward. Leaving Kleia and O'Conn and her grandchildren saddened Kti, but she believed the people would flourish with their leadership.

The long journey to Samos Island gave them time to plan. They agreed Eumaios would launch his vessels on one more search for Laertes. Then their wedding would take place with Neaira and the shrine women of Hera in charge.

Once Kti arrived and shared their good news, Neaira rushed headlong into wedding details. "Relax and ready yourself for the rituals, Mother. Eumaios will return in ten days with or without Laertes. You both agreed, if you remember, for me to arrange the wedding while you retreated with the shrine women. Now, Mother, go. Worry not a bit about the details."

As Neaira pulled Kti to her feet, Kti could not decide whether to smile or frown. "I guess I am nervous about the ceremony, although it makes no sense to be so."

"And Mother," Neaira continued, "I shall give you in marriage with or without Laertes. All of the islanders love you. We will cheer you on. We hope to find Laertes, but know he needed time to understand his failure to find you and Kleia. He told us little of his journey home. After several attempts to find you in the Western Sea, even beyond it, he left here distraught. We know you would be happier to have all of us around you, but Mother Gaia works in her own time."

"Dear practical eldest daughter, so much like the strong women of our family, I submit to you. I can relax for the first time in many moons."

Caution about the future lingered, however, as her memories took her to the fateful night of her challenging northern journey. Then she remembered how much love and deep insight about the Mother's Way brought her back stronger.

"I wonder," she said, "if the world will find the peace our Mother wants for it. Though we have lost so much control to the warriors and their whimsical gods, they have never supplanted the Mother. She will endure, but she will adjust as she must through the ages. The equal partnership of spirit, mind, and body will prevail. Strong women will see to it."

Neaira nodded. "But I am curious if my generation will keep the partnerships alive. Many among the unsettled population roam the middle sea. Their violent bent makes me worry for my own son, who has just received the rite of manhood."

"But you have a solid marriage with Theo."

"Of course, of course." Then Nearia shuddered.

"Why are you shaking?" said Kti.

"Just thinking of what you must have experienced."

"Turn your thoughts to the happy time of my approaching marriage rite and feast."

"Dearest Mother," Nearia said with a grin, "now you must go to the shrine."

Kti made her way to the shrine. She promised herself quiet

contemplation, healing in the dream chamber, and Gaetha's leading her through an examination of her life.

This marriage, so important to her, completed her journey. Not that the others had not been sacred, this sacred marriage, she knew, fulfilled her destiny. She felt young, alive, yes, virginal— why not? Nearer to full wisdom, she experienced great joy. Her heart's eye opened wide to her new life. She knew Eumaios took a similar inner journey in their time apart. Ten days hence, each would bring healthy wholeness to their union. How blissful, yet how solemn and profound, their time would be.

"Here on this beautiful island, indeed a sacred spot, wise Gaetha, why does the happiness I feel give me uneasiness?" Kti said on the last day at the shrine.

The ancient one had known Kti for many years. "Woman, child, woman, child, woman," Gaetha uttered from a trance, "deep, deep in the chasms of the earth answers come to your questions. You will find them." Mother rocked with her eyes closed.

Kti had never seen her so. Gaetha always discussed problems with an open gaze. Past seventy years now, she had grown frail in her body, but remained forever young in many other ways.

What transpires here before me?

When Gaetha focused her eyes, she showed no sign of remembering the words she had just uttered. "You will marry, but your life will not be yours, nor will Eumaios' life be his. You will come to the shrine to tend to the people. I have awaited your return, Kti. Old now, before long I must go to the Mother's vast star yard. Taking my place as Sibyl, Sophia will continue to honor the work you both do. I shall roam in the wilds of the East. I have gone into deep counsel with the Great One, our

Mother. She agrees that your marriage, most sacred, readies you both for your roles. The shrine women join me in welcoming you to your work. The Mother chooses you."

Kti stared at Gaetha in amazement.

"We cannot foretell what will happen," Gaetha continued. "Whether or not you will write the rituals on the tablets as you have done the history, we do not know. That will be discussed, once you and Eumaios come to us."

Kti knew they must do as Gaetha pronounced. She wanted to protest their unworthiness, but she dared not speak for fear of offending not just the ancient woman who sat before her, but also the Great Mother herself. "I treasure your words. I shall present them to my dear husband. We shall visit, as you suggest."

"Dear child," the old one wheezed, "we unwind our lives as we must. You do not choose your tasks. Your tasks choose you."

When Eumaios gazed into her eyes on the day of their marriage, Kti felt bliss, natural and complete. On their journey to nearby Ikaria, they spent long hours in embrace. They explored each other's bodies, uniting them as one. Their union took them to the core of the earth and expanded them to dance in the rhythms of the sky.

She wondered if the lutes, lyres, and flutes, all playing out the blessing of their union, were real or merely her imagination. After a week, they set sail for Tigani and home. As their feet touched the sandy shore, they joined hands.

Kti gazed into Eumaios twinkling eyes. "Now we go to the shrine and our work."

Once more, you are me, dear one, in your bones.

CHAPTER THIRTY

The shrine grounds, in springtime beauty, surrounded Kti as she strolled with Eumaios toward the astral arch. She took her place in a nook of the shrine to begin her work. For several days they counseled those who came to them. Then they sought out Sibyl Gaetha.

"The people who come need help," said Kti. "We advise them, but we see in them a dependency that cannot be good "

"It surprises us that many give up their initiative, make offerings, or expect miracles," Eumaios said. "What has happened to their judgment?"

Kti waved her arms about. "When I studied at Gaia's Parnassus and when I first came here, I found whole, even-healthy, people who took charge of their lives. This time, I find it hard for people find their own answers to their problems."

Eumaios nodded. "They expect us to give the answers. They practice behavior foreign to our experience. We feel incapable of helping."

"Simple human needs or disagreements, we can handle. We can arbitrate the conflicts," Kti said, "but I have not found a way to help a person who says, 'Give me the answer. I am not to blame for my hurts.' I listen, then I question, but I never say, 'the only way to work out this is that.'"

Eumaios threw up his hands, "We wonder if we help anyone."

Gaetha arched one eyebrow. "You witness the changed world. These people have been displaced, exiled, buffeted about by circumstance. They have endured hunger, many deaths among their kin, and separation from loved ones. Your work, because it reflects your experience, much like theirs, excels ours. You have good instincts and an ability to adapt. We have observed you enough to know we already profit from what you do. Please continue. We need you."

Kti glanced at Eumaios as they titled their heads toward each other.

Gaetha paused, then spoke again. "Now we speak of another task. Please join us in conclave tomorrow to discuss whether or not to record our rites. We continue in the spirit of the gatherings at the Artemision. Some still oppose the transcribing. Others believe the time to keep rituals secret and oral has passed."

"But scripting is too important to abandon it," said Kti.

"Scripting keeps our words alive because it addresses the waning arts of remembering and transmitting orally," Eumaios said. "Keeping records gains importance, even urgency. Our men who follow the warriors' Way keep all kinds of records—contracts, treaties, histories, laws, codes, and inventories—to give order."

"Some rulers perpetuate the fabrications of their tellers," Gaetha said. "They carve their story on rock pillars or tablets to belittle or ignore the heritage of all people, especially those of us who keep the Way of the Mother. They make rules that bind us without letting us question the mandate. Those in charge voice their version of the story with boasts not truths.

"I have been very careful when I script to give a full account," said Kti.

"We know you write tales and legends to preserve and expand the words of the tellers to integrate a broader view of what has happened. Your experience will help us make wise decisions about our rituals." Gaetha held up her right hand. "I agree that being bound by the written word might limit the ability of the people to keep the rituals alive in their inner being during daily practice. The frozen written word takes vitality from the rituals. You may remember, Kti, that some shrines, when we discussed scripting many years ago at the Artemision, already insisted their words were the only true words."

"Yes, I do remember that," Kti said.

"Whether we script or not, some script the rituals and others more likely will. Some versions will endure, but if we do not record at all, we will lose our rituals. With these views in mind, we must discuss what scripting will bring to our Great Mother. We shall welcome your advice."

The conclave resulted in an agreement that Kti and Eumaios, both accomplished tellers and scribes, would, as a first step, integrate more directly into their work the words of the rituals, especially those in the rites of adolescence, of adulthood, of marriage, and of burial. They would consult the shrine women as they recorded but would have freedom to write as they saw fit. In the days that followed, Kti and Eumaos spent their time helping the people, scripting, and working with Neaira and Theo with the family trade.

One day, Eumaios said, "My dear, you tire easily lately. Are you all right?"

"Yes, I am tired, but content. My body feels the draining energy of our many tasks. More to the point, I am with child. I think this child will be your first."

Kti frowned, as she delivered her last words, for she did not know if Eumaios had lain with another. They had never discussed his past. "But, Eumaios, you have a right to your past... also a right to keep it private. Please disregard my observation. I act like a jealous girl who wants to be assured of her first place in the heart of her mate. Lately, I have been listening to too many young girls."

Eumaios took Kti's hand. "Kti, we married, soul to soul, when we were young. I never thought of another as my mate. You rightly formed liaisons with two others before me, but you have always been my only love."

Nothing more needed to be discussed.

After the birthing that followed in due course, Eumaios stretched his arms to hold his son above his head. "We have certainly broken precedent in giving you a name, dear son. Welcome to the world, Ktimaios. With the blend of your mother's name with mine, you begin a new form of naming."

Then he turned to Kti. "What a family we have. All of your children, dear to me, I consider mine and welcome ours to add to our brood. You, my dear, look fit. How are you, really?"

"Take away that look of concern. I am healthy. I have peaceful calm around me. Walking each day to the shrine and back has kept me strong. When I came to this hillside, little did I realize I would travel so much to the valley. I am glad Neaira lives in the home Aunt and Uncle left. It serves as a good place to rest. With Kleia staying in the North so far away, my sons with Conn already in the stars, and my two boys, Laertes and Arkos, still lost, only Neaira and her family, and now this little one, can bring us comfort."

As she spoke, she glanced in many directions as if in search of her sons, both so long away.

"Yes, Kti, they will find their way back," Eumaios spoke as if he sensed Kti's thoughts. "Not being able to account for our loved ones leaves a hole in our hearts. When I returned to Ortygia to find my parents, they often expressed how they kept hoping for my return. Many years passed before they welcomed me, confirmed my birthright, and blessed my return to you."

Kti leaned toward him as Eumaios shook his head. "Can you imagine the agony I felt, how much I blamed myself for not seeing you safely on your way to Samos? How much I feared you lost to us forever?"

She took his hand in hers and stroked the back of it.

"My heart leaped when young Laertes came back to tell us of your route," Eumaios said. "We searched, but think how many years passed before Conn's ship came to port on Ithaka Island. When the captain gave me your stone as he told us of your tragic loss of your new family, I knew I must come to you. Conn was a good man. Otherwise you would not have chosen him. I almost wish I could have known him."

Kti collapsed into Eumaios arms.

As Eumaios mused on his memories, he held Kti close. "Someday we will hear of Arkos and Laertes."

"Yes, I know that good news will come. But now, let us relish the life of this young one as we launch him well into this realm." She tilted her head back to gaze up at him. I anticipate a joyful time with my husband and our newborn son."

Neaira came to the bedside. "Mother, you must rest now. Father, please give me instructions for the days I am here to see after you. Mother, enjoy freedom from your shrine and household cares."

Neaira and Eumaios, with Ktimaios in his arms, left the room, to give the new mother a time for peaceful sleep.

For a time, Kti's eyes remained wide open. "I see them, Mother Gaia. You will in your time bring them back to me."

Then closing her eyes, she drifted off to sleep.

The West beckons.

CHAPTER THIRTY-ONE

In the months that followed, Kti and Eumaios helped at the shrine. Still, they found moments for themselves. They enjoyed young Ktimaios. "His eyes are like yours, dear Eumaios. He will see deeply into the Way of the Mother as you do."

"And his hands are yours, dear Kti. His work will interweave many lives as yours does."

Their neighbors' praises brought them extra joy. "He is such a happy child, so loving, so peaceful. How did you make him like this?" to which they would say, "Ktimaios came to us that way. We thank Mother Gaia every day for him."

Desire to see his first steps and hear his first words motivated them to rush to their mountain retreat after their shrine work. Often, Neaira brought her growing family to visit. She played her own tunes on the lyre as Kti told stories or did her weaving. Eumaios sometimes listened from a distance while he scripted. Contentment reigned in their home as well as in the village. Kti and Eumaios, known by the villagers as the wise couple, thanked Gaia for their halcyon days.

Kti and Eumaios sat in their garden playing with Ktimaios on his third birthday when a man of familiar stride approached.

With the early spring winds, Ody had brought his swiftest ship into port, paused to alert the others, then rushed to their mountain home. "News of oncoming hordes requires that everyone on this island seek safer waters."

Kti stared at her brother with widened eyes. "How can this be? The waters have been peaceful for some time."

"I will explain on the way to port or after we are on board ship. Your sailors await your orders to sail."

"I will go at once to port while you close the household, Kti," Eumaios said.

"The fleets of Neaira and her husband will sail with us as far as a western port on Krete Island where their children manage part of the family trade. The shrine women have sailed to the Artemision. Kti, your citadel Pronni beckons you."

In the hidden cave room, Kti stowed the tablets of the shrine history and the ritual of adolescence she had scribed when her shrine work allowed. Those and other household treasures filled the workroom. The great side arms of the mountain home closed against the mountain to hide their home."

The home secured, Ody hurried Kti to port to join Eumaios. "Dear sister, the ships await. The winds favor us. Pen convinced me you would be safer with us in Arkadia than at your Pronni citadel on Kephallenia. Promise me, if you sense danger there, you will come back to us or join Telemakhos and Polykaste on Parnassus. Your household, with their gear, awaits you on board. Other villagers will go to their relatives spread to all corners of our great sea. The rest will sail to Krete." He rested his fists on his hips. "No more talk, let us sail."

Ody may be a bit gray-bearded and weathered, but he cuts a commanding figure.

"Most who stir our waters once again, no doubt, leave the western isles in shambles. They have already moved to us in Arkadia. They forced old Nestor from his lands and port at Pylos. All his family, with those not massacred, live close to us." Ody spoke as they moved with speed.

Breathless to keep up, Kti said, "What of your safety at Pen's citadel?"

"So far we remain safe." Ody kept his pace. "Pen rules well as she tends the lands—a regular farmer. I help her, but mostly I explore our ancestral lands of great Kyllene just next to her holdings. At last, I find peace after my weary travels. No one speaks of the seas. Few recognize the parts of a ship when I reminisce. I have found my haven, the place the shade of Teiresias spoke of in my dream of the underworld, where I was to plant my oar."

As they settled on deck, Ody spoke more of unsettled times. "Nestor and his household were lucky to escape the invaders, but they abandoned their goods, stock, stores, and records. The same tribe threatens Sparta, the territory of Menelaos and Helen. Among the marauders come ancestors of our own tribe, those prolific followers of Herakles."

Kti looked up from tending Ktimaios. "If I remember correctly, long, long ago, Herakles and his followers migrated to the north and east to make a better life."

Ody looked to the sea. "When his canny cousin Eurystheus displaced him as leader of the people and foisted upon Herakles legendary labors and feats, many times exaggerated by the tellers, Herakles took his people away. Now, many generations later, Herakles' ancestors believe they have first rights to our lands."

Kti watched Eumaios, who had finished organizing their

fleet, jump on board from a fast-moving small boat.

Seating himself beside Kti, Eumaios took Ktimaios, who greeted him with outstretched arms. "Thank goodness we are organized and under way."

"Eumaios, Ody tells me that among the marauders are ancestors of Herakles reclaiming lands once theirs before they migrated."

Ody turned to face Eumaios. "They spread fear throughout the Peloponnese. Few penetrate our remote lands locked away from seaports. Still the returning tribe brings others from famine or quakes to claim land. I try to calm them, our family roots closely linking them to us. We seek peace, but we live guarded lives."

Kti listened to Ody as she settled young Ktimaios into a sheltered sleeping place. "I am sorry about Nestor's plight. I pray you stay safe."

A swift journey brought them around the outstretched fingers of the southern Pelops' land. They headed north, making good time to the port where Ody kept his ships. There, Ody headed inland, leaving Kti and Eumaios to take charge of the lead vessel of their fleet as they sailed toward Kephallenia.

"We must dock at Sami north of my land," Kti said. "Erato will give us safe haven while we check the Pronni citadel."

Eumaios nodded. "Though close to home, we must remain cautious. Let us not risk any of our lives."

Some days later, Kti and Eumaios approached the Pronni citadel.

"Extensive repair will make the citadel livable," Kti said. Stopping, she signaled caution. "Someone camps here. I see evidence everywhere."

"Yes, the fire still burns, and the smell of food fills the air," whispered Eumaios as they slipped behind a standing wall. "Quiet, someone approaches."

Kti held her breath.

Rejoice. A lost one returns.

CHAPTER THIRTY-TWO

A man strode toward the fire. He carried two rabbits looped into a rope and shouldered a doe. His hunting gear hung from his shoulder.

Kti gave Eumaios a questioning look, then motioned him forward.

"Do you speak our language?" Eumaios held out his hands to reveal no weapons.

"Yes, I do. I visit here while we trade in these waters. I have hoped to hear someone utter words in my native tongue."

"Are you from here, then? Why did you leave?"

"Taken from here, only a boy, on board a ship with my mother and sister, I jumped overboard to swim for help. I wandered the world, found my older sister with her family on Samos Island to the east, then began searches from there that led to nothing. Distraught, I took my trading ship to eastern ports only to be shipwrecked. Once again I sail and seek my mother and sister."

Kti contained herself no longer. She rushed from her hideaway, threw her arms around the young man, and sobbed with joy. "Truly, my own child, my Laertes, you have returned."

Stories unfolded from both mother and son. For a time,

Laertes could not accept his mother's marriage to Conn and his sister Kleia's to Conn's son. His heart, for many years frozen in hatred toward their abductor, slowly thawed. "After the turns of my life, I forgive the man who took us. After all, he won my mother's heart."

Kti recounted stories of their journey beyond the pillar, of their sojourn in the green isles and of the thriving kingdom, the domain of Kleia, now called Maeve. He gladly accepted Eumaios, whom he had not at first recognized, as his new father, royal in his own right, heir to his family's kingdom.

Together they walked to the south port.

"The Mother blesses us that we found each other on this day, for we sail home tomorrow," said Laertes. "As we talk, our entourage strikes the tents spread at the southwestern port from which we sailed with our captors many years ago."

Kti and Eumaios kept stride with Laertes, who gave a nervous peek at his mother. "I shall describe the beginnings of my journey after I jumped overboard, but not before you tell me, dear Mother, of my brother Arkos, lost to us when he searched for Father. We learned Father's fate, alas, when Uncle Odysseus brought Father's ashen bones back to us. I visited the family burial tomb in the valley but found it covered. May I hear now that Arkos has returned safely?"

Kti, basking in the joy of Laertes' homecoming, blinked as she looked down. "Long lost to us, I hesitate to call his name for fear he may feel the words and long for us from his assigned star place. Still, my heart tells me he lives... he will return to us. We cannot discuss what we do not know, can we? Let us turn instead to your life. First, tell me of your stay on the island to which you swam."

With a glance at her tear-filled eyes, Laertes grinned as he lingered no longer over Arkos' absence. "My experiences on the island reminded me that the Great Mother lives in people everywhere. Except for the rituals you both taught me, ones I learned among the people who rescued me prepared me well for life."

"It surprises me that you found the island inhabited," Kti said. "Conn told us no one lived on the island. I had a hard time forgiving him for leaving you, but before the weather blocked him, which meant he needed to sail past the great barrier to reach his family encampment. He reassured me you had chosen your destiny."

"He spoke correctly. No one occupied the island. Let me explain. I struggled in the waters, but I reminded myself of my task so I could keep swimming. My body felt sharp rocks. I had reached the shore."

"It must have been dark by then."

"Sparse moonlight shone from the just waxing orb, enough to light my way to shadowy, massive stones standing like beacons along the shore. I slept behind a stone shelter. With morning's light, I stirred, hungry and thirsty. I scanned the horizon but saw no vessel."

"How did you cope with the stark landscape, the searing sun?"

"I suffered from sun sickness, sought the shade of the stones formed much like a shrine altar, and collapsed once again. When I awakened, the sun stood high overhead. I dared not move because I sensed another presence. I feigned sleep, but through drooping lids saw feet standing beside me. With one quick movement, I tackled the figure. To my surprise the tackled figure laughed, stood upright, and leaned against a nearby giant stone. The stranger, a young girl about my age, showed no fear. We stared at each other. She hurled me a skin water pouch. I drank. I wondered if we could communicate."

"Did she say anything?"

"She said, 'I can speak your language, Hellene'."

I was amazed. "How can you know my origin or my language?" I said.

"Did she explain?"

"She described my dress, my sandals, my ring. She told me, 'I have seen many of you in our port to the east. My mother befriended one, married him. Together they birthed me. What brings you to our stone shrines?' Thus, began my sojourn with Cesme and her people, for she led me to her mother, who with her sacred companions once every ten years, tended their Great Mother's seven deserted shrines and even older sacred caves."

"Where did they come from?"

"Most of them settled in lands near a thriving harbor citadel farther east on a much larger island. Cesme, on her first journey to the outpost islands, like her mother before her, trained to make the next ten-year journey. She was learning the ways of cleansing from her mother."

"Where did you go?"

"We traveled from shrine to shrine, purifying each in turn. They kept the sites pure in hopes of re-inhabiting the land so they could worship at them once again. Cesme, her mother, her mother's mother, and many more generations before them had tended the stones. Their ancestors abandoned the island when warring tribes came. Those wars, famine, or earthshaking moved her people in many directions, although heretofore on the islands they farmed, thrived, and lived in peace."

"Those warriors must have done a great deal of damage."

"Cesme's tribe believed the invading people had desecrated the altars with animal sacrifices, perhaps with sacrifices of humans. She told me, 'When the occupiers finally abandoned the islands, our journeys to purify the altars began'."

"How far did you have to travel?"

"Their work complete, we boarded vessels for a rough journey. After five days, we reached their home. From their larger port, I could sail to Samos Island. You would have found the life among these people compatible with your own. From the rituals I witnessed, I learned that their ways involved loving attention to ancestors. As we do, they used well-trained leaders to advise the people, help them resolve conflicts, and live responsible lives."

"What did you discover of the Great Mother as you traveled with them?"

"In their temples, they counseled from behind doubled walls of stone through constructed holes. They had multiple ritual centers at most sites. In one they experienced and celebrated the beginnings of life. In another, they gained wisdom through rituals and counseling of their teachers. When they needed spiritual sustenance, they dreamed and healed there. The third formation transformed them to realms beyond our human existence."

"Their ways, so similar to ours, encourage me, for Gaia exists everywhere we travel in forms we recognize."

"Cesme reminded me often of the limitation of language when I tried to put their Way into words, but I agree we have much in common."

"It would be exciting to visit Cesme someday,"

"Oh, Mother, that you will, I believe. They live in Ortygia now." Laertes glanced toward Eumaios.

"Laertes, you were in my native land," said Eumaios. "I hardly believe it."

"Yes, your native port was my departure point when I left Cesme and her people. Neaira confirmed that when I reached her port on Samos Island. Had I known, while I was there, I would have sought for your parents."

Holding Eumaios' hand, Kti followed Laertes gaze.

"Now we approach our encampment," Laertes said. "My life changed when I met Seleme, my dear wife who comes to greet us."

They turned to see a lovely woman along with two lively children coming toward them.

Kti clasped Laertes hand. "Do I have a whole family to meet? How exciting."

She pointed to the ships beyond the approaching family. "I marveled the first time I watched the unloading of ships like yours. Goods floated ashore on rafts, atop buoyant bladders of mammoth sea leviathans the likes of which I had never seen."

A woman of beauty appeared before them. With raised eyebrows, she peered at Laertes.

"Mother and Father, my spouse Seleme," Laertes said with pride. Then to his wife he added, "Seleme, you are in the presence of my mother, Ktimene."

The two women embraced without words.

"And here, greet my new father, Eumaios, an old friend, my first teacher who in my youth showed me the Way of the Mother."

Eumaios enfolded Seleme in his arms. In turn, the children,

Jamil and Mahti, cuddled with their grandparents.

The enlarged family sat to await a forthcoming meal. Servants brought olives, delicate wines, and tender squid, octopus, and fish from the waters nearby, all prepared with the spices of the orient. Then meat that Laertes had snared was served. Last, came figs with goat cheese accompanied by more wine.

Kti shifted her gaze from Laertes to Seleme, and then back to Laertes. "You must tell us the story of how you met."

PART SIX

LAERTES

ANCIENT CANAAN
(ASHKELON)

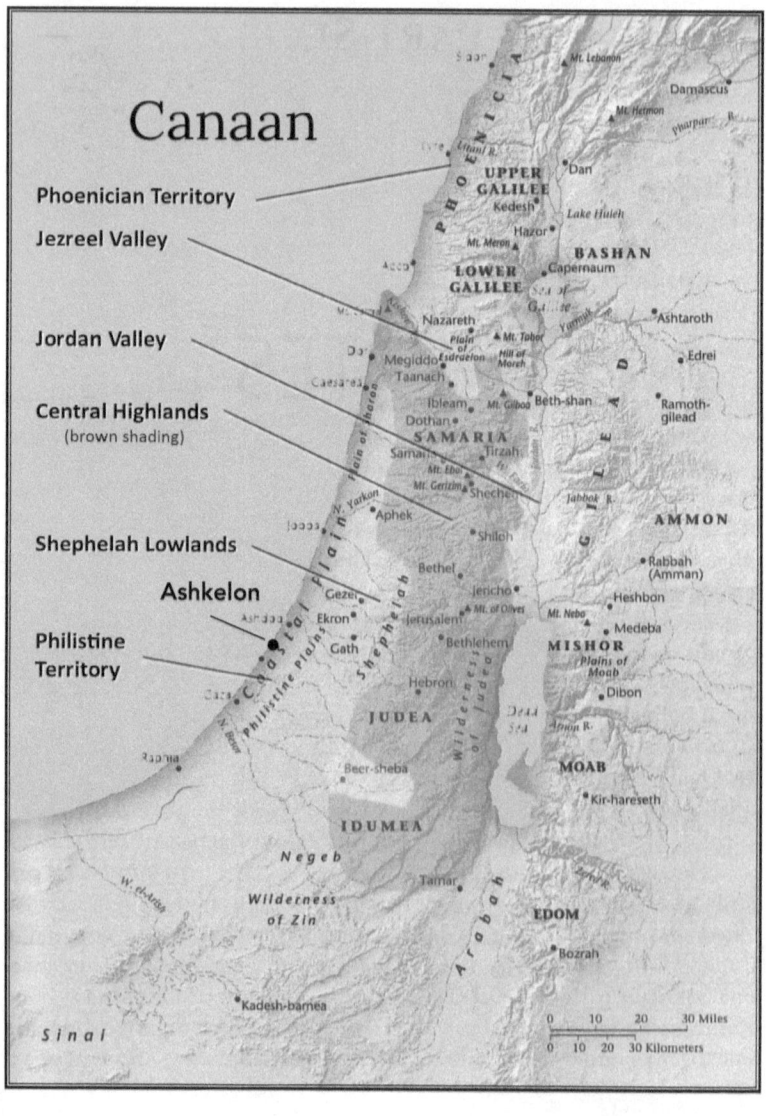

Canaan

Phoenician Territory

Jezreel Valley

Jordan Valley

Central Highlands
(brown shading)

Shephelah Lowlands

Ashkelon

Philistine
Territory

Many stars form our family.

CHAPTER THIRTY-THREE

At the rail of a trader headed to the Near East, Laertes peered at his first mate. "Six journeys in the waters of the Great Sea found no traces of my mother and sister who, along with me, were captives of Keltic traders. I still search, but for my livelihood I work in the family trade."

Before the mate answered, a massive scraping sound came from below.

"We are grounded!" Laertes shouted running to the fore of the ship. "All hands, on deck."

"More bad luck!" Laertes muttered under his breath. To the mate he said, "Stuck, with no land in sight."

Hand over his eyes, the mate scanned the horizon. "But look, a ship, a ship, we are saved."

All on deck shouted and waved. The ship changed course and four men boarded. Laertes met the captain, a swarthy, scar-faced fellow, who showed steady sea legs.

"We exchange our cargo for your pulling us off this rock," Laertes said, "or if our ship is not seaworthy, a journey to the nearest port for help."

"Not in a bargaining position," the captain smirked. "I claim your cargo and all of you as my prisoners. You will be rowing me to the next port in chains if you do not come voluntarily."

Strong arms wrapped around Laertes' shoulders. His crew struggled but were overpowered and roped together for the transfer. Loosened rope in between, each carried cargo.

Laertes whispered to the nearest crew, "Pass on a message. Cooperate now. Loosen ropes as you can, but do not give away your ability to run. Escape at the next port."

The rescuers-turned-captors secured their ropes to the rowing benches. Hard work brought them to an unfamiliar port south of their destination of Ugarit. Eye contact signaled readiness. Over they went.

Laertes shouted, "Run in all directions. Make your way home."

Alone among strangers, Laertes darted through the streets. He stopped in the shadows of an alleyway to catch his breath. "Great Gaia, guide me."

His head downward, Laertes blinked. "What sparkles? A dazzling stone that must have an owner to seek out."

Before Laertes bent down, a young girl ran toward him, an older woman behind her, breathless. "I search for a family gem my parents gave me. I missed it when I returned from my walk. My chaperone and I took shelter here. Have you seen it?"

Laertes bent forward, swept up the stone, and placed it in her delicate hand.

Eyes wide, she stared. "You must come with us. My parents will thank you for your honesty. Another might have ground the stone under foot."

Laertes's lips twitched. *I am blessed with a hiding place. No one will suspect as a runaway a young man accompanying two women.*

"My name is Laertes, and I am a ship's captain from Samos Island who trades in these waters, but my ship was grounded off course. I do not know this port."

"Sir, I am Seleme, and this is my companion, Markela. You have reached Ashkelon, the southern-most port of Canaanite land, the home of my people, the Danites. We stay at our town home where my father can tell you more."

★ ★ ★

LAERTES SAT ON AN ELABORATE gilded bench with lions carved on each arm, the front paws forming the hand rests. He studied the intricate carvings and mosaics on the ceiling. His shoulders jerked when a man said, "They are beautiful, are they not?"

Laertes stood and shook the extended hand. "I am Laertes, son of Eurylohkos and Ktimene. My trading ship, grounded near here, sails from Samos Island. If you are a trader, you may have brought goods to our port."

Laertes' host nodded. "I am Jacob. I bring goods from my lands to this port, but I cannot claim that I trade along the seaways. We farm." He pursed his lips. "I understand from our daughter, Seleme, that you rescued her from a scolding. Losing the gem upset her, but recovering it relieved her. You have our deep gratitude."

Laertes glanced down at his hands and clothing. "Please forgive my appearance. When we were grounded, a scalawag and his men boarded us. They took us as galley slaves after they confiscated our goods. We rowed two days, wondering if we could escape at the next port."

He tapped his temple with his forefinger. "Not the smartest of captors he was, so we ran from them in all directions when we landed. I found refuge where your daughter looked for her jewel."

"We do not condone pirating. Please know we are grateful that you are an honest man. The jewel belongs to Seleme's ancestor. Following the decease of my wife who now leads our tribe, Seleme will take her place among our people. An important, irreplaceable piece, this gem symbolizes her succession."

Laertes gave a slight bow. "It pleases me that I could return it."

"My dear wife, Andrite, who leads us and sees after our spiritual life, will want to give you thanks, also."

"First I must seek lodging, then a market for purchasing clothing, I am not presentable for such a meeting."

"My dear young man, you will bathe here and find garments laid out that will suit you well. Then I shall bring my wife to meet you and have one of our household lead you to lodging for ships' captains."

Laertes met Andrite of whom he saw features that molded her daughter.

"You have blessed this household with one of its sacred treasures," Andrite said. "Our artisans will embed the gem in a secure mounting, you may be assured. We give you this small token of our appreciation, a traditional mosaic. Now Bildad will lead you to suitable lodging."

"Thank you, dear lady," Laertes said. "Such kindness as you both have bestowed surpasses the hospitality that I am able to give in return. Should we meet when I am more favored, I shall reciprocate. Give my regards to your daughter, the very image of you."

A new day comes for your forming star child.

CHAPTER THIRTY-FOUR

At morning's light, Laertes received an invitation to dine with his benefactors that evening. He entered a world of ease and splendor. At first, he mistook the opulence as frivolous but witnessed the household industry produce an abundance that was never wasted or indulged.

During dinner conversation, Laertes shared his experiences as a trader beyond their region and as a member of a family who kept the Way of the Mother alive in a changing world. When he told of his escaping Keltic captors to find help for his mother and sister and of his frustration in not finding them, the family all murmured in anxious tones.

Andrite stared at Laertes. "What happened to your family runs parallel to the kidnapping of two children of our ancestors when they settled for a time across the Great Sea in an isolated valley of Arkadia."

Laertes raised his hand. "How interesting, my grandmother's family has ancestral roots on Mt. Kyllene in Arkadia. Please do go on; I am sorry to interrupt."

"The two children were not far away, the boy hunting small game and the girl, as usual, following him. The family called to them but received no answer. They searched and searched but never found them. They learned from native people that slave-trading renegades had taken children from their villages. They believed the children had been swept into the captors' ship. A chase proved fruitless. After many searches, our heartbroken ancestors returned to this land but sent out many search parties thereafter. Even these many generations later, we hope for closure."

Seleme turned to Laertes. "When my ancestors came back to our lands, they continued to follow the Way of the Mother even though hill people, the grandsons of Abraham who had moved into our fertile valley from their scrubby lands, insisted we follow their One God. Some of our tribe blended with them, but my family resisted their Way."

"Our strength and, alas, our weakness," Jacob said "was that our matriarch had married Abraham's youngest grandson, Benjamin. Their relationship prompted Benjamin to open his heart to all ways, but he also wanted peace with his brothers, so he welcomed them into the valley. For a time, the family hoped to blend the Mother's Way into the tradition of the One God by emphasizing that he had a loving mate, Shekenah. But the more radical hill people would not accept a mate equal to their God."

Bowing his head, Laertes said, "Your family, too, has suffered a great loss and trials with your way, just as we have."

With a wry smile, Jacob shook his head. "The disappearance of the children makes me all the sadder that you cannot find your lost ones, Laertes. We pledge to help."

As the evening wore on, Laertes could not overcome his sadness. After thanking them for their hospitality.he took his leave of the family. "Tomorrow, I shall find a way to rescue my ship, connect with a caravan to negotiate for goods, and find my way home to continue the search."

★ ★ ★

TO SET HIS PLAN INTO MOTION, Laertes stepped from his lodging the next morning into the sunshine. He met the eyes of Jacob.

"What a surprise to see you this morning."

"Young man, my family has a proposal for you," Jacob said. "Soon we return to the countryside. We need assistance with our trading efforts. Our children need to learn more of the languages of the larger world. Consider joining our household as trade advisor, a tutor of languages. In exchange, I shall help you salvage and repair your ship, connect you in trade negotiations with our caravan masters, add some new vessels to your ship to form a fleet, and become a financial supporter of joint efforts. What say you?

"Such a generous offer," Laertes chuckled, "I must accept. The opportunity to stay might give me the best base for forwarding my own trading interests while finding news of my mother and sister."

Besides, I am quite taken with lovely Seleme and wonder if we might have a future together. I shall venture into her world to see what might be possible.

Laertes found Seleme and her sibling to be quick students. "You know more languages than most of the seaworthy men who ply these waters."

"And you know our language better than when you came," Seleme said with a sly grin.

Laertes studied her closely. "What are your dreams, Seleme?

Have you selected your path?"

"The first question is easy. Just as my ancestor did, I would see the world. Sailing away for distant shores, pitching my tent wherever the winds take me, that is my dream."

"Is your wanderlust ever to be? Does it match your path?"

"Ah, my path. That is harder to see. Someday I am destined to lead my people. Will it be here, I wonder?"

"Mm, somehow I see your having both your dream and your path," Laertes said. Smiling, he stood. "Now I must find your father to discuss our trading ventures."

I know she feels about me as I do her.

Laertes relished his position in the family. He assisted when Antrite's mother dwindled in health and the family blessed Antrite as leader. But the death and succession caused tension among the valley tribes. Some wanted Seleme to marry into a neighboring branch of the family. That match, they reasoned, consolidated the power with the fortune of the families.

Believing his presence kept Seleme from bending to such plans, Laertes decided to leave. *I do not want to go, but I cannot stay to cause strife in such a beneficent family. I love Seleme, but I cannot stop plans if they are best for the family.*

That evening Laertes approached Seleme's parents. "I plan to leave soon. Your children are accomplished in their language studies and can practice with each other. Your part of the trade thrives. Now I must grow it. Also, I need to see my family."

Antrite patted the chair next to hers. "What else is on your mind, Laertes?"

"You know me too well. My being here impedes your resolving tribal tensions." Laertes dipped his head. "I love Seleme,... I believe she loves me."

Jacob clapped his hands together. "Then it shall be done. We approve. If she will have you, you must marry. You two match each other in every way."

"We are little disturbed by the pressures of others. None among them is so worthy of Seleme as you are." Andrite stood. "We have long seen the logic of such a union."

Laertes gasped, eyes wide, while Antrite fetched Seleme. Before he knew it, Laertes gained what he had long dreamed of: Seleme's assent.

Later that night, Laertes pounded his pillow. "But how can I, who can not find my own mother or sister, presume to take on the responsibilities of such a marriage? Someday Seleme will be the leader of her people. Union with another branch of the tribe, well established in the region, will bring peace far more than our marriage."

★   ★   ★

SHORTLY PAST MIDNIGHT, LAERTES threw together his belongings, mounted a fast horse, and galloped away. *A cowardly act, I know, but still the path I choose.*

For days, in the darkness of a room deep in the heart of Ashkelon, Laertes both wept and slept. Urgent knocks came to his door, but he ignored them. Then a key turned in the lock. Weakened by hunger and fever, he could not raise his hand.

I should have blocked the door.

He discovered later that Seleme and her chaperone each day they came to order his room, let light in, but most of all to give him water or what food he would take. Seleme massaged his body with pungent oils. For days, she repeated her ritual. She spoke to him of his energy returning. Many times, she told him of her love.

Still he did not stir nor speak.

She fed him herbal potions and health-giving foods and slipped sharp, slender needles into the key places of his body to release pressure, a process she had learned from Eastern women who came with caravans. She took his hand to lead him around the room.

One day, Laertes felt weightless and opened his eyes. The room filled with a bright light even though his mind told him near darkness shrouded it. *What is happening? I am hovering over my body. I see order restored to my quarters. I see my immobile body beginning to move. I see Seleme beaming love into my very soul. I am falling, melting into my body.*

"Seleme, you have brought me back to life. You free me from my darkness. I live for our happiness."

"Ah my love, you have come back to me. We shall finish your recovery at the nearby seaside."

Strolling along the beach one day, Laertes fit Seleme's delicate hand into his much larger one. "We have entered into a sacred space that binds us eternally. I shall never leave you."

Several days later, Laertes opened his eyes wide when Seleme stepped from her marriage litter. He sighed at her delicate beauty, took her to the marriage altar, and began the life of his dreams.

★ ★ ★

KTI MARVELED AT THEIR LOVE STORY. "The story will live forever in our chronicles."

The next morning Kti awoke to find the family in traveling gear. She held tight to Eumaios as the young family boarded their ship.

They offered parting words. "We shall return to trade at the next greening season."

"Did this really happen?" Kti said, her satisfied smile greeting the sunlight of early day. "Let us spend the year preparing for a grand reunion by calling Neaira home. Maybe Kleia will come, too."

PART SEVEN

KTIMENE AND
EUMAIOS

THE ISLAND OF SAMOS

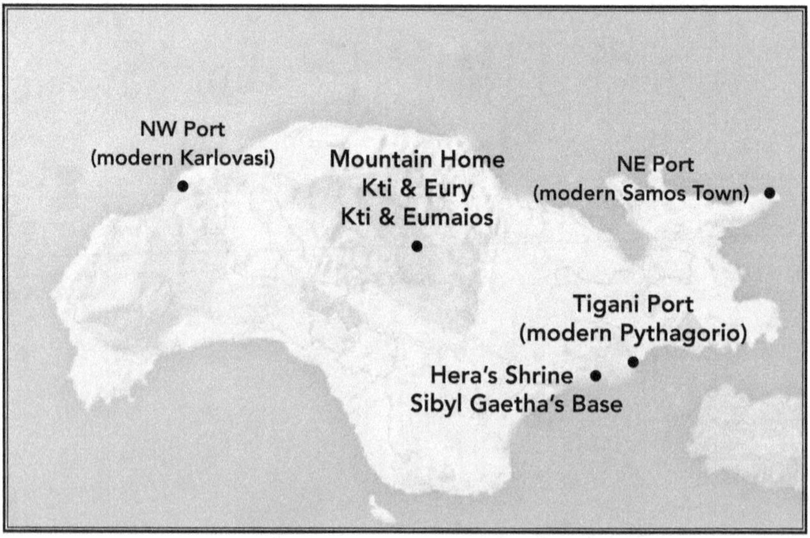

NW Port
(modern Karlovasi)
●

Mountain Home
Kti & Eury
Kti & Eumaios
●

NE Port
(modern Samos Town) ●

Tigani Port
(modern Pythagorio)
●

Hera's Shrine ●
Sibyl Gaetha's Base

A completed pattern, star stuff dances.

Chapter Thirty-Five

As the earth awakened the next year, Kti and Eumaios walked the grounds of the Pronni citadel as they inspected their restored home. Kti gazed at the ceiling of the Great Hall. "I did not think we would see the walls or inner timbers raised to their former magnificence. The hill people, our household, and many builders from across our trading territory have outdone themselves."

Eumaios held Kti close as they stood at the rebuilt fire pit. "We have made headway with the orchards as well as our vineyards. Soon they will be at peak production."

"Laertes and Seleme will return soon. I have word from a Samos ship captain that Neaira, Theo and their three young ones will accompany the Levantines. A stay on Kephallenia will give them respite from their trading trips."

Before the gathering, a ship docked showing both a protective eye and an eagle subduing a boar, the banners of Pen and Ody. Kti concluded that her brother's entourage had arrived for a visit before traveling to neighboring Ithaka. For some time, Kti had expected them to return from Arkadia. When Telemakhos became custodian of the Parnassian stronghold, he stayed on Parnassus more than on Ithaka. He had urged his parents to return.

"How welcome their visit is," Kti said. "Let us go to port to meet them."

A messenger stepped from the ship. "My lady, our vessel brings the ashen bones of your brother, famed Odysseus, King of Ithaka and Arkadia. On this ship comes Queen Penelope. Her son, Telemakhos, and his family follow from their Parnassian citadel."

"How can this be?" cried Kti.

"Dear sister," said Pen, "I must respond, for this messenger, too stricken with the sadness of our mission, falters. I barely can speak myself."

Already numbed at the news, but still aware of hospitality, Kti embraced Pen. "Come first, dearest Pen, to the citadel to refresh while you rest. Then we shall talk."

With the wise counsel of a sister, thoughtful even in the flush of fresh grief, the small entourage of Pen, a few attendants, and ancient Phemios the Teller proceeded to the citadel.

Pen, her deep gray eyes tear-filled, with dark circles, joined them on the terrace. "Long days have we traveled," she said, "first by land from our inland home, then by sea. Many times, before his death, Ody said to me, 'Take me home for burial if you find my remains. I may be lost on battlefields or in shipwreck that washes my body to a distant shore. If you can, though, honor my body, then take my bones home.' His most recent reminder came shortly after he brought you back from Samos Island. Intruding tribes had depleted lands to the south of us. First, Nestor's kingdom fell. Even now, invaders threaten Sparta. We might soon be threatened in landlocked Arkadia. Of that I shall speak more, but now I share plans for Ody's burial."

Kti embraced Pen, then led her to a cushioned chair. "Be

seated here, dear one, and tell us what you can." She held tight to Pen's hand and sat beside her.

"Ody," Pen said, "will rest in the rocky layers of the valley tomb below. His bones will be with your Eury, his beloved parents Laertes and Antikleia, and his ancestors. Ody will rest at last in a tomb to be built on Ithaka. First, I honor his wish to rest in this valley, but he belongs to Ithaka. I brought his brooch and cloak that saw him through many battles and trials before he came home to me so long after Truva fell. His release allows his star to form among the others, their pattern repeated here on earth."

Glancing at Eumaios, Kti shook her head. "We will arrange the burial rituals according to your wishes, Pen." Her wandering words gave her relief from the shock of her loss.

Between tears and calm, Pen recounted Ody's last sea journey to the western isles beyond the great pillar. "Your telling, dear Kti, of your sojourn with Conn gave Ody yearning for the shores of the green isles, the home of a mysterious people who live on the island of the winds and guide the flow of life. Soon after you left, he put forth a case to depart with a remnant of his loyal retinue. I assented, for he still needed to subdue the demons of his restless wits. The shock of the slaughter of his warriors haunted his night dreams. After Truva, he came home to me in body, but his spirit wandered. After long ordeals of his journey home, full of physical and mental and spiritual testing, he struggled to rejoin a world of peace."

Pen bit her lip. "How he suffered. I thought the sea journey would give him relief. He assembled his sailors of years' past, those elders who had not fought in Truva or those who came back another way. 'Why have I lived when I could not save them all?' he repeated. He needed to complete his return, to make peace with the sea, you see. I welcomed him back from the West when the springtime greening came to our mountain home."

"What a dangerous journey he undertook," Kti said. "Now he knows of the land I love,"

"You will be pleased that he saw Kleia, now Queen Maeve, along with her family. He met other leaders of the northern Great Mother whom Kleia honors. He witnessed, on a sacred hill, the induction of Kleia's husband, O'Conn, as primary leader among the many other leaders of the tribes assembled. He marveled at how the people at the high-hill assembly worked out their strife in peace."

"It warms my heart to learn he was there with them, even for a short time."

"That your child helped bring about this model of governing, he said, affirmed what your own name foretold of your progeny. Indeed, they had forged a civilization there that works. He visited magic places of the blessed isle to renew his soul. Kleia and O'Conn, he saw, had begot a line to carry their ways forward."

"Are they not blessed? Who could have imagined this outcome for these two?"

"Upon his return, with a calmer spirit, he explored the valleys of the great Argive rivers to the south to visit Nestor's sons. He went to Sparta to see Menelaos and Helen. Soon though, he announced he must travel the valley of the Styx River, then upward to the peaks of Nonakris whose icy crags feed our rivers with their springtime melting. He planned to scale the highest peak of Nonakris, the Great Kyllene. There he would find Sibyl

Amphito of Lusi, a woman of great wisdom. She would give him further guidance for his days among our people. His talk of forming his heavenly star disturbed me. I implored him to seek Amphito's aid in guiding his spirit to peace here with me."

"Ody always could see beyond what others could envision."

"Resolving to go to the mountain gave him some comfort. Before he made his trek, his spirits eased. We spent many happy days of that springtime and summer. After he helped gather the harvest, he took his leave. He assured me he would return safely before the winter snow. He begged me to go with him, but I knew he must make his journey alone."

"Ody was a careful man when it came to planning and strategy," Kti said.

"You are right. He returned before the snows came. He told me he wandered among the barren boulders. The stately trees, those great pines among the rocks, had sapped the sparse water. As he trekked, he saw specters of the past: battles, sea journeys, dreams or real happenings that followed him home to us. He found Sibyl Amphito. She told him, in his descent, he must discover those things that would give him lasting peace. But he could not summon words to tell me what he encountered."

"His spirit calmed. We enjoyed deep love again. We planned ways to install the practices of the people of the western isles. We strenghtened the Mother's Way among our people. The specters came back, at first, in his dreams. Then they visited his waking hours. At times, calm returned. One night he awakened me, his eyes glazed over as his breath came with labored gasps. He clutched his chest as though his great heart had burst. His lips twisted as he said, 'No more trouble, love. I leave now for my star. Keep my love with you. Take my bones home.' Then he breathed his last."

The two sat in communal silence, as tears trickled down their cheeks.

After a time, Pen spoke again. "I caressed him. I rocked his body. I called him many times, 'My own dear, dear love.' I repeated his name until I could not say anything. I closed his eyes, those probing wise eyes, prepared him for the great pyre, and called a great funeral feast with games he would have relished. By then, deep winter kept us bound to our home. Alone I mourned our young daughter, who, try as I might to nurse back to health, died in the cold of winter that came on swiftly. I buried her on the land she would have governed. When spring came, I set sail for Parnassus to be with Telemakhos, then came to bring Ody's ashen bones here. Our dear son's entourage follows close. They will be with us to complete the burial rituals."

Kti sighed before she spoke. "We shall welcome Telemakhos as we prepare the tomb."

Pen wrapped her arms around her body. "Then this great man, my dearest husband, will be freed. Telemakhos will go to Ithaka to erect Ody's earthly shrine. I predict my husband will have many shrines erected to him throughout the wine-dark sea."

"I want to tell you everything, my plan to return to Arkadia, live among my people, carry out the Way of the Great Mother to integrate into our Argive ways some of the Northern ways Ody admired. I must rule our people as Father, Mother, my only sister Iphthime, and our infant daughter have a place in the stars. Iphthime's daughter will carry on when she comes of age. Then I will work with the Argive shrine women of Hera or with

Amphito at Lusi. I shall be buried, when the time comes, in Arkadia beside our daughter. But you must come to me before that time, to visit."

Kti nodded. Pen fell silent for a long time, until the mellow light of the evening sun encompassed them as they rested in her silence.

As she stared toward the setting golden orb, Kti wondered, *Will it come to pass as she says?*

Your courage gives you peace.

CHAPTER THIRTY-SIX

"Now Ody must complete his star forming," Kti said. "In our ritual robes, we shall commemorate his bones and conduct his burial rites. Later, our time will come to remember Ody, our friend, our brother, our childhood companion."

Eumaios took her hand as they walked to the shrine room. "He filled our childhood and our mature lives with joy intermixed with pain."

After the rituals, Kti led Pen, their arms entwined, to the great hall for feasting and remembering. "Linger here as long as you wish. Visit Ody at the tomb alone or with us."

"Yes, Kti, I shall stay while Telemakhos constructs Ody's Ithakan tomb near the palace that we loved so much. I shall go there to view it, then return to Arkadia."

Each day at dawn, Kti stayed behind while Pen strolled into the valley. One morning, nestled in Eumaios' arms on their upper terrace, Kti watched Pen's descent. "How patiently she honors her dear husband, her strange husband whom she loved so deeply."

What Pen thought or felt, Kti could only guess, for she said little.

Often, in silence, Kti sat with Pen by the fire pit in the great hall. When they spoke, they recollected the years awaiting the return of their husbands. These times transported Kti to desolate memories of the long healing she endured after the deaths of both Eury and Conn. One day she dared to say, "I know the toll the death of Ody and that of your infant daughter takes upon you, Pen."

Pen's large gray eyes fill with tears. "Ah, yes, dear sister, you have experienced journeys into the valley of death. Though helping me with my journey may bring back sad memories, please know that being with someone who has traveled that journey gives me solace."

"You were there for me to help Great Gaia pull me through my time of grief," Kti said as she squeezed Pen's hand.

In private, Kti spoke to Eumaios of Ody. "I hold dear so many memories of our childhood. Those memories bring me joy, as does the journey to Truva to discover with Ody Helen's absence there."

"My thoughts land on the years I spent supporting the Ithakan household and keeping Ody in the rituals as we prayed for his safe return," Eumaios said, sounding wistful. "But of late, I have remembered assisting Ody in his triumph over the suitors who had gathered at their Ithakan citadel to gain Pen's marriage bed. That memory still gives me great pain as I try to justify the carnage of that day mixed with some solace of knowing that order came to the kingdom as a result."

Kti took Eumaios' hand. "I am grateful you were there to help. I am grateful, too, that the Council of Elders supported Ody as he brought order to his household, an effort that calmed the people who lost sons both in battle. He regained his place as a leader of the people."

Through the days of Pen's visit, Kti prepared for the return of Laertes and Neaira with their broods. One day, as she worked, Pen took up a napkin Kti had designed for the gathering.

Kti smiled. "Oh, Pen, please join me in the stitching. Your handiwork has always surpassed mine."

"You shall have my help," Pen said with a smile, "until I receive word the shrine for Ody on Ithaka is complete."

As Pen's visit wound down, Kti visited the tomb with Pen. "I am honored to accompany you."

"Today I must complete Ody's last wish, though I pause to share something with you. When he returned from Great Kyllene, he wanted to travel to Pronni immediately to see you, Kti. He told me Sibyl Amphito always spoke of you as Kallisto and often, when she mentioned your name, she went into a deep trance. She ordered Ody to send both of you to her. But he worried because the Sibyl would not reveal why you must come. I hope you will come to me in Arkadia, Kti, but I hesitate to advise you to go to Amphito. I fear we will lose you both to madness. Still, I knew I must tell you of the strange request. Ody would have wanted it."

Kti took Pen's hand. "I know Amphito's request gives you concern, Pen. You know we must come. Yes, one day we shall make the journey to you. If she lives, we shall visit Sibyl Amphito at Lusi. Now, though, while we tend our son, Ktimaios, we will enjoy our other children with their progeny. They give us great happiness, as Telemakhos and his thriving family give you joy. Perhaps Arkos will return to us someday."

As she spoke, Kti looked to the East, for she always knew Arkos would come from there.

The two women, deep in their own thoughts, walked arm in arm to the citadel. At the evening meal, Ariel entertained them with the telling of the early ancestry of their lines while Phemios, his old teacher, dozed at the hearth behind him. Phemios, as did they all, jerked, rousing when the dogs barked.

"Has some of the family come early?" Kti said.

In bounded a weathered man, with a sentry close behind, mouth agape, ready to announce him. His familiar manner and stance, shrouded in long years of absence, first stirred old Phemios, who moved toward him to greet him. "Old man, surely you no longer trade these waters. I had thought you long dead. What brings you here?"

Before the man could answer, Phemios bowed toward the family. "Please forgive my forwardness, queenly ones, but here stands Kentros the Trader, a ghost from the past. You may remember how often he came to trade in these waters. He told us the news during your childhood days when wise Queen Antikleia and good King Laertes ruled."

The family shifted in their seats as Phemios rambled.

"I well remember his first visit here. At this very hearth, we traded stories long since woven into my songs. Young Odysseus had just been born to relieve the gloom of the death of the eldest babe, Arkos, who left us so soon in the winter chill. Kentros' visit added great joy to the birthing of the man we just honored in burial. How good he should come at this time."

Before Kentros or the family could speak, Phemios, in an unusual burst of energy, spoke to the grizzled man. "When first you came, you had one ship, but the last time I saw you, I remember at least ten. You had docked your traders at Samos Island where I had come with Eumaios, now lord of this citadel, at the side of our own fair Queen Ktimene, to fetch our lady and her household to safety from marauders threatening their shores. You put in at port that day on your way to safer waters."

The trader raised his hand as if to speak.

But Phemios continued. "Just after the great victory at Truva, we saw you, when all the people of the seas stirred in chaos as they found their way home or settled new lands. Not many reach our age, friend Kentros. I have trained young Ariel here to help this family enjoy their evenings with rhythmic story. Now, I reside with Queen Penelope of Ithaka and Arkadia. This will be my last voyage. But I cease these rambling words of an old friend. Now, I simply say, welcome."

"I must acknowledge my old friend's words with care," Kentros said, "for what I tell you might one day enrich the telling lore."

Laughing, Phemios nodded.

"Yes, good friend, we have much to share," said Kentros.

Then he addressed them all, but deferred mostly to Kti. "Thank you, Queen Ktimene, image of your dear mother, for welcoming an old man to your warm hearth. I have news that will gladden the household. I just left the forward ship of a great trading fleet that docked at the Port of Ortygia, the homeport of your own father and mother, Eumaios. I learned the fleet will soon arrive here from the far west beyond the pillar. Your young Kleia, now called Maeve, together with her husband O'Conn, leads the fleet. They come, I am told, for a rare visit in these waters."

Kentros bent slightly at the waist. "But, dear family, I come foremost to pay tribute to the great man just placed in the valley tomb. News of the death of wise Odysseus has spread far.

Prepare for many to pay homage. His story will live on. He will be remembered as the greatest warrior of this era."

Then Kti raised her hand in greeting. "Welcome, good friend. You bring us happy news. I have hoped for Kleia's visit. Her timely arrival coincides with the visits of Kleia's siblings. Laertes, her twin, and Neaira, their older sister, who come soon with their families to enjoy one another and to welcome their youngest brother, our Ktimaios."

"Good Kentros, I thank you for your kind words," said Penelope. "Odysseus always respected you. I am honored that you have come."

"To these welcomes," said Eumaios, "I add my own. You speak of Ortygia, my home. Do you bring news of my parents?"

"Your parents have reached an ancient age. Although frail, they express happy thoughts that you will come soon to show them their grandson. They have long desired to meet your spouse."

"Ah," Eumaios said, "for a fortnight I have dreamed of their calling me home. We have discussed my dreams and will leave for Ortygia soon after the gathering of our children. You confirm we must."

With that, the family invited Kentros and Phemios to table while Ariel entranced them with ancestral lore.

Clasping her hands together, Kti grinned. "Let us not tell Neaira and Laertes of Kleia's coming."

Pen swirled in joy. "What fun it will be to see their faces, if only I could stay that long."

Eumaios joined hands with them. "If not, we shall describe the grand surprise when we see you next."

Phemios and Kentros danced to the accompaniment of

Ariel's instrument. Eumaios clapped in time with the music. Kti and Pen watched in amazement.

"What next?" Kti said, laughing so hard she gasped for breath.

Forming stars bring joyous songs.

CHAPTER THIRTY-SEVEN

Two days after Kentros sailed eastward, Kti and Eumaios, with Pen, greeted the family trading ships. Their hearts warmed with each arrival. First, Laertes and Seleme came down the plank of their lead ship. Follwing them came their two children—their miniatures, but taller than last year—Jamil and Mahti. Amidst embraces, their servants erected tents along the shoreline for their retinue.

Close behind docked sleek traders of the Samian fleet. From the first ship came stately Neaira. After her bounded Theo and their two strapping boys, another Laertes, after Neaira's grand-father, and Askanius, after a family ancestor. Both boys, at home on board a ship, helped secure the fleet. Neaira held the hand of an alert young maiden, who slipped from Neaira's grasp to run to Kti for an embrace.

Neaira spoke a formal greeting. "Dear Mother and Father, welcome this thriving child, your own namesake, Mother, a young Ktimene. She already rules our home."

Then she added, "How good it is for all of us to gather here. We greet you, dearest Aunt Pen, mourner of a great hero, our uncle. Kentros delivered the sad news to us at sea just a day ago so that the shock of it would settle. Thank you for sending him to us. After we purify ourselves, we shall go to the tomb to bid Uncle Ody farewell."

After the families offered tributes to Gaia for safe arrival, they organized the children for their evening's sleep. Then the adults gathered for a welcoming meal, good conversation, and the oncoming night breezes that cooled the terrace.

Ancient Phemios, to the hushed listeners, sang of early tribes settling Arkadia. He recounted how warring people ended the golden times of peace until a blending of the people erased the strife. At dawn they joined Pen at the tomb for a leave-taking ritual to bid her farewell.

Privately at the departure, Pen lamented to Kti that she would not see Kleia or her family. Her last words to Kti were, "Please come to me when you can."

Aunt Erato and her family visited from neighboring Sami. On the fourth day, Telemakhos and Polycaste came. He reported that Penelope found them on Ithaka, paid homage to Odysseus at his home shrine, then left them resolved to carry on in Arkadia as she and Ody had planned.

"Especially does she want a visit from both of you," Telemakhos said with emphasis.

A few days later, Kti strolled with Neaira into the nearby vineyard to sit among the shaded vines of an arbor. "How are the shrine teachers faring these days?" she said.

"They have restored the shrine grounds and thrive once again." Neaira said. She slumped her shoulders. "But Mother, they need you and Eumaios. They send urgent pleas that you return to counsel the people."

Kti lifted her hand. "Dear one, our dream is to return. First, though, Ktimaios must reach manhood so that he, not Eumaios, can be installed as ruler of Ortygia. Also, we must arrange for Kleia or her youngest daughter to take charge of this citadel."

"That will be a long wait, but I know they will welcome you. In the meantime, we will do our best to help."

Hands clasped, they took slow steps from the arbor to the terrace for the evening meal. Kti said, "Knowing we are needed will help the time pass."

Later that evening, Kti watched Seleme approach while Eumaios and Laertes visited and Erato talked with Theo and Neaira. Kti clasped Seleme's hand. "How well you blend into our family, Seleme."

"We have much in common, I believe," Seleme said. "Just as I recently saw to my mother's burial, you have received the ashen bones of a brother, then sent him on his journey to the stars."

"Great Gaia consoled me just as you, no doubt, gained solace from your Great Mother. Keeping our ancient great ones with us gives us strength."

"Laertes talks of the challenge, now many years in the making, of the Sky Gods to the Mother's Way. We admire how you have preserved the Way of the Mother. We have the same challenge to our Mother. What have you found helps most in these times of change?"

Deep in thought, Kti came to an answer after several moments. "I have forwarded the common beliefs of the two ways, those of the Great Mother and of the Sky Gods."

"Tell me how that has helped you with your brother's death."

"Although we have not found common discussion about the afterlife, we both adhere to the same way for burial in our family tomb, for remembering with honor our loved ones," Kti said. "If the warriors believe Ody has gone to his place in the Underworld's Elysian Fields to sit among other great heroes to discuss great deeds, so be it. For my part, I doubt this life continues with an eye to the past deeds."

"What is your path in the afterlife?"

"The great mystery of death's leading to ultimate transformative rebirth holds more hope for me. As I spark into a star, I pray I shall have freedom of enlightenment in an all-encompassing unity."

Leaning forward, Seleme said, "How do you as leader of your people help them to enlightening unity?"

Taking Seleme's hand, Kti looked into her deep brown eyes. "Our Way does not punish for disobedience. Instead it guides our dreams and visions with good counsel that leads us to our point of origin. With our Way, I can help people make better choices about how to live. Some of the responsibility of finding wholeness recedes if people are told they must obey rules but lose the reasons why, the rationale of the Sky gods."

Kti shook her head. "I have spoken enough. I would know your thoughts about your Way. You will bring richness to my simple knowledge, I know."

"Your gracious words allow me to enter the discussion with openness," said Seleme. "I like your ways of expressing your views."

Kti smiled at her.

"I have studied with our practitioners of Mother Astarte," Seleme said. "As matriarch and teacher of Astarte, I follow the Way before Ba'al, the storm god, so similar to Zeus, supplanted her with some of our people. I have visited the Red Tent where the women of Yahweh, the one God, practice rituals very different from the public rites of the one God. There Shekenah, spouse of the one God, has powers. The women relish their private time away from the men when they bleed or birth children, both of which deem them unclean. They laugh at the stigma but perpetuate the time to give them privacy."

"How encouraging to hear that the women of your followers and those of the Red Tent have a path to the Way of the Mother."

"She has been diminished among the neighboring tribes, but women everywhere in our lands keep the Mother alive. I pledge to join you in preserving the rituals. Some who teach the men belittle our goddesses by making them playthings of a ruling force. Instead we teach that both forces work in harmony and benefit all of us."

"All of our lives we learn," Kti said. "Sharing what we know makes life fuller.

Then she said, "Thank you, Seleme, for bringing Laertes back to good health. He was acquiring skills when, so young, he left us, but he had much yet to learn. Your touch surely saved him a difficult rebirthing, should he have taken the drastic measure of self destruction that often appears to be the only choice at such a time."

The women embraced, knowing well that each opened to whatever the Great Mother brought them. For that matter, they had a healthy view of what the warriors could add and what they could learn from the Mother. They joined the conversation of the others. Shortly all adjourned to their quarters for dreaming sleep.

Convergence blends patterns for young ones.

Chapter Thirty-Eight

The next evening, before the feasting, a servant approached Kti and whispered to her. She gave half a smile, then turned to her guests. "I shall return shortly."

No sooner had she left, she re-entered the room. Two strangers accompanied her. "Neaira and Laertes," she said, her eyes misting, "Behold your sister, Kleia. Here stand Kleia, called Maeve among her people, and her husband, O'Conn. Their lives thrive in the West. Their coming, I kept as a surprise."

She motioned to the wine steward. "We welcome them with new wine. Bring it forth that we may offer the great forces our thanks for their safe arrival."

The family toasted but stared in stunned silence. Then joyous laughter blended with embracing. With Eumaios next to her, Kti beamed as she watched their family celebrate.

Her smile broadened when Kleia took O'Conn's hand to guide him to Neaira and Theo, who threw their arms around each in turn. Out of the corner of her eye she caught sight of Laertes striding toward the terrace. She held her breath but released it when he returned.

It might be hard for Laertes to accept O'Conn as brother. As the son of the man who took us from our citadel, even I am reminded of the hard times of the journey.

Kti breathed in once more as Kleia and O'Conn approached Laertes and Seleme. She squeezed Eumaios' hand.

Kleia's eyes danced. "Brother, you are tall and handsome, but that must be so to win such a lovely one as the stately woman by your side." She threw her arms around them both pulling O'Conn to them. "Ánd here is my dear spouse, O'Conn, whom you will love as I do."

Kti relaxed her hand when Laertes returned the hug and in turn embraced O'Conn. In easy conversation they listened to accounts of Laertes finding Seleme and Kleia finding O'Conn. Kti whispered to Eumaios whose bemused glance took in the scene.

"This lovely child infuses good spirit," he said. "They have won the day."

Kti relaxed even more when the evening's lively exchange turned into teasing.

"Sister," said Laertes, "you mix into your talk strange words of the North that Mother brought to us, too."

With glee, she said, "Your accents, if not your words, reflect strangeness, unlike mine."

The laughing banter and feasting lasted into the night. At last, Kti beckoned the servants to lead everyone to sleeping quarters.

In the days that followed, some went to the port to direct their captains or to see after their vessels, sometimes joining their crews in short trading trips. The children joined the adults in the great hall or on the terrace for visits, but mostly their nurses or their tutors found ways to engage them in interchanges with their cousins.

Some went to the ritual center with Eumaios or Kti. Some sought one or the other for private visits. For many hours they discussed the wellbeing of their peoples and their ways of governing and conducting rituals. Some went with Eumaios or Kti to the hill people.

One day, Kleia walked with Kti to the ancestral tombs then farther to the lake below Mount Aenos. "Mother," she said, "I still miss your wise counsel. Freya and I have blended well with the people. I speak of Freya, for I know you miss her. She thrives. Her husband manages a large fleet. He established trade with her brother, who inherited the family land according to the laws of their father. Her brother, well acquainted with his mother's Way, had sympathy with the Way as we hoped he would. After his father died, he urged his mother to visit her people in the North. Their lands, he said, would be hers to pass on to Freya, should she come. If not, they would go to the female line in the family."

"It gladdens my heart to hear of Freya. Did she ever sail into the waters of her family?"

"Freya traveled to her brother. She visited her mother in the North. Ready to travel to her star yard, her mother asked Freya to conduct the burial rituals. Freya stayed with her mother until she placed her mother in the customary hollowed log and recited the final ritual."

"She lamented long ago that she would not be with her mother when she died," said Kti. "How good that she was there."

"Freya's husband came for her the next spring thaw," Kleia said. "She asked her brother to care for the land that came to her. He will welcome her or her progeny when they come again."

"Your account of Freya gives me much comfort and takes

me to happy times with Conn in the green lands." Kti beamed at her daughter. "I marvel at you, my wise child. You are still young but have grown even wiser."

As they wandered, they talked of Kleia's inheritance of the citadel. They planned for her daughter Kallisto, when the time came, to see after it as a trading point of which Kti and her own Conn had dreamed.

Another day, while Kti played with Ktimaios, she thought of each of her children in turn. She thanked the Mother for guiding them so well.

To Eumaios, who sat beside her, she said, "Being surrounded with our growing family reminds me of our good fortune. When they return to their own lives soon, then we will journey to your father and mother. Still I lament that we have no news of Arkos. Perhaps one day that will change.

"In time, we shall know, Kti. All the family searches for Arkos."

The late summer brought fair winds for sailing. Laertes and Seleme journeyed with Neaira and Theo to Samos Island, then onward. Next, the westward seaways favored the journey to Ortygia. The Hyperboreans, with their fleet, sailed alongside Kti, Eumaios, and Ktimaios. They planned to visit for a time, then sail home.

Kti breathed in the sea air as she cradled Ktimaios. She moved into the crook of Eumaios' arms "What a joy it will be at last, my love, to meet your parents. They birthed you, my greatest treasure. I love them beyond reason already."

Eumaios blinked and held Kti and his child closer. "They will love you, not because I love you, but because your spirit brings forth love in everyone you meet."

Kti burrowed her head into Eumaios' chest and thought she heard music. The voice within her said, "Such a good sign, the song of the wind, makes the journey magic."

All stars conspire to bring you knowledge of your progeny.

CHAPTER THIRTY-NINE

Kleia and O'Conn stayed with Eumaios and Kti at Ortygia long enough to greet Eumaios' elderly parents. Then Kleia and O'Conn mustered their fleet for the trek west.

Before boarding, Kti visited with Kleia about the naming ceremony at Parnassus of Kleia's generation and those of the next. "Many of the shrine women remembered your birth in the stone circle. I am delighted the shrine women confirmed Maeve, your name in the North."

"Yes, Mother, also the shrine women gave my daughter your childhood name, Kallisto, which matches her temper. That she will inherit the citadel at Pronni, according to the Way of the Mother, seems just right. She will know shrine work, telling, and scribing as you do. Her name suits her perfectly. I marvel at how well the shrine teachers read us."

Leave-taking gave Kti one last moment to embrace Kleia, O'Conn, and the children. Kti told Kleia of her joy in finding her and her siblings making their mark in their worlds. She and Eumaios blessed them as their fleet sailed away. Kti's final words to them echoed over the waters, "Return as often as you can, my loves."

The Ortygian family forged a bond with Ktimene, the

daughter they never had. They agreed that Ktimaios, their heir, as soon as he reached the age of four, would spend his summers in Ortygia to learn the customs of the people. Eumaios would accompany him.

Kti found Cesme to thank her for bringing Laertes back to them after his escape from the Kelts. She arranged that the family be recognized at court for their work among the temples to the west. When she sailed away, she knew the future goals of all of their offspring, save one, Arkos, still lost.

As springtime came, Kti settled refugee shrine women of Eleusis at the far western rim of Palli. They had grown impatient with the spectacle imposed on them by warrior priests from Athens who connected the city to the shrine with a sacred way. Kti planned retreats at their peaceful haven when she did not go to Ortygia with Eumaios and Ktimaios.

In the ensuing years, Kti and Eumaios built their trade as they enjoyed visits of their children.

In Ktimaios' twelfth year, Kti, in the company of her neighboring kin, traveled to Ortygia to attend a series of celebrations. She left her ship at Palli where she sailed with her cousin Pallinder.

"I am glad to travel to Ortygia with you, cousin. Eumaios and Ktimaios have been there throughout the winter months that marked the final days of Eumaios' parents. Soon after we arrive, we shall honor their recent passing. Then Ktimaios receives the rite of manhood and joins in marriage with Menaja, Cesme's granddaughter. The ultimate celebration, the installation of Ktimaios as ruler of the realm, will climax the celebrations."

In all of the ceremonies, Kti marveled at how well the shrine women of Ortygia, Kephallenia Island, and Mount Parnassus blended the rituals. The presence of her relatives from Palli, Kranni, Sami, and her own Pronni marked the closeness of the heirs of Kephalos and added to the festive harmony.

After the solemn rites and feasts, Kti embraced her son. "I am proud of you, so much that I give you my special blessing."

Ktimaios took his mother's hand. "Dear Mother, I am honored to be your son. You have shown me the ways of the spirit that will help me guide my people well."

Before the week passed, the entourage took their leave of King Ktimaios. As she left, Kti told Eumaios, "I shall be glad for your return to me in a few days."

Eumaios embraced Kti. "I have missed you these many months. I shall not delay. A security force stands ready to protect you until then. This time no stranger will take you away."

Some days after her return, Kti looked up from her morning meal on the terrace. She met the eyes of her herald, fully expecting him to announce the return of Eumaios' ship.

Instead, his eyes wide, the messenger said, "My lady, three strange ships enter our eastern port of Poros. I have never seen such vessels. The many-colored banners that flutter in the winds bear strange emblems. We cannot tell their origin."

Intrigued but cautious, Kti asked her attendants to accompany her to port. She also requested that several armed sentries stand by.

When the leader came ashore, Ktimene looked at him with raised eyebrows. "Cousin Pallinder"—for surely the man before her looked exactly like her cousin— "I left you less than a fortnight ago in Palli. How can you be here? Why do you travel from the east on strange vessels?"

The stranger spoke in the dialect of Kti. "My lady, surely

the powers confuse you, or perhaps that trickster Hekate has withdrawn the shades of reality to whirl you beyond the limits of this world. I have sailed from the Far East. I believe, if my memory serves, Palli is to the west. My trading fleet comes to explore my rights to use these lands for my trading."

"Sir," Kti said as she signaled her sentries to be at the ready, "these lands, occupied since the time Kephalos, came to his son, Pronnus, many generations ago. Through the Mother line they passed to the Queen of this citadel, the sole heir of the land. What gives you a claim to trading rights here?"

Undaunted by her words, the stranger said, "My lady, I come seeking a woman I left as a young lad just reaching manhood, to seek my father."

Kti's hand flew to her throat, while her words held a cautious edge. "I know of this lady. She would have me extend you hospitality. Please dock your ships. After you are refreshed, for surely your journey has been long, we shall take a midday meal on the upper terrace. We must know of your origin, your abiding place, and your mission."

"I shall join you soon, dear lady. As we eat, I shall tell you my story to give you reason to welcome me to this citadel."

"Let it be so." She signaled her attendants to conduct their guest to the bathing room and a chamber for rest before she received him.

Can it be? Can it be? She watched him leave her. To give him credence, his familiar gait, his build surely resembled that of the family. Still she must be cautious.

East meets west to complete the earthly pattern.

Chapter Forty

While the household prepared the table for her meal with the stranger, Kti greeted Eumaios, who had entered the citadel from the western port.

"Thank the Mother Goddess, you arrive," Kti said as she told him of their guest.

Eumaios embraced her. "I will be at your side to hear the words of our guest and to help you confirm his identity." Before he left to refresh himself, he told her of the transition of rule in Ortygia. "You would be proud of our Ktimaios."

The two of them gathered to meet the stranger on the terrace.

"Indeed, many years ago," Kti said, "I sent a son to search for his father, though reluctant to allow one so young to take on the mission. You see before you my husband, with whom I joined many years after my brother, now gone to the stars, brought back the bones of my first husband, the father of that long-gone son. My brother confirmed that all his men, including my husband, died at sea while homeward bound. The husband who sits with me here remained loyal to this family. After the death of my parents, he gained his freedom, much property, a fleet, and the right to return to his own kingdom. After that, he asked me to be his bride. As teachers of the Great Mother, we were mates of the soul who continued to watch a thriving family grow. We always hoped that the eldest son of this household would return to us one day."

Kti resumed her testing. "As an affirmation that you might be associated with this household, first, give us your name. Then tell us the names of those I have just mentioned as a sign of your claim."

"Strange woman, in troubled times, always wisely cautious," he said, "my name is Arkos; yours, dear Mother, in childhood, Kallisto, in maturity, Ktimene."

Kti's eyes filled with tears, while her heart leapt in her chest.

Arkos, a stranger no longer, rushed his words. "My own father, Eurylokhos, after my many searches of which I shall later tell, I suspected had truly been lost. I learn with great sadness that, without my farewells, my father rests in the valley with Uncle Odysseus, my own Grandmother Antikleia, and Grandfather Laertes. Son of Odysseus and Penelope, Telemakhos, companion of my search, went as far as Pylos, then Sparta those many years ago, when we sought our fathers."

He gestured toward Eumaios, who sat next to Kti. "This man, whom I now proudly call Father, none other than Eumaios, brought us back from Samos Island to this citadel as I reached early manhood. I took the mantle as first assistant of the port in the absence of my father, still returning from the war at Truva."

Kti leapt to her feet. "My son, my son, my long-lost son, how I have yearned for you. I have many stories to tell you."

Mother and son clasped each other in a tight, long embrace.

Arkos tilted his head back so he could look into her face. "I must know how Uncle made his way before his time to the valley tomb. I must also know the whereabouts of his son, Telemakhos, the companion of my youth. Does his mother, your dear friend, Pen, who also bravely awaited the end of the war, still reside in nearby Ithaka?"

"We will talk of much that has happened in your absence." Kti linked her arm through his as they strolled across the terrace.

"And what of my siblings? I see we have much to share to bring to light the moons that have rolled by to form our life paths. I have my own story to tell."

"I am pleased that you can match your mother's gaze as well as her testing," said Kti.

"And you, dear Mother, in the fashion of your namesake Kallisto, who became the great bear among the star imprints, I honor as my ritual name giver." Then, bounding to the edge of the terrace, he called out, "Here I stand on the spot where you named me Arkos. The cave I made my lair, I found just below your favorite place, here, from which you could see the waters of the seas around us."

"I see, dear bear child, you have not lost your laughing, gentle ways." As Kti spoke, she snuggled closer for many more embraces.

Kti told Arkos what had transpired in the many years of his absence. He accepted Eumaios as Father while lamenting the loss of a father he never found.

"I will go to the valley to pay tribute to Father and to thank the Great Mother for bringing him home. I will honor all those buried there."

He marveled at the tales of his siblings, at the story of Conn, and his mother's sojourn in the Western Isles. "As we gather this evening, I would like to bring one of my retinue. Then you shall hear of my own journey back to you."

"Please do as you suggest," said Kti.

"On my way to the ship, I go alone to the tomb. My first time to the tomb must be my own." As he headed toward the doorway, Arkos said, "Until this evening then, I take my leave. Just before the stars shine forth with the crescent moon, we shall join you for feasting, then telling. Fix my bed chamber, please, for two."

Happy to see her son so capable of playing games, she grinned after he vanished. "Our son has a wife."

As dusk came, Kti asked for torches to illuminate the way of Arkos with his entourage from the port. From the rampart, beside Eumaios, she watched their newfound son approach the main gate, amid swirls of bright colored cloth, iridescent and opaque. Banners glistened in the last rays of the sun to flash reds, blues, or yellows against a background of white. A small parasol sheltered a miniscule woman from the sun's waning rays.

All the lady's attendants wore flowing robes with high-topped collars. Each garment, richly jeweled, brocaded, and intricately stitched, displayed multi-foliate flowers scattered among exotic, long-tailed birds.

The lady's embroidered flowing cape revealed a design of an open-aired arcade with sloped roofs that came to lifted points. Detailed stitching included images of young women, bedecked in flowing robes with fluttering ribbons, on the lawn of the arcade. Jagged mountains, from which cascading water-falls rushed through trees, formed a protective circle around the women. Overhanging clouds gave the scene majestic beauty and an aura of mystery. Arkos wore finery that echoed the deco-ration of the lady.

When the young couple entered the upper gate, Arkos led forth the porcelain-skinned woman. Her wide, dark eyes sparkled below elegant glistening jet-black hair, pulled back and dressed with sea pearls and shimmering stones extended on tiny wires to let them jiggle in the rhythm of her movement.

In an instant Kti accepted this woman whose enigmatic smile below her sparkling eyes warmed Kti's heart. *How far, my dear, will you stretch my world and what abides there?*

See your imprint on the East.

CHAPTER FORTY-ONE

A t the massive portal, Kti held out her hands in welcome.
Arkos spoke first. "Mother and Father, I present my
spouse, Ling. Her full name, Lei Su Ling, designates her
origin in the Lei family."

He took the arm of the lovely woman to whom all attendants kowtowed. "She knows much about you. She has heard
about my life here and on my birth island, Samos. Ling scribes
and speaks our language well."

Standing straighter, Arkos expanded his chest. "I taught
her."

Kti took Ling's hands into hers, noting their delicate
strength. *Much like the texture of her attire, strong yet fragile*, Kti
thought as she embraced Ling. "You have brought our long-
absent son to us. My heart sings a welcome to you. While your
attendants prepare your quarters, we shall dine as we learn of
your path together."

Kti gazed at Arkos and Ling in turn. "We lament that you
missed the recent gathering of Neaira, Kleia, Laertes, along
with their families. At the time of your search for your father,
the twins, Kleia and Laertes, still young, you likely remember
least. Now Laertes lives in the land of Canaan near Ashkelon,

a busy port near Egypt. Kleia abides in the western seas on a green isle the tellers call Hyperborea, the origin of the winds. Both bonded with leaders of tribes that occupy the lands they claim as home. When they visit with their growing families, they bring life to our lofty citadel. The world becomes smaller as we link our trade to these places."

Then Kti cast her eyes on Arkos. "But your journey has taken you even farther than your siblings, Arkos. Please tell us of it. Ariel, our young teller, sits here to take in the account of your quest. Your journey outward, then back to us, must be a part of the family lore."

Eurykleia, the faithful nurse, stirred from her place beside Ariel. She made movement to retire.

Arkos turned to her. "Ah, gentle nurse, rest now. You will hear my story from Ariel." He embraced her fragile frame with a gentle hug.

As the ancient one made her unhurried way from the hall, she said, "You, the gentlest of the children I tended, I wished to see before my journey to the stars. Mother and son finally connect, pattern perfect now. Our loving queen, your mother, ever yearned for you." With deliberate steps, she crossed the terrace, an attendant lighting her way.

"Before I tell my story, dear parents," said Arkos, "I must tell you, Eumaios, how much I admire you for your loyalty to my family. My mother bonded with you in spirit many years before you achieved full union. We happily acknowledge you, Father, and our newest brother, Ktimaios, who rules the kingdom of your parents."

"I am pleased … grateful for your generosity," said Eumaios.

"How difficult it must have been to have you, their only

child, taken from them. I foresee a time when such enslave-
ment must end. During this trading journey, we shall visit your
homeland to meet our brother and the homelands of Neaira,
also Kleia and Laertes. I remember the twins as thriving children. Neaira, as I, fast attained adult ways to assist you with
household, trading, and shrine matters, but the twins lived
without a care, much as the young ones in Ling's home when I
arrived in her land to enjoy the company of her cousin, Chan."

Kti took Ling's delicate hand. "Finding Ling fulfills you,
dear son."

"I discovered Ling in my early days at the farthest point of
my journey eastward in my search for Father."

Squinting, Kti tapped her head. "Such a journey is hard to
imagine."

"With the fast-coming maturity of our young ones, Ling
urged me to travel into the lands of my roots. I yearned to find
you, Mother, if indeed, you still lived. You needed to know of
my years away, of my existence still on this earth."

Ling, mostly silent except for pleasantries, said with firm
pride, "Arkos speaks too modestly. When he came many years
ago to our land of Chen, he fast became invaluable to our court.
My father ruled a vast region. Growing our trade fit into his
plans."

"Clearly, you two share a bond that suits you as ours has
always suited us," Kti said." She peered into Arkos' eyes. "But
Arkos, why did you not come back home with Telemakhos
before going East?"

"I believed Father may still live, so I made haste to find him.
If he did not sail with Uncle Ody to Kephallenia after his planning mission in Truva, he may have sailed into the Dark Sea."

"Aunt and Uncle sent word you stopped on Samos Island. But then we lost you." Kti gazed into the distance.

"Oh, Mother, I did not mean to worry you. I simply was driven to find Father. From Samos Island, I sailed to Truva where both Nestor and Menelaos told me they had last seen Father. My thoughts ran like this: 'He could have stayed behind to continue his trading, to make deeper explorations and to amass local materials for rebuilding Truva'."

Arkos settled deeper into his chair. "Here is my story, told as it happened."

PART EIGHT

ARKOS

CHEN
(ANCIENT CHINA)

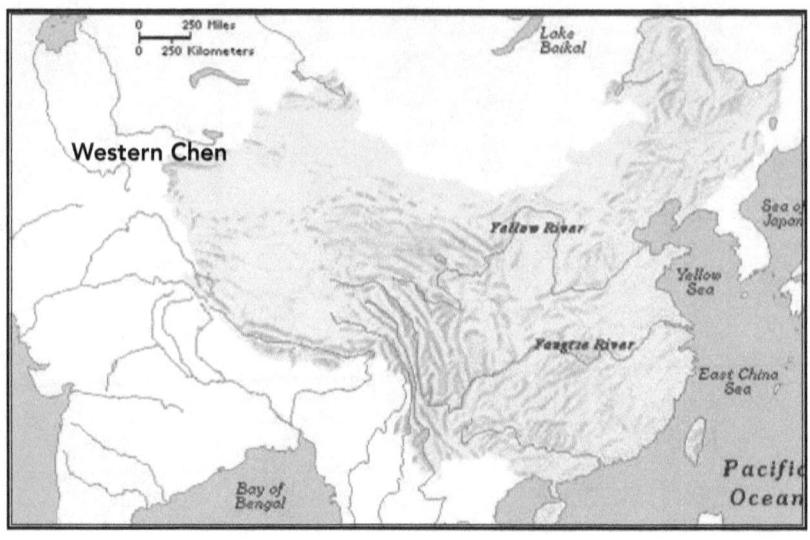

Chapter Forty-Two

A ship sat in the dock. Arkos shouted to a hand busy with the rigging. "Greetings sailor, where does this ship travel?"

"She travels as far east as possible on these dark waters. When she docks, most aboard will join a caravan that trades with peoples of immense resources. We have taken some like you with us then and again."

"That sounds promising. Take me to your captain."

Upon meeting the captain, Arkos requested more information from him.

"Yes," said the captain, "your father might have joined a remnant of Odysseus' men who decided to settle beyond the eastern shores of the Dark Sea. Some, I hear, went farther beyond the mountains of another easterly sea. They planned to build a major stopping center for caravans forging routes to sources of gold, ceramics, textiles, spices, jewels, and bronzes."

Nodding, Arkos grinned. "Father might have joined them. He always pressed to the limits. If you have a space, I shall sail with you."

The bargain struck, Arkos sent his plan with a trader sailing to Samos Island.

The trader said, "Have you heard that maurauders who

swamped the ports of Samos Island met their end in a battle with Egypt's powerful Pharaoh?"

"Yes," Arkos said, "Trade is brisk again."

"I shall deliver your message to Aglaeus whom I know well."

After many days by ship or land, Arkos found permanent settlers, Hellene remnants among them. He did not find his father but was encouraged when one of the men said, "One who fits your father's description traveled over the rugged mountains to the mysterious land of Chen."

"I shall go there with the next caravan."

Once he arrived in Chen, Arkos' trading blood stirred. He made note of amazing goods: shiny cloth, intricate bronze pieces, and delicately carved jade and ivory. He spoke with a friendly local man. "I seek the best trading center of the area."

The man greeted him with a hearty laugh and a beckoning gesture. "Follow me to the gathering place of the Lei family men. They thrive in trade."

If my father is anywhere, he is there.

A disappointed Arkos did not find his father, but he attracted the attention of Lei Chan and his friends, who enjoyed hearing his tales of the West, an edge of the world so different from theirs. Arkos located lodging and promised to join them every evening.

One night, Arkos met Chan's distant cousin from the provinces, who had just arrived to study at court. Arkos saw through the disguise that revealed a young woman's shape. He shook his head. "Chan, what ruse is this?"

"I present my cousin, Lei Su Ling, who wanted to hear your stories. As a court woman, the daughter of the emperor, she cannot go out in public. Ling is my closest friend, save you, Arkos."

Arkos reached out to give Ling a gentle shake of his hand, but instead found himself flying backward. "Oof, my back."

Slapping his knees, Chan buckled in laughter. "Friend, never enter an Eastern woman's space. You will always find yourself flying through the air."

Arkos caught a twinkle in Ling's eye. She squinted her round eyes, her lips curled upward. "Welcome to my world of Chen, western trader."

★ ★ ★

ARKOS SPENT MANY EVENINGS in the company of Chan and Ling. As the enterprising trader from the West, he attracted attention throughout the trading area. Soon the head of the Lei family asked Chan to present Arkos at court.

Arkos gave a deep bow. "I am honored to be in your presence. Your nephew has warmly welcomed me."

He delighted in the lilting voice that responded. "Lei Chan tells me you are a trader. Perhaps you would welcome a tour of the Lei lands. We might have some enterprises to interest you."

Arkos walked the lands with Chan. In one shed, his eyes widened. "So here I find the durable, vibrant cloth of great mystery. How strange that these worms can spin threads to make the shiny cloth. That cloth, precious jades from the mountains of your lands, and rare teas and spices from your terraced hillsides will enhance the trading caravan I am organizing in a warehouse nearby."

"Ah, friend Arkos, we make more items that will interest

you. The hewers of advanced metal produce intricate implements—mirrors, tongs, or needles that you may not have seen."

"We possess nothing that rivals these useful items, nor do
we have anything like these massive bronzes from molds far
more advanced than ours. Your goldsmiths craft designs that
surpass any I have seen on cups, bowls, and ritual objects, some
inlaid with ivory, lapis, jade, or other precious gems."

Chan patted his friend on the back. "Arkos, my dear western
companion, we shall do magnificently as trading partners."

Winking at him, Arkos nodded. "Yes, Chan, we have
immense opportunities."

Arkos discovered he could not see Ling at court because
women of the house remained confined unless summoned.
Even then, to speak to a chaperoned woman at any public gathering, he must be formally presented.

In the evenings, though, Ling continued, in disguise, to join
the duo. Arkos practiced their dialect, as well as others from
traders. Chan and Ling, in turn, learned his language.

Arkos witnessed their writing on rolls of pulped trees from
which their artisans formed scrolls to use with special ink and
tools, all filled with sacred mystery. "Ling and Chan, I am
pleased to observe that your way of writing connects to your
ancient, revered immortals."

"Our immortals, both male and female, shared wisdom
with our ancestors," Ling said. "No rivalry marred their peace or
their freedom. Along with statecraft, Father urged me to study
ancient spiritual practices. I studied accounts of both the male
immortals and the immortal sisters, the latter, lost except to
women cloistered in out of way mountain hermitages."

"When I make the journey home, I shall take some scrolls

to Mother so that she can script our ancient wisdom to make a compact record of the tellers' lore as her mother told it to her. That will disrupt the warrior's code to its core and bring the Great Mother back to equality with the warrior gods."

Star twin, Kallisto, your eldest, the small bear,
completes your earthly circle.

Chapter Forty-Three

The emperor presented Arkos to the central female figures of the family, Ling's grandmother, the Dowager, and her aunt Lei Su Wei, Chan's mother who had become, at the death of Ling's mother, the emperor's confidante. Their excitement prompted them to introduce Arkos to all of the young daughters, as well as the Emperor's wives and concubines.

One evening as the trio sat in the trade center, Arkos laughed when Ling said, "I know the protocol of court sounds complicated, but we women perform our roles to adhere to the present customs. We do little in public. Our power resides behind the scenes. I have freedom in this disguise."

She paused. "When I see you at court, we must signal in stealth from behind the fan."

Even though he suspected Ling reciprocated his feelings, Arkos knew he must not betray to her or to Chan his growing love for her. The time fast approached for Ling to marry her elderly cousin, long ago, her betrothed. As his first wife, his marriage to Ling would bring the family branches closer.

"I must view Ling as treasured friend, even though I have dreamed of our life together." He shook his head. "I must abandon thinking of elopement with her and a life together on the trade routes."

Arkos felt emptiness beyond relief when Ling stepped from the marriage litter adorned in regal red to take the hand of her husband.

In the years that followed, Arkos watched Ling bring forth a male heir to solidify the family. Then came a young daughter, betrothed to Chan, the next in line to rule the family dynasty if Ling's son had no heirs. Arkos had helped the emperor gain family harmony. Still, Ling's marriage did not calm his heart.

Arkos lived at his trading center built west of the Lei lands. He visited Ling and her husband as surrogate uncle of the children. He became a trusted trade advisor to her husband. Never in those years did he overstep his position.

During his visits, Arkos stayed with Chan, who welcomed him as a brother. On one visit, Arkos learned from Chan that he and Ling's young daughter had confirmed their betrothal. "She and I will be married soon. She fast becomes a favorite of the inner court. She lives up to her name, Lei Wei, given in honor of her grandmother and my mother, her great aunt."

On a later visit, Arkos witnessed the affirmation ritual that would unite Chan and Lei Wei. The night of the ceremony, vigorous shakes awakened Arkos from his deep sleep.

Chan's face loomed over him. "We are summoned to Ling's side. Her husband has died. Their household is in chaos, as Ling faces a claim from her husband's brother to take her into his household as a second wife. Such an act, a brother's right, he asserts, gives him guardianship of her young son, the heir of both family branches and future emperor. Ling calls us to her side as her father's emissaries."

Upon their hasty entry to her chambers, Ling said, "I shall

never agree to enter the brother's household."

"You are ill, Ling, and your hands shake," said Arkos. "We must take you home. Chan, can you arrange it immediately?"

Following Arkos' lead, Chan saw her illness as a way out of the immediate union. To avoid disgrace, Chan told the family, "Ling will return to her father, the Emperor, for a time to mourn, to recuperate from an illness that has swamped her."

The family raised no objection to his announcement.

Arkos watched Ling's illness move into darker periods. "Oh, Chan, I fear for Ling's survival."

Arkos smiled his first smile when Chan said, "She has rallied some. The Emperor is sending her into the mountains to live among the sisters who practice ancient arts of body and spirit control that will enliven her."

★ ★ ★

WHEN ARKOS LEARNED THAT, in time, Ling's recovery was possible, he said, "Chan, I must take my leave to search again for Father, to make my way home. Instead of bartering my goods to a caravan master, I shall take them overland myself, sail to Truva, and load them onto a vessel that will stop at Samos Island. From there, I shall take a family ship to Kephallenia. I hope to return before many moon spans."

At Truva, Arkos made arrangements with a trustworthy captain who agreed to dock at Samos Island. The tides delayed departure.

"I shall explore the new city as I search again for Father," he promised himself.

Truva flourished, but Arkos found no one who remembered his father. Before the ship sailed, he resolved, "I cannot go forward. I must return to Chen." He bartered his goods for a fair price before he journeyed to Chen. "I shall collect one more load to trade. Besides, I must attend Chan and Lei Wei's wedding."

In his heart, Arkos realized Ling drew him back. "She must be mine if she consents. Even if I cannot have her, she must not return to the brother of her late husband. She will never be content in that household."

Arkos arrived at Chan's two days before the wedding.

"Dear friend, Arkos," Chan said as he slapped Arkos on the back. "Now that you return, you must stand up with me at the ceremony."

Arkos bowed. "I shall be honored. Does Lei Wei have the beauty of her mother?

Tilting his head, Chan grinned. "Did you connect with your family and your father?"

"No, dear friend, but with the weather delaying departure, I had time to return for the wedding." Then Arkos took a deep breath and let it out. "Has Ling recovered, succumbed to her illness, or …"

Before Arkos could finish the question, Chan motioned toward the inner chambers. "See for yourself."

Arkos followed Chan into the garden. His eyes filled with tears. He knelt beside a bench surrounded by blossoming peonies. "Ling, you are—"

"Yes, Arkos, I am well. My heart beats faster now that you have come back to me."

Following a long silence, with Arkos holding her delicate

hand, Ling's words spilled out. "After my long illness, my father convinced the family of my departed husband that I remained too fragile to enter their household. Father arbitrated an agreement that my son would stay with my departed husband's brother, who would serve as guardian. My son would visit me only one season of the year. His heirs, from a marriage they would arrange, would inherit the rule of the kingdom. Chan or his progeny remained next in line after my son and his progeny. That meant my father's kingdom would revert to Chan, should no heir be born. The brother would keep my late husband's lands."

Arkos' eyes widened. "What does this mean? You are not married?"

"I returned to manage our inner apartments since both my grandmother and my aunt have gone to our ancestors. That role will end when Chan marries my daughter. Then Wei will manage the inner life of the court."

Arkos, not relinquishing Ling's hand, looked toward the Emperor and Chan, whose faces were covered with broad smiles. He barely took in the Emporer's words. "A widow is free to marry as long as her father condones the match. We leave you two so that you may learn of Ling's healing and other important matters."

★   ★   ★

ARKOS TOOK SOME MOMENTS before he could speak with calm. "Ling, tell me of your healing time." He listened to her with rapt attention.

"My spirit opened the longer I stayed away. The mountains and valleys of that peaceful place brought me many days of shadow, floating clouds, snow, or rain, then shadow again. The bright peonies of springtime, the chrysanthemums of autumn, even the ever-present lotus did not stir me. Nor did the harvests of tea and rice bring me to my ripeness. The winter cold pricked my skin, but my body stirred little. I awakened from my slumber as the late springtime came. Life coursed through my body just as it does through the bear mother who, during hibernation births a cub, then welcomes it upon awakening."

"Ling, dear one, I wish I could have been there to help."

"No, to heal, the ordeal was mine alone. I faced the tiger, the dragon, and the ghosts of my ancestors. When the dragon's fire turned the phoenix to ashes, I went beyond my demons, then, like the phoenix, came back to life. At times, I soared as if turned into a firebird myself. I joined the students of the Way to learn more of the arts that would replenish my body. Father brought me news that I may return to his household with my daughter, but that my son must join my late husband's family."

Ling hesitated, then swallowed hard before she continued. "The arrangement gave me freedom, but I lamented the loss of my son's constant presence. Father and Chan brought me home. I had periods of despondency. I entered into intense exercises to empty myself. Our physician gave me herbs. She arranged massages and needles. Only when you, my dear Arkos, walked into the garden did my world fully brighten."

Ling plucked a peony. "This blossom reminds me of the beauty of the moment. The petals resemble the opening of my heart. Arkos, how many years, dear friend, have we shared our innermost thoughts on every subject but ourselves? You know I love you past reason, past passion, to the inner core of my being where an empty vessel always resides ready to receive wisdom and ultimate reality."

"Let us," together they chorused, "unite in marriage."

★   ★   ★

KTI SPOKE, HER HAND OVER her heart. "Your story touches me. It will reside in the archives with the other historys of our family."

"Dear Mother Kti," Ling said, "I understand well, with my son's absence, how much sorrow you must have felt while Arkos did not return."

"In the moment of my return to Ling," said Arkos, "we could speak no more. I took her into my arms. We agreed we belonged together. Her father blessed the marriage, a quiet simple ceremony. We planned to travel, enter trade, and be productive. We enjoyed the arrival of a son and daughter, twins."

"Mostly I traveled in disguise as a male," said Ling, "a role with which I had become familiar. In our fifth year of marriage, we learned of my dear son's death, which made Chan the heir to my father's kingdom. Alas, my father died thereafter. We returned to bury him and to attend my daughter, Wei, seriously ill after delivering a stillborn daughter. Sadly, she did not survive. Dear Chan offered a solution to the lineage. Would we agree to his betrothal to our daughter? We made the agreement, subject to our daughter's assent when she reached womanhood. The time had come to seek you. Arkos had spoken many times of our coming. Now that we have found you, we shall come again with our twins."

The young couple uncovered a package they had carried to dinner. Kti looked at Arkos.

"Dear Mother, we bring you a gift. It will enhance your writing."

As Arkos spoke, Ling's delicate fingers released the twine. Arkos unfurled a scroll and handed it to Kti.

"What have we here?" she said.

Arkos turned to Ling. "Ling will demonstrate, with inks and a scribing instrument, how you must use them when you write. I learned the technique, but she is more skilled."

Kti took Eumaios' hand. "What an amazing way to scribe, so concise, so compact for storing. I shall carry some with me in my traveling bag."

Eumaios nodded. "Yes, my love, we must master the technique."

Kti embraced Arkos and Ling. "Thank you, dear ones, for such a magnificent gift. With these scrolls, we must convince the Sibyls to script the rituals."

PART NINE

JOURNEYS

THE ISLAND OF KEPHALLENIA

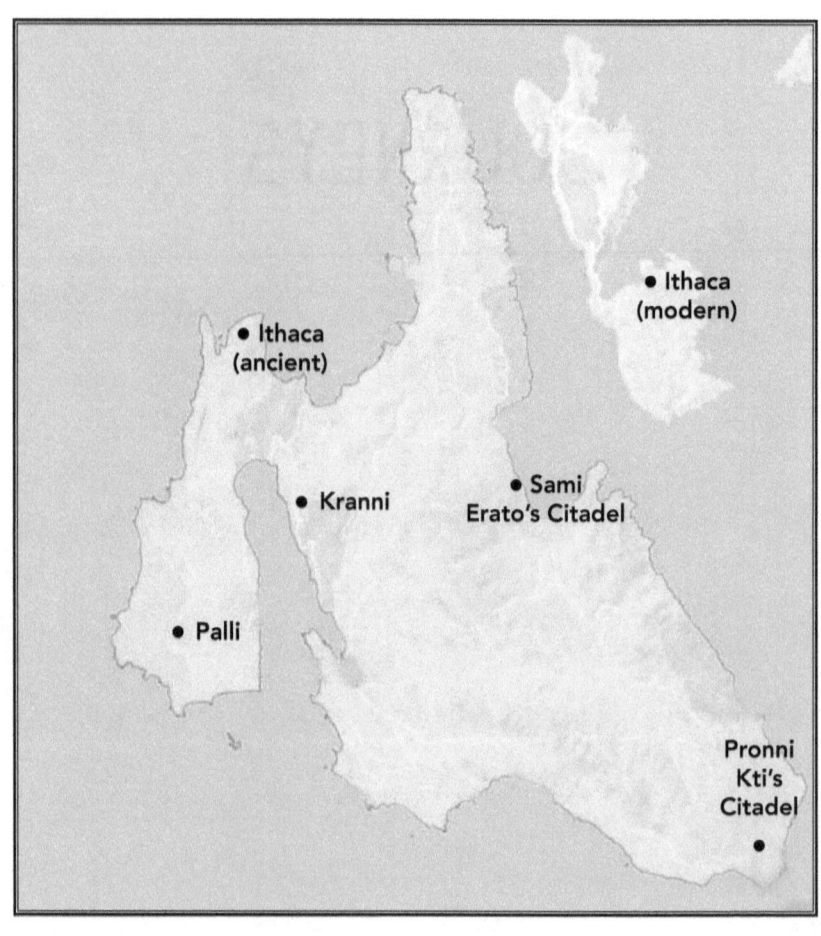

A promise kept.

Chapter Forty-Four

Kti sighed when Arkos and Ling said they would leave within the week. "How can I ever let you go, dearest Bear Child and dearest Ling? You have brightened our lives beyond my imagining."

"Mother, we can visit more if you sail with us to Samos Island," Arkos said. "We plan to stop to spend time with Neaira there."

"Now is too soon," Kti said. "First, we must prepare the citadel for Kallisto, Kleia's young daughter, who will be the guiding light of its future. Kleia will bring her next springtime. Once we leave here, we will make our independent journeys. Eumaios goes to our son in Ortygia and I to Parnassus. We shall be initiated into the Council of Elders in these separate places."

Arkos held up both arms. "Would that we could wait for you to do these things, but we must return to our young ones and to our trade."

"Besides, dear ones," Kti said, "we promised Pen to visit her on our way to Samos Island. We must keep that promise."

A few days later, the young couple bade farewell with assurance of seeing them often. "Samos Island will always be one of our stops,"

Kti welcomed her daughter Kleia and Kallisto, as planned, in the spring. With them, she and Eumaios toured the citadel along with its ports and grounds.

"The beautiful hillside home, with its lands protected by Mount Aenos, have given us many years of pleasure, dear Kalli. We leave it in your good hands. You have skills as a scribe and a teller; thus, I leave my histories of the branches of our families with you insofar as I know them. Continue them, guarding this precious treasures in the lore of the Great Sea."

Kalli embraced her grandmother, lingering in her arms. "I shall absorb energy from you and your ancient ancestor, both of you my namesakes. That energy will help me carry on your work. What a magnificent legacy you have left me."

Kti held tight in the embrace. "You will have assistance from Askanius, Neaira's son, who has trading in his blood. He has already left Samos with a small trading fleet to join yours here. Both of you will do well here."

Kleia joined their circle. "I shall miss you, dearest daughter, so I plan visit at intervals to enjoy what you accomplish here."

Upon his arrival, Askanius bounded from his lead ship with eager stride to receive the greetings of Kti and the others. When his eyes lit on Kalli, Kti knew he would be at home. He whispered to her, "If she will have me, we might wed. Time will tell."

Kalli greeted Askanius with an embrace. "Welcome, dear cousin. I predict we shall work well together."

Kti smiled as if she could see into a bright future. *Ah, better than I imagined.*

Kti, along with Eumaios, Kleia, Kalli, and Askanius, joined hands to pronounce the blessings of Mother Gaia on this new day for the citadel. With raised arms, Kti said, "Mother Gaia, guide Kalli and Askanius as they manage the trade and the life of the citadel."

Kti and Eumaios took their leave. At the lofty citadel of Parnassus, Kti looked forward to seeing Telemakhos before going to Gaia's shrine for reception into the Council of Elders. Eumaios traveled west to Ortygia to give Ktimaios word of their plans and to be seated with the Council of Elders, the first rite he would receive in the land of his birth. Cesme would bestow the rite.

Before harvest, Kti joined Eumaios at Pen's port to go inland. "Oh, how I have missed you, my love," she said.

They held each other close. Then Eumaios whirled her around as he looked into her eyes. "Seldom apart of late, this separation was unbearable. Let us always stay near one another."

"No more separation," Kti said. "Now, we trek to Pen and then to Sibyl Amphito, if she lives."

Eumaios squeezed her tighter. "Onward for those visits, then to Samos Island."

They camped in the mountains the first night, arriving at Pen's by midday. The rolling mountain meadow above a snug fertile river valley to the south gave them their first view of Mount Kyllene to the north.

Eumaios spoke of Ortygia. "I told Ktimaios and Menaja we would hold them ever in our hearts. They assured me that they would see us soon on Samos Island."

After a moment, he continued. "When Cesme gave me the Rite of Wisdom, I sat with their Council of Elders. Her bestowing the Rite helped me make a significant leap toward my destiny."

"My love," Kti said, "I gained insights to give me solace

whatever our future holds. When Sibyl Pythia gave me the Rite, I understood how our paths have given us true blessings. Our children form a protective, southern circle around the foremost reaches of the earth to connect with the coils of the dragon that encircle the northern star yard where Kallisto, the great bear, holds a central place."

As she spoke, her arms and her swaying body, as if in ecstatic trance, bent toward the west to Kleia's green land. She swept her arms eastward toward Ktimaios' Ortygia, then onward to Pronni, now nurtured by Kleia's child Kalli. Next, she arched to the east toward Samos Island, Neaira's port. Tipping farther east, she designated Laertes' Levant. Finally, leaning ever more eastward, she completed the great imaginary earthly bounds to mark the lands of Arkos' Chen.

"Each child fulfills what my name foretold," she said. "They all influence great peoples and perpetuate the Way of the Mother."

She bowed her head as if in communion with the Mother to say, "May Wisdom ever keep them and their progeny strong."

When they reached the meadow near Pen's citadel, Kti looked again to the high mountains. "I remember Mother's account of springtime watering of the meadows. She told me of thaws from the peaks of Nonakris forming watery cascades from melting ice that sent upward a mist to shroud the peaks. Sun and moonlight intermingled with the mist as it glistens upon the jagged ice masses that pointed downward just before they crack and form, drop by drop, first a gentle trickle then a cascading stream."

Eumaios said, "The nourishing water has produced the abundant harvests we see in these meadows, does it not?"

"Yes, my love, it does. We will see cascades of water as we follow Arkadia's River Styx across the valley to reach the mountains where the Sibyl resides. The Styx flows, in its opposite direction, into the great river Arkanius which, in turn, spills into the eastern sea at Naphali."

"That will be our port of departure, right?"

"Yes," Kti said, "Telemakhos and Polycaste told me Pen will make the journey from her home with us to Naphali. From there, she will go to Hera's shrine near Argos where she will abide with the shrine women."

"That shrine must be in the path of warriors."

"The Argive shrine thrives despite its nearness to many warrior strongholds. Throughout the reigns of Pelops' children, the shrine women have kept peace during times of unrest. They maintained the Way while plots of revenge shifted the power at Pelops' citadel at Mycenae. Recently the conflicts favored Agamemnon, then Aigisthos, now, once again, Agamemnon's son, Orestes, who reigns with Menelaos and Helen's daughter, Hermione."

"What about Elektra? Did she find her rightful place?"

"Elektra, the daughter of Klytemnestra and Agamemnon, I learned, now serves at the Argive shrine. The people of Mycenae, Argos, Sparta, Pylos, and our citadels in Arkadia connect, but in between, the lands are filled with wanderers."

"Should we be worried?"

"I do wonder if we will make it to the port for our departure to Samos Island."

Kti arched her eyebows. "We shall soon know."

After Pen welcomed them, they caught up on their diverse lives. Kti spoke of Telemakhos and Polycaste's report of the unsettled condition of neighboring tribes. "I am glad we left our scribed family history in the care of Kalli. We will not scribe the rituals until we reach safety."

Eumaios added, "We will use a more compact system. We have many scrolls that Arkos and Ling brought when they came from Chen."

Pen gazed in wonder at the scroll Kti unfurled as Eumaios spoke.

"While we visit, we want to explore the rituals that gave us a seat with the Elders. Those rituals, though from different shrines, gave us valuable insights."

"What were the rituals like?"

"The rich mix of women's voices at Parnassus helped me feel the blessings of life in this realm but drew me closer to life beyond. I realize how previous rituals have prepared me for this time. As no men came to the Parnassian ritual, Eumaios received the rite in Ortygia. I understand men still take part in the ritual to the south where you received it. I know from the discussion of the Parnassian council that men came to the rituals at all of the shrines before the warrior code came."

Eumaios chimed in with a gleeful tone. "Ah, yes, Menaja, young Ktimaios' wife, arranged for Cesme, her grandmother, now a Sibyl, to administer my rite. My eyes opened more."

Pen stirred the dying embers in the great room pit. "My experience changed my life. I prepare my niece, young Penelope, the child of my sister, Iphthime, to occupy this citadel."

"What will you do after she comes?"

"Then I plan to work at a Mother Shrine. Joining the Elders inspired my decision. I plan to study more deeply with the shrine women at Lusi. Amphito invited me to come to her when she conducted our transition ritual last year. She needs to share her work there just as Gaetha wants you both at the Samian shrine."

"Will you stay there long?"

"I do not know where I shall work, either in Amphito's mountain retreat or at the Argive Heraion. When springtime comes, I will go to the mountain. The children already conduct the planting and harvesting."

As she spoke, a flame flared from the ashes in the fire pit to light the great hall. A woman appeared before them.

"Helen, are you magic?" Kti said gazing at the aura around her that the flickering flames projected.

"No, I am real." Helen laughed.

"Your joyous laughter enlivens us as we near slumber," Eumaios said.

"How did you pass safely through the wandering tribes?" Pen said. "I would never be so brave."

"In due time, you shall know all," Helen said.

Kti, through a broad smile, said, "How can we ever know all about you, dear friend?"

Catch Helen's star if you dare.

CHAPTER FORTY-FIVE

Kti peered at Helen with raised eyebrows. "Really, how did you travel through such dangerous territory?"

"No one noticed me along the tree-draped trail," Helen said. "I walked in the late day sun, touching the ripened grapes while the workers sang their tribute to the harvest. Doves settled nearby cooing the evensong. With a lone serving woman, I passed unrecognized among the harvesters. I wanted to arrive here before the torch lighters led you to your rest."

She embraced each, then settled into the cushions of the couch that surrounded the fire pit. Her words rushing onward, she said, "I doubt you know yet of the death of my dear Menelaos. He died bravely defending Sparta. The funeral games, the days of public mourning,... most of all, the days of private reflection kept me bound to Sparta."

"We would have come to attend the games, had we known," said Pen.

"I dared not send messengers for fear of their being captured. Had any of you come to Menelaos' rites, you would have met your death. I have eluded all the greedy pests who thought I should choose one of them to reign beside me. No one knows, save my inner circle, I have left. I like it that way."

Kti said, "Helen, you are a wonder."

Helen's face glowed in the firelight, "What joy I felt, Kti, when I heard on the winds that you both visited with Pen."

She beamed at them, then gazed into Pen's eyes. "Pen, Pen, how long have we been apart, though so close? Roaming bands infest the roads around us, ready to strike at will. My servant's cloak covered me well. No one gave me a second glance. I thank the good Mother of the Shadows who protected me."

Pen busied herself with acts of hospitality. "Helen, welcome, welcome, you must take a repast with us before we all retire. I know you tire from your journey. I speak for all of us when I say that the death of Menelaos saddens us."

In silence, they ate while they absorbed Helen's news.

Then the three of them each told Helen of their losses, their joys, how their lives had changed as a myriad of events had unfolded

"Your accounts give me balance, courage to tell of Menelaos' last deeds."

After a moment, Helen dabbed her eyes, then spoke. "Menelaos—warrior, trader… adventurer to the last—died not even a moon span ago defending our home. He had joined Orestes and his allies in an entanglement with the followers of old Naphlius, now dead. That treacherous father of Palamedes had given marauders free reign at the port of Naphali. Now Orestes has it back."

Helen frowned and tightened her fist. "May the Great Mother test his twisted soul before rest finds Naphlius. "

"How did Naphlius become part of the story?" said Kti.

"His Kretan ancestors married into a family of our tribe who maintained the port of Naphali. The line ends with his death. He turned against us, his adopted tribe, when he could not accept that his son, Palamedes, betrayed us at Truva. Naphlius believed the warrior band headed by Agamemnon and Menelaos, even Odysseus, poisoned the minds of the troops against Palamedes. That son became a clever tactician himself as well as a student of Daedalus, from whom he learned the secrets of inventive sciences and numerology."

"Oh, how could anyone believe that of my beloved brother or the others." said Kti.

"We all know that Nauplius visited each citadel to spread rumors of our husbands' infidelities with camp followers or captive slaves. I missed his wily visit while I languished in Egypt. My sister, Klytemnestra, some said, believed him enough that she colluded with Aigisthos to murder Agamemnon when he returned."

"What terrible results that unleashed," said Eumaios. "But what was the truth?"

"Orestes, dear child, after his father's death, killed Aigisthos, then rashly his own mother whom he thought willingly joined Aigisthos to reinstate the line of Thyestes at Mycenae. When Orestes learned of Klytemnestra's innocence, that only Aigisthos murdered Agamemnon when he and his men ambushed the great commander as he approached his citadel and that Klytemnestra was captive in her own citadel, Orestes succumbed to madness."

"What happened to him?" said Kti.

"He entered a long period of deep grief at the loss of both his parents. He sought purification at many shrines to keep him from Mycenae until emissaries, allies of his father, and our own Hermione, his betrothed since childhood, convinced him to return as ruler of Mycenae. Sorting out that travesty took many months. Once Orestes understood the truth, he joined the other tribes to secure Mycenae from the followers of Aigisthos. With the death of Nauplius, marauders he had welcomed either departed by the seaway or ran wild through these lands."

"Now what is Orestes doing as ruler?" said Pen.

"With the port once again in his control, Orestes is trying to bring peace to all of us. Those who had followed Herakles into the East many years ago still trouble us. They say they left willingly to establish a colony near Truva and another in the north. Now they claim our lands as their homeland. Everyone harbors the wish to return home, even after many years. Menelaos tried to make peace with them, but when they persisted, he died bravely defending Sparta, a stray arrow hitting his great heart."

Helen paused, narrowing her eyes "Now comes the interesting part. Those men, lust filling them, after they murdered my brave Menelaos, entered our citadel, their object to subdue me. I heard them shouting as they came, 'Rape Helen, whore of Menelaos.' They believed the story of my presence in Truva, a wife of Paris, then, after his death, wife of his disgusting brother, Deiphebius, you see. For that matter, they likely knew of my childhood dalliance at Eleusis with the chieftain."

"What lies!" muttered Kti through clenched teeth.

"Tellers relish repeating that story. Menelaos fell when they stormed our home. The guards drove them away. I ran into the worship center, put on my shrine robes, and gathered the holy women around me. All of us, in solemn garb, sang the mourning chant for Menelaos. They still surrounded us, but they allowed us to mourn. For days we carried on the rites, conducted the funeral games, recited our prayers. The shrine women continue that practice in my absence. Warriors dare not breach our holy ground, especially our exiled kin who know our Way."

Helen's tone turned triumphant. "The invaders have installed themselves around my lands. They resort to sending emissaries. So far, I have worn my widow's garb or holy robes, retreated with the shrine women whom I lead, stared down their emissaries until I sent them away."

"Has Orestes come to your aid?"

"Orestes tried to penetrate their camp but to this point has only managed messages. When I leave here, I plan go to Mycenae to join them. Together we will gather a force and drive out the invaders. They will be surprised, should they ever enter Sparta before we return. Perhaps we shall wear them down. Otherwise we shall have to fight them, I suppose."

Pen signaled her household to lead them to their sleeping chambers. "Helen, you leave us much for dreaming. We shall have our private moments of remembering Menelaos, a good man to the end. We shall spend the days of your visit discussing many things before you go."

Kti took up a torch and handed it to Eumaios. Then she stretched. "We have so much to learn from each other these few days we have together."

Yes, wise ones all, you touch your source.

CHAPTER FORTY-SIX

The next morning Pen, Kti, and Eumaios told Helen of their induction into the Council of Elders. Kti turned toward Helen. "Now, Helen, tell us of your experience when you took your place on the Council."

"Well, my dears, no males joined us," Helen said. "Sparta exudes male bravado that boasts and struts. How males receive rites at any level remains men's business. My father, when he married Klytemnestra's mother, who little followed the Way of the Mother, allowed males to go to leaders of the Sky Gods, some to Zeus, some to Poseidon, both of whom usurped the traits of Mother Gaia. Menelaos, claiming he had larger battles, let his warriors initiate the young men, although he wisely followed Mother Wisdom. He never doubted everyone should study Her ways, but he had little inclination to reform. The women will someday bring Wisdom of the Mother to our men, young or old. All males will benefit. Needless to say, no men in Sparta received the rites of the elders when I received the ritual two years ago."

Kti, with head bowed, said, "What has happened since your induction?"

"We have brought one group of women into the Council,"

Helen said. "We planned to bring men in this fall. The renegades who surround us have taken the children they could snatch from their homes to separate centers for the boys and the girls to receive education. What nonsense. When Orestes and I return victorious, we shall remedy that. I practice the Mother's rites in our ritual center where no male dares step without my command. Only ridding the territory of the occupiers will resolve the problem."

"Who is on the Council?" Kti said.

"An ancient shrine woman with a few elders around her constituted our council until I with three of my attendants, all younger than any of the aging wise ones, came to the rite. The Sibyl of Troezen, Aethra, led our induction. You, Kti, will remember that she mothered the chieftain, the father of Iphigenia. Because of the turmoil around us, we benefited from the deeper meaning of the rite, especially the idea of transformation. Perhaps in these days with you, we can form our own council, share our various reflections, to bring me closer to the fullness of the rite. Intellectually, I know its power, but I have yet to experience the deepest journey into my heart's eye."

"Amphito, who led us, personifies what I want to become," Pen said. "Soon, I shall go to her to complete my spiritual quest."

"Ah, Pen," Kti said, "you make me even hungrier to start our journey into the mountains. We hope Amphito will agree that we cast into writing the rituals of the Mother. When we settle on Samos Island, I want to spend my time with that project, but having the blessing of most of the Sibyls helps. Pythia of Parnassus has agreed to my writing them as so many have distorted them into public spectacle."

"We hope Amphito will join Gaetha, Pythia, and Cesme in

agreeing," said Eumaios.

With a wry twist of her lips, Kti shook her head. "We know the danger of written rites taking on rigidity to prevent them from resonating in the ages to come. Speaking the rituals keeps them alive to deeper thinking, reflecting, and knowing. Still the Mother never condoned the distortions now practiced."

In the days that followed, the four internalized their knowledge of the sacred ritual. They grew in using it in everyday actions.

On the last evening of her visit, Helen took a small pouch from her travel bag. "Kti, Menelaos and I presented you and Eury two golden chests. One had items to fulfill earthly desire. In the other, the figures reminded you of the stages of gaining spiritual needs. I know you have used them well. I give you and Eumaios additional trifles for the ruby crested chest. For the emerald crested chest, I give you another figure. She represents Gaia who presides as the unity behind all other manifestations of the Mother."

Kti stared at the small figure, eyes wide. "What stone has such sparking depth?"

"Formed from a stone that came from the Mother house at Siwa in the deserts of Afrik, she has origins deeper into the earth much farther south. When our craft center split the stone to achieve the proportion of the other three in your chest, I asked our artisans to fashion this figure to enjoy a place on the small pedestal above the central figure. When light shines upon it, the figure beams all of the colors to remind us that all colors collect within Gaia to shine forth enlightenment."

"How did you find it?"

"Pharaoh's holy women, not long ago, when I returned to

them, took me to Siwa, the most ancient center I have visited. I found it there."

"What a trip that must have been," Eumaios said while he handled the small figue.

"They tell me, though, that deeper into Afrik other centers, more ancient, keep the Way alive. Perhaps one day we shall know."

Helen turned to Kti. "And, Kti, I release you from your oath to keep secret my whereabouts during the skirmish at Truva. You must tell the true story. No parties live who might be hurt by Hektor's and my decision to send a substitute with Paris while I remained in the Pharaoh's sanctuary."

Kti nodded, then she and Eumaios thanked Helen for her thoughtful gifts.

"I shall see that my history gives a faithful rendering of your sojourn in Egypt, Helen. I wonder if you might come to Samos Island one day soon after the unrest settles in your land. We can travel to the mainland to see Iphigenia. I understand she has moved from the Artemision to Tauros, although some say she resides in Bauros.

Helen smiled enigmatically at the mention of her daughter, a love child with her chieftain. "What a good idea, "she said, "but I might see her father before I see her."

All turned to her, mouths agape.

"I have had an emissary from him from Athens. He has become their current Theseus, as they call their rulers after the first Theseus who so long ago subdued Krete on behalf of the Athenians. His birthright made him ancestral heir through the Troezen line of his mother's people. He has asked me to join him in Athens as his queen. He promises aid against the hordes that surround my palace in Sparta. What do you think of that?"

"Well, well," Kti said, "you two certainly matched well those many years ago at Eleusis."

"If I go there, I will see that their cultural center gathers accurate records of the tellers' stories. I shall make Athens a safe place for a library of the tellers' lore. Kti, your history belongs here."

"Not a bad idea." Kti tilted her head. "After all, Kephalos, Father's founding ancestor, had origins in Athens of those earlier days when the small village first paid tribute to the Kretans for the accidental death of the Minos' eldest son. Kephalos brought to the western wilds his Kretan bride, Prokris, who had found her way to Athens when the Kretan empire collapsed."

"If Athens becomes my home, I shall begin the collection," Helen said.

"I understand the value of such a center as a gathering place for historys of all of our people," Kti said.

Helen left amidst many wishes for her future happiness. Her laughter echoed throughout the valley as she disappeared into the mist. Soon she would see Orestes, her dear nephew, and her own Hermione, his wife.

"Who knows what Helen will do next!" Pen, Kti, and Eumaios spoke in chorus, their own laughter following Helen through the valley toward Mycenae.

Ascend the mountain. Gather your star stuff.

CHAPTER FORTY-SEVEN

In late autumn while the sun still warmed the day to erase the chill of night, Mount Kyllene, highest peak of Nonakris, beckoned Kti and Eumaios. Kti preceded their farewell by saying, "Pen, we shall return for the harvest rites. No winter snows come yet to great Kyllene. We can reach Amphito at the top, visit with her, then descend to the safer hillside for a night's rest before returning to you in three or four days."

After strapping supplies and rolled warm blankets to their backs, Kti embraced her dear friend. "Pen, we know you remain concerned about this journey. I remember your telling of Ody's unsettled state when he returned from Mount Kyllene, but Pen, we can meet the twists of our mental states as well as the ardor of the journey. Besides, the weather should welcome us for days to come."

"I know," Pen said, the drawing out of her words betraying her concern. "Still, do take care. I have told you of Amphito's wisdom. Her insights will penetrate to your inner core. She deeply affected me at Hera's Argive shrine. She brought something fresh to my heart. She gave me inner peace, even joy, for the first time since Ody's death. She freed me to enter my last phase here with certitude."

Final embraces saw the couple on their way.

They traveled through the valley of swift-flowing Styx, climbed the sloping hillsides, and ascended Kyllene. Before darkness, they found Artemis' sacred grove, surrounded a singular hut. Before the hut, an ancient woman sat beside a glowing fire.

Kti thought she slept, but before they could greet her, she spoke. "Daughter Kallisto, I have been expecting you and your Jamin."

Eyes wide, Kti turned to Eumaios and whispered, "No one knows the name I gave you in the naming ceremony so long ago, or so I thought."

Kti acknowledged Amphito's greeting. "I was named Kallisto after my ancient ancestor; now I am called Ktimene. When ancient Kallisto disappeared in these mountains, her parents cared for her son Arkos, whom they found wandering near the bear caves. Those who ruled after Arkos called this land Arkadia to honor him. Alas, they did not find Kallisto although they searched for her. Her disappearance remains a mystery."

Amphito raised her bony hand. "I know all of that, child, as well as your lineage and progeny. No need to do the customary recitation. I see your life clearly as well as that of your mate. Come closer. Sit." Thus, began Amphito's oracular teachings.

Eumaios and Kti sat at her feet for many hours. She related the deeper meaning of the rites, enriching each as she spoke. She spoke of the destiny of all the children, ending with that of Ktimaios of Ortygia. She unfolded the life of Kallisto, daughter of Kleia, beyond her life at Pronni citadel on Kephallenia Island.

For a day they listened to Amphito, until she ended their visit with strange words. "The web of your lives now enters another realm."

"Yes," Kti said, "we go to the shrine women of Samos Island to assist them in their work—"

"Do not misunderstand me. They do their work. You do yours," said Amphito with impatience.

Trying again to reach her meaning, Kti said, "We benefit greatly from the last ritual we received, the one our cousin Penelope told us you pronounced last year that placed her at the table of the Council of Elders at Hera's Argive shrine. During our recent visit with her and cousin Helen and now, with you, we have strengthened our grasp of the ritual. For all your words of wisdom, we thank you."

Amphito gave her half a smile. "Our words give insight, yes, but Penelope and Helen find their own way to the stars. The shrine women in many parts of the world and the many matrons who preserve the Way in their households find their paths. Your work belongs to you."

"Tell us more of why you summon us," Kti said. "Guide our next steps."

"Kallisto and Jamin, your journeys brought you here to me. Now, go on the trail you just traversed to the sacred cave below. If you do not find it, you will wander until at last you ascend again to search it out. Otherwise you descend into darkness, into Persephone's realm for great trials."

With that, Amphito waved them away.

"What cave? We saw no cave along the trail."

"You have eyes to see," Amphito said as she plunged into an inner journey, no longer reachable.

Her haunting words sent them on their way. They left her their last offerings of cakes made from newly ground wheat, honey fresh from the hive, and wine from the first squeezes of grape.

Baffled by her words, in silence Kti and Eumaios spread lunch in a bower farther down the mountain. Around them, among stately firs, almond trees stood naked, their limbs stripped of leaves by the late fall winds. Soon they began their descent.

"We must attend carefully the upcoming passage," Kti said, "through the most dangerous point of our descent."

"Hug the mountain," Eumaios said, "otherwise we will plunge downward to certain death, the Styx below washing us away."

"Ah, a safe place to rest," Kti said as they moved under a mossy overhang above the trail.

A great crashing sound roared above them. First, small rocks, then, massive boulders careened over their heads to send a second avalanche of large stones. Loud cracking sounds warned them that the overhang that protected them shirred off to join the other boulders.

Eumaios, in an effort to move them both closer to the mountain's wall, lost his footing. Kti grabbed his hand. They stepped inward as the mountain ledge disappeared. Falling rocks echoed below. After a time, stillness returned to the mountain.

Before Kti could orient herself to her surroundings, one more thunderous avalanche plunged them into cavernous darkness.

Star touches star. Sky and earth converge.

Chapter Forty-Eight

Kti and Eumaios, both conscious after their inward plunge, checked their condition. The bone of Eumaios's right ankle had ripped through his skin. Outstretched to regain balance when Eumaios moved them inward to the mountain wall, the leg endured the buffets of many boulders. His bruises and cuts would heal.

"I must attend your leg right away," Kti said.

She touched her pouch, glad it remained at her side. The other hand felt a flat rock floor beneath them, not a precipice. She grasped Eumaios' body around the waist, tumbling with him deeper into the cavern. Their packs full of their supplies and blankets fell with them.

A small opening furnished light from outside. She found their travel torches. With flint, she added torchlight to the natural light. She lit a fire from hastily gathered twigs and heavy limbs placed in a stone circle she formed. The fire gave warmth, with a place to prepare for setting the bone. Her heart gladdened to see their water pouches hanging compactly against their bodies.

"I find myself unharmed, ready to tend your wound. We shall make this shelter a healing place for you. Rest, if you can, dearest, until I am ready."

With practiced motions, Kti gathered healing tools from her pouch. She lay nearby strips of cloth from her inner garment, a cover from her cloak, and straight limbs to form a splint. She worked with speed and efficiency. To ease pain, she administered to Eumaios a potion from her herb pouch.

"Prepare to withstand the pain," she warned, then snapped the bone in place. She closed the wound, wrapped it, and applied the bracing tree limbs. Eumaios lost consciousness, the potion she had administered giving him relief.

While Eumaios slept, Kti explored the cave. She found well-preserved ochre, ash, and charcoal wall drawings. She read the art as best she could.

One striking drawing showed a man and a woman, hands joined, at the opening of a mountain cave. In the next, the man, a bow with arrows quivered, carried a stag around his shoulders. He leaned over a woman who lay on a slab with a small human figure separating from her body. An imprint of a bear appeared on the babe's small chest.

In the next drawing, the woman held the small infant close to her, the child's head bending toward her breast to receive nurturing milk. The last one depicted the woman lying inert, her image regally garbed. She held in her clasped hands a sprig of yew, the tree of death. The man knelt at her side, tears, much like leaves, flowing from his eyes.

Kti gasped to see such detail in the drawings.

Then she looked to the floor below the cave drawing. A stone slab, an apparent cover, protected whatever lay below. Kti cleared away silt that had drifted from the ceiling of the cave and lifted the slab to find a fragile skeleton.

Could this be the birthing cave of Arkos, the son of my ancestor, Kallisto, the home of the couple, and finally, the burial cave of Kallisto?

She uttered a prayer to Mother Gaia on behalf of the person who lay before her, placed there with loving care.

At that moment the earth shook. More boulders rumbled down the mountain. Some blocked the cave's mouth.

A blessing as well as a curse, she thought.

The barrier would shut out some of the night chill while it blocked the sunlight of the day.

An injured Eumaios would face the greater challenge of climbing out of the cave when he could travel. Most of all, the boulders would muffle their cries to guide rescuers who would surely come.

Eumaios stirred little the first day. When he did, she had food ready for him. She apportioned their supplies. To ease his mind, she said, "We have food for several days. Do not worry. Now take more of this healing potion so you can sleep."

Eumaios closed his eyes tight. "Ah, Kti, I blame myself for this whole debacle."

"You should take no blame for nature's tricks."

She diverted him with an account of their incredible surroundings. Then as drowsiness overcame him once again, she said, "We find ourselves exactly where we belong. Here. Now."

Then she added, "Sleep, dear one, let yourself heal."

Again, as Eumaios slept, Kti moved about the cave, a torch with a long burning punt in her hand. She found a skeleton of a man near the woman's slab. Dressed as a hunter, he appeared to have placed his body with forethought. She saw no evidence of a small child's bones. She knew to use her torches sparingly.

Still, she must know her surroundings.

Eumaios awoke again, calmer in spirit. She described her discoveries: the two skeletons and the schema on the walls of the cave. "If this is not the birthing cave where Kallisto brought forth Arkos, surely here a man and a woman with child tarried until disaster struck. I have found a large chart that traces ancestors from places I cannot fully decode, but most interesting, I found what I believe to be Kallisto's name. I have found symbols for a name next to hers. It is—"

"Jamin," he said. "Ever since Amphito uttered the name, I have been haunted by many memories of my being called Jamin as a boy, but more to the point, I remember sitting at Ortygia's court listening to a teller recount a tale that links the name to an ancestor, a woman, a freed slave who became the beloved of our most revered ancestor. She came from a land mass far away in the East."

Taking a deep breathe, he stopped for a moment. Then with an astonished tone, he continued. "I hear it now. I do not believe it. I only half listened to the tale in the dream, but now the lines come clearly to me."

"What are the words?"

"The teller spoke in a woman's voice: 'I was separated from parents who brought their people to a distant land from their farmlands and sloping hills where we tended herds, farmed, and traded. We traveled to the new land for a safe haven from the fierce brothers of my father, Jamin. My father, the youngest brother, instilled jealousy in his brothers because his father favored him. The brothers, save for Father, rigidly followed one god. My parents, who practiced the religion of the Great Mother, opened our home to all religions. My mother, a treasured princess, led her tribe. Father's brothers took the lands near ours that came as Mother's dowry. Rather than bend to his brothers' ways, Father accompanied Mother and her people in search of new lands. We settled in a vast landlocked valley surrounded by mountains. One day, my brother disappeared on a hunting foray. In search of him, I strayed from the family. Captured by slave traders, I found myself sold into the household of this court. I never saw my family again.' Those details of the teller's account of my ancestor, I hear most clearly."

Eumaios added, "Why had I not linked this story with your own and Kallisto's disappearance, along with that of Laertes' Seleme and her Levantine family. These connections of the sister to me and the brother to you ring true. Our union, it seems, reconnects our family roots, Kti."

Kti gazed into her spouse's eyes. "My dear, if what you say did not make such good sense, I would believe you are under Amphito's spell."

Eumaios took in a deep breath. "I see clearly, my love."

"I know you do, for so do I. I shall take out a scroll and write a bit of history while you sleep," Kti said. "Rest is healing. We must travel soon to share our discovery."

PART TEN

KTIMENE

Complete.

CHAPTER FORTY-NINE

The next morning after their small breakfast, Kti gazed at the wall. "I must add to the family lines. During your healing days, I shall busy myself with that task. Then I shall scroll the rituals of the Mother. With Amphito's agreeing, we now have the blessings of four Sibyls. The scrolls, ever with me, await my words. I know the Great Gaia will guide me as I scribe."

Through a sleepy haze, Eumaios said, "I am glad the scrolls tumbled into the cave with us."

"I am amazed how far Seleme's people, surely ancestors of both of us, traveled across the inner sea," Kti said.

"Yes, my love, Eumaios said, his voice growing weaker, "they formed our family lines, no question.

Kti turned to practical matters. "Our food and water will last seven days. In my explorations outside the cave, I added to the firewood, surveyed how to move off the ledge, and gathered more berries, seeds, nuts, and herbs from the mountains."

Eumaios nodded.

"When you are able to move," she said, "we can maneuver down the trail. Now you must complete your healing."

"If the good weather holds until I am able, we shall leave

before the seventh day."

"Yes, by then, a search party will come to assist in the descent."

While Eumaios slept, Kti used the ochre, ash, and charcoal that created the drawings so long ago. She added color of the berries she harvested to enrich the mix. She added the male and female lines from Jamin and Kallisto to Arkos and his mate through to their own Arkos, Neaira, Kleia, Laertes, Ktimaios, and to their children. She included Eury and his family, and Conn and the two dear star children she and Conn lost. She filled out the line of her father, Laertes, from Kephalos and Prokris.

Once Eumaios awakened, he added to his line. She drew new branches for both Helen and Pen. The web spread far across the wall. At the end of the third day, she gazed at the record. The center of the web, where Jamin and Kallisto resided, two bears appeared to imitate the constellations. The other generations flowed from them.

This earthly family imprints the stars of the heavenly constellations, our sparkling star yard.

Late on the third day, when she changed Eumaios' bandages, she choked down a gasp, trying not to show distress. Red streaks climbed Eumaios' leg. She did not have the potent herbs to fight the infection or the tools for amputation. They would have to let the infection take its course to a certain end.

Eumaios saw the lines and gave a slight nod.

They savored the moments of their lives, their dreams, and their hopes. "We thank the Great Mother for such rich blessings," they chorused to end the death ritual. On the sixth day, eased by herbs that allowed him to drift to peaceful sleep,

Eumaios died.

Alone Kti made her plans. First, she gave Eumaios the burial rites they had delivered so many times to others. Afterward, she placed his cupped body at the opening of the cave to prevent contaminating her space.

She wept and groaned at moving him. She protected him from predators and left the body ready to carry from the mountain for a proper burning, then burial in the family tomb.

She wondered about descending from the mountain to Pen or ascending it to seek Amphito. When she tested the trail, she found it blocked on both sides. *Otherwise help would have come already.*

She reapportioned her supplies, foraged for food, and brought more twigs and limbs to dry for her fire. *Winter will come soon. I must prepare.*

After completing successful scavenges, she turned to scripting. For days she wrote on the tiny traveling scrolls. She completed, at last, as best she could, texts of the history and the rituals of the Mother.

To the last ritual, the one she so recently received at Parnassus that gave her peerage in the Council of Elders, she added some turns that reflected the visit with Amphito and her rich discussions with Eumaios, Pen, and Helen. The words of the rituals flowed unhampered, ink and instrument cooperating with her swift-moving hand. *Surely Gaia has blessed my work to give my words wings.*

Kti lost track of days until the first snow came to increase her water supply.

The winter solstice approaches, she thought one dreamy day.

She had marked each day. Soon she must face her death.

She ate and drank sparingly the little remaining in the cave. Still she counted each bite with each drink, a feast that honored the Mother.

To fend off numbness, she often stomped her feet, rotating them in great circles as she did her hands and fingers. Fierce winds came. Snowdrifts mounted outside the cave. She collected water that dripped from icy formation during rare sunshine. The ice, a blessing, formed a barrier to fend off the wind.

She turned to her dear Eumaios, whose body, now encased in a sheet of ice, lay frozen in the position of a new born babe, just as she placed him. On the night of the solstice, the full moon lit the cave from its icy portal. Kti, for warmth and comfort, cupped herself in Eumaios' curved body. Never since his death had she done this, but on this night, she knew she must.

Kti's dreamlike sleep in the arms of her beloved brought her a vision of her cave drawings now completed. Each family name, connected by lines, turned into a star, or so it seemed. She followed a moonbeam to the inscription of their own name, "Eumaios" and "Ktimene." She saw her added notation of "Jamin"—a name she had given her loving spouse so long ago, but now knew belonged to him in his childhood and to his ancestor, indeed her ancestor. She saw "Kallisto" with her own Ktimene.

"It is complete," she said, or thought she did. Then she settled into a deep sleep, nested in the bends of the body of the dear man who for all those years had protected her, strengthened her, and drew her closer to the Mother.

She whispered, "Oh, my Eumaios, oh, my Jamin."

Solstice day brought the beaming sun into the cave. She stirred. Eumaios stirred.

The beam drew them both from the cave. They moved upward, on the beam of the light, gaining strength. As they looked back, great stones once again tumbled down the mountain. Walls of snow and ice traveled with the boulders. The entry of the cave, again curtained, disappeared behind a newly formed wall of stones.

Only a ridge remained. There, two bodies slept in a great embrace.

Their eyes shone. Hand in hand, along the sunbeam, with abandon, they danced to the rhythm of the skies. They moved across the sky from brightness to brightness that dotted the darkened spaces. On and on they danced among the stars of all the constellations.

At last, they took their place within the orbit of the great and small bears, those beacons of comfort that had directed travelers along the sea routes. Kti, Kallisto once again, saw star points of her many ancestors imprinted in the sky much as they were on the wall of the cave. Eumaios, now Jamin, sent her glimpses filled with love. Infant star stuff, they danced in a continuous spiral among their welcoming ancestors. Finally, they held their places side by side, at one with the universe.

EPILOGUE

On the evening she expected Kti and Eumaios, Pen sent runners up the trail to meet them. They reported no sighting of the couple. They discovered, instead, an avalanche at the narrow gap on the trail below where Ody had told her he nearly plunged to his death. Pen could not bear to believe the sheer drop above that point had claimed Kti and Eumaios.

For days, the runners checked the area. Additional avalanches blocked the trail nearer the citadel. They searched the ravines within their reach and skirted the stony barriers of the avalanches to reach Amphito's hut. There, they found a cold firestone and no sign of life.

On an excursion to the northern rim of Pelops, the runners found Amphito on the warmer side of the mountain where she spent the winter west of Korinth. She offered little help, but muttered from a trance, "The stony trail."

They thought she said, "The cave."

Maybe Kti and Eumaios had found shelter along the path, but no one remembered a cave. The runners went as far as they could down the trail until more avalanches blocked the path. They traveled home a safer way.

Blizzards came. Their search stopped until spring thaw.

A slow and arduous task, they cleared the boulders and debris. Before the freeze had released the whole mountain, they found Kti's and Eumaios' frozen bodies huddled together on the narrowest point of the path. Kti's hand clasped Eumaios's hand. Both huddled in their cloaks and blankets.

Clearly Eumaios had been injured. Kti, they discovered, administered to him as best she could. They found no evidence of their supplies or other objects they had carried with them, save the pouch that Kti always kept at her side.

Pen and Helen honored the couple, placing them on a massive funeral pyre to assure their bodies reached the staryard. They knew deep down they had already joined the ancestors.

Some days later, they pronounced the Mother rites with Amphito, who came to them from the mountains with holy men and women devoted to Artemis. Amphito assured them that Kti and Eumaios completed their life's work. "They move to a rhythm beyond our understanding," she said.

A small party took their ashes and bones to Pronni where the children with their families and many others came to place them in the family tomb.

Pen's Telemakhos, with Polykaste, and Orestes, with Helen's Hermione, joined Helen and Pen at Pronni. The great feast lasted for many days.

Traders spread the news of their deaths. Tribal leaders and shrine women came from Dodona, Parnassus, Lusi, Samos, Argos, and Troezen. Others traveled from the far away Artemision, the Pharaoh's temples, Tauros, and Siwa. Only Arkos could not join Neaira, Kleia, Laertes, and Ktimaios and their families.

Months later, Arkos, Ling, and the twins came. He moved his father's bones nearer to the couple's bones. He noted that Kleia had placed Conn's bones closer. No one knew Kti had placed in her pouch small bones of her ancestors from the sacred cave. Now they mixed with the others in the tomb, the pouch with its contents remaining at Kti's side.

When Helen and Pen examined the pouch, Helen found the four figures of the Mother. "They kept Kti strong during her final days," she said.

The blood of each child of Kti, true to her prophetic naming so many years earlier at Parnassus, flowed into the veins of high kings of Ireland, the ruling houses of China, the rulers of established houses of Canaan and the territories surrounding it, the Island kingdom that became Sicily, and the ranking families of the Greek mainland and many islands. Tracing these bloodlines requires many accounts beyond the tale told here.

To this day, no one has discovered the scrolls.

AFTERWORD

Bronze Age writings abound. They come from archaeological, historical, linguistic, mythological, and critical researchers and poets and fiction writers. Why another volume, then, set in the Bronze Age?

Some time ago an ancient woman entered my life. She jumped off the page of the ODYSSEY, one of the most familiar epic poems of any age. She lives in six lines crafted around 750 BCE. The school of writers or a writer many call Homer wrote the lines from the words of the oral tales of earlier ages. We do not know if this woman was always present in the oral recitations, nor do we know how she received her name in the epic.

One classics scholar told me she was likely a formulaic nicety that helped the teller remember lines. Another told me that her name could mean "founder of civilizations." He suggested that I should retire immediately and write a novel to tell her story.

I heeded the latter, but not right away. She is present in the same lines of all extant accounts I have seen. Below, she comes to life in the *ODYSSEY* Book 15, lines 333-338, of the translation of Robert Fitzgerald:

> For she had brought me up with her own daughter
> Princess Ktimene, her youngest child.
> We were alike in age and nursed as equals
> Nearly, till in the flower of years
> They gave her, married her to a Samian prince,

Taking his many gifts.

Eumaios, the swineherd, speaks these words when Odysseus, in disguise, tests Eumaios's loyalty and gauges what is happening at his Ithacan palace from which he has been absent for twenty years fighting on the plains of Troy and making his way home. No other mention of Princess Ktimene, sister of Odysseus, appears in the epic.

Soon, I began my quest to find Princess Ktimene in other ancient manuscripts or in other types of records found in the Mediterranean area. Little appeared in any extant record that has come down to us. She filled a space for the most part on compiled family trees. Some modern writers discovered her and gave her brief voice to comment on or praise her famous brother. What I could not find affirmed that such a woman needed a story and that her story should depict what might have been the experiences of a woman who lived and functioned as the daughter of a ruler on a remote island in the late Bronze Age.

From mid-1200 BCE to the beginning of the next century BCE—the time and place of the novel—the world around the Mediterranean Sea and beyond witnessed transitions in its customs and its governance. Ktimene's ancestors, who had migrated from the East by choice or by force, had gone through social, political, ecological, and economic changes.

Later to their settled lands came warrior cultures to populate places already the home of the network of tribal families to which Ktimene belonged. We call the region today the Peloponnese after Pelops, legendary founder of the Myceneans, the major tribe of the area in that time. The Mycenean warriors joined other warrior cultures, such as the ones developing in Corinth, Thebes, and Athens. As winners, these tribes slanted in their favor the lore that comes to us today in epic form.

One can glean the story of the earlier people only between the lines of the epics. The differing ways of worship give a good example of sorting the views of earlier settlers from the latter. The warrior cultures brought with them the Sky God religion of Zeus and placed him and his entourage on Mount Olympus. They incorporated into their system the local deities to suit their needs and their penchant to control people.

The Olympians competed mostly with Gaia, the Great Mother, whose forms at local shrines represented aspects of her nature mainly as Aphrodite, Artemis, Athena, Hera, and Demeter. These deities migrated with the earlier tribes and blended with existent nature cults of indigenous people or of some of the migrants.

Hence the followers of the Great Mother honored the bear, the hawk, the eagle, and the dove, along with other creatures. They also found meaning in the flora of the region or in the things they saw in the sky or sea. In their attempt to disrupt the shrine worshippers, the warriors threw the mythic structures into chaos.

Other differences in the cultures are instructive. The earlier tribes may have migrated as their eastern trading economies and agrarian settlements grew too large for the home territory to support. They were pioneers with a frontier spirit, living beyond the boundaries of customs they left behind, or they adjusted customs that I reflect in their rituals of birthing and naming, their inheritance and leadership systems, and their death rituals. The warriors who invaded later set forth inheritance and leadership protocols that favored the Mycenean male, as opposed to the prior ones that contained matrilineal, matrilocal, or egalitarian elements. The Myceneans gained their land mostly by force instead of by tribal migration, the primary method of the more peaceful, agrarian people in the record.

Soon the Myceneans brought captured peoples from Crete and from the widespread ports of call of their traders, turning the Peloponnese into a rich melting pot. They often built alliances through arranged marriages among powerful families and allowed the practices of diverse religious and political customs. The culture slowly shifted to the warriors' ways.

Ktimene would have been among those who subscribed to the waning systems; thus, I depict her as trying to preserve what she could.

In my story, the pulls between the old and new disrupt the more peaceful ways of the shrine women of the Great Mother. Migrations become even more intense in the unsettled times. Some tried to enter the Black Sea for trade, but the settlement called Truva, or Troy, blocked the traders. The attempt to subdue the Trojans, often called the Trojan War, and the ongoing disruption of populations form a backdrop for Ktimene's story.

The themes of transition, disruption, connecting alliances, and maintaining and building personal and social relationships among diverse peoples inform the lore of the time and the fabric of my story.

I take a stand on several controversial issues debated among scholars to this day. I contend the Great Mother shrines functioned and influenced matters into the time of the novel, even though the Olympian religion asserted more and more mandates for change. I believe the shrine centers communicated with one another and remained quite vibrant in their practices. I keep the inheritance, social, and governance struggles more in flux between patrilineal and matrilineal systems than do most scholars of this time. I recognize, however, that in different places the patriarchy dominated for many centuries before the time depicted in the novel.

I opt for a broad and sophisticated trading system that extends beyond the Mediterranean to the East and to the West instead of a localized, restricted one. I believe that refugees and exiles proliferated and disrupted the more peaceful areas and that slave trade escalated. I contend that the earliest oral traditions, crafting chores, and religious rituals belonged to the women. I agree with many modern climatologists that famine, earthquakes, and other natural disasters added to the turmoil.

The frontier survivors, among whom I count my heroine, kept cool heads and held deep spiritual convictions of their more settled shrine religions and tried to live peacefully with the religion of the Olympians. Into such an era Ktimene found her way to her own star. The star image is mostly my own invention, but it rests easily in a time when navigating the waters by stars would suggest the echoes on earth of the sky patterns.

Tellers who entertained in the citadels of the Myceneans kept stories alive. Their legends, with mythic overlays and multiple versions as time passed, inform the basic story line of my novel. I shine a light on anachronisms of later tellers who conflated times or used the legends for their own purposes. I found that implied meanings can be guessed by examining the gleanings from writers in the Homeric tradition as well as from accounts found in Herodotus, Pausanias, Plutarch, Strabo, and many others closer to Ktimene's era. I present next an approximate timeline of my heroine's life and a glossary to help with the characters and places. The glossary and the text of the novel use some Greek spellings; however, I have modernized many spellings and meanings.

Ktimene grew up on Kephallenia, an island on the western fringe of a changing world. Frontier people—edge dwellers, as I think of them—enjoy pushing the limits even while they maintain a strong sense of justice with a perspective to judge what to keep and what to discard in a changing world. They never fear change. They live well in the present moment. They know how to survive.

Ktimene's people withstood buffets of change as they often did not receive the first blows. Instead, the blows came to those on the front lines. My story shows how one woman lived and thrived in such a tumultuous setting and time.

GLOSSARY*

AND

TIMELINE

A

Admetus: (1) daughter of Peloponnesian ruler, Eurystheus; before the time of the novel, teacher at the Artemision, a center in the Near East, only a column of which remains today near Ephesus; (2) (invented) leader at the Artemision.

Aegeus: Athenian ruler who sent his heir Theseus to subdue the Kretan Minotaur, later to plunge to his death into the sea that bears his name when black sails signaled defeat although Theseus succeeded; refuge giver to Theban Oedipus and Corinthian Medea.

Aenos: mountain located between Pronni and Sami on the Island of Kephallenia where tall pines grow for shipbuilding.

Aethra: Troezen shrine teacher/queen mother of Theseus, heir to Athenian Aegeus; Troezen mother (invented) of the chieftain father of Helen's child who rules Athens late in the novel as another Theseus (invented).

Agamemnon: son of Atreus; ruler at Mycenae; brother of Menelaos; husband of Klytemnestra; father of Iphegenia (some say) as well as Khrysothemis, Elektra and Orestes; commander that topples Truva who returned to be killed by Aigisthos, or Klytemnestra or both.

Aglaia (invented): shrine teacher of Hera at the Heraion on Samos Island with whom Ktimene attends a conclave at the Artemision.

Aglaeus (invented): husband of Penthenia; uncle to Ktimene and Eurylokhos through different family lines; manager on Samos Island of the family trade.

Aigisthos: Mycenaean heir of Thyestes, head of the out-of-power line of Pelops; ruler of Mycenae after he murders Agamemnon and claims Klytemnestra; victim of Orestes, son of Agamemnon and Klytemnestra who, for revenge, murders him and Klytemnestra.

Akhaians: aggregate name for troops that accompany Agamemnon to regain Helen at Truva (Troy).

Akhilleus: son of Pythian ruler, Peleus, and the nymph, Thetis; Myrmidon leader at Truva; avenger of death of Patroklus by killing Hektor whose body he returns to suppliant Priam, Truvan ruler/father of Hektor; chooser of short hero's life instead of long-life oblivion.

Amphito: (invented, a Sibyl by that name is mentioned in the lore): Sibyl residing at Lusi at the shrine of Artemis in northern Peloponnese.

Andrite: (invented), Leader of the Canaanites before her daughter, Seleme (invented)

Antikleia: child of Neaira and Autolykos whose lineages connect her with Arkadia and Parnassus; wife of Laertes with whom she rules at Pronni on Kephallenia Island; mother of the heroine Kallisto/Ktimene, Arkos (invented), and Odysseus.

Antipe: (invented), mother of Eurylokhos, who marries Ktimene, and Erato (invented), who is a friend of Ktimene, and inheriter of Sami.

Aphrodite: Near Eastern primal mother of fertility and love; Olympian goddess trivialized as wanton daughterr of Zeus; most beautiful in the "Golden Apple" myth for which she gives Truvan Prince Paris Spartan Helen as prize; emblem holder of the scallop shell, myrtle, dove, girdle, mirror, and swan.

Apollo: Olympian son of Zeus who evolves from Near Eastern sun gods and who enters Zeus' Olympians as sister of Artemis; patron to prophets, musicians and poets; claimant of Delphi and other centers once belonging to goddesses; emblem holder of the lyre, laurel crown, hawk, raven, and fawn.

Ares: warlike god of Thrace incorporated into the Olympian system; lover of Aphrodite (some say husband); with his sister, Eris, a stirrer of conflict; emblem holder of spear and sword.

Argonauts: Mythical sailors who went into the Black Sea to Kalkis to take the golden fleece (to conquer a northern trading port), the myth growing over time to include most famous heroes of the Bronze Age and beyond, as well as the Olympian/classical version of the Medea story; their ship was said to be designed, built, and navigated by Laertes' ancestors from Samos Island (some attaching it to Ktimene's father).

Argos: major city in the Peloponnese eclipsed by Mycenae; ancient site of major shrine of Hera.

Ariadne: daughter of the Kretan Minos who, in her main myth from the Zeus tradition, for love helped Theseus subdue her brother, the Minotaur, a factor in the Minoan fall; also depicted as abandoned by Theseus or left, at her request, on Naxos Island from which she traveled to the Near East to become a shrine teacher or, in later myths, to join Dionysus to be crowned his queen of the heavens.

Arkadia: Peloponnesian area named after Arkos, tribal ancestor of Ktimene; mythical place suggestive of a "golden age."

Arkos: (1) Kallisto's child reared by his grandparents to become leader of early tribes, later called Arkadians to honor him. (2) Ktimene's brother (invented) who died before the birth of Ktimene. (3)

(invented) Ktimene's son, Autolykos, named Arkos in manhood.

Artemis: Olympian huntress daughter of Zeus; assistant at births, one being Apollo, her twin; earlier, Near Eastern overseer of menses, childbirth, and midwifery who carried the sacred bough and silver bow; holder of emblems of date-palm, stag, bee, deer, wild goat, boar, and quail; before Zeus, honored goddess with shrines from Arkadia to the East's Artemision.

Artemision: major Near Eastern shrine of Artemis that pre-dates the Mycenaean age (Only one column remains today near the old city of Ephesus).

Ashkelon: trading city on Near Eastern western rim; key stop on Egyptian trading routes where caravans sell locally or ship west; touch point of shipwrecked Laertes, son of Ktimene, after escaping captors.

Ashtoreth (Asherah): Canaanite goddess of fertility related to Ishtar; holder of a lotus and a pair of serpents.

Astarte: Assyrian goddess of love and fertility related to Ishtar and Ashtoreth.

Athena (or Anatha, Sumarian Queen of Heaven): of Eastern roots, adopted daughter of Olympian Zeus who claims Athena as born of him alone not her mother Metis; patron of spinners, weavers, sculptors, builders, potters and protectors; wisdom keeper in centers on Krete, in the Peloponnese and at Athens, Izmir and Delphi; emblem holder of the olive tree, snake, and owl.

Athens: settlement on mainland Greece strengthened after warriors intermix with earlier settlers; later powerful center of trade and culture rivaling Sparta, but a village still in the novel.

Atreus: Mycenaean ruler at the expense of his brother, Thyestes, to cause strife among heirs; father of Mycenaean Agamemnon and Spartan Menelaos collectively called the "Atrides."

Atrides: See Atreus above.

Aulis: port of eastern Greece where fleets of Agamemnon depart, with favorable winds, to conquer Truva or to rescue Spartan Queen Helen.

Autolykos: husband of Neaira, his joint ruler at Parnassus; father of Antikleia; grandfather of Ktimene; mythic trickster and thief; claimer of Herakles as father.

B (Note: The Greeks use the V sound for B sound; thus, see Greek names and places under V.)

Baldar: Nordic God of the Valhalla System.

Benjamin: (invented, but in the Hebraic history, the youngest son of Jacob, son of Abraham), Family name of Jacob and Andrite , father of Seleme, who is the spouse of Ktimene's son Laertes.

Bridge: 1) A shrine figure in Gaelic lore; 2) daughter (invented) of Maeve/Kleia, (invented) and O'Conn (invented), name given to Kti by Kelts.

Byblos: trading port in the Near East thriving in the time of the novel.

C (Note: The Greeks use the hard K sound for C words; hence see Greek names and places under K

Canaanites: occupiers of Syria-Palestine, a region, mostly under Egypt's control in ancient times; home of hill tribes who follow Abraham and his one god and of other valley tribes, farmers and traders, who follow other religions.

Carians: tribe in the Eastern area that encompasses present-day Turkey and in Krete until a cataclysmic earthquake and tsunami helped diminish the culture, now called Minoans who were taken to the Peloponnese, returned to the East, or sought refuge in Kretan hills.

Celts (Kelts): tribes likely originating in the steppes of Eastern Europe, also called Kimmerians, Urnfield people, and Gauls; enterprising traders and explorers believed to enter the western seas and land rims as far west as Iberia and Ireland; later than the novel, settlers of northern Europe.

Cesme: (invented): member of a tribe whose ancestors migrated from Malta to the east, likely Sicily; tender of the stone temples of Malta who discovers Laertes (invented) after he jumps ship to go for help; grandmother of Menaja (invented) wife of Ktimaios (invented), child of Ktimene and Eumaios and king of Ortygia, now geographically the tip of Syracusa, Sicily, hence queen of Ortygia; Sibyl of Ortygia (invented).

Chieftain (invented): father of Helen's child, born while Helen studies at Eleusis; ruler of Athens named after first Theseus whose dates rule out his fatherhood of the child of Helen of the lore although most accounts suggest he is.

Clay Disc of Phaistos: not definitively translated disc housed in the Heraklion museum in Krete, but found in the ruins of Phaistos, a

Minoan palace in western Krete.

Conn (Konn) (invented): Keltic trader and explorer; captor of Ktimene, her twin children--Kleia and Laertes, and Freya, from Kephallenia; second spouse of Ktimene, the two entering into a sacred marriage; father of O'Conn (invented) by his first wife, victim of a tribal massacre.

Crete: See Krete.

D

Daedalus: wise Kretan inventor who created the labyrinth for the Minotaur; escapee of the wrath of Minos, with his son Ikarios, after assisting in the Minotaur's death to continue his inventive ways. See other accounts for his rich history.

Danites: Seleme's tribe of Canaanites that pre-dates the occupation of southern Canaan by the Hill people.

Dark Sea: name for the Black Sea, or Euxine Sea, a trading prize of the people who control its entry, in the time of the novel, the Truvans then the Akhaians.

Demeter: protector of agriculture, fertility and marriage with symbols of wheat sheaf, torch and sacrificial bowl; holder of Eleusis long after the Olympians who never fully integrate her; mother of Kore, or Persephone, whom Hades takes to the underworld causing Demeter to decay nature until the Olympians agree that Kore spend only the winter there.

Diomedes: Argive ruler of Tiryns who fights at Truva where he goes with Odysseus and Ktimene (in disguise) to the Truvan temple of

Athena to confirm Helen's absence or presence and to scout taking the Palladium, the image of Athena believed to give victory to the possessors.

Dione: Pelasgian-creation-myth Titan who with Krius forms one of seven pairs of divine creations of Eurynome; ruler over the planet Mars; loser of power to the Olympians; shrine holder at Dodona where Ktimene visits.

Dionysius: Of Near Eastern descent, Olympian son of Zeus and the mortal Semele whom Zeus saves when Hera tricks Semele into incineration; in some traditions, mate of Ariadne after she was left on Naxos Island; teacher of the vine culture; possessor of dualities of grace and madness, clarity and confusion, bliss and torment; representative of grapevines, bulls and ivy.

Dodona: religious center in northwestern mainland Greece that houses shrines of Titans, Dione and Themis, but that Zeus attempts without success to eclipse by trying to take Dione as consort until his followers move south; example of the power struggle between the Earth Mother religions and Olympians.

E (Note: In Greek, the symbol H stands for Eta, giving modern-day H words an E beginning and sound.)

Eileithia: A healing deity believed by some to be the originator of modern medicine; holder of the veil brought to Odysseus to save him from drowning when his raft capsizes, thus "spiriting" him to the island of the Phaecians, the last stop on his way home.

Elektra: Daughter of Klytemnestra and Agamemnon, sister of Orestes.
Eleni (Helen): goddess-like daughter of Spartan Leda and Tyndareus

known for her beauty and insight; Spartan cousin of Ktimene; spouse of Menelaos.

Eleusis (Elefsina): ancient shrine of Demeter that gave Athens status as it grew into a center of power at which time Eleusis moves from its dedication to the pre-Olympian Demeter to serving the Olympians.

Erato (muse of lyric poetry, love): 1. sister (invented) of Eurylokhos, Ktitmene's first husband; close friend of Ktimene; ruler at the neighboring citadel of Sami on Kephallenia Island. 2. Hera's shrine teacher (invented) with whom Ktimene goes to the Artemision.

Eumaios: loyal swineherd who tends the herds at Pronni and Ithaka whose name implies god-like service to earlier Earth Mother figures; taken from Ortygia, a young prince, who is sold to Antikleia and Laertes from whom he gains freedom after loyal service; third spouse of Ktimene.

Eurystheus: father of Admetus; heir to the Peloponnesian royal house; nemesis to Herakles.

Eurykleia: nurse to several generations of the family of Laertes and Antikleia.

Eurylokhos: prince of neighboring Sami next to Ktimene's Pronni; first spouse of Ktimene; Odysseus' main officer.

Eurynome: (invented): sister of Aigisthos; member of the Argive/ Kretan trading family that Ktimene and Eurylokhos visit on their way to Samos Island.

F

Fates: ancient arbiters of life--Klotho, Lakhesis, and Atropos—in the philosophical creation myth that says Darkness came first to unite with Chaos to form Night, Day, Erebus, and the Air, Night then forming, among others, the Fates.

Freya: Nordic consort of Od with implied earlier role as arbiter of love and fertility. Ktimene's household servant (invented), bought by Laertes after Freya's uncle sold her to a ship's captain when he saw her as a threat to a new inheritance system that supplants women's inheritance rights.

G

Gaia (Ge): oldest divinity, Mother of gods, wife of starry Heaven; progenitor of the earth and the human race from Chaos; giver of insight in incubating sleep and oracles; pre-Olympian goddess at Delphi whose cow symbol suggests Egyptian or Eastern roots.

Gaetha: Sibyl of Samos, shrine teacher and confidante of Ktimene.

Glaeus (invented): cousin to Ktimene and Eurylokhos; eldest son of Penthenia and Aglaeus; supervisor of the family trade from the largest port at Vathy on Samos Island.

Great Bear: constellation; sky domain of Kallisto, ancestor of the matrilineal line of Ktimene, who mothered Arkos, the little bear, uniting leader of tribes in the central region of the Peloponnese named after him "Arkadia."

Great Egg (Universal Egg): source of creation which Pelasgian myth of Palestine or Egypt says came into existence when Eurynome arose naked from chaos as undifferentiated androgyny and, lonely, danced with Boreas or the great serpent to hatch sun, moon, planets, stars, earth with its plants and creatures, the latter splitting into feminine and masculine for future creations.

H

Hades: Olympian ruler of the underworld, earlier Persephone's domain of renewal, whose cap of darkness, chariot, horse, and scepter reflect his nature. Olympian account of birth order of Hestia, Demeter, Hera, Hades, Poseidon and Zeus suggests a female integration of indigenous goddesses into Olympus.

Hekate: Near-Eastern wise elder of the dark of the moon who joins Artemis, waxing maiden, and Selene, matron, to form a tri-part goddess; leader of souls to the underworld for unbinding into transforming mystery; Olympian dark one whom humans placate with offerings at crossroads leaving Hermes to claim many of her traits.

Hektor: Truvan prince; son of Priam and Hekuba; husband of Andromake; father of Astynax; exemplary hero with the best traits of warriors; death receiver of Akhilleus who kills him to avenge Hektor's killing Patroklus; according to some, took Helen to Truva instead leaving her in Egypt.

Hekuba/Hecabe/Hecube: wife of Truvan King Priam; mother of Hektor, Paris, Kassandra and many other children; after the fall of Truva, slave of conquering Myceneans.

Helen (Eleni): See Eleni.

Helios: Titan sun god born to Hyperion and Thetis who with his multiple eyes sees and reports all he sees.

Hellas/Hellenes: The designation the Greeks prefer for their country/ people, since "Greek" was a late Turkish derogatory term.

Hephaistos: Olympian son of Hera and Zeus (or other lineages); smith-god designer of metallurgy including Akhilleus' armor and Olympian ornamentations; husband of Aphrodite who cuckolds him; keeper of fire, hammer, anvil, forge, and bellows.

Herakles: averter of ills, savior, healer, city protector; claimed by Dorians, Egyptians, Scythians, Tyrians, Phoinikians; ancestor of heirs who return to claim the Peloponnese; Olympian child of Alkmene, wife of Amphitryon, whose form Zeus takes to make her his last mortal conquest; assignee of labours by his ruler cousin, Eurestheus, when Hera foils Zeus's plan that Herakles rule, after Zeus promises that the first-born rule.

Hera: Olympian sister/wife of Zeus; avenger of Zeus's dalliances; pre-Mycenaean goddess at Argos, on Krete, on Samos Island, and in Thessaly; keeper of the veil, pomegranate, scepter, peacock, cuckoo (Zeus's wooing form), the seasons, life stages, and moon stages as well as of all nature, all life and all elements.

Hermes: trickster with winged sandals, brimmed hat, ram, and tortoise-shell lyre as symbols, Olympian god, earlier Egyptian Thoth, truth arbiter; son of Maia with Zeus; displacer of Hekate as underworld guardian; protector of travelers; patron of commerce and messengers.

Heraklion: trading center for Knossos, pre-Mycenean Minoan palace, which likely received its name from the people of Herakles.

Hermione: daughter of Helen and Menelaos; in some accounts, wife of Orestes who rules with him at Mycenae.

Hittites: tribe of the Near East that dominated its northern areas south of Anatolia.

I

Idomeneus: From Knossos on Krete Island, Athenian who led the conglomerate occupying Greeks in the time of the novel; leader of a fleet that sails with the Atrides to Truva.

Ikarios: (1) son of Daedalus, Kretan labyrinth designer; winged escapee with Daedalus who helps subdue the Minotaur; flier too high, the sun fatally melting his wings; likely worshipper of "Kar," the moon-goddess of Karian tribe. (2) father of Penelope, husband of Periboea likely of Karian origin; ruler in Arkadia who approves Penelope's marriage to Odysseus provided his daughter, Iphthime, stays nearby.

Ilium: another name for Truva (Troy) and its environs.

Iphigenia: daughter of Klytemnestra and Agamemnon or of Helen and an unknown chieftain; sacrificial victim when Apollos's diviner reads signs that the winds prevent sailing from Aulis to Truva or evader of sacrifice when a deer's sacrifice allows her escape to become a Near-Eastern priestess of Artemis.

Iphthime: sister of Penelope; daughter of Ikarios who remains near her home citadel; wife of a local chieftain.

Indus River: important boundary of the lands of the Far East.

Inanna: in the Near East, the Sumerian Great Mother figure; queen of heaven.

Ishtar: Mesopotamian Goddess of life, death, and rebirth, who in the

Assyro-Babylonian world became the deity of love, fertility, healing and war, often related to Ashtoreth and Astarte.

Isis: Egyptian Goddess of life, death, and rebirth who is worshipped out of Egypt even into the Roman times.

Ithaka: site of the palace and extensive lands of Odysseus and Penelope that some believe to be the present-day Ionian island of that name, but recently called into question as the western isthmus of Kephallenia (Smithsonian) or as Lefkada (Dorpfeld), etc.

J

Jacob: son of Abraham whose progeny lead the "Twelve Tribes of Israel;" worshipper of one god whose beliefs encompass the Near East, then the West, with perhaps five generations separating the tribes' spreading across the "world" and the time of the novel (1250 BCE).

Jamil (invented): son of Seleme and Laertes.

Jamin (invented): name Ktimene confers on Eumaios in a rite of adulthood; family name before, at the age of four, a Phoinikian serving girl kidnapping Eumaios from Ortygia to give in exchange for her passage home, the shipmaster, at the serving girl's sea death, selling him to Laertes.

Jason: recipient of several mythic accounts, this story using Jason's leading the Argonauts into the Dark Sea to capture the Golden Fleece, supplant a Dark Sea culture and open trade.

K (C)

Kallisto: 1. Pelasgian mythic mother of Arkos who establishes tribal land rights in Peloponnesian Arkadia; only daughter of Nonakris and

Lykaon; adept of Artemis who breaks her vow of chastity with Zeus or another to disappear, her son, Arkos, found in the hills; the Great Bear constellation. 2. (Invented) Ktimene's childhood name given to honor her ancestor. 3. (invented) Kleia's daughter, hence Ktimene's granddaughter, who inherits the citadel at Pronni.

Kalypso (covered or veiled): early form of the Great Mother that Olympians diminish to enchantress holder of Odysseus on her island of Oceanus to slow his return home.

Kassandra: daughter of Hekuba and Priam, rulers of Truva; receiver of the gift of prophecy from Apollo, but the curse of never being believed when she spurns him; priestess of pre-Olympian Athena whose deep insights make her a wisdom teacher.

Kastor: brother of Helen who takes her to Sparta after she gives birth at Eleusis.

Kentros (invented): trader and bringer of news who comes to the citadels of the Great Sea.

Kephallenia Island: island in the Ionian Sea off the western coast of Greece named after Athenian warrior, Kephalos, the head of the male line of Ktimene.

Kephalos: warrior when the Minoans fall to Athens (@1400 BCE, some say later); husband of Minoan "princess," Prokris; receiver, for military achievement, of an Ionian Island named after him Kephallenia where he, Prokris and four sons settle, the sons inheriting quadrants named after them Krani, Palli, Sami and Pronni, the latter, the land of Laertes, father of Ktimene.

Kios (Chios) Island: island off the west coast of present-day Turkey situated north of Samos Island, trading outpost of Kephallenian families; claimer of Homer as a famous inhabitant in the era @750 BCE when the oral tales of Ktimene's era @1250 BCE achieved written status.

Kirke (Circe): Olympian enchantress who waylays Odysseus' men to turn them into swine until Odysseus, resistant to her spells, frees them; assister of Odysseus's journey to and from the underworld where Teiresias foretells the future; a Great Mother form.

Klamakis (Invented): husband of Eurynome (invented), cousin of Klytemnestra and sister of Aigisthos; manager of Greek family trading in western Krete where he and his family inhabit the summer villa, Hagia Triada, formerly the retreat of the Minoan ruler at Phaistos.

Klytemnestra: Helen's step-sister, born of Tyndareus and a citadel woman (some say of Leda in an egg her husband fertilizes at the same time Zeus fertilizes the egg bearing Helen); wife of Agamemnon whom she purportedly murdered upon his victorious return from Truva to become wife of usurping Aigisthos, other versions saying she became his wife under duress; victim of vengeance of Orestes, her son, who murders her and Aigisthos.

Klio: muse of history; shrine teacher (invented) of Hera on Samos Island who befriends Ktimene.

Knossos: main palace of the Minoans that falls to Athenian Theseus, successor of Aegeus as ruler of Athens after 1400 BCE, when earthquakes north of Krete sank a portion of present-day Santorini to cause a tsunami that weakens already declining Minoans; in the time of the novel, seat of government held by Athenian Idomeneus.

Kore (maiden): Olympian designation for a youth; pre-Olympian designation for Persephone, the youthful form, or daughter, of Demeter, as the forming ascendancy of seasons and the benign but stern arbiter of the underworld; with her mother, holder of shrines on the Peloponnese and at Eleusis.

Krete (Crete): island known today as home of Minoans; location of active trading centers of the Mycenaean era in which the novel is set.

Kronus (Cronus): Titan king of Gods whose parents are Uranus and Gaia; mate of Rhea, his sister; who, knowing that a child born of him will subdue him, swallows his children until Rhea substitutes a stone Zeus, who subdues him, rescues his siblings and replaces him.

Krysothemis: daughter of Klytemnestra and Agamemnon.

Ktimene (founder of civilizations): heroine of my novel who has one citation in the Odyssey. For more information, see the Afterword and the story I give her.

Kydonia: ancient northwestern port of Krete, today Chania, the capital.

Kyllene: one of the peaks of the northern Peloponnesian mountain range of Nonakris, named to honor Nonakris, mother of Kallisto, matrilineal ancestor of Ktimene; home to numerous shrines dedicated to Artemis, the most important at Lusi.

L

Laertes: 1. ruler of Kephallenian Pronni with Antikleia; father of Odysseus, Ktimene, Arkos (invented). 2. ancient trader from Samos Island; navigator of the Argonaut; ancestor of Laertes, Ktimene's patrilineal Kephallenian ancestor. 3. son (invented) of Ktimene and

Eurylokhos; twin to Kleia; spouse of Seleme; settler and trader in the Near East.

Lei Su Ling (invented): spouse of Arkos, eldest son of Ktimene and Eurylokhos, from western Chen (modern western China) in the Far East.

Lelegians: tribe of the Peloponnese before the Myceneans, likely of Near Eastern origin; occupiers of southern Arkadia, their center at Sparta; peaceable tribe that intermixed with Pelasgians and Carians.

Lephteria (diminutive of Greek word for freedom) (invented): priestess of the Demetrian Shrine at Eleusis who assists in the birth of Helen's first child and later brings the child to the Artemision.

Levant: general designation for the coastal trading and inland farming areas of the southern Near East.

Little Bear: constellation, near the Great Bear, placed to honor Arkos, ancestor in Ktimene's matrilineal line.

Loki: Nordic trickster god.

Lusi: shrine dedicated to Artemis in the northern mountains of the Peloponnese; residence of the Sybil Amphito.

Lykaon: husband of Nonakris; father of Kallisto (Arkadian ancestor of Ktimene's matrilineal lineage) and many sons; chieftain in the ancient northern Peloponnese.

Lykos (invented): First son of Ktimene and Eurylokhos; in manhood, receiver of the name Arkos; short version of Autolykos, the name of Lykos' maternal grandfather.

M

Mahti (invented): daughter of Seleme and Laertes, son of Ktimene.

Makis (invented): son of Penthenia and Aglaeus; manager of the northwestern port (present-day Karlovasi) of the family holdings on Samos Island.

Mallia: Kretan port and trading center that serves Knossos.

Mazdeans: ancient Near-Eastern group that subscribes to a balanced, enlightened Godhead which equally divides its attributes to the male and female parts of nature and that influences many religious strands.

Medea: wise teacher/ruler of Kalkis, Black Sea area the Argonauts conquer; in Olympian tradition, wife of Jason whom he discards for a Korinthian princess provoking her to murder their children and his bride; refugee of Athenian Aegeus whose son she attempts to kill, once again to escape; pre-Olympian, Eastern wise teacher, not a trivialized, alleged murderer.

Menelaos: brother of Agamemnon whom he accompanies to Truva as spurned spouse of Helen of Sparta; enlightened husband of Helen and receiver of special insights and truths of the Old Man of the Sea who helps the sons of Odysseus and Eurylokhos search for their fathers.

Mentes: apprentice grandson of wise Mentor, the disguise Ktimene uses to make a journey with Eurylokhos to Truva.

Metis: mother of Olympian Athena; whom Zeus swallows with her unborn child to claim he alone birthed Athena; pre-Olympian Earth Mother form with close affinity to Demeter. Artemis.

Minos: ruler of ancient Kretan people who, in the hero myth, fell to

Theseus of Athens; possible title of a series of rulers, the name given by conquering Greeks, the original name lost in pre-history.

Minotaur: son of ruling Minos whom Theseus subdues in a labyrinthine chamber; vulnerable male heir of Minos vulnerable as Theseus needs to kill him to claim Krete for Athens; in the earlier tradition of the Great Mother, Ariadne, the matrilineal inheritor, benefits from his death as he is patrilineal heir.

Mycenae: high hillside main citadel of the Mycenaean warriors located on the eastern coast of the Peloponnese.

Myrmidons: tribe of Akhilleus.

Mytilini, or Lesbos: island with thermal springs between Samos Island and Truva that serves as rest stop for sailors.

N

Naphali: major port serving the citadel of Mycenae.

Naphlius: father of Palamedes who refutes verdict of treachery that cost Palamedes his life at Truva; vengeful spreader of rumors about the Mycenaean leaders who allowed port entry of enemies of Mycenae.

Naxos: Island in the Kyklades where Theseus leaves Ariadne after Krete falls.

Neaira: 1. In an earlier pre-Olympian form, feminine of Neairus, the Old Man of the Sea, who controlled the seas and its creatures. 2. Ktimene's grandmother; wife of Autolykos with whom she rules the citadel at Parnassus. 3. daughter (invented) of Ktimene and Eurylokhos who marries Theo, son of Penthenia and Aglaeus, and continues family trade.

Nephys: Egyptian goddess; sister of Isis.

Nestor: ruler of Pylos on the southwestern shores of the Peloponnese; leader in the Truvan conflict.

Nonakris: mother of Kallisto, ancestor of Ktimene; wife of Lykaon with mountain range in the northern Peloponnese bearing her name.

Nut: ancient Egyptian goddess whose body arched forward to form the skyways so that she births the sun each day, launching it forth from her mouth, and receiving his fiery chariot back at dusk.

O

O'Konn (O'Conn)(invented): son of Konn (Conn) by his first wife; husband of Kleia, daughter of Ktimene and Eurylokhos who takes the name Maeve; first High King of the Green Isles.

Od: god of Valhalla; mate of Freya, a Nordic goddess whose origin pre-dates him.

Odysseus: brother of Ktimene; son of Antikleia and Laertes; husband of Penelope; father of Telemakhos; major role player in Homer's Iliad and Odyssey.

Olympus (Mount): home of the gods headed by Zeus usually located atop a mountain range on the eastern coast of Greece just north of Athens although Cyprus also claims one.

Olympian System: god system headed by Zeus that the Mycenean warriors bring to Greece to displace or drive underground the goddess system of the subdued indigenous tribes.

Orestes: son of Klytemnestra and Agamemnon; avenger of the death of his father and ultimately ruler at Mycenae, some say with Hermione, daughter of Helen and Menelaos.

Orkemedes (invented): tribesman of Antikleia who escorts Ktimene to Eleusis to assist Helen in childbirth.

Ortygia: island home, possibly at the tip of Syracuse in Sicily, from which a serving girl takes Prince Eumaios, son of Ktesios, a boy of four, to be sold as servant of Antikleia and Laertes.

P
Palamedes: son of Naphlius reputed to know the ancient arts attributed to Daedalus; warrior who traveled with the Atrides to Truva where he faced death for treason.

Pallinder (invented): cousin of Ktimene who rules at Kephallenian Palli, one of the quadrants Kephalos divided among his sons.

Palli: Western Kephallenia that belongs to Kephalos' son Pallus; site of home shrine to Trimetria.

Paris or Alexander: son of Priam and Hekuba of Truva who survives exposure mandated by Priam when he learns Paris will cause the downfall of Truva; judge of Aphrodite as fairest goddess from among Hera, Athena and her who will receive Spartan Helen as prize, an act that fulfills his destiny.

Pasiphae: mate of Knossian Minos; mother of Ariadne, Phaedra, Minotaur and others; wise shrine leader and ruler of Krete. Note:

Theseus subdues Pasiphae's mad son, the Minotaur, said to be born as a result of Pasiphae's coupling with a bull, perhaps a report of a misunderstood viewing of the rite of sacred marriage.

Parnassus (Mount): site of Delphi, prominent shrine of Olympian Apollo; earlier home to the Sibyl Pythia, taken into Olympian orbit as a priestess of Apollo, pronouncer of oracles but earlier a Sibyl with a teaching center of Gaia and Athena; citadel of Autolykos and Neaira.

Peisistratos: son of Nestor of Pylos.

Pelasgians: tribe of Pelasgus (ancient or seafarer) that with Lelegians and Carians migrated from the Near East to the Peloponnese before the Myceneans to form peaceful settlements; ancestors of the families that intermix with the Myceneans.

Peleus: parent with Thetis, a sea nymph, of Akhilleus, hero of the Myrmidons who help Myceneans conquer Truva.

Pelops: founding father of the Myceneans; conqueror of tribes of lower Greece called, after him, the Peloponnese.

Peloponnese: See entry under Pelops.

Penelope: daughter of Periboea and Ikarios; wife of Odysseus; cousin and close friend of Ktimene; devout follower of the Great Mother.

Penthenia: aunt who welcomes Ktimene to Samos Island where she and her husband Aglaeus handle the family trade.
Periboea: wife of Ikarios of Arkadia, mother of Penelope.

Persephone: daughter of (or form of) Demeter in pre-Olympian myths; guard and guide of those who entered the underworld;

Olympian queen of Hades, Zeus's brother, who kidnapped (raped) her as his underworld mate.

Phaedra: a daughter of Pasiphae and Minos, given as mate to Greek in charge of Crete. Phaedra (invented): maid in household of Eurynome and Klamakis.

Phaistos: palace of the Minoan overseer of western Krete that served as the site of the government and of religious rites; deserted ruin during Mycenaean occupation.

Pharaohs: rulers of Egypt.

Phemios: teller at the court of Antikleia and Laertes who taught the art to Odysseus, Ktimene, and Eumaios and who later served at Ithaka.

Philoitios: loyal herder of Laertes then Odysseus and Ktimene.

Phoenix: seasoned leader and historian of warfare at Truva.

Phonikians: Near Eastern traders so named to imitate their speech; rounded-ship traders who competed with the Greek traders.

Pollux (also known as Polydeuces and with his brother Kastor, called the Discouri): Helen's brother who came to take her back to Sparta after the birth of her child at Eleusis.

Polycaste: Nestor's daughter who marries Telemakhos and joins him in managing the citadel at Parnassus after the deaths of Neaira and Autolykos.

Poseidon: child of Kronus swallowed with other siblings who, when rescued by Zeus, joins his family on Olympus as ruler of the sea; pre-

Olympian with other origins; trident bearer; bull and horse tamer.

Priam: king of Truva; father of many children with Hekuba, most prominently Hektor, an exemplary hero, and Paris, abductor of Helen; charger of high fees for steerage and passage into the Dark Sea for trade; possible heir of Herakles.

Prokris: wife of Kephalos; legendary daughter of Minos; mother of Pronnus, Pallus, Krannus, and Samos, inheritors from Kephalos and Prokris of Kephallenia.

Pronni: citadel of Pronnus, son of Kephalos and Prokris forming the main male family line of Ktimene.

Pronnus: son of Kephalos and Prokris who inherited Pronni on Kephallenia Island where he built the ancestral home of Ktimene.

Pylos: Nestor's western port on the Peloponnesian coast (actually two sites on the western coast of the Peloponnese are designated for the city).

Pythia: Sibyl of Delphi in the shrines of Parnassus in pre-Olympian times; Olympian pronouncer of Apollo's oracles.

R
Rhea (earth): Titan mate of Kronus with whom she rules the heavens; mother of the Olympians who rule when Rhea sets aside Kronus' son Zeus instead of allowing his father to swallow him.
S
Sami, Same: portion of Kephallenia Island given to Samos, son of Kephalos and Prokris; home of Eurylokhos, the husband of Ktimene and the first officer of Odysseus; domain of Erato (invented).

Samos Island: island near modern-day Turkey known throughout the ancient world for its shrine to Hera; trading center for the Kephallenian families; home, in early marriage, of Ktimene and Eurylokhos and later of Ktimene and Eumaios.

Seleme (invented): Eastern ruler of a tribe outside the orbit of the Abrahamic tradition; wife of Laertes, son of Ktimene and Eurylokhos; mother of Mahti (invented) and Jamil (invented).

Sibyls: wise women serving major shrines of the Mediterranean, possibly connected with Near Eastern Kybele; important teachers of Ktimene: Pythia of Delphi; Gaetha of the Samian Hera; Cesme (invented) of Ortygia; Amphito of Lusi.

Sophia (invented): priestess at the shrine of Hera on Samos Island; friend of Ktimene.

Sparta: Peloponnesian citadel ruled by Tyndareus, father of Helen; citadel next of Helen and Menelaos.

T

Teiresias: blind seer of the ancient world whom Odysseus consults in the underworld about his future. See additional information of reliable researchers of myth and symbol.

Telemakhos: son of Odysseus and Penelope who searches for his father, fights with him to subdue the suitors who pursue Penelope, and finally holds the citadel on Ithaka Island as well as one at Mount Parnassus; nephew of Ktimene; husband of Polycaste (invented).

Themis: Titan sister of Kronus with shrines throughout the

Mediterranean area, one of them at Dodona.

Theodoros (invented): youngest son of Penthenia and Algaeus who helps with the family trade on Samos Island; husband of Neaira, eldest daughter of Ktimene and Eurylokhos; in his generation, manager with Neaira of the family trade.

Theseus: law giver and ruler of Athens after Aegeus as his heir born of Aethra of Troezon; subject of Athenian hero tale that gives him a major role in the conquest of Minos around 1400 BCE, a period before the scope of my novel but within the teller's art then; in the novel, name given to succeeding rulers of Athens, the chieftain, who impregnates Helen, becoming one; mainly my way to account for the time span between the first Theseus and the chieftain.

Thesprotia: purported to be one of the entries into the underworld, the one I use being the entry port leading to Dodona.

Thessalia: vast untamed territory to the north of Attica, the site of Athens; home of a major shrine dedicated to Hera; area possibly named after Thessalos, a son of Medea.

Thetis: sea-nymph wife of Peleus, king of Thessaly; mother of Akhilleus, the hero of the war at Truva who subdues Hektor to avenge the death of his companion, Patroklus.

Thyestes: brother of Atreus whom Atreus supplants as Mycenaean ruler thus perpetuating a feud between two branches of the house of Pelops; ancestor of Aigisthos, his heir, who kills Agamemnon, victorious commander at Truva, to rule Mycenae with Klytemnestra.

Tiamet: goddess of the Near East.

Tigani: ancient port on Samos Island, now called Pythagorio; trade base of family of Ktimene and Eurylokhos.

Trimetria: triple-form of the Great Mother who guides Kephallenians; a variant of Demeter, a designation of Metis's triple nature.

Troezen (Troizan): port-city of the eastern Peloponnese; home of the first Theseus and the chieftain who impregnates Helen.

Truva (Tros, Illium, Troy): citadel and key port of northwestern Anatolia (modern-day Turkey) that controls the entry to the Dark Sea.

Tyndareus: father of Helen and her siblings; ruler of Sparta.

U
Ugarit: port on the western coast of the Near East that serves many caravan routes from the East as a distribution center.

V
Valhalla: home of the Nordic Gods.

Vergine (invented): shrine teacher at the shrine of Hera on Samos Island; friend of Ktimene.

Z
Zakros: port of Krete that controls the trade of eastern Krete.

Zante Island: island south of Kephallenia Island in the Ionian Sea, likely Zakanthos Island today; home of the giant tortoises that nest in western Pronni.

Zeus (Dias): ruler of the Olympians after overcoming his father, Kronus, until he is eclipsed in the age heroes; with his brothers, usurper of Great Mother powers of the Pre-Olympians whose thunder bolt may imply origins as a weather god, or storm god.

*Much of the GLOSSARY echoes Robert Graves although unconscious borrowings come from other sources absorbed throughout the years.

TIMELINE

Note: Dates are speculative as the novel is set in the shadowy prehistoric period of the late Bronze Age that usually ends around 1100 BCE.

@1250 BCE—Birth of Kallisto (named after her Arkadian ancestor and informally called Kalli until coming of age, when she receives the name Ktimene, her adult name, informally Kti) to Antikleia and Laertes, rulers of the area designated Pronni of Kephallenia Island in the Ionian Sea off the western coast of mainland Greece
1237 BCE—At Mount Parnassus, the adult naming of Ktimene, informally called Kti thereafter
1234 BCE—Marriage of Ktimene (Kti) and Eurylokhos (Eury), prince of neighboring Sami; move to Samos Island to help with the family trade
1233—Birth of Autolykos (first, nicknamed Lykos, later, at initiation into manhood, named Arkos), first son of Kti and Eury; start of war with Truva
1232 BCE—Birth of Neaira, first daughter of Kti and Eury
1226 BCE—Birth of Antikleia (Kleia, later Maeve) and Laertes,

twins, to Kti and Eury at Parnassus

1224 BCE—Kti's return to Pronni to open port and await return of Eury from Truvan war

1222 BCE—Arkos searches for his father, Eury

1220 BCE—Marriage of Neaira to Theo at Pronni and her return to family trade on Samos Island

1214 BCE—Return of Kti's brother, Odysseus (Ody) with bones of Eury, who died in return from war

1212 BCE—Conn, the Kelt, kidnaps Kti, Kleia, Laertes and Kti's companion Freya with plans to sell them; Laertes jumps ship to go for help

1212 BCE—Marriage of Kti and Conn; miscarriage of son on way to the Green Isle

1211-1208 BCE—Kti's sojourn in Green Isles until death of Conn and their young son; marriage of Kleia (Maeve) to O'Conn, soon to be the first high king of the tribes of the Green Isles

1207 BCE—On Samos Island, marriage of Kti and Eumaios, freed, rewarded and now recognized prince of Ortygia

1206 BCE—Birth of Ktimaios to Kti and Eumaios on Samos Island

1205 BCE—Return to Pronni; reunion with Laertes from home near Ashkelon with Seleme, his queenly wife, and their children; death of Odysseus, Penelope bringing his bones to Pronni for temporary rest in family tomb; Pen's delivery of a message Odysseus received from Sybil Amphito calling Kti and Eumaios to Mount Kyllene, Kti's ancestral home

1205 BCE—Reunion with all of family except Arkos at Pronni

1195 BCE—Installation of Ktimaios as ruler of Ortygia; marriage of Ktimaios; return of Arkos with spouse, Lei Su Ling of Chin (China)

1194 BCE—Installation of Kallisto (Neaira's daughter and Ktimene's granddaughter) as owner of the citadel at Pronni, installation of Eumaios and Ktimene to Council of Elders, reunion with Pen and Helen of Kti and Eumaios at Penelope's citadel near Kti's ancestral home on Mount Kyllene after all of them have received the rite of the

Elders; death of Menelaos, Helen's spouse and brother of Agamemnon whose line is in the hands of Orestes rules at Mycenae

1194 BCE—Visit of Kti and Eumaios with Amphito, Sybil of Lusi, thereafter fulfilling their earthly tasks and returning to their star home

Acknowledgements

Creating this work evolved over a long period of teaching the ancient epics, finding Ktimene, and being haunted that she did not have a story. My interest accelerated when I guided the first phase, the oral epic tradition, in a 1989 National Endowment for the Humanities session for public school teachers and librarians entitled from "From Tales of the Tongue to Tales of the Pen." My job was to demonstrate how the Odyssey was transmitted from oral recitation to a written epic.

In l989, the leaders in the Summer Seminar, as well as participants and our national speaker, to whom I give thanks, encouraged me to find my heroine in extant works or create her story. Although still working full-time, I gathered background books by enhancing my private library, ordering books as needed from interlibrary loan and acquiring a library grant for which I thank the Texas State Alkek Library, San Marcos. For assisting in finding materials and books, I especially thank Margaret Vaverek, the faculty outreach librarian. In the early stages, encouragement abounded when I spoke of my intent to give Ktimene a story. I thank those who gave me that early push.

In 1999, when modified retirement came and a semester of down time allowed, I headed to Greece to gain a sense of place. I am deeply grateful to Dolores and Nik Pergioudakis who invited me to stay with them in Peraius where I gained insights into Greek life, while I used the British Consulate library and studied more deeply artifacts in the Archaeological Museum, the Benaki, the Academia Archives, the Goulandris Museum, the Acropolis Museum, and other appropriate sites in Athens and the Islands. Often one or the other accompanied me to translate and to give context to artifacts. They also drove me to sites on the Peloponnese, especially to the ruins of Temples of Artemis in the northern mountains and to Delphi and environs. When they could not accompany me, some of Dolores' advanced English language students came with me.

Of those, I especially thank Leesa and Katerina and her family. Above and beyond their hospitality in their home, Dolores accompanied me and helped me find and settle into housing on Samos Island where I stayed for six weeks to do research and visit local sites as well as museums and local bibliotechs.

I thank my hosts Heraklia and Kostos who did much more than furnish me a room. Both Dolores and Nik traveled with me to Kephallenia Island where I would stay for another six weeks. They drove the entire island with me and helped me find excellent accommodations with a family whose young daughter assisted me. Thank you, Erato.

Near the end of my stay on Kephallenia, Dolores called to see if I would show a friend the neighboring Island of Ithaca. Having been a widow for over ten years, little did I expect the friend to be my future spouse, but, indeed two years later, Kent Haynes, a widower who lived only forty minutes from me in the United States, although we had never met, and I married. For many years afterward, De and Nik welcomed us in Greece. Thank you, Kent and Dolores and Nik—our guardian angels—for many things.

Just before I left Greece, I kept a long-arranged appointment with one of the women who had mounted an exhibit I had seen in 1995 at the Archaeologlical Museum regarding ancient Greek women and goddesses. When I asked her questions that evolved from that exhibit and from my studies and travels, she encouraged me to continue my project which by now I realized must be a novel. Her repeated refrain to questions about whether or not something could have happened to my heroine echos still: "I cannot say it happened that way, but I cannot say it did not." I thank her for her encouragement and support,

I returned stateside with my journals that sketched possible scenes and began a period of subliminal mind wandering about the novel while Kent and I developed our relationship. We traveled back to Greece in the next year and almost all subsequent years to the present while I wrote, re-checked some sources, read with Kent what I had written, re-wrote, revised, edited and finally asked trusted readers to look at what I had written. I most sincerely thank my late sister Sally, Ann Marie and later Nancy, Dolores, Lynn, and my daughter Ann and son John for their suggestions and encouragement.

I also thank dear Kent for his many read-throughs and suggestions, and another Nancy for inviting me to read from my novel at various stages. I thank Susan, Kathleen, and other colleagues who told me I could write fiction, not just guide students to analyze it, and my patient family for sticking with me during the long gestation period of the novel.

Thanks to Becky for introducing me to Cynthia Stone, who took me on for final suggestions and seeing me to print. And yes, Cynthia, I thank you for your excellent guidance during my last revisions and edits. I alone take credit for the path I chose for my heroine, a path that often deviates from or brings to question the traditional reading of the period but that has traction in sources up to the present,

ABOUT THE AUTHOR

Born in Illinois, Luan Brunson Haynes was transplanted to Texas at the age of twelve. Following graduation from Northwestern University with a bachelors' degree, she spent fifty-plus years in academe, ultimately earning a Ph. D. in English at Texas Tech University. Then she served as professor of English at Texas State University for the next thirty-seven years. In addition to teaching assignments, she held the office of Department Chair for eleven years and Associate Dean of Liberal Arts for fourteen years. The capstone of her years at Texas State was being named Distinguished Professor Emerita. The apex of her professional life came while serving on the council and as president of the Association of Departments of English, an arm of Modern Language Association that serves universities at home and abroad.

Along the way, she took on research and traveling to deepen her knowledge of an era she taught in her world literature class, with the aim of writing in retirement. Finally, she has completed a novel set in the late Bronze Age recounting the experiences of a woman who needed a story.

She resides in Wimberley with her husband and enjoys her grown blended family and friends when they visit. In addition, they travel in Europe each year for three months, mainly in Greece.

The author with her husband Kent,
sailing toward the Greek island of Skopelos
Photo by Dolores Reyes Pergioudakis

www.ingramcontent.com/pod-product-compliance
Lightning Source LLC
Chambersburg PA
CBHW021132260626
47169CB00005B/1573